EARLY PRAISE FOR
BLOOD TO RUBIES

"*Blood to Rubies,* Deborah Hufford's meticulously researched and exquisitely imagined epic of the forces that shaped and misshaped the Oregon Territory, is nothing short of phenomenal. Her narrative is a rich quilting of lives, Native and White, whose cultures met and clashed in the early days of the West. It is poetic and sensual and tragic and utterly riveting. Mark my words, this is destined to be a classic. "

—**WILLIAM KENT KRUEGER**, *New York Times* Bestselling Author of *This Tender Land, The River We Remember*, and more than twenty other novels.

"A scorching saga told with crushing intimacy and rock-ribbed characters. . . layered between love and war."

—**KATHLEEN GRISSOM**, *New York Times* Best-selling Author of *The Kitchen House* and *Crow Mary*

"The world needs to know this heroic and powerful story of Chief Joseph and his struggle to save his people."

—**PETER BUFFETT**, Composer of Oscar-Winning *Dances with Wolves* Fire Dance scene and Emmy Award-Winning *500 Nations* and Author of the *New York Times* Best-selling *Life Is What You Make It*

"A spellbinding debut . . . both gritty and lush . . . impossible to put down."
—**LESLEY KAGEN**, *New York Times* Best-selling Author of
Every Now and Then and nine other novels

"Deborah Hufford's brilliant debut novel presents a lyrical, sweeping tale of cultures destined to collide, made personal and very, very human through characters who embody dignity, hope, aspiration and the heartbreak of deep loss. *Blood to Rubies* will raise a reader's heart, break it, then raise it again with an artist's subtle touch. This book is memorable, its characters vibrant, and its message as current today as it was when this story unfolded. It merits multiple readings, careful thought and a place on a library's highest shelf.

—**GREG FIELDS**, Author, *Through the Waters and the Wild*
2022 Winner, Independent Press Award for Literary Fiction

"Fluent and raw! Hufford takes you below the surface of an old west story and tramps you through our nation's youth with all its vicious tendencies and human fallibilities laid bare in graceful, poignant, and blindingly honest language. Deborah Hufford is an author to watch! "

—**DIANNA ROSTAD**, *USA Today* Bestselling and
Award-winning Author of *You Belong Here Now*

"*Blood to Rubies* brings the romance of the West to vivid life. Hufford's timely and detailed rendering follows a dozen characters from their origins, in Nimiipuu villages or eastern cities, by way of ships and wagon trains, boxing rings and brothels, mines and photographer's studios, to their part in this historic conflict. Fascinating photographs add depth and resonance to this broadly woven tale. "

—**KAREN FISHER,** Author of *A Sudden Country,* PEN-Faulkner Award Finalist and Fishtrap *Writing the West* Instructor

"*Blood to Rubies* is spectacularly reminiscent of *Dances with Wolves* in its powerful depictions of the land and Native Americans' sacred relationship to Nature. It breaks your heart. We are inspired to understand why the earth is so precious to Native Americans and why it should be to us all."

—**GARY KELLER,** Location Scout for Oscar-winning *Dances with Wolves* and Kevin Costner's Emmy Award-winning *500 Nations* and Founding South Dakota Film Commissioner

Blood to Rubies takes you on Chief Joseph's epic journey through the most rugged terrain on the planet. The book is so real and so powerful, you feel as if you are riding with Joseph's band in 1877."

—**SANDRA BRONCHEAU-McFARLAND,**
Chief Administrator of the Nez Perce National Trail
and Nez Perce Tribal Member

"As a Nez Perce elder who has been on the Chief Joseph Annual Trail Ride nearly thirty times, retracing the exodus of Joseph and our people, I can attest to the crucial importance of that historic event in Nez Perce culture. Some youth in our Chief Joseph Foundation programs ride this trail as a rite of passage *Blood to Rubies* does justice to this saga and to the bravery of our people."

—**BONNIE EWING**, Nez Perce Elder, Founding Board
Member of Chief Joseph Foundation, Mentor to Tribal Youth, and Descendant
of the Nez Perce Chief Twisted Hair who saved Lewis and Clark from starvation
and freezing to death in the Bitterroot Mountains in 1805

"Deborah Hufford's *Blood to Rubies* is a beautifully rendered, sensual adventure of the struggle of Westerners moving to tame the Oregon Territory. This immersive story is richly evocative of a post-Civil War time frequently misrepresented in American Western movies, including the lives of indigenous peoples. Painted on a sweeping canvas of unspoiled plains, forests, and mountains, we are immersed in the grand and the grotesque, the lilting and the lascivious, the honest and the raw."

—**MICHAEL MILLER, Ph.D.,**
Author of *High Bridge,* the story of Matilda Joslyn Gage, suffragist inducted into the Wolf Clan of the Mohawk

"*Blood to Rubies* is a panoramic portrayal of humanity's endless effort to better one's station in life and the tragic price paid by those whose destiny it is to lose everything in the struggle. Beautifully written, it is an important epic that should forever be included in the telling of our nation's history."

—**J. STANION**, Author of *My Place Among Them*, the story of John Iron Horse, twelve-year-old survivor of the 1890 Wounded Knee Massacre, who is subjected to an Indian boarding school but finds there a sympathetic teacher

"The story of Chief Joseph comes alive in this sweeping American saga of frontier carnage and courage. I could not stop reading as the story unfolded page by gripping page."

—**LYNN SELDON**, Author of *Carolina's Ring* and *Virginia's Ring*, the first two books of a war fiction trilogy, and many other titles.

BLOOD TO RUBIES

Deborah Hufford

VIRGINIA BEACH
CAPE CHARLES

Blood to Rubies

by Deborah Hufford

ISBN 979-8-88824-072-4

Published by

köehlerbooks™

3705 Shore Drive
Virginia Beach, VA 23455

800-435-4811

To my husband and hero,
Evan Jones,
who saved my life by
donating his kidney.
Without him, I would not be here.
And neither would this book.

FOREWORD

ALLEN V. PINKHAM, SR.

Descendant of Chief Joseph and Leading Esteemed Nez Perce Elder

Even though *Blood to Rubies* is a fictitious tale in the Northwest territory in the 1800s, it rings true. It is deeply researched and depicts little-known facts and Native perspectives that most Americans have never read. The tale blends itself artfully with historical truth. It is a fascinating story of the tragic—but also heroic—saga of Chief Joseph and the Nez Perce War of 1877. It is well-done.

Can historic prose capture the real essence of a tragic event? At times I think not. But this author breathes life into events that are unimaginable and gives voice to individual Nez Perce and their courage to keep fighting against overwhelming odds.

This book is especially pertinent to me because I am the descendant not only of Chief Joseph but of another warrior in the War of 1877, my ancestor Wahlitits. He and his equally courageous wife and their unborn baby died fighting at the brutal Battle of the Big Hole. This horrific scene—and so many others during the war—are depicted powerfully in this book and honor my ancestors for their bravery.

The author also honors Nez Perce women, who have often been overlooked in the War of 1877. They were very brave. Some fought alongside their husbands, dug rifle pits, ran horses and provisions to warriors out in the battlefield, tended to the wounded, buried the dead, risked their lives in the struggle, and often died in battle.

During President Thomas Jefferson's tenure, he stated: "If the Indian raises his axe against us, we will do the same and it will be a just war." But there is never a just war when you take something not your own.

We knew the white man was coming to our territory long before Lewis and Clark came among us in 1805. When we acquired the horse around 1700, we asked, "Where did this animal come from?" It was said, "The water," meaning "the bitter water, the ocean." A strange creature had brought the horse. This book honors our horse heritage and our development later of the Appaloosa breed, which became central to our culture.

Through trade and travel, we learned that "the creature" spoke a language we had never heard before. It had eyes like fish, and some had their faces on upside down and were pale of skin. And they smelled.

As time moved on, we learned more, and the creature became a human being that numbered as many as the stars. Our Nimiipuu word for them was "Sayapo." They were a tribal people that came from east of the Big River that flowed south (the Mississippi). Our wise men and oracles said the Sayapo would bring some good things and some bad things to us.

They had metal and glass and gunpowder and books and written language. We were curious to learn more, and we traded with them. But it was also predicted that the rivers would someday run red with our blood, which came true. And it was said they would draw lines across our earth and say this is our land and this is yours. And that came true. We made many other predictions that came true. Yet we are still here. And we call ourselves Nimiipuu, meaning "We, the People."

This book honors the Nimiipuu and gives a poignant yet nuanced account of how our people looked at the newly come to our land and how we tried to meet that change. It is a respectful telling of the resilience of our people and the leader most famous among us, Chief Thunder Rolling from the Mountain, better known as Chief Joseph, my ancestor.

Allen V. Pinkham, Sr.
Christened *Pa xat hi ka tin*, Nimiipuu meaning "Five Rays of Light"
Former Chairman of the Nez Perce Tribe and Leading Elder

AUTHOR'S NOTE

Read more about Allen Pinkham, Sr., and his work keeping the flame of the Nez Perce culture and other Native cultures alive as a Board of Trustees Founding Member of the Smithsonian's National Museum of the American Indian (NMAI), a Chairman of the Nez Perce tribe, the Founding Chairman of the Chief Joseph Foundation, and his many other important works in land rights, environmental science, tribal health, cultural history of his people, and his leadership on North American tribal councils on my author site, DeborahHufford.com.

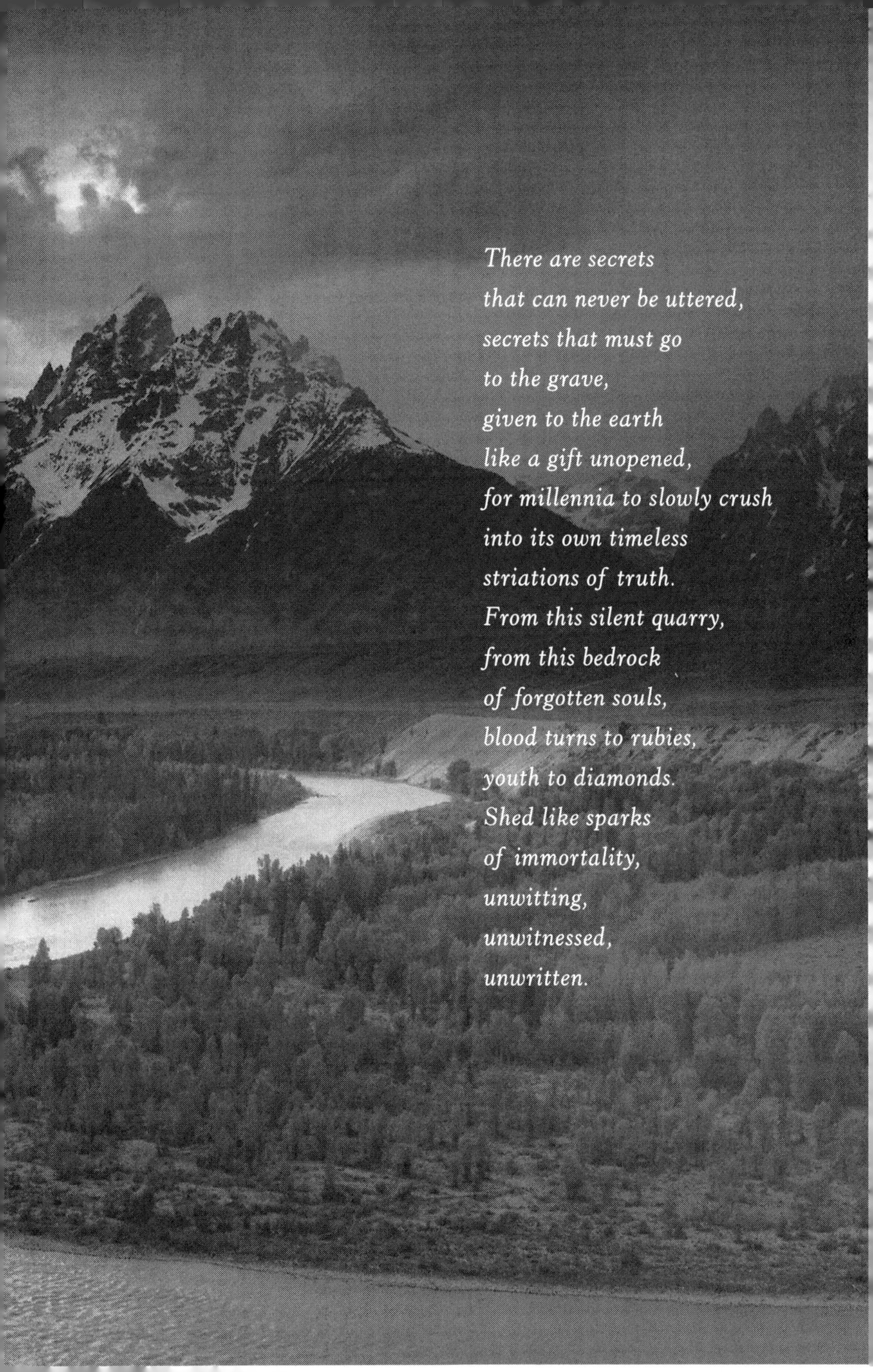

There are secrets
that can never be uttered,
secrets that must go
to the grave,
given to the earth
like a gift unopened,
for millennia to slowly crush
into its own timeless
striations of truth.
From this silent quarry,
from this bedrock
of forgotten souls,
blood turns to rubies,
youth to diamonds.
Shed like sparks
of immortality,
unwitting,
unwitnessed,
unwritten.

ONE

PRELUDE

THE END WAS NEAR, but he did not fear it. His heart was full, his time on the earth complete. He had been granted a life of epic proportion, lived to its fullest measure. Now death waited for him in the wings like a patient usher, the symphony of his years dwindled to an ellipsis of quiet strains. Old bones, old breath. Impediment its own consciousness. Then, finally, the end, 103 years. A man who had seen much.

His last day was simple in the small town of Spotted Horse, Idaho, 1948. As he did every night at six, he shuffled into the Maple Leaf Café, bent as a gnarled walking stick, and sat at the chrome-rimmed counter. A cheese sandwich on white bread and a glass of milk waited for him on the red, faux-marble Formica. He grasped the sandwich with spidery fingers and clamped toothless gums over the bread, stamping out half-moons, leaving a rind of crust on the plate. Cold milk left an unacknowledged rim around his sinkhole lips.

Hunched on the stool in an arthritic stupor, he peered up. A large black-and-white photograph enshrined in an ornate, gilded frame and coated with decades of dust hung on the grease-pocked wall. The picture showed an Indian marriage on a mountain cliff. The old man stared at the photograph as he chewed. Through fogged cataracts and cigarette smoke, the thinnest of echoes sliced through time, tickling his brain like an ancient feather. It plunged down a fissure in his memory, where whole worlds had fallen.

Beside the picture hung the mounted head of a rare white buffalo, musty gray like old carpet and moth-eaten in its truncated majesty. Its marble eyes, dulled by grease, cast a ghostly, ghastly gaze, as if its spirit had traversed beyond its tortured post nailed on the wall and back to the open prairie, leaving only a husk.

The old man wiped his mouth with a paper napkin, scratched at his crystallized stubble, then shuffled out. His old John Deere tractor was parked in front of the café in a space tacitly reserved for him. He climbed onto the torn tractor seat and turned the key. The engine block rumbled, belched diesel soot, and shook tiredly into motion.

Under the axle between the large tractor tires, a three-legged terrier, rheumatic and nearly blind, rose for the trip home. A long time ago, he'd named the dog Willie, but he no longer addressed him. Theirs was a silent bond expressed in daily rituals. Old man, old dog, old tractor. A fixture on the streets of the small town. Passing, then gone, but always there.

His dilapidated cabin sat several miles outside of town, on a gravel road in the mountains, surrounded by overgrown weeds and rusted carcasses of broken machinery. He climbed from his tractor and shuffled past a small cemetery, oddly well kept, at the edge of the tangled yard. Two small boulders squatted like stalwart toads between two elegant gravestones. The engraved granite faces marked time, dragging it forward beyond living memory, beyond forgetting. The old man touched one of the gravestones in passing. He opened a tattered screen door, and the little dog followed, scurrying as the door slammed hollow behind them.

Inside hung a somber gray pall. Stacks of newspapers and books teetered precipitously, sustained only by virtue of their chaos, the narrow path through the catacomb violated by an occasional stray book or crumpled paper.

Beyond the eccentric squalor, black and white vintage photographs spanning a half century and a life rich in adventure blanketed the walls. Some framed, some thumbtacked to the broken plaster, their corners brittle and curling with time. Fragile remnants of vanished dreams. There were portraits of famous people: Wild Bill Hickok, Sitting Bull, George Armstrong Custer sitting on a dead grizzly. There were photographs of great events: the Pony Express, the San Francisco fire, the first transcontinental railroad. And there were pictures of majestic scenery. One frame enshrined a 1938 *Life* magazine cover with a mountain scene. The cover blurb read, A FRONTIER PHOTOGRAPHER REMEMBERS AMERICA'S WEST.

One photograph, larger than all the others, hung above the stone fireplace—a beautiful woman with blond hair like a lion's mane tousled by the wind, her face cast toward the sun, sweeping her hair to the side with a tanned arm. Her other hand grasped a Winchester rifle. She wore men's dungarees and a white cotton blouse rolled to the forearms. A leather belt cinched her waist, the end drooping like a hound dog's tongue. It was not her beauty that was so striking but rather the look in her eyes, mightily independent and piercing in intensity. For all her youth, she was clearly a woman who had not suffered fools.

Somewhere under the pallets of debris lay a negative plate—only the negative, for the photograph itself had been thrown frantically in the fireplace long ago. In it, the Bitterroot Mountains towered beyond a meadow blanketed with flowers. The image had been blurred, however, for the photographer had knocked the camera in haste, and the smears of tall buffalo grass seemed like undulating hair or waves of fire.

Two images emerged from the whorls of grass, double-exposed in ghostly mime. One was the ominous darkness of a grizzly bear running, its massive form besmudged by its speed, though its long, extended claws remained eerily in focus, leaving trails of lethal force like scratches across the page. At the far corner of the frame, in front of the grizzly, was the head of a little girl, barely higher than the grass. The photographic plate remained buried but forever present beneath the crushing sediment of a life's work.

A squarish rocking chair sat before the fireplace. On its arm was a black, lacquered Chinese box painted with the image of an Oriental slave girl surrounded by admiring men, its edges burnished by wear.

Had a visitor ever set foot in the cabin, that visitor would have been struck by the extraordinary mésalliance of such remarkable photographs within the rumpled cottage. The photographs were his legacy. Occasionally, unexpected thoughts from another time bumped around in his knotted brain. He did not know why they came to him. Even in his quickening years, he fell into them like trap doors to paradise. And they surrounded him in the vivid exuberance of his youth. And he remembered.

TWO

PRISM OF THE SUN

THE FIRST TIME Frederick saw her was in the summer of 1871. He was riding through the Bitterroot Mountains along a spiny ridge above the Salmon River. He'd been on the Oregon Trail and wandering the western frontier for nearly ten years, photographing pioneers, immigrants, Indians, those fleeing despair, and those looking for hope. He himself didn't know what he was looking for, only that he was tired and yearned to settle down.

His horse and pack mule were picking their way along the rocky path when he noticed a woman floating in a mountain pool below. He squinted against the sun, surprised to see that she was nude. The surface of the water was calm, and she swam in long, slow strokes across its glassen surface.

From the mountain trail, she looked like a water nymph. Her long, golden tendrils were dreamy and otherworldly, like mermaid's hair, undulating with every stroke.

He drank her in like a thirsty man. Then his photographer's sensibilities took hold. He dismounted and pulled a tripod and large box camera from the mule's pack. Setting up the tripod among some branches, he had a clear view for the camera. He pulled a large negative plate from a leather pouch. The wet-plate process was cumbersome, but it had become as effortless as breathing for him. In his fingers was a decade of repetition, and they flew in a familiar cadence of movement and memory.

First, he glazed the glass plate with light-sensitive collodion, then dripped the excess back into the bottle, for it was expensive. Next, he immersed the negative into a closed sleeve of silver nitrate to marry the two solutions. All this had to be done inside a curtained box, a portable darkroom mounted on his mule. It took him only seconds to prepare a plate, but he trembled, his arousal spreading to his fingertips. *Like an excited schoolboy gripped in secret want*, he thought, embarrassed at himself.

He was twenty-six years old and had never seen a woman naked, at least in the flesh. Only girlie postcards. Here, now, in this bouldered terrain of scarp and crag, was a woman he never could have imagined, her flesh lucent and luxuriant as carved marble, but supple. She was the most beautiful creature he had ever seen. A butterfly with shimmering water for wings, a mountain-lake seductress—part siren, part seraph—beckoning from the water.

He crouched under his camera shroud, slipped the coated glass plate into the camera, and removed the lens cover to expose the plate to light. The woman lay still atop the water, her arms outstretched. In his private darkness under the shroud, the chemicals etched their magic on the plate. It could take seconds or minutes to capture an image, the vagaries of which both vexed and exhilarated Frederick. But the sunlight was bright, and the woman remained motionless on the water's surface for long enough, he hoped. Then he inserted a plate holder into the camera and pulled the negative out, protecting it from light.

As she swam toward the shore, he worked feverishly, hoping to capture her nude outside the water. She rose from the lake, the water hugging her thighs, then ankles, shedding droplets like watery sparks, finally relinquishing her to earth and sky. As she stood at the water's edge, her hair gleamed, rippling down her back like hammered brass. Water beaded on her taut skin. She moved with an animal grace that seemed to him extraordinary for her genteel sex. Tall and strong.

Perspiration dripped from his brow as he readied another plate. The sun reflected off the water, eclipsing her profile in a glowing aura. Magnificent! He clicked the shutter, her head bent back, her face and breasts glistening, her eyes closed as she basked in a sculptural mood.

He was surprised when a horse walked into the frame. Frederick recognized the horse as an Appaloosa, a breed of the Nez Perce Indians who lived in the mountains. The animal was spotted like a snow leopard, white with jagged black splashes. This image of a horse and nude woman in the wilderness seemed like a dream. How could it be? Frederick breathed hard, sweat burning his eyes as he rushed with another plate.

The horse bent his nose toward her outstretched fingers. Just as he touched her fingers, Frederick pressed the shutter. He imagined the plate hungrily soaking up the image, seeking out the nuances of light and form, committing each luscious subtlety to posterity, fixed as stone. He never tired of the miracle of it.

This was his last shot. He was not tempted to watch the woman dress. Somehow, the idea seemed an invasion of her privacy. But warmth rushed to his loins. He did not turn toward her but, in his mind's eye, relished the image of her stepping into her petticoats. And his thrill hardened.

He packed up and beamed in ebullience that he had captured such extraordinary images. He wondered what he could possibly do with the photographs. They would be scandalous in respected circles. And he knew he would not sell them for erotic use, although pornographic postcards were a booming market. He felt a possessiveness, a protectiveness toward this lovely creature and would not subject her to the vulgar instincts of men.

As he turned, he glimpsed a dark smear in a brace of birch across the gorge. He peered through the foliage, squinting, and was startled to see a tall white man looking back at *him*. Their gazes met snapped together, as if the plunging expanse between them were fused by a fine steel thread of secrecy pulled tight. Together they had imbibed the clandestine beauty of the mountain siren. How long had the man been standing there? Had he seen Frederick photograph the woman? At this thought, a wave of guilt ran through him. But the man doffed his hat ever so slightly, as if in polite acquiescence, then disappeared into the trees.

Frederick returned to his work, coating his three glass plates with sodium thiosulfate to fix the images. The plates were delicate and expensive and even more precious to him now with their secrets. Heating the solution over a small flame until blood warm, he poured the varnish across the plates, then stowed the negatives in metal sleeves. They would be safe there until he could develop the images on paper.

After packing his equipment, he sat down against a tree to lunch on stale bread and cheese, washing it down with jug wine. A flock of blackbirds exploded from a copse of aspen, scattering like black beads of a rosary flung into the blue sky. He soared with them in his exhilaration. He'd been at the right place at exactly the right time and captured the photographs of a lifetime.

THREE

SILK & SIMPATICO

AFTER HIS mountain-lake diversion, Frederick rode down from the Bitterroots into Spotted Horse, a pioneer town nestled in the lap of the mountains. He boarded his horse and mule at the livery, where the blacksmith directed him to the Spotted Horse Hotel. As he checked in, the proprietor ordered a boy to lug his equipment up the stairs to his room.

"With care, please," Frederick warned. "There are glass plates."

The room was not bad. The proprietor's wife had made the place clean and cozy. He noted her feminine touches. Calico curtains and a quilt on the bed. A framed picture of lambs and a child in a meadow. The wallpaper, though stained from the gas lamps, had a pleasing floral design. There was even a small vase on the chest of drawers, filled with wild cornflowers and daisies.

He sank his road-weary bones into the cushions of a rocking chair in the corner. As he pulled off his boots, he reveled in the comfort offered by this small bit of civilization and felt the pull of settling down.

Savory smells wafted up from the kitchen. He soon feasted on hot corn bread from the oven, drizzled in honey; boiled potatoes swimming in butter and gravy; garden string beans; and juicy roast beef that had—refreshingly—not been cooked to the consistency of saddlebag leather. When he was offered a piece of hot apple pie, he thought of his mother, and his homesickness mingled with the sweetness of the filling he loved so much. After asking the proprietor to compliment the cook—his wife, as it turned out—Frederick left to visit the local saloon, the Rusty Spur.

The town watering hole was always a good place to get the lay of the land. And he was thirsty as much for company as he was for drink. The saloon was a friendly place, smelling of stale liquor, smoke, and the familiar rankness of unbathed men. A table of locals welcomed him to their poker game and shared their gossip as if he were an old friend. He settled in, said little, listened much, lost at cards, and was surprised at how relaxed he felt with his new drinking buddies.

The next morning, Frederick awoke refreshed. He had a feeling about this town. While traveling of late, he had entertained thoughts of setting up shop somewhere. He smelled bacon and coffee downstairs and heard dishes clattering in the kitchen. His stomach gurgled with anticipation. After a hearty breakfast, he stepped out onto the boardwalk, the bell on the hotel door clanging behind him. His next stop was the bank, to inquire about storefront property for rent. The banker had good news.

"As a matter of fact, there's a one-room business with lodging above on main street. It's been vacant since the clothier there died from pneumonia—and too much whiskey," the proprietor added under his breath. "Some of the soft goods are still on the shelves, just like he left 'em. The fella didn't have any kin," he added. "What line of work ya in?"

"Photographer," Frederick answered. "Do you think a photographer could make a go of it here?" he asked, a little worried the answer might not be what he wanted to hear.

The bald banker took off his spectacles and rubbed the bridge of his nose. "Well," he said, "about a year ago, a photographer set up shop and had plenty of business until a cattle rustler was identified in one of his pictures in his front window. The rustler shot that poor fella for his trouble. He's out north of town now, pushing daisies."

Frederick visibly winced, and dismay clouded his face.

"But I wouldn't let that dampen your spirits," the banker quickly said. "The rustler's dead too. Folks didn't cotton to 'im killing the town photographer *or* stealin' cattle. Lotta folks go through here on to Indian country and Oregon. When they heared there was a photo-making machine in town, they often as not stopped in to get their picture taken. For posterity and such.

"One thing for certain," he concluded. "Ya got vanity workin' for ya, and that's a powerful motivator. Folks really hanker to see their mug. Look at it for hours."

His dead predecessor notwithstanding, this was all the endorsement Frederick needed. He told the banker he'd rent the store and lodging above. When could he move in? Immediate occupancy. He put cash down, and the banker gave him two keys.

"Welcome," said the banker, shaking his hand. "When you get settled, we can post a notice up on the bank front. And let Mr. Moss, the newspaper editor, know too. He'll print an announcement. That'll get some business through your doors."

As it turned out, no notices at the bank or newspaper were needed. Before he could set up shop, Frederick had an inquirer at the front desk of the hotel. He met with the handsome woman, who, the innkeeper later informed him, was the madam of the local cathouse.

He mused at how news could travel so quickly from bank to brothel. *But any business is good business*, he concluded, *as long as the customers don't shoot me*. He agreed to meet with the madam after he got settled several days later.

When he creaked open the door the next morning, the sun threw a dusty trapezoid of light onto the worn plank flooring. His shadow spread across the floor, then bent and angled over the shelves of folded garments. His new studio filled him with contentment as he began clearing the shelves. But he sensed an odd displacement of the man who had once owned the store, the residue of the dead man's touch in the folded clothes, the energy of his effort in their fibers.

Frederick wondered how his own legacy would stack up against the humble aggregate of folded garments. Such sleepy offscourings of a life, they were the only remnants left by the merchant. An ornate cash register remained on the counter like a barometer of the dead man's worth. *For all its iron stridency*, he thought, *it seems a tinny measure of mortality*.

He put the folded clothing respectfully aside in the back room and swept the place clean, set up his equipment, and readied for his first customer, Madam Lillian Bordeaux. But he quickly realized he had a problem: he needed backdrops for portraitures. And he knew, judging from the madam's well-coifed person and stylish clothes, she would want an elegant background. He was concerned that she would not be pleased with the results, and this would not be good for business, especially with such a well-connected customer.

When Madam Lillian arrived in an emerald-green dress and her dark hair in a stylish chignon, smelling of perfume and soap, he nervously welcomed her.

"You are my first customer, madam. I'm afraid my studio is not set up yet, and I haven't acquired all the needed equipment and props. Is there a setting in your establishment that might serve as a proper backdrop for such beauty?" he asked, unabashedly playing to her vanity.

"Oh, I see. Are you looking for payment in something other than cash?" she smirked, her voice soft as smoke.

"Certainly not, madam!" He hadn't even thought of *that*. "I only desire that your pictures turn out properly." He felt himself blushing. Madam Lillian smiled broadly at his obvious embarrassment.

"Well, in that case, my boudoir will make the perfect backdrop. I dare say, most of the men in this town will recognize the setting. And now their wives will have a chance to see it too, in your photographs!"

The next day, he toted his equipment across the street and up to Madam Lillian's boudoir, which he was pleased to see had all the requisite silks and accoutrements for an opulent set. He helped her arrange the folds of her full skirts across the cushions of her velvet chaise, the undercarriage of her skirts frothing with lace. He directed her to position her shoulders turned slightly, regally, and her right elbow to rest upon the back. The rest Madam Lillian did herself, having an instinctual sense for poses both pleasing and provocative. Peering through the lens, crouched under the black cape draped over his camera, he could see that the portraiture would indeed be comely.

"Aw, lovely, lovely!" he purred under the cape. Madam Lillian's eyes brightened with his praise. He was impressed by her theatrical embellishments—saucy or shy in the bat of an eye, and on a whim, she would snatch up a silver-handled mirror or tasseled atomizer as a prop. But her finest inspiration came with the last shot; she lowered her silk gown to expose white shoulders and the doughy plentitude of her cleavage, across which she brushed plumes of buffalo grass pulled from a bouquet.

He had never witnessed such staged seductiveness and for a fleeting moment noted the contrast of her contrivances with the oblivious sensuality of the mountain-lake siren. But the viewfinder kept him focused as he captured his subject in a demure gaze softened further by the plumes against her skin.

Madam Lillian's dusky radiance translated lavishly on film. He set up a darkroom for developing the large prints in a closet in the back of the store. When he finally illuminated the room with a gas lamp, the prints seemed to light up, bringing to life on paper the woman's luminescent flesh. He sat admiring the images for some time.

There was a problem of propriety here, he recognized immediately. Firstly, much as he wanted to, he could not display the portraits in his storefront windows, for some townspeople would not look upon them kindly. Secondly, because the photographs were taken in a brothel, there was sure to be the assumption that the photographer had partaken of the services.

And lastly, and this was perhaps the thorniest problem of all, Madam Lillian would be a hard act to follow. The setting and subject were so beautiful that any other woman in the town would be hard pressed to compete. No, this would not do. A morally fallen woman in such elegance raised her to status unbefitting. He could already hear the reputable dowagers of the town clucking. Putting on airs! How dare she! And worse, how dare *he*! He would be an accomplice in an unforgiveable crime: affronting female vanity.

When Frederick presented the photographs to Madam Lillian, her face lit up. "Oh my, these are grand, Mr. Cortland! Simply grand!" she said, beaming. Frederick was relieved but also worried, since he had to tell her that despite their loveliness, he could not display her photographs in his storefront. But he had fretted for naught.

"Well, of course you can't put photographs of a madam in a storefront! Mrs. Shaw and Mrs. Denton would form a tar-and-feather committee and run you out of town on your mule!" she laughed. "No, my pictures are going in my parlor! I have just the right frames for them. I dare say, more eyes will see them in my parlor than in your storefront, Mr. Cortland. You'll do well by me. Mark my words. And should you ever change your mind, you're welcome to visit me, on the house. You'll find I do good work too!"

She smiled slyly and touched his cheek with her fan, soft as the flick of a moth's wing. Then she strutted out the door even more resplendent than when she had entered.

For all of Madam's charms, Frederick was taken by those of another; the memory of the mountain-lake phantom burned inside him like a phosphorous glow. It had always been his custom to develop albumen prints immediately upon producing negative plates. But, strangely, and for the first time, he had not developed the prints promptly but hid the glass negatives away in the storeroom, among the folded garments of the deceased clothier. He often glanced at the closed door and relished the anticipation of the images, as if the woman herself were waiting for him behind the door. He had never experienced such titillation. The longer he deprived himself of the secrets of the plates, the more inflamed his passions burned. The more luscious his own seduction.

FOUR

BURIED TREASURE

MADAM LILLIAN was good for her word. At her urging, and on the merit of her parlor photographs, her clients brought their wives and families to Frederick's new business. He quickly became busy, photographing portraitures, christenings, weddings, picnics, barn raisings, quilting bees.

There were somber occasions too. Funerals of babies who died in childbirth or of the croup, children who'd been bitten by snakes, trampled by oxen, or poisoned by toxic weed in cow's milk. Photographing babies was hard for Frederick. He found himself swept up in emotion and could barely compose himself as the family gathered around him, sobbing quietly, the mother draped in dark sorrow.

He hid his emotion in the dark privacy under his camera's cape. But through his lens, the babies seemed like dead little angels, fossil cherubs of lost hope.

He photographed adults, too, who died in ways as varied as fate could fancy, although dysentery and tuberculosis were most common. His subjects had not been photographed in life, so posing in death was a last chance for the family to save their image for posterity. He tried to preserve a tangible memory, albeit pasty and gray with the pallid pigment of death.

It was delicate business, for he served as preacher, doctor, and undertaker at once. Recently, the Mitchell baby had died of dysentery. They were poor, the infant garbed in a ragged dress and laid out in a tiny, handmade coffin on the kitchen table. Frederick began his work. He combed the hair and then, with a smudge of shellac, formed a curl around his finger that settled on the child's forehead. A bit of rouge on the little round cheeks. A tad of gypsum powder on the eyelids. If death had been painful or prolonged, the suffering was difficult to conceal, the eye sockets shrunken and wrinkled like cupped shoe leather.

Placing a special possession in the baby's hands softened the image for the family. "Do you have a rag doll? A stuffed lamb for your little one?" he asked quietly. They had nothing. He picked a frond of lily of the valley and placed the delicate flowers in the infant's tiny fingers. Mrs. Mitchell began to sob silently and tried to compliment him in broken words.

There were many who could not pay. Instead, families showered him with produce or chickens or quilts or other prized possessions, which he declined, knowing the measure of their sacrifice. He was welcomed to dinner and invited to socials. And so, he integrated quickly with the townspeople, and in their greatest moments of happiness or sorrow, when emotions ran strongest and loyalties cemented, he was there to document the events.

The town suited Frederick, and he suited the town. Spotted Horse was the final stop west before crossing the Bitterroots and Rockies. The town was backed up against the mountains like a bullied child against a schoolyard wall. Many folks had ended up there by happenstance or tragedy rather than inclination. It was a hash of cultures: immigrants and native Indians, roughneck mountain people and refined easterners, the poor and the better off, the good-hearted and the good-for-nothing, preachers and whores, ex-slaves and ex-soldiers.

A cacophony of tongues filled the streets. Gesturing became a language all its own, filling the voids of meaning between cultures once separated by hemispheres but now splintered together in jagged symbiosis.

The Irish hated the English. Cattlemen hated sheep men. The God-fearing loathed the heathen. Ex-Confederate detested ex-Union. The Chinese were despised by all, and ex-slaves scorned and savaged. All struggled to survive in the growing town, sprouting a motley garden of humanity that made for a strange Eden indeed on the frontier.

Frederick was most fascinated by the original inhabitants of the land, the local Nez Perce Indians. As a child, he had admired famous frontier artist George Catlin's illustrations of Indians and relished Lewis and Clark's accounts of their interactions with Natives. He'd imagined meeting these strange beings on the frontier one day.

The Nez Perce had saved Lewis and Clark from starvation. The members of the expedition had eaten their horses and been reduced to eating candles by the time the Nez Perce found them in the mountains. The tribe nursed them back to health, built them canoes, then showed them the Northwest Passage to the ocean, the very reason for their expedition. Nimiipuu Natives, mounted and on foot, ran along the bluffs, whooping encouragement, first along the Clearwater, then the Snake, and finally the wide, rushing Columbia that swelled with anticipation to the sea. Lewis and Clark wrote of their generous hosts: "We can justly affirm to the honor of this people. They are the most hospitable, honest, and sincere people that we have met on our voyage."

Frederick considered it fate that he was now settled only miles from where Lewis and Clark had been saved seventy years before! All his childhood readings, all his imaginings, all his travels the last ten years had led to this place, and it seemed right and true. Now these Natives stood before him *in the flesh,* Indians whom Lewis and Clark had heralded "the most hospitable, honest, and sincere people" they had met on their voyage.

They posed for his picture-making machine, dressed in their most cherished attire, their horses lavishly adorned. Frederick saw what William Clark had described: "Stout likely men, handsom women, and verry dressey in their way."

They were spectacular Native specimens: broad shouldered, tall, and regal. The garb of their shamans and medicine men was especially flamboyant, with headdresses of eagles, wolves, mountain lions, or elk. Frederick's mind swam with the prospect of the profits he would make from such images. Money did not attract him, per se, but it enabled him to travel and take more photographs and buy more equipment. The eastern market had a voracious appetite for postcards of the shining frontier and its disappearing "savages." Frederick felt an urgency to capture these images—that he was at a crossroads of history.

One day, Frederick was shocked when an old, fair-haired, blue-eyed Nez Perce man walked through his front door, bedecked with the head of a rare white buffalo. The man introduced himself as Hall-lay-too-kit, meaning Daytime Smoke. But then he thumped his chest, saying emphatically, "Me Clark! Me Clark!"

My God! Frederick thought. *Could it be? William Clark's son? This half-breed old man, son of the great explorer!*

He anxiously beckoned the man to sit in front of the camera. He looked at the magnificent man-beast and felt a sudden, searing knowledge that he was touching history. That he could freeze time between the past and the future, at a point riven with terrible irony. The people of this old man's mother had saved the explorer and showed him the Northwest Passage. His father, in turn, had opened the floodgates of history to their very destruction. Frederick could not reconcile his exhilaration at photographing the Nez Perce and guilt at what he knew the future held—and at his making a profit from their demise.

FIVE

WESTERING MUSE

FREDERICK WAS BORN in St. Joseph, Missouri, the westernmost supply point for the Oregon Trail. While the frontier town of St. Louis was dubbed "the gateway to the West" by the eastern press, St. Joe was the floodgate, releasing rushing torrents of humanity from all corners of the planet to spread westward, first like rivulets, then as ever-expanding rivers of hope.

Since the age of eight, Frederick had assisted his father in photographing travelers beginning their trek to the Oregon Trail:

immigrants and easterners, missionaries and mercenaries, dreamers and desperadoes, and everything in between. Frederick had brushes with fame, from literati like Mark Twain to "illiterati" like Jesse James, whose tarnished luster attracted newspapers across the nation. Access to these notable acquaintances, compounded with the fact that they were passing through to lives of adventure and leaving him behind to everyday drudgery, fostered a powerful wanderlust.

In April 1860, when Frederick was a teenager, the first Pony Express rider left St. Joseph from the Pike's Peak Stables to deliver a leather bag of mail to Sacramento, California, on the shore of the Pacific. Frederick and his father were at the stables early in the morning to photograph the event. Throngs of people, horses, and buggies waited with excitement for the start of the ride.

The next year brought more excitement. Impending war had been a festering boil on the nation's future. In April 1861, the boil was finally pierced when Fort Sumter exploded into active war. The inevitable had finally happened.

That month was Frederick's seventeenth birthday. Spring lilacs leafed out, their confetti buds bursting with luminous fragrance. Soon after, caravans of settlers arrived in St. Joseph to join the wagon trains going west. Every passing day and every passing portrait of the western-bound heightened the allure of the frontier so much that he thought he might burst in frustration.

On his birthday, Frederick gathered the courage to tell his father he intended to go west. His father's lips curled wistfully under his mustache.

"I was wondering when you would tell me, son," he said. With pride, he put his hand on Frederick's shoulder. In the previous year, his son had sprouted up to nearly his height, and he was beginning to see Frederick as a young man.

"Your mother will be heartbroken, you know. But, frankly, if I was your age, I'd do the same thing." He smiled at his son. Frederick was stunned.

He had expected his father's disapproval. "I'll help you, Frederick," his father continued. "But you have to promise me you'll try to stay out of harm's way. There are a good many charlatans out there. You've helped me photograph some of them! Many more come to a sad end than a happy future in the frontier. But I can't fault you for wanting to go."

He patted his son's back affectionately, then gave him a stack of negatives they had shot that day of immigrant families going west in covered wagons. "Take these to the back room. We'll talk about this later. Let me talk to your mother. She won't be happy."

But Frederick's mother needed no convincing. Only weeks earlier, pro-Southern bushwhackers had dynamited the railroad trestle outside St. Joe's and sent a train plunging into the water below, killing twenty passengers. The war had come to their own back door.

Frederick's mother could see that the choice for her son was simple. If he stayed, he'd be conscripted into an army, although which one depended on whatever Federal or Confederate renegade remnants absconded with him first. Missouri fomented with extremist factions from both camps—Quantrill's guerillas on the Rebel side, John Brown's vigilantes on the Yankee side. They overran the state like feral hogs, and young men were as likely to be killed for their boots as conscripted. Civilians in Missouri had been savaged or lynched by one or the other side for real or imagined crimes—made no matter. No one was safe, and the real reasons for the war were hard to reckon.

The first year of the war had seen bloody battles: Bull Run, Shiloh, Antietam. Frederick's childhood friends came back in boxes or missing limbs, years older than their age, their youth having abandoned them on the battlefield. Sunken, distant eyes spoke of the horrors they had seen. Casualties were more often lost to typhoid or dysentery than in battle for any righteous cause.

The next year, in May 1862, just after he turned eighteen years old and after a year of planning and saving money and buying equipment and a mule, he was ready. He packed up the camera and equipment his father had given him, then headed due west on a dirt path rutted as a washboard, to the Oregon Trail.

Frederick's first subjects were the pioneer families on the wagon train who became his traveling companions and friends. Soon he was being asked to capture all manner of events and personages. This was when he first found himself ruefully profiting from the misfortune of others, for much of his business came from photographing the dead, the wan by-products of once-bold ambition.

His first experience photographing a dead body was early on the trail near Kearney, Nebraska. A young couple who intended to be wed in Kearney were crossing a rocky riverbed in their buckboard when the wagon lurched. The young woman was thrown from the wagon in front of a wheel, nearly severing her head. Her fiancé was bereft beyond despair. He begged Frederick to photograph them together for a wedding portrait. Frederick was aghast. But the young man's entreaties were so pathetic he could not refuse.

The ladies in the wagon train dressed the woman's corpse in her wedding dress, with prairie flowers in her hair and her face behind a veil. But her head dangled from her neck like a limp rag doll. With difficulty, Frederick and the young man sat her upright in a chair, then placed a butter churn handle behind her. The ladies wrapped a lace tablecloth from her trousseau around her crushed neck and the handle. Frederick placed a bouquet in the hands folded in the dead bride's lap, then positioned the groom behind the chair, his hands on his fiancée's shoulders and his arms on either side of her head to prop it up. The young man had an uneasy sensation of holding her head disembodied in his arms and began to weep.

Frederick waited until the groom gathered his composure. Standing behind his dead bride, donning his Sunday best with his hair slicked down with pomade, he lifted his chin and nodded to Frederick that he was ready.

As Frederick crouched under his cape, peering through the viewfinder, he could imagine the woman to be alive and happy in her new-married state. His was an act of mercy, for the young man could not lay his love in the grave and leave her behind, buried on the trail, without an image to remember her.

When Frederick was done, they carried the bride to a hastily made coffin, the young man crumbling once again into sobs. Once she was lowered into the ground, Frederick read some words from a book of love poetry he had. He chose part of a poem written by Henry King, a seventeenth-century English poet who had himself lost a young wife to early death. He recited over the open grave:

Sleep on, my Love, in thy cold bed
Never be disquieted!
My last goodnight! Thou wilt not wake
Till I thy fate shall overtake:
Till age, or grief, or sickness must
Marry my body to your dust
It so much loves; and fill the room
My heart keeps empty in thy tomb.
Stay for me there: I will not fail
To meet thee in that hollow vale.
And think not much of my delay:
I am already on the way,
And follow thee with all the speed
Desire can make and sorrows breed.
Divided, with but half a heart,
Till we shall meet and never part.

SIX

CONFLUENCE OF FATES

FREDERICK'S CHILDHOOD imaginings became flesh on the trail. Growing up, he had soaked up a love of history from his grandpa, who first introduced Frederick to the work of George Catlin after purchasing illustrated volumes of the artist's work. The huge tomes, replete with 300 color engravings, depicted the many Indians Catlin had painted across the West in the years following Lewis and Clark's expedition. The artist believed them to be a "vanishing race" and felt an urgency to document as many tribes as possible.

When Frederick was packing for his journey, his grandpa gave him the books as a going-away present. "You're sure to meet some of these characters in your travels," he said with a smile. For Frederick, the books had the ring of truth, of unvarnished love of knowledge, unfettered by prejudice. He trusted their accounts implicitly, and the images they painted were as true inside his head as life.

So, on the trail, when he met Natives *in the flesh*, it was as profound as seeing ghosts come to life before his eyes. But *these* were not insipid, paper-thin specters, flat, fleeting, half formed. No. They were creatures of the earth, the here and now, rooted, stalwart, strong. Their presence held a strange power for him, like demons and angels become one on earth, painted and garbed in such raiment as from another world.

Indians would greet the wagon trains to trade for food, tools, or fabric, or simply out of curiosity about the strange white people coming to their lands. They would touch the hat of a white man or the fabric of a woman's skirt, sample the foods they smelled cooking in camp pots, or pick up a scythe or lantern, examining it with a perplexed look.

Early in his travels, Frederick encountered an Omaha brave in eastern Nebraska who wore buckskin leggings fringed with human scalps. The man's face and bare chest were daubed in red pigment. The Indian's name was Snake Fight, and he had two rattlesnake skins wrapped around his waist, their heads and tail rattles crossed in front over his loin cloth. The young warrior was curious about the photography equipment on the mule and touched the shiny brass lens and iron plates in wonderment. Frederick could only offer him a photograph as a memento. But the man was pleased with the gift and left beaming.

Frederick enjoyed the intense curiosity Natives showed with regard to his photographs. It sometimes protected him from potential danger. He felt like a god presenting them with miracles, such was their awe. Even hostile Indians let him alone. It was bad medicine to kill this white shaman who could capture life and hold it frozen in his hands. His reputation spread among many Indian tribes, and he became known as Sooyáapoo, "Man Who Makes Magic Pictures," a moniker he liked very much.

Frederick marveled at Native fashions and their ingenious use of natural materials. When he asked Natives to pose for him, they returned dressed in elaborately beaded, fringed, or painted regalia, their palette from nature's richest colors, the equivalent of the white man's Sunday best.

It never occurred to Frederick that such vibrant colors might be wasted in his black-and-white photography until a Shoshone chief asked him where all the color had gone in his pictures. Thrusting his forefinger at his own brilliant war paint and colorfully beaded chest, the chief glowered with disapproval at the colorless photographs.

Frederick's shoulders fell in disappointment. How could he explain the limits of his camera? He pointed to the heavens, then to the chief's war paint and bright attire, and pointed to the sky again, attempting to convey that these colors came from the Creator. Then he patted his own chest and nodded his head back and forth as if to say, "I am only a man. I cannot make the Creator's paint." The gruff chief's face softened. Then his braves pointed out that his enemy had already posed, and didn't he want whites to know that he was as mighty? He was finally persuaded.

Frederick felt the shades of black to white and a thousand grays in between managed to capture life fully, albeit in a different dimension of nuance. *My images are luscious in detail,* he thought, *and dignified in their palette of stone.*

He was fascinated by the Native styles of hair. As a boy, one of his favorite illustrations by George Catlin was of the Iowa head chief White Cloud, whose face was greased solid red, save a black hand across his mouth and cheek. He sported a giant bear claw necklace and a spectacular pompadour like bristling red fireworks atop his head, the hair coated with bear grease and buffalo dung to stiffen. Frederick mused that male vanity was the same no matter the race and thought of white men he knew who preened over their pomaded locks and lamb-chop sideburns.

Besides the elaborate headdresses fashioned from the heads of buffalo, wolf, bear, or other beasts known for fearsomeness, medicine men sometimes chose creatures for their beauty; Frederick remembered a Pawnee headdress of a swan, its neck arched gracefully, wings spread across the man's shoulders as if he himself could take flight.

When Frederick was first traveling with the wagon train through Nebraska territory, the wagon masters wanted to rest the animals and repair some wagon wheels, so Frederick decided to explore. They had entered the land of the Cheyenne, Shoshone, and Crow. The wagon master told him there was a friendly Crow village a couple of miles from the wagon train if he followed the river.

Frederick was particularly inspired by Catlin's painting of Crow Chief on his horse. The image was so extravagant that some might have believed the artist had taken unbridled creative license had Catlin not had a reputation for accuracy and minuscule attention to detail. The image depicted the chieftain and his rearing bay stallion with feathered matching bonnets of flowing black hair so long that it swept the ground. Frederick held no fantasies he would find such a phantasm in the Crow village, but he hoped he might photograph Indian life with tipis or horses.

But his excitement was serrated with fear. The Crow were generally friendly with whites, but their warrior culture was fierce, and they mutilated their foes. He reminded himself he was no longer a boy reading about frontier adventure. Now he was living it. Realization quivered up his spine that he might be riding toward a gruesome end.

Fortunately, Frederick found a clamorous welcome from chiefs and warriors gathering for council and adorned in finery that rivaled that of Victorian royalty. But these were warrior dandies with deadly charms. They wore feathered symbols of their counted coup, notched or marked in pigment to show their courageous exploits and kills in battle. When a Crow chief greeted him wearing a feathered war bonnet that touched the ground, Frederick knew this man was courageous indeed, for every feather represented an exploit.

The photographer noticed that some braves and even women and children had medicine bags made of small animals or fetuses of larger mammals. Pouched beaks of pelicans, swans' feet, and rattlesnake skins with heads intact were reincarnated into beaded bandoliers.

He saw an infant in a cradle holding a baby rattle. He touched a brave's shoulder, pointing to the rattle questioningly. The man beamed and grabbed his own crotch, jiggled his hand, then put his two hands on each side of his head and pointed his index fingers forward to indicate horns. The rattle was the decorated, dried gonad of a buffalo bull, Frederick surmised, in hope the virility of the beast would magically endow the tiny boy. Its million wizened spores held powerful medicine.

Riding back to the wagon train at sunset, Frederick's heart was full, his mind dancing with the visions of Native life he'd seen for the first time. The Crow were allies of the Nez Perce. His grandpa had once recounted Lewis and Clark's meeting the Nez Perce chief Red Grizzly Bear, called Xaxaac-Ilpilp. The chief wore a sweeping hide at once magnificent and macabre, covered with human scalps and fingers of enemies slain in battle. For this, he was known as "Bloody Chief."

Frederick could not know that he would someday photograph the sons of Chief Red Grizzly Bear *and* William Clark, standing together, shoulder to shoulder, weary old men armed for war against the whites, a war their white and red fathers had sworn against over a peace pipe a world before. But the confluence of fates had already set in motion the end of one civilization and the beginning of another. The silver nitrate of Frederick's photograph would etch its eerie enigma like the shadow of a shaman dream.

SEVEN

VERMIN & VERITÉ

FREDERICK'S STUDIO business was soon flourishing. He welcomed all walks of life and reveled in the diversity of subjects presented to him. A Negro couple, Capurnia and "Honey Boy" Stewart, brought in their five children for a family portrait. He was impressed with their crisp and fashionable attire. Capurnia was obviously in charge and arranged her brood artfully in front of his camera before he could intercede.

"This is the way I picture our portrait," she stated. And it was clear there would be no discussion otherwise.

"Very nice indeed, madam," he said and disappeared under his cape.

His customers included merchants, miners, and farmers of many extractions, especially English, German, and ex-slave, as well as Basque sheep herders and Chinese families who ran laundries.

In his weekly poker games, Frederick made quick friends: Bull Bamrick, an ex-Confederate colonel, and Red Striker, a strapping, red-haired Scotsman and former Union spy. But Frederick's favorite was Willie McGee, the farrier and livery owner, a stout, bandy-legged Irishman from the rugged western reaches of Donegal. Willie was what folks called a "character." His powers of loquacity were legion. Profanity and scatological speech flowed out of him, especially when lubricated by whiskey. A tongue so sharp could clip a hedge, as Willie might say.

His words clipped the sensibilities of a good many townsfolk, too, and he had been extracted in various undignified fashions from every saloon in town. Once, when the British saloon keeper warned the English-hating Willie to watch his language, the result was a string of vulgarisms to make a pirate blush. "Fuck the King's English and the English king, too! I'll not curb me tongue for any but me lovely wife, God rest 'er soul." He leaned into his words with the resolve of a surly drunk, then melted into a pool of rememberings, for the only thing that could quiet Willie's tongue was his dead wife's imagined ghost asking him why an unworthy soul such as himself survived his much worthier spouse.

Frederick discovered Willie in the saloon one day, recounting his glory days in the rat pits of London. Willie bred rat terriers, not only to control the rat population in his livery but also for sport. It was in the rat pits of the London Rookeries that Willie found true joy.

He had raised a little orphan terrier pup he'd named Mabel—after his mother—and she quickly proved a ratter of exquisite skill and pathological zeal. At the rat emporium, Mabel's talent blossomed. When he set her down in the dingy pit filled with 100 rats and the clocker started his watch, she leapt into the seething melee and made handy work of it, killing 100 rats in record time.

In Spotted Horse, Willie held ratting days at his livery, where he and all races of men pitted their dogs against the livery rats and wagered on the carnage. Children came too, and Willie gave them hard candy while they watched.

Willie turned to Frederick: "Bring your camera. Everyone has a good time but the rats!"

For all Willie's braggadocio, he had a soft side. Frederick knew Willie took cow's milk to a prattle of poor children and lent his mule to the struggling Clarence Forester and hired an orphan boy who had lost his mother and father on the Oregon Trail, providing a little room for him at the livery.

Willie had found him sleeping under straw in his hayloft, dirty and ragged as a sewer rat. Once he'd cajoled the boy to at least share his name and where he was from—Chester, from Texas—he asked a kindhearted prostitute to give Chester a bath. "Nothin' more, mind!" Willie added. "I'm not payin' for 'im to dip his wick!" Willie gave her some of his old clothes for the boy. "Burn his stinkin' rags. Smells like he dropped his braces in the shitter."

She brought the boy back clean and clothed. Willie made a makeshift bed in the hay with a tattered old blanket. "This'll have to do for now. But you'll be warm at least." So began Willie's new role as an adopted father.

It did not occur to him at the time that this was indeed the choice he'd made. He was not a patient father and bemoaned to Frederick that the boy was "useless as a crocheted piss pot! He's afeared of critters, especially rats," and could not be trusted to grease an axel or true a wagon wheel. "And here I am, like a boar with tits, trying to suckle a child. What the hell was I tinkin'!"

When Willie hired Frederick to photograph his terriers with the dead rats they had dispatched on ratting day, laid out rank and file outside the livery, the boy showed interest in Frederick's camera. He hung back, his hands in his pocket, watching intently as Frederick changed plates. Frederick noticed the boy's curiosity and explained in simple language how the camera worked. The boy looked at him with big saucer eyes, entranced.

The next day, Frederick talked to Willie about hiring Chester to clean his studio and run errands. Willie was skeptical: "You'll have to show him the business end of a broom." But he shrugged, secretly relieved he would no longer be solely responsible for the boy's welfare.

Frederick appreciated the cantankerous little Irishman for the contradiction he was. *Kindness is as kindness does*, thought Frederick, and Willie had an Irish sense of fairness even his unruly tongue would abide.

EIGHT

FAR SIDE OF PARADISE

WHEN FREDERICK arrived in Spotted Horse, he had been on the trail for nearly ten years after leaving his parents' drugstore in St. Joe's. He yearned for a place to make his own. But settling down had unexpected liabilities. Years of memories caught up with him. When he finally slept in the same bed for more than a few nights, he relived scenes he'd long since forgotten, sometimes bolting upright in the night, panting, drenched in sweat.

It started with buffalo: great herds standing in cold morning mist like furry locomotives snorting steam in the crisp air. But then the scene melted into grotesque dimensions; from a distance, big gray boulders dotted the prairie like a glacial dumping, so many it was hard to imagine how they got there. Only when he got closer did he realize the boulders were huge, headless mounds of raw flesh, the skins and heads hacked away by white hunters. Majestic beasts stripped of their mighty mantles, reduced to rotting flesh. And the putrid smell of death engulfed his dream.

He dreamed of human graves too. An endless trail of them. Some families chiseled cherished family heirlooms into coffins or markers. They piled rocks over graves to keep wolves and other predators from the body. But after they disappeared over the horizon, the snarling beasts dug up and desecrated the dead with indelicate efficiency. Often travelers came upon fresh graves violated, bones protruding, ants swarming gray, awful faces and gathering greedily about the eyes and mouth.

One scene resurfaced mercilessly. On the trail, a little girl and mother had discovered a disinterred grave with torn blue gabardine and long golden braids exposed in the dirt. He had watched the mother pick up the braids. She washed them in a nearby stream until they gleamed like gold nuggets, patted them gently, then wrapped them in a kerchief next to her Bible. But in his dream, the dead girl returned, reincarnated through her hair, wearing her blue gabardine dress, gossamer and airy like the prairie sky until her face shriveled black and her broken, sharp teeth grimaced.

Human skulls bleached by rain and sun were also common on the trail. They bore carved inscriptions of Bible verses or poetry. What in a more civilized land was barbaric desecration became raw tidings from those who had already passed through to those who followed.

After a long day on the trail, looking for graves and reading inscriptions was a favorite pastime of the children. Their fascination with death was innocently devoid of the true horror. Epitaphs told of death by Indian attack, prairie fire, snakebite, cholera, avalanche, freezing, thirst, poison, broken heart, murder, and suicide.

Frederick also had happy memories. A boy a little younger than himself had a pet ox named Old Brock he'd raised from a calf. Brock had been part of an eight-ox team, but six were lost to exhaustion and sickness. When Martha, Brock's partner, collapsed, Brock sank to the ground with his mate and refused to go on. The boy's father said Old Brock had to be shot, but the boy pleaded not to kill the grieving ox.

The boy stayed back with Brock through a snowstorm. Days later, Frederick saw the tiny silhouette of ox and boy distant on the ridge. Everyone yelled with joy and waved their hats, galloping toward the wayfaring pair, hugging each other, crying to see such a sight.

Truth was, Frederick had lived ten lifetimes. He'd photographed the mundane and the monumental and nearly every race of immigrant and North American Indian tribe north of Kansas. He'd seen folks in fortitude and foible and tried not to judge, for more often than not, they'd been thrown into circumstances for which they had no earthly defense. They coped as best they could, with what crude tools they had in the wilderness.

He remembered the whispered entreaties of families at night, asking God to protect them from Indian attacks and sickness and other hard prayers. The cumulus of westering pioneers followed pain-rutted paths to raw wilderness.

The Indians, in contrast, seemed both wise beyond white scholarship in the ways of nature and ignorant and curious as children in the ways of whites. He photographed Indians with enthusiasm but, again, not without guilt, for he feared for the red race.

Photographing landscapes, however, brought him a wild, guiltless joy. The Bitterroots were awash in paradisal possibilities. He thirsted to capture their beauty. The Nez Perce would show him their secret vistas with obvious pride, canyons scooped out of the mountains, swooping down in breathtaking rushes, emptying out their magnificence onto vast prairie. He understood the Indians' elemental longing for the land and buffalo.

He enjoyed his mountain forays most in fall, when autumn's burnished hues drank up the canted light. The crunch of leaves and melancholy decay engulfed him in gold-washed reverie. He felt as if he had been led to the far side of paradise, beyond the reach of whites and civilization to a realm utterly wild, untended but ordered as the world was meant to be. And he an interloper but for the beneficence of his red brethren.

NINE

WHISKEY & WRATH

IT HAD BEEN TWO MONTHS since Frederick had arrived in Spotted Horse—since he had secretly photographed the lake siren. He'd become oddly consumed by the hidden negatives and found himself stuck between compulsion and inertia. He mused at his quandary. How had such a neurosis lodged in his mind? And him a photographer, a lover of images!

Frederick was drinking in the saloon when Willie beckoned him to a game of poker. Willie was in full throat, bragging of his prize ratter, Garm, appropriately named after a hellhound of Celtic lore. He was recounting how Garm flushed out rats in their tunneled lairs when a woman burst through the saloon doors.

The doors flapped violently in the wake of her anger as she halted in the middle of the room.

Tall and lithe, she was electric with a strange, vital energy. A blond mane tumbled about her shoulders. She wore men's dusty canvas pants and a simple blouse rolled to her elbows, revealing tanned arms and strong, sure hands, one with a rifle, the other a clenched fist. Her sapphire eyes were burning glass, searing through the sudden silence as she searched the room.

Her glare settled on a man at the bar. Bystanders vacated the path of her ire, leaving the man squarely in the gunsight of her wrath. She stalked toward the man until she was an arm's length from him.

"You roughed up an old man this afternoon," she snarled.

The man thrust a drunken, surly expression her way. "That blind ole bastard. He ran into a barn door, lady. We all saw 'im do it. Funniest damn thing." He turned to his two companions with a drunken swagger. They elbowed each other and smirked.

"You beat up a defenseless old man," the woman seethed between clenched teeth. Her voice quavered like prairie grass before a storm.

The man laughed. His companions aped big, toothless grins at such sport. Then the man turned to his accuser, the smell of his whiskey breath and rotting teeth full force in her face. She winced.

The man leered. "Whatcha gonna do 'bout it, lady? Puttin' on a man's duds don't make you no man, and I ain't figurin' to fight no lady cause"—he got a mischievous look in his eye—"'cause I'm a gentleman!"

He took hold of his suspenders and puffed out his barrel chest in mock pride. His companions burst out laughing, slapping each other at the gall of their unkempt companion calling himself a gentleman.

"You are a slovenly swine and a coward, too," the woman said, still calm.

"Look, lady, call me anything ya want. Then get the hell out. I got drinkin' to do. And I ain't got no hankerin' to listen to a woman's goddamn prattle."

"You need to learn some manners," she answered. Without warning, she gripped the rifle in both hands and smashed the butt into the side of his head. Like a Hun with a scimitar, she followed up with violent blows to his crotch and ribs.

My God! She fights like a gladiator! Frederick thought. He had never seen such violence from a woman.

The man reeled from the blows, his eyes wide with pain and the astonishment that a woman had rendered it. He fell in a heap on the floor, groaning, his head spurting blood as if it had sprung a leak.

She whirled and swung the rifle stock at the heads of his two companions, hitting one of them squarely in the face, blood exploding out his nose. The other ducked, barely missing her lightning assault. He scampered frantically on his hands and knees in staccato desperation toward the exit. She cocked her rifle, took aim, and grazed his buttocks. He writhed on the floor, howling, grabbing his bloodied backside.

"If you ever touch my father again, I'll kill you!" she hissed. Then she glared challengingly at the other men in the room, ready to unleash her wrath on any who dared make a peep. The whole room seemed to recoil. She stormed to the door, then was gone.

Through the window, Frederick saw a spotted Appaloosa standing in the street, a lead rope hanging in the dirt. The woman jumped up on the horse with the grace of a Sioux warrior. The horse reared forward at her nudge, and his pounding hooves left bullets of dust in the road behind.

In a flash of recognition, Frederick realized the woman was the naked siren he had seen at the mountain lake—but this time, clothed and armed! He flushed and turned back to the table. Wiping his brow, he looked up and caught the gaze of a dark-haired man sitting across from him. Frederick quickly lowered his eyes.

But something tugged at his memory. He glanced up again to find the man's gaze still fixed upon him. Then awareness struck: his fellow voyeur from the mountain lake!

The man saw that Frederick had at last made the connection. His lip curled slightly in wry recognition, and his expression brightened, like sunlight after clouds have passed.

"Now, *there* is a magnificent woman," the banker, James Slickum, said, turning back to the card game. "A real wildcat in a petticoat—well, if she ever bothered to wear one, that is!" he chuckled.

"She made short work of those rascals, just like my Mabel in the rat pit," Willie said. Then he nodded to the prostrate man still moaning and holding his bloodied buttocks. "Poor fucker. Looks like he shit nettles!"

The entire table laughed.

"Who is that woman?" the dark-haired man asked.

"Sorrel Lanning," answered the banker, assessing his cards as he talked. "She and her old Irishman father homesteaded some land in the valley several years ago. Funny pair, those two. But they're makin' a go of that farm. Raising horses for the Army." He frowned at his cards and scratched his chin: "I don't believe Seamus could get a dress on that young woman if he hog-tied her. My Ethel and the church ladies were scandalized last year when she showed up for the turkey shoot in men's dungarees. She damn near won, too!"

"I'm bettin' my money on Sorrel this year," a bald man with big whiskers said.

"That'll be somethin' to see!" Willie said. "Tom Munroe's won three years in a row. That'll burn his ass to lose to a woman!"

The men guffawed at the irony, for Tom was big and bombastic and fancied himself a ladies' man.

Willie smirked. "He may be donkey-rigged until Sorrel Lanning gets done with 'im!" He held up his little pinkie, then drooped it metaphorically. The table roared.

"Last year's shoot was the first time we ever saw her," the banker said. "Tongues been wagging ever since. Ethel says she couldn't put up a jar of jam if her life depended on it. But she can work as hard as any man and can shoot a gun and ride a horse better, too."

"Married?" the dark-haired man asked. The men laughed.

"Every man in these parts has given up trying to court her," the banker continued. "She doesn't give a tinker's damn for men, 'cept for Seamus. She's like a poison oasis in the desert. A pity, really. Such a beauty."

"Yes," the dark-haired man said, glancing back at the doors. Frederick's thoughts wandered to the lake. He once again felt the blood rush warmly to his face.

The dark-haired man laid his hand down—a straight flush, with the queen of hearts leading. The royal lady on the card stared up in an immutable, Mona Lisa half smile, as if she knew their guilty secret.

That evening, neither man could drive the blond firebrand from his mind.

TEN

MOTHERLESS CHILD

SEAMUS AND SORREL Lanning had become father and daughter by fate, not birth. Sorrel's true parents, Patrick and Bridget Cleary, were Irish immigrants from Donegal. When the potato crops failed, the two boarded a teeming boat bound for America, leaving behind millions perishing from starvation and disease. Bags bulging with cherished possessions, hearts burgeoning with hope, they were dumped into slums as crowded and filthy as the boats. But there was work. They had left a land of death and doom. Anything was better than what remained behind.

Bridget became pregnant with Sorrel during the voyage. Already thin and malnourished from the famine, her seasickness was compounded by morning sickness and a racking cough that shook her slight frame mercilessly. She got off the boat gaunt and weak, a bony shadow of the girl Patrick had married.

Patrick got work at the ironworks, and husband and wife moved into a tenement brimming with families. The smell of boiled potatoes and cabbage filled the halls. From tenement windows, mothers flapped rugs that wagged like the tongues of hungry children and flung slop out on a ragged hedge of garbage. Everywhere was squalor. But still, there was comfort in the familiar strains of language and old ways.

Bridget was not strong enough to work or even stand. Tuberculosis, the doctor said. He applied leeches to the patient to bleed out disease, then prescribed bed rest and laudanum. The latter would help quell her bloody cough. The Irish ladies next door assured Patrick that they would watch over Bridget until the baby came. By the time the baby was born, Bridget had no strength left for the effort. The doctor feared for both mother and child.

"Sweet Mother Meery." Mrs. McGillicuddy shook her head. "It's beyond me what the good Lord be thinkin' puttin' a baby in that woman's womb, sick as she is. It'll be the death of 'em both."

The ladies said rosaries and lit votive candles en masse for Bridget Cleary and her unborn child. When the child came, the Lord was obliged to answer half their prayers. The baby was small but healthy. Bridget held it in a blanket and smiled a tepid but genuine smile, then told Mrs. McGillicuddy that God and the angels were calling her, but she was glad she got to see her baby before she went—God's final gift to her. And then she closed her eyes and was gone.

"Ready she was. She went peaceful," Mrs. McGillicuddy told Patrick, who had run home from the ironworks. "And God left you a beautiful girl, healthy as a spanking-pink pig."

But Patrick did not hear the assuaging words. He only looked at his dead wife in the bed, beads of sweat still on her hollow face, and wondered how on earth this skeletal, gray corpse was all that remained of the beautiful wife he had married in Galway three years before.

Lucky it was the baby was strong, for she mightn't have survived either, Mrs. McGillicuddy said. "Poor motherless waif. Whatever is to become of her?" she added, shaking her head, then making the sign of the cross. "Mother Meery, help 'er."

Mrs. O'Brien down the hall had a new baby and enough breast milk for Bridget's baby. The buxom, once-upon-a-time scullery maid had so many children that she no longer had time for scrubbing floors. Father Gerald liked to say she was "blessed" with a new baby perennially. "Blessed, indeed," she would mimic caustically after Father left. "I wish the good Lord would bless us more in bucks and less in babes. Mouths need feedin', and the cupboard's bare as my arse." All the ladies laughed at her irreverence.

But Mrs. O'Brien was a good soul and said it "weren't any more work to feed one babe as two," and she would chat to the ladies in the tenement hallway, cradling both babies in her arms, her big breasts like two mounds of ice cream, each with a red cherry that glistened with the infants' suckling.

Bridget had requested her baby girl be named Sorrel, after an eccentric grandmother she had loved dearly and who had provided her the funds for passage to America. Little Sorrel thrived under the care of the tenement ladies and wandered about the place as if she had ten mothers instead of none. Patrick worked hard at the ironworks and had no energy left at the end of a fourteen-hour day for the toddler. But he did the best he could.

Patrick met Seamus at the ironworks. He was a blessing for Sorrel, for he took a liking to her and she to him. All the ladies took a liking to Seamus, too, for he liked women and noticed things other men did not.

"Ah, Mrs. McNaughton, you're looking beauteous today. What've ya done to yer hair?" he would say with doting charm.

"Ya flirt, Seamus. Nothin' at all! This ole mop's same as it ever was! But yer lovely fer askin'. Me ole man never noticed I had any hair whatsoever!" she laughed.

"Now, what'd be cookin' in yer kettle, Mrs. Donnelly? Smells sweet as me mother's lamb stew in heaven it does! And me with a killin' hunger!"

The ladies were glad to invite Seamus for a bite and never begrudged him the meager food in their pantries, for he was generous with treats for the children and would surprise the mother of the house with a clutch of flowers or oxtails from the butcher, knowing how little they could afford such niceties. When he sat at their tables, he played with the children and helped with the dishes after the meal.

"Saints be praised, Seamus Lanning. That all men could be good as you! The women of the world would be a happier lot," an appreciative mother would exclaim.

Seamus came home with Patrick often—after hours at the bar, to be sure—with a package of beef kidney or tongue or beef tips for stew, along with potatoes. And he would cook a feast. Sorrel came to love Seamus as her own father.

Work in the ironworks was exhausting and dangerous, and the workers, the majority Irish, quipped that if Ireland was hell, this surely was purgatory. Sorrel was five when her father was killed in the factory, crushed by a crucible filled with molten iron. He lived for an hour after the accident and was conscious enough to ask Seamus to care for his little girl.

Seamus was getting on in years, and he knew he wouldn't last in the ironworks much longer. The bosses had let men go much younger than he, albeit with less capacity for hard work. But his time would come soon. When Patrick was killed, fate forced Seamus's hand, for now he was responsible for two mouths. Seamus moved into Patrick's flat. He stopped going to the bars after work and went straight home. He would fry up liver or cow tongue and onions or cook oxtail soup and boiled potatoes and talk to Sorrel about her day.

He bought an illustrated fairy-tale book and read stories to Sorrel every night before tucking her into bed and kissing her good night. He was by nature a nurturing soul, and fathering came comfortably. But he fretted over his heavy responsibility and wondered what on God's green earth he was ever going to do. He would turn out all the lights and sit by the window, drinking whiskey and smoking. Looking out onto a grimy, city nightlife rank with smells of garbage and burning coal, he mused at his peculiar situation. A father at his age! After several shots of whiskey, he would put out the butt-end of his day, frazzled, little left, and fall asleep.

ELEVEN

MOLTEN DREAMS

SEAMUS DECIDED to look for a job as an exercise boy or stable worker before the inevitable happened. He had worked with horses as a youth in Ireland and missed their touch. He had a natural way with the beasts and would quickly prove himself if given the chance. But such jobs were hard to come by and more likely given to free darkies than to Irish, their reputation for drink and wildness preceding them.

Nevertheless, on Sundays, Seamus made the rounds to stables, looking for work. He took Sorrel with him for luck and in hopes the presence of the child—and their clean clothes and polite manners—would convince an employer of his dependability.

He finally landed a job as a groom at a stable close to the old Bathgate Estate near Fordham. The job did not pay as well as the ironworks, and he would have to rise even earlier. Since a groom's work started at 4:30 a.m., he had to get up at 3:30 to catch the trolley for the forty-five-minute ride to the stable. Despite this, his new job was a joy to him; his soul bloomed anew. The feel of those noble creatures was as primal and immanent to his being as the silken Irish mists hanging on the heath. They were in him, part of him. And he wondered how he could have ever lived without them.

It was all glorious: the smell of fresh straw, the munching of oats, the insistent whinny when the feed didn't come quickly enough, the smell and feel of lineaments. He loved, too, the steam rising off a horse's body after a dawn workout, the creak of freshly soaped leather, and running his hand down a Thoroughbred's leg to feel for telltale heat or bruising—even the sweet scent of horse shit. The textures, the scents, the sounds of horses aroused in him memories of Ireland, and in his sleep, his old brain trolled busily for the lost rememberings of his boyhood. He was young again, strong, in the morning of his days and filled with the honeyed hope of youth. Then he awoke with a tinge of disappointment to find himself in an old man's hut of bones.

He loved his job so much that even on Sundays, his day off, he took Sorrel to the stable, a trip that she looked forward to all week, for she shared Seamus's passion. She had a natural way with horses—"Just like her old man," the grooms quipped. Pride filled Seamus's chest. She was only five but fearless around the half-ton beasts. She helped her adopted father hot-walk the horses or wrap their legs or calm fractious stall mates in her tiny voice. Together, they trimmed their feet and rubbed speed into their legs. Wherever she was needed, she was eager. The grooms kidded Seamus that he'd better watch out; his daughter would have his job in no time at all.

He marveled at his good fortune at having found gainful employment at a stable, and he in his twilight years. But he had an Irishman's ironic regard toward the future, for he was filled with unflagging hope that his luck would hold, yet dogged by a fear his luck would run out.

Indeed, the dream was too good to be true.

One Monday, Seamus took the trolley just off the Bowery. When horse-drawn fire engines and mounted police suddenly galloped past, he called out to a man standing at a trolley stop, asking what the commotion was about.

"Those damned Irish are rioting and burning everything in the goddamned city! And they're lynchin' niggers!"

Seamus had seen plenty of riots in the city in recent years. The streets quaked with draft riots and labor riots and race riots, all inextricably linked somehow, although the nuances were mostly lost. Seamus read in the newspapers later that the final ignition point had been a dock strike by Irish workers protesting poor wages. When the employers hired black strikebreakers, a bloody melee ensued. Then federal troops—most directly from the battlefield of Gettysburg—were sent to crush the rioters.

It seemed the entire island of Manhattan was combusting, from the Irish slums of Five Points in lower Manhattan to as far north as Central Park. After burning the provost and draft offices, the rioters moved on to lower Manhattan and set fire to Horace Greeley's *New York Daily Tribune*. The mob surged on to the *New York Times* but were thwarted by the newspaper's sentinel Gatling guns. They tore through wealthy blocks, ransacking mansions, then targeted Brooks Brothers, the city's leading clothier for the wealthy. The company had a huge contract with the government to produce Union Army uniforms and was embroiled in a labor dispute with 400 garment workers. Representing everything the rioters hated—anti-labor, the wealthy, the draft—Brooks Brothers was looted, then set ablaze.

Seamus got off at Clarkson Street and turned the corner to find a mob dragging a black man out of a bakery. There, in the middle of the street, the man was bludgeoned and kicked to unconsciousness. Then he was strung up by his neck, his body gyrating in death throes until finally still.

The mob, its bloodlust still not sated, doused the dangling body with kerosene and set it on fire. The black, greasy smoke and acrid stench roiled and billowed and twisted, as if tortured by the knowledge of its own terrible nature.

The putrid smell of burning flesh engulfed Seamus, and he shuddered uncontrollably, retching as he stumbled down an alley in terror. Seething waves of rioters flooded the streets, and armies of police marched toward the onslaught. He ran as fast and far as his old lungs could take him—behind him, explosions and gunfire. His heart pounded like a frenzied bird flapping its wings against its cage.

The mob advanced up the street. At the end of the block, huddles of black children from an orphanage screamed and cried, herded into a mismatched caravan of carriages and buckboards come to their rescue. The motley chariots of deliverance galloped away, whips cracking and urgent hooves echoing on cobblestone.

His heart pounded as the mob invaded the orphanage, throwing furniture out the windows, smashing galaxies of glass to the street outside, and setting all afire. He shook at the thought of what could have happened to the children had they been in their beds when the invaders came.

Seamus ran until his lungs nearly burst in his chest and the streets fell quiet. He was beyond the madness. He walked several miles the rest of the way home and stood in front of the tenement, not ready to go upstairs. The smell of burning hair and flesh clung inside his nostrils. He could not escape it. He tried to compose himself before seeing Sorrel. She was such a smart little thing, and so intuitive, just like a horse. When he walked into the room, he could not hide his discountenance, and her child's eyes were wide with fear. He told her there were riots in the city but that they were far away. They were safe.

The next morning, newspaper headlines blared what he had seen with his own eyes. The trolleys were not running, so Seamus walked most of the way to work that morning, through blocks and blocks of ransacked streets, flames licking from smoking ruins.

When he arrived at the stables, he was horrified, for the barns had been burned to their foundations in the rampage—the horses left screaming and rearing in their stalls, the grooms helpless to save them from the smoke and flames. Only the skeletons of blackened stalls remained, steaming carcasses of horses inside, the hair singed completely from them. Occasionally, a carcass would groan, expelling fluid and steam from its cavity. His beloved stable was now a molten nightmare of putrid flesh and charred dreams.

TWELVE

THY KINGDOM COME

THE RIOTS LASTED for several days. Like many, Seamus lost his livelihood and future. But what visited the old man and his little girl next had the feeling of singular damnation, as if the devil had chosen them for special punishment and lurked in the tenement with them.

Two weeks after the stable burned, Seamus came home from a fruitless day of job-hunting. He picked up Sorrel from Mrs. McGillicuddy, but the little girl did not show her customary eagerness to see him. She was strangely distant. Her body was wired with tension, and her watery blue eyes had taken on the cast of ice, hard and clouded. Seamus thought perhaps she was sick and felt her forehead for a fever. He leaned down to gather her in his arms, but she shunted away. Then he glimpsed long streams of blood running down the inside of her leg. He gasped and whispered hoarsely: "Child, what has happened!"

No sooner had he expelled the frantic words than a terrible fear scuttled down his chest and settled in the pit of his stomach, twisting his gut. He lifted Sorrel's skirt, even as she pushed his hand away, and he could see that the little girl had been damaged, violated in an unspeakable way. Her petticoat was caked and clotted, nearly black with blood.

Seamus gasped again and pulled Sorrel toward him in an urgent embrace, as if he might absorb her pain and take away the hurt. But she stood stoic and staring into space while he sobbed onto her little shoulder.

Seamus boiled some potatoes in silence. Then he sat down in front of her.

"Darlin', please tell me who did this. You must tell your da," he pleaded. But her face was a wall of intransigence. He sighed. "We will go away from this place so you are safe," he said. "The devil who did this will burn in hell. He will burn in hell for eternity, and God will punish him."

But even as Seamus uttered the words with grinding resolve, he wondered why God had forsaken his little girl. The next day, Seamus told Mrs. McGillicuddy in cryptic but nonetheless unequivocal words what had happened. She covered her mouth and blanched at his meaning.

"There is a demon among us," he said, "and I must move Sorrel far from this place. Can you keep a close eye and keep her safe until I find a new home?"

She nodded solemnly. "Aye, Seamus. Upon me mother's grave, nary a man'll touch her. Upon me mother's grave. You can be sure of it."

Seamus looked now at every man in the tenement with suspicion, as if behind a smiling face and jovial manner lurked a monster. For an instant, he had a flash of paranoia and wondered even at Mrs. McGillicuddy, for it had been during her watch that Sorrel had been violated. But his mind quickly came to her defense: she had been an angel after Sorrel's parents died and very generous in helping Seamus. How could he question such a good woman? No, the devil was a man; he was sure of it. He could not squelch his rage at the unknown, even toward his closest friends, and it consumed him like a curse.

Tens of thousands were fleeing the city, many heading in the only direction that offered hope: west. Just the year before, President Lincoln had signed the Homestead Act, which provided 160 acres of public land in the western territories to anyone who could live on and improve the land for five years. The act opened up the floodgates of humanity eager for open spaces, for free land, and for a second chance.

Seamus felt the city crushing him. He could not return to the iron mill. He was getting old and had a daughter to care for.

Across the country was free land, if they could only get there. Seamus asked Sorrel if she might like to go west and start a horse farm. It had been several days since he had discovered her horrible secret, and she had not been the same child since. But at the mention of horses, her eyes sparked, and she ran to him and hugged him hard. It was the first time she had shown any liveliness, and Seamus was struck by the change.

Seamus gathered his sparse savings and combined them with the meager cash Patrick had collected in a cigar box. He pawned the few belongings he could from the flat—Bridget's silver tea service, Patrick's porcelain shaving mug, and an heirloom ruby necklace from Sorrel's eccentric grandmother.

Within a week's time, they had packed their bags and boarded a westbound train out of Union Station. Seamus was relieved to settle into their seats after all the jostling and pushing. As the train moved away from the melee, they settled into cushioned comfort and the rhythmic, velvet clack of the steel rails. Sorrel stared out the window of the accelerating train. The lamplights of the city slashed through the night, then gradually melted to dark. Soon, she was asleep.

It took them two weeks to reach Chicago, then St. Louis, and, finally, Independence, Missouri, the trailhead of the Oregon Trail. From there, they joined a wagon train after purchasing a wagon, a horse team, and supplies.

Sorrel's transformation was immediate. They had come from the cramped, dark squalor of tenement life and stepped through the gates of heaven. The land boasted beautiful, grassy stretches of prairie occasionally veined with tree-lined river valleys. The fresh air smelled of wild sweet clover and prairie flowers, and a vast, cottony sky soared above them. Sorrel loved the wide-open spaces, the horses, the adventure. She was flourishing, and this filled him with joy. He had not realized that the city was suffocating them. He felt the solace himself, the rightness of going west.

In the evenings, after he and Sorrel unharnessed the team, fed them, and hobbled them to graze, Seamus would cook, and Sorrel would run out on the prairie to explore.

Sorrel did not have a doll but had noticed that other little girls in the caravan did. One evening, she gathered scraps of cloth Seamus had packed for mending clothes and grabbed a pail, then went in search of some little creatures to be her dolls. A mouse would be good, or a baby rabbit if she could find one, she told Seamus.

She tromped to the edge of the marsh and saw a big frog jump, and then another. They weren't exactly cuddly, but they would do. She laid down a bed of marsh grass at the bottom of the pail for their bed, then worked at constructing her little family for nearly two hours.

Seamus found her with a pail full of three big bullfrogs wearing little diapers she had constructed from scraps of plaid flannel. "Look, Da! My new babies!" Sorrel lifted her pail proudly. "They were naked, so I made diapers for them."

Seamus nodded, and she demonstrated her scientific diapering procedure, holding them gently upside down and stroking their white bellies. They seemed to like this and would lie still to be diapered, splayed out like little bandy-legged, barrel-chested boxers ready for a massage, Seamus thought. He chuckled under his breath. When she put the warted, double-chinned fellows upright in their finished diapers, they croaked like gruff old men, and Seamus could see more distinctly the resemblance to crusty Irish boxers he'd known in the past.

"They are the finest wee ones to ever wear diapers," Seamus announced in his hearty brogue. "The little people will be jealous to see your fine frog babies!" He grinned to himself for days at his little girl's ingenuity.

Sorrel and Seamus sat together on the buckboard for hours as their big, bonneted wagon swayed on heaving axles from dawn to dusk. Like the ships Sorrel's and Seamus's parents had taken to America, the earthbound galleons pitched and yawed across the ocean of prairie. Men and women, children and dogs, old and young, oxen and mules and horses—all inched across the endless grass in wagon trains. Seamus found comfort in the labored creaking of the wheels turning in the rutted trails. It was the sound of the future coming. Time melted into geography, then destiny. The West was their promise, their prayer: *hallowed be thy name, thy kingdom come.*

THIRTEEN

INTIMATE ILLUSION

FOR ALL HE HAD witnessed through a lens, Frederick had no experience with women and intimacy. He was now twenty-seven years old and had never been with a woman, flesh to flesh. In fact, he had not even kissed a woman. So the negatives of Sorrel still hidden in his backroom had ignited his obsession like kerosene on fire.

Many months after seeing Sorrel in the lake, Frederick caught another glimpse of her, this time swimming with an Indian woman. He was riding the same trail above the same lake when he caught sight of them. He pressed his eye hard against the spyglass to focus, breathing in chopped gasps, his eye socket perspiring against the lens rim. He tried to hold his breath and steady the spyglass. They were swimming nude and frolicking. He heard their voices in two languages, lilting in laughter as they splashed each other. Then they swam to the shore and lay down in the pebbled shallows, hip to hip, their eyes closed above slight smiles. Their long hair fanned out in the shallows, the Nez Perce woman's black, glistening like obsidian.

Frederick's eye moved hungrily over their bodies. Both were lean, tall, angular, their hip bones rising gently above the water. Nothing like amply fleshed postcard women. The Indian woman's skin was bronzed and beautiful, her muscles ropy. She rolled to her side and touched Sorrel's stomach. The blond woman opened her eyes and turned to her. Frederick's heart jumped. He gulped. They kissed and were soon tangled in flesh—strong, long limbed, muscle braided in passion.

He did not know such physical intimacy existed between women. Frederick longed to capture their entanglement through his lens. He stood stone still, the spyglass fogging up. Heat filled him from chest to groin. He wiped the lens quickly, then pressed it hard against his eye socket, his brow beaded in sweat. His mind froze their movement like a camera shutter, their bodies burned into his mind's eye with jeweled radiance.

They groped each other, hands hungry. Arms and legs intertwined, shadows of water and lissome flesh, dark pools of pleasure.

Frederick's privates were engorged and pulsing for release. His breathing labored, his heart pounding, his body surged so intensely he nearly collapsed, and wet oozed inside his trouser leg. He had never experienced such unbridled bliss.

Frederick's obsession became so fevered that he was vexed by his enchantment. *Traveling alone for so many years breeds perversity*, he pondered. He'd heard tales of mountain men and fur traders who, in their isolation, had taken on strange ways of seeking pleasure. Coupling with animals was common and often said to be less meddlesome than having a woman.

Willie, of course, was ready to retell such tales in all their glorious depravity. During a poker game, he told of a mountain man who happened upon a woodpecker hole at the same height as his "peckerwood," as Willie called it, snickering at his clever turn of phrase. The man rimmed the hole with bear grease, and it "fulfilled the duties of an ever-faithful wife for many years, without listening to prattle," quipped Willie.

Frederick was appalled at the story, his eyes popping wide like a schoolboy who'd just seen a girly picture for the first time. He worried that others would misconstrue his blushing for guilt, or worse, priggishness. He certainly considered himself a gentleman and found such stories abhorrent. But humans have a fundamental curiosity for depravity. He couldn't resist listening.

For all Willie's wayward musings, he had never related such a scene as what Frederick had just witnessed! *Women with women*. It seemed to him beyond imagining, even for men with the most lascivious minds. Maybe aberrant female attachments were less common than those of males? Or perhaps they were beyond the world of men, mysterious, even menacing. Somehow, their passion did not feel salacious to him, but rather sacrosanct, inviolable. He felt no urge to share his discovery but kept it cosseted, growing more resplendent with each remembering.

Of course, he *did* have other secrets, but they were far less enigmatic. He kept a special collection of photographs inside a cigar box, hidden under handkerchiefs. They became an incubus of obsession—swathed, coddled, layered in years of his own adoration, dog-eared from his fondling. Some were daughters or wives, one a schoolteacher, all in perfectly innocent poses, and all his alone in his imaginings.

He recognized one day a similarity in the women: each was blond, slender, and resolute in her gaze. Perhaps because his mother was blond. They say men seek out women with their mother's qualities, trying to replace her, replicate her. *Seems natural enough*, he thought. He loved his mother and she loved him. But he had a gnawing fear that his fondness for the pictures was deviant.

Oddly, he was the consummate professional in his work. Calm, charming, smiling. He put his subjects at ease, as long as he had his camera as his prop, perhaps his crutch. But without his camera, in the presence of a young woman he felt exposed, utterly helpless to even look her in the eye.

His paper ladies kept him company. They were accommodating, approachable, available to him without effort. Now the blond siren waited for him in the back closet of his studio, hidden in the metal-cased negatives. The more time passed, the more enticing his secret. He was caught between depravity and deprivation, each strangely heightened by the other. He had traveled down an inexplicable path and now was lost to go back.

Slowly, logic laced with curiosity interceded. One Sunday, he decided to develop the prints. He smiled at the irony of conducting this unseemly activity on the Sabbath. But the forbidden fruit made his anticipation sweeter.

In his darkroom, he first floated a sheet of paper in albumen, a solution of egg white containing a chloride, then in another tray of silver nitrate. He then set the paper into a printing frame, aligning the glass negative over the cradled sheet. Now for the magical part: setting both in the sun to let light and chemicals marry on the paper!

As often as not, the image could be lost to bad chemicals, errant light, or other vagaries of the delicate process. To lose this image would be to lose a rare treasure. His heart throbbed as he waited. The image would not reveal itself until he took the framed paper back into his darkroom, rinsed it, then toned it in gold chloride that smelled like bitter almonds. All this in total darkness. His hands fumbled, so he slowed to the deliberate pace of a careful novice. Finally, he fixed it in sodium thiosulfate to fuse the image to paper forever.

Now the moment of reckoning. He opened the door and walked into the sunlight with the dripping print. He trembled at what he saw: a nude, golden-haired woman, pale as Venus, an angel reposed in a bed of dark diamonds. The water-laden print gleamed with details so sharp as to come alive. The woman was no longer fantasy but flesh, the water an agate dream of his own desire, echoing, lapping over itself in strident dimension, engulfing him in waves of reverie. He was awash in fresh infatuation.

FOURTEEN

IRON SHARPENS IRON

AFTER SORREL interrupted the poker game, Frederick learned the name of the mysterious dark-haired man. He worried the fellow would broach the topic of their shared secret, but he found Ransom Fallon to be discreet.

He liked Ransom immediately. Quiet and thoughtful, he had come from a roughneck past, as Frederick would discover later. When the poker game broke up, the man extended his hand to Frederick.

"I thought I would introduce myself." Only the slightest bemused smile crossed his lips. "I understand you are a photographer. That must be interesting work."

"Yes, I've seen a great deal," Frederick said, smiling. He knew they were both thinking of the naked woman in the mountains.

Ransom was dark complexioned with olive skin, black, wavy hair, and black-fringed, gunmetal eyes. Their translucence gave his face a dusky, unfathomable quality. He had a scar near his left eye, and his nose had been broken. But the deformities fleshed out the handsomeness with enough imperfection to convey character, implying a past shaped in part by violence and misadventure.

Ransom had grown up in a Welsh mining village. Later, in America, iron factories and railroad work had sculpted his physique into rippling musculature. But it was boxing that bestowed him with a careful, animal grace.

Frederick's grandpa had told him about Wales, a mysterious realm full of paradox. The Welsh, his grandfather said, were both poets and pugilists, with a propensity for bookishness and brawling in equal parts.

"Ah, the land of King Arthur!" Frederick said.

"You know it?" Ransom asked, surprised.

"I grew up reading about King Arthur's court, castles, battles," Frederick said.

"I grew up playing in those castle ruins!" Ransom interjected. "They are everywhere. Wales is very much like this land. Rugged. Beautiful."

Frederick remembered Welsh settlers in Missouri and eastern Kansas. "They share a common bond with their Celtic brethren, the Irish," his grandfather told him. "Both suffer under English oppression."

The Irish, when not allowed their native dancing, held their arms stiff to the sides like dead sticks but moved their legs like their feet were on fire so the English occupiers could not see them dance through the windows of their homes, his grandpa said: "The Welsh, too, are not allowed to speak their own language, so they sing deep in the mines. Chorister quarrymen. They call it *eisteddfod*."

Frederick recalled the memory: "Do you sing?"

Ransom smiled broadly at this acknowledgment of an honored Welsh tradition. "Yes, I enjoy it."

"What brings you to Spotted Horse?"

"I acquired the rights to the old McGregor mine," Ransom said, leaving out the fact that he had won it in a poker game.

"Well, welcome." Frederick felt quick kinship with Ransom. If he had to share his secret with anyone, it was at least safe with the Welshman.

It was not until weeks later that Frederick learned more of Ransom's background. He'd been forced to make a hasty escape from Wales at the age of sixteen. He had intended to go to Ireland but hid on the wrong boat, which landed on the wrong continent. But the raw young America suited him.

He found ready work in factories and on railroads. But he knew that such grueling manual labor sucked the strength and soul from even robust men. He had seen his father and generations before him ground up by the mines.

The only constant in the maelstrom was chance. Games of chance were common in the city, from oily back alleys to opulent gambling halls. Ostensibly, Ransom was swept up in the ribald human current. But he realized that he must rise above the common flowage or drown in it. As a boy, he had played back-alley craps—covertly, to avoid the disapproval of his parents and ensuing strappings—but soon graduated to poker. He liked these games, especially the excitement of risk and the easy society. He had a natural aptitude for the cerebral nuances of the game.

Gambling was not his only means of income. By virtue of his size, he was thrust into the boxing ring. At first, he fought boys in neighboring villages, then graduated to men who traveled the circuits, looking for "fresh meat," boxing's butcher-shop vernacular for new opponents. "Fresh meat" meant mostly brash young men, reduced with little effort to bloody inertia. But Ransom was not one of these. He was able to capitalize on his opponent's low expectations.

He discovered that his boyhood skills honed in Wales were lucrative in New York, a haven for boxing and gambling. After a brief bout of profligacy prompted by the tragedy that chased him from Wales, he began to apply an insurance adjuster's sensibility to gauging risk. He avoided higher-stakes games. He molded a persona that was cordial, quiet, and refined. Opponents often assumed he was more successful than he really was and folded in the face of his suave countenance.

But his refined persona rankled rough clientele with less finesse and less capacity for losing money gracefully. Ruffians who lost assumed his smoothness was in fact calculated cheating. In such cases, pugilistic experience was helpful.

After the Civil War, the country was aflame with gold fever in the

Black Hills, Idaho, and California. Ransom knew too well the meager prospects of mining, but he also knew opportunity was inherent in new civilizations.

After crossing America via factories, boxing rings, gambling halls, and railroad gangs, he landed in San Francisco. Elegant at its core but ragged at the edges, it was built from magnificent wealth intermingled with ghastly poverty. Ramshackle buildings thrust up belligerently from the wharf. Squalid back alleys twisted through the city like hog bowels. But there were fashionable districts, too, with shining new buildings and elegant street fronts. The city had an air of going somewhere.

San Francisco was swimming in nouveau riche. Gambling tables were whirlwinds of activity. Liquor and ladies of leisure fueled the fever. Ransom's approach to gambling was mannerly in a city given to excess. He had only mediocre success east of the Mississippi but found that a patient player could make a passable living in San Francisco. He stayed sober and paced himself, much like he did in the boxing ring, pulling back, gauging his opponent, waiting patiently for the right moment.

He had learned patience from his mother and preferred gentle pursuits—reading, theater, the company of women. Women picked up immediately on his quietude, his curiosity, his philosophic acceptance of human fault and foible. He liked people. He especially liked women, and they especially liked him. He hungered for the emollient side of life that was feminine and nuanced, to escape the testosterone stew of male bombast.

FIFTEEN

THE BOWELS OF HELL

SEVERAL WEEKS after the poker game, Frederick was dining at the hotel when Ransom walked in and asked if he might join him for dinner. While eating, Frederick asked Ransom about his childhood.

"Well, I grew up in generations of miners. My father joked that little Welsh boys were born covered in soot."

He recounted that the mines claimed boy children out of the womb and claimed the girl children, too, because they were bound to the males. Dreams went no further than the lights from their headlamps on sweating black walls.

"As a little boy, I saw a mule being lowered down a mine shaft in a sling, poor beast. Eyes rolling in terror. I can still hear his pathetic brays echoing down the shaft," he said, shaking his head.

His da said the mule would never see the light of day again, that they'd pull him up when he was dead and his work in the mines was done.

"I remember thinking there wasn't any difference between that poor beast and my own father," he said. "Suddenly, I felt like I was being buried alive. Like I imagined that mule felt. Then I vomited on my father's boots."

As a little boy, Ransom had nightmares about being down in the mine and coming face-to-face with the devil. "Pastor Owen preached fire and brimstone. I used to think the mines were so deep that hell wasn't far below, and if I dug too deep, I'd fall in," he laughed. "I asked my da once if ya had to be dead to be in hell. He laughed and told me to be good and I needn't worry of such matters."

He had once whispered to his mother, knowing intuitively that his question would be blasphemy to his father, "Must all Welsh boys work in the mines, Mama?"

"The mines are a terrible thing, Ransom," she replied as she tatted a sock. "But they are the only way to feed our families. Your father and the other men make the best of it. That is the way it has always been. But for smart boys like you, there are better things in life. And you must strive for them. You must read and study and not take the grog and not play cards and fight and idle your youth away. If you study, you can go to school. Learn another trade. Then you can have a fine house and not live in filth and darkness and ignorance all your born days."

So, he vowed to please his mother and escape the mines. But what he had intuited about his father's opinions on a non-mining life was borne out as Ransom's studious tendencies became evident. His father was not a roughneck. Indeed, he admired reading and learning, churchgoing and singing. Nor did he wish less for his son. What he feared was that his son was striving for the unattainable, that his dreams would render him useless for real work. Mr. Fallon knew what was inevitable, even if his wife didn't.

But inevitability can find itself playing dangerous odds against a mother with resolute dreams for her favorite son. And Mrs. Fallon was a resolute woman. Her son was born with more vision and drive than a mine shaft could contain, and she knew it.

She sought out teachers and professionals in the town and neighboring estates who had books and borrowed them for her son. He consumed them as quickly as she could bring them to him. There were books on history and engineering and farming and geology and architecture and America and business and the classics. The plans she held for her boy she kept to herself. But Ransom understood them implicitly and accepted his mother's gentle urgings and gifts of learning.

His father's vision for Ransom was of stone, but just as stone yields to water, so Ransom's father saw his son slowly slip from his iron grip. Mrs. Fallon's gentle ways were winning, and Mr. Fallon had little stomach to fight her.

Mrs. Fallon's prayer that her boy would have a life outside the mines would be answered, but at a price that tore at her heart forever.

SIXTEEN

TREAD THE EARTH LIGHTLY

THE LONGER FREDERICK was in Spotted Horse, the more he felt he was living the adventures he had read about in youth and thought how fateful landing in the town was, as if it had called to him.

The nearby tribe called themselves Nimiipuu. But early French fur traders had mangled the name to "Nez Perce," French for "pierced nose." It was a misnomer since they did not pierce their noses. But the misnaming was the least of the white injustices to the tribe.

Now Frederick was meeting these very Indians in the flesh. Two teen Nez Perce boys had ridden into town from their village miles away to explore white-man curiosities at Mr. Marston's general store on Main Street. Mr. Marston helped them pick out colorful hard candies inside his glass case.

Frederick and Mr. Marston exchanged amused glances as the boys tasted the sweets, tentatively, wide eyed. Peppermint and lemon drops brought the most dramatic reactions. After they decided on several candies to take back to their village in a small, brown, paper bag, Frederick showed them some photographs. He had a bin of rejects, photographs that were blurred or flawed, that he used as currency for "paying" Indians to pose for him. They had never seen these "magic pictures" before and were awed he could "stop life" on his white man "hide." He convinced them to pose for him in his studio.

The boys returned to their village and shared Frederick's photographs. Days later, a Nez Perce man showed up to request Frederick come to his village to make photographs. Draped over his right shoulder was an otter fetus with two heads from whence his spirit name came: Two Head Otter. The man wanted Frederick to photograph his young son on his prized buffalo horse.

The son was thirteen summers but had already ridden on a buffalo hunt. "Qoqaalx! Qoqaalx!" Two Head Otter exclaimed to Frederick, gesturing his son's height, which was shorter than himself, and then mimicked shooting a bow and arrow. Frederick knew qoqaalx meant "buffalo." Two Head Otter believed a magic picture of his son would bring strong medicine.

Frederick rode to the village—a half day's ride—on an ancient Indian trail through mountains and forests. He saw a grizzly and her cubs and later an elk herd. A doe, innocent of her loveliness, drifted among the trees. Occasionally, he spied mountain goats perched high on mountainsides, white specks on gray, sharded rock.

Clambering up a steep slope with his horse and mule, he topped the ridge and gasped at the valley below. Frederick had never seen so many horses; thousands of them blanketed the earth.

The Nez Perce were among the wealthiest tribes on the continent in equine assets. Frederick remembered reading about Lewis and Clark's admiration of their horse culture. Now—now—he understood why they had been in such awe. Thousands of moons before, Nimiipuu first acquired horses from southern tribes who had traded with Spanish conquistadors in the hot lands. They learned to hunt buffalo with their new mounts and bred them selectively for coloring and toughness. Some had spots over their entire body, like leopards. Wild patterns were prized not only for their beauty but also for the strong medicine the spots had to protect them in battle.

Whites called the horses Appaloosas for the Palouse River running through Nimiipuu lands. But the Nez Perce called them *maamin*. Frederick thought how apropos, for the word sounded like "mother." Indeed, like mothers, their horses had become the source and soul of the Nimiipuu, their well-being and their wealth.

Frederick's horse nibbled the feathered tops of the tall prairie grass as they cut through the herd. Frederick noted the robust condition of the horses. Flesh on their ribs, sleek muscled, coats shiny. It was summer, and spring foals frolicked and gamboled, squealing their high baby whinnies in fractious play, smelling each other and then suddenly kicking up their heels. Several followed Frederick's horse and mule with outstretched noses, snorting at the strange intruders. The horses were of every hue and pattern, but the starry spots of the Appaloosas flashed conspicuous constellations of color.

Frederick rode into the village, children whooping and jumping with excitement around him. It seemed the entire village knew of his coming. Two Head Otter welcomed Frederick with his arms spread. His son stood behind him, dressed in a handsome beaded buckskin tunic and fringed leggings. The son's name was Storm Horse, his father conveyed through pantomiming swirling wind with his arms. "Storm horse" signified a tornado in Nimiipuu. Two Head Otter's wife translated in cobbled English, and Frederick nodded understanding.

Frederick was showered with food and gifts and given his own tipi. Men, women, and children gathered. The photographs amazed them. They had never witnessed such a thing and touched the photographs to feel the world inside, wondering if they might come alive, such was their wonder.

He set up his tripod and camera with boxed curtain. Two Head Otter's family tipi bore painted images of horned buffalo heads and a huge sun. Frederick decided to include the tipi in his photograph. He saw the father's face glow with pride as his son rode his horse before the camera. The horse, splashed with striking, piebald coloring, was a gift for his first buffalo hunt. "Maamin. Taz maamin," Two Head Otter said. *Appaloosa. Beautiful appaloosa.*

His pride reminded Frederick of his own father's when he'd first announced he wanted to go west. His heart ached at the memory. He would include Two Head Otter in the photograph, looking up at his son. Honor the son and honor the father. Frederick would send the picture to his own father. He would understand.

Frederick learned much on his visit to the Nez Perce village. One explosive incident served as an education in tribal rivalries. Among the photographs he brought to the village was the image of a Bannock chief, a dreaded enemy. Several braves became agitated, pointing at the chief's bow, which was adorned with a scalp. Frederick realized in horror that the scalp was Nez Perce. From their gestures, hugging their chests and pointing to the sky, Frederick surmised he might have been a brother or relative.

Now he understood the outrage of the braves. The Nez Perce's wealth in horses made them a common target. Fundamentally peaceful, they had become fearsome warriors by necessity, for they were surrounded by hostile tribes. Their bitterest enemies were Bannock, Snake, and Shoshone. To the north, the Blackfeet and Gros Ventre. To the east, Assiniboine. To the west, Spokane and Coeur d'Alene.

The Nez Perce did not customarily mutilate or display bodily relics of slain enemies. There were fearsome exceptions. Bloody Chief, one of the chieftains Lewis and Clark had met seventy years before, had been adorned with enemy fingers, and Twisted Hair had worn a cape of thirty-four Shoshone scalps. Despite their ghastly garb, the explorers deemed them friendly and honorable.

The Nez Perce, too, had been impressed by the white-skinned men. The explorers and chiefs swore their friendship and shared the peace pipe. Old Chief Twisted Hair gave his solemn vow: "Our hearts are good." The news of the promise spread among the Nez Perce and passed from generation to generation as a mark of honor.

Frederick watched that legacy unravel as whites consumed Nez Perce land. The explorers and Nimiipuu did not know the ultimate irony of their promise, nor how Nez Perce hearts would come to be tested.

SEVENTEEN

THUNDER ROLLING FROM THE MOUNTAIN

TWO HEAD OTTER belonged to the Wallowa Lake tribe led by old Chief Tuekakas, a leader who had indefatigably protected ancestral land from whites. Frederick came to know Chief Tuekakas's two sons, the oldest of which was named Hin-mah-too-yah-lat-kekht.

"Thunder Rolling from the Mountain" had been baptized by a Christian missionary as Joseph. Born in a cave during a violent thunderstorm, he was destined to be a steadfast spirit in a maelstrom. Joseph exuded a quiet wisdom and not a hint of superiority.

Joseph's younger brother, Ollokot, was more buoyant and gregarious. The two young men understood their destinies: Ollokot was to be a warrior, Joseph a chieftain.

Both had splendid physiques: Joseph stood six foot three. His brother was nearly as tall. They had the sculpted cheekbones of the Nez Perce, aquiline noses, sumptuous lips, and square-cut jaws. Sinuous necks fanned out to enormous shoulders. Athletic games in youth and years of bow hunting made their arms thick as tree limbs, their thighs muscled whipcord.

When Frederick first came to Joseph's village, the young chief welcomed him in pieced-together English, Nimiipuu, and Chinook Wawa, an old jargon used between fur traders and Northwest tribes. Late in the evening, Joseph asked Frederick a question, and a brave named Red Rock Lizard translated: "Hin-mah-too-yah-lat-kekht asks, 'Why whites come to our land like grasshoppers?'"

Frederick thought for a moment. "They are hungry for a new life," he said, and picked up a handful of dirt. "Fertile soil. Freedom. New life." But Red Rock Lizard stared at him, confused.

Frederick pondered. How could he explain how so many whites lived in poverty and disease and squalid cities? How could he explain that this beautiful land was like paradise?

He scrunched up his shoulders and body to look small and skulking. His eyes darted all around as if in fear. Then, suddenly, he raised his arms to the sky, his eyes wide with wonder. He smiled broadly, breathed deeply to take in fresh air, open spaces. He brought his raised hands together as if thanking the Creator.

Suddenly Red Rock Lizard's face brightened in recognition. He turned to Joseph and nodded to the sky, repeating: "Ilaka wispa. Ilaka wispa."

Joseph nodded and smiled sadly at Frederick. "Yes. Yes," he said. "This . . . land of . . . goodness. You call 'heaven.'"

Frederick had often observed the difference in how whites and Indians regarded land. The Nez Perce lived nestled in the Bitterroots, the lap of the Rockies, where stone-studded, velvet meadows swelled in the shadows of jagged giants. The land yielded abundance, but nature's bounty was flanked by ruthless beauty that taught them humility and reverence, too.

The Nez Perce did not understand the white notion of owning land. How could Mother Earth be owned by such temporal beings when she was forever? How could she be owned by those beholden to her for life itself—whose feeble flesh and brittle bones she took back into her womb? It was with puzzlement that Natives observed the encroachment of the strange whites, skin pale as the underbelly of a fish, whose wagon trains scarred the land with rutted veins.

The whites marveled at the lush hills and sweeping meadows blanketed in blue camas flowers and yellow mule's ear. But the hills were only a gentle prelude to the stone treachery of the mountains. The Indians knew the seasons of this treachery—when the mountains would give them shelter and solace amid the high whistling winds and when the mountains would crush them with snow and ice and killing cold.

Again and again, the mountains swallowed up the whites, froze their bones, and starved their livestock, hurtling wagons with whole teams of horses down rocky slopes. The Nimiipuu believed the mountain spirits were angry at the whites and punished them, that the whites were foolish to defy the reign of the seasons and the mountains.

It was a curious thing, nevertheless, the sheer idea of defying the nature of things. As if whites no longer heard the breathing of the earth. They stripped the hillsides of trees, butchered the buffalo and beaver, mutilated and gutted the land. They left a swath of carnage and mindless defiance behind them.

So when the dry autumn prairie, teased by their insolent campfires, ignited into an angry inferno and swallowed entire caravans, the Indians were not surprised. When rivers, swollen and roiling from spring thaw, raged through canyons and swept away wagons and oxen and human refuse, they wondered why whites taunted the earth.

The Nimiipuu showed them safer routes and tried to teach them the ways of the earth so they would not perish. But whites did not honor the wisdom of the Indians nor the ways of the earth. And so they died, or suffered the loss of loved ones, for their obstinacy.

Chief Tuekakas had skillfully avoided signing treaties ceding land. His people hunted and lived freely in the lush hills of their ancestors, peaceably trading and coexisting with whites. But when gold and silver were discovered near the Orofino River, a chasm split the tribe; many Nimiipuu chiefs signed treaties. Only seven chiefs—Chief Tuekakas among them—refused to give up their land. But how could they stand on the mountainside in the face of an avalanche?

Days before Tuekakas died, his two sons were returning from their annual buffalo hunt with the Crow. It was autumn on the Lolo Trail, a trail worn by thousands of years of ancestors through the steepled pines of the Bitterroots. They had in tow packhorses loaded with buffalo meat, skins, and heads, as well as weapons and finery for which they had traded with their Plains brethren.

They stopped at the Sacred Medicine Tree, *pottoosway*, a lofty Ponderosa pine, ancient and majestic, with a huge ram's horn embedded in its trunk. Generations revered the tree for its supernatural powers, kneeling at its great roots, leaving offerings of thanks or entreaties for success on a hunt or in battle, for the birth of a child or healing of a loved one.

The brothers walked up the path padded in pine needles. A hawk called out in the watered sky, and buttery echoes reverberated between the canyon walls. They came to make a request of the tree: the healing of their dying father or, if that was not to be, a passing that would bring him peace.

Sunlight poured down through spiny branches. But suddenly, a cloud scudded darkly over the sun, and the tree turned skeletal and foreboding. Joseph and Ollokot glanced at each other, grim faced. They rose wordlessly and touched the tree as hope fled from their hearts.

When Joseph and Ollokot returned to their camp at the fork of the Wallowa River, their father lay dying inside his tipi, swaddled in bear skins beside a crackling fire. The chief was weak and raspy, his chest rising and falling like an ocean tide. His sons began to keen in a low chant, and it seemed to the old man beautiful and sad. Like the distant howling of wolves under the stars, a celestial sprinkling in a sugared night sky.

"I fear not for my own passing, my sons." He ground out the words. "My heart is heavy for my people." He took a deep breath. "Nimiipuu oracles have foretold vast change, much struggle. You know this. My own dreams tell me this," he said. He suffered greatly with the hard reckoning that lay ahead, lodged like a hatchet between the prophetic and the profane.

Once, in the fullness of manhood, his soul had been a mighty cyclone. Those had been days of plenty when buffalo roamed as far as his eyes could see, the rivers were thick with salmon, and his people prospered and lived in peace. But now the whirlwind of his spirit, like the cornucopia of his people, had spiraled down to a tip so tenuous it had dissipated into air, like displaced memory, like a lost frontier. And there was no help for it.

He felt the air above him crowded with souls. He gulped, his chest rattling. Then his breath wisped upward, floating with a curl of smoke out of the tipi and into the vast sky. Tuekakas died with young Joseph at his side. It was autumn and exactly sixty-six summers since Lewis and Clark had smoked the peace pipe with the Nimiipuu.

Before his last breath passed through his lips, he entreated Joseph to keep a promise: "My son," he choked out, "my body is returning to Mother Earth. When I am gone, think of your people. They look to you to guide them. Always remember: your father never sold this land. You must stop your ears when they tell you to sign a treaty. Soon the white men will be all around you. They have their eyes on this land. This land holds my body. Never . . . never sell the bones of your father and your mother."

EIGHTEEN

STOWAWAY HEART

FREDERICK'S STUDIO was thriving, but he desperately needed more supplies, especially decorative backdrops. He had seen an advertisement in the San Francisco *Bulletin* for a studio in Chinatown that painted backdrops for the Chinese theater and photography studios. He decided he would take a trip to San Francisco. He had never been to the bustling city and was intrigued. While in San Francisco, he would visit Ransom, who was there on business.

Frederick was surprised to discover that Ransom had done quite well for himself. He spent his earnings on small investments, books, an occasional fine meal, and modestly priced, tailored clothes. And he was a member of the Mechanics Institute Library on Post Street, a grand, Italianate building with arched windows and scrolloping Corinthian carvings. Frederick met him there, and they shared a drink surrounded by marble columns, leather-bound books, and tufted, rosewood furniture. All bespoke a gentlemen's club of distinction and scholarly pursuit.

In this genteel enclave, over the whirling topaz of bourbon, Ransom recounted the dark deed that had sent him fleeing from Wales. As a teenager, he had accidentally killed an English landowner guilty of raping a young woman named Bronwyn, whom Ransom had loved since childhood.

"I escaped to a Welsh seaport and hid in the hold of a ship bound for Ireland. I was going to send for Bronwyn," Ransom told Frederick. "But I soon learned the ship was going to America. Then, Bronwyn discovered she was pregnant. To save her honor, she married a schoolmaster in a nearby village. But she died in childbirth."

In one harsh blow, he had lost his love, his family, and his homeland and carried his disembodied sorrows with him to a new world. Loneliness corroded his heart. He became a creature of the streets, gambling parlors, brothels, boxing rings, drowning himself in drink. He smothered his incandescent emotions with ebullience of the flesh.

But his cobalt heart was like an urn filled with fire but starved of air. One night, lazing in a window under the moon, he remembered a moonlit night in the castle ruins with her. She had said he would make something of himself. He vowed on her honor that he would.

He went west. Once he got past Missouri, he augmented his lean gambling earnings with railroad work. One day, he was slinging a sledge side by side with other filthy, sweat-drenched Irish and Chinese on a rail line that extended as far as the eye could see on an endless prairie. The landscape was featureless, of such vast monotony it overwhelmed him with despair. He was no one, in the middle of nowhere, going no place at all.

When the man beside him stood up to stretch his back and noticed specks moving across the horizon like ants, Ransom stopped too. It was a wagon train going west. Before he knew it, he had thrown down the sledge and was striding toward the foreman's wagon to grab his bedroll and all his earthly belongings he still kept in the duffel his mother had packed for him years before. Once and for all, he was going west—way west.

The foreman barked at him: "What the hell are you doing! Get back on the line, goddammit!" But Ransom kept walking, bare to the waist in the tall grass, his sweat-slick back rippling in the sun. He began loping, then running, toward the wagon train that would take him to California.

Frederick reveled in the spectacle of San Francisco. It bustled with rickshaw drivers, laundry carts, fish vendors, and Chinese coolies loaded down with huge baskets on bamboo poles balanced across humped shoulders.

Women clad in tight, brocaded silks and with satin-black coifs shuffled demurely down boardwalks. Other women of lower status in coarse blue and black cotton, their hair tightly braided in long queues, sold flowers and vegetables and trinkets. Everywhere were colored lanterns and signs in Oriental calligraphy. He was mesmerized by the carnival.

He stopped at a storefront piled high with baubles and hand-painted cloisonné. Amid the riot, he spotted two little girls, twin toddlers, their round little faces perfect as porcelain doll heads. They smiled shyly, then disappeared behind the stacks. An old man quickly came to his side and bowed a greeting. The man was slight, barely five feet tall. His face was ancient with wrinkles, his chin hair bound into a tight, grizzled braid that curled like a scabrous rat tail. He held in his hands a shiny black box, ornately carved and hand painted.

"Magic box," the man offered in soft, broken English. "Very nice. You like?" he cooed, pointing a finger resembling a bird's claw at the lid. It was exquisitely painted with a scene of a Chinese slave girl surrounded by admiring men. The man's eyes twinkled, and he held up the same finger as if to say, "There's more!" He held the box under Frederick's gaze: "You try open magic box."

Frederick gently placed his thumb on the rim, but it would not open.

The old man smiled. "Special box. Hold secrets." He pressed the side of the lid, and it slid slightly to one side. Then he pushed at the middle of the side panel, which moved inward. He pressed a concealed locking mechanism, then lifted the lid with a long, yellowed fingernail. Inside, the box was lacquered in black with gold filigree. It had many compartments. The old man held up his hand again. He was not done with his demonstration. "More secret. Very special box."

He opened the lid of one of the small compartments and lifted it completely out. Underneath was a key. He placed the tiny key in a lock and, to Frederick's astonishment, pulled from the bottom of the box another secret, black, lacquered box. It was nearly as large as the main box except that it was very shallow. The false bottom was perfect for secret papers, love letters, money, or—Frederick instantly thought—clandestine photographs. A place where no one would ever find them. For ten years now, he had kept his special photographs in a cigar box, but the images of the mountain-lake siren were special. They were for his eyes only.

"This box magic box. Keep many secrets. Never tell," the old man said. Frederick felt his face flush suddenly and a rush of paranoia, as if the ugly little man had clairvoyant powers.

He asked the old man how much, and they exchanged currency. The man instructed him once again in the complicated sequence. Frederick followed the knotty fingers, then tried the sequence himself. The old man watched and corrected as his student fumbled. Finally, Frederick committed the process to memory.

As the old man handed him the box, he stroked it gently, bidding it adieu. When he looked up, he was no longer smiling. Frederick thought he saw something in the man's expression, something akin to regret or sorrow. The man averted his gaze, his eyes suddenly vacant, hooded like dead leather. He turned, shuffled silently through a beaded doorway, and was gone.

NINETEEN

BEST PORTION OF A LIFE

IT HAD BEEN A YEAR since Old Chief Tuekakas had died. The Wallowa Lake tribe, now under Joseph's leadership, had spent the summer months on a successful buffalo hunt in Montana Territory with the Crow. Spirits were high.

The trek had taken them through breathtaking land. Wallowa Lake opened to Hells Canyon, the deepest gorge in North America. Beyond that, the tribe had followed the ancient Lolo Trail carved torturously through the Bitterroot and Clearwater mountains. Seated in the laps of the august giants were rolling meadows and prairies, veined throughout with rushing rivers teeming with salmon. They then followed the Yellowstone River to a land of geysers and bubbling pits, steaming mists, and eerie rock formations. Now they returned through the same.

Sings Like Lark had cooked her family's favorite meal, and they dined on tule mats outside their tipi. The sweet aroma of camas bulbs roasting in a pit wafted out to the hungry children playing horses in the meadow. The roasting meat was even more enticing. Succulent buffalo steaks sizzled on the fire, flames licking the crisp edges. Men and children hovered over the savory crackling, rubbing their stomachs.

Playfully, Sings Like Lark rapped the knuckles of her husband, Tall Tree, with her wooden spoon as he tried to sneak a bite-sized morsel of meat hanging temptingly from a skewer, a morsel he claimed was roasting just for him.

Tall Tree feigned a frown at his wife's scold and turned to his friend: "A mighty warrior defeated by his wife's wooden spoon!"

As a special treat, Sings Like Lark had baked *oppah*, a sweetened long bread, and picked a bowl of huckleberries. She and her daughter, Flying Horse, had dug up bulbs of wild hyacinth, too, a favorite for their sweet, nutlike flavor.

She set out the clay dinnerware and utensils and drinking cups carved of ram's horn, then spread the food in festive array. The oppah bread sat like a chapel of warmth on a wooden breadboard. At the center she placed a horn vase of colorful wildflowers: scarlet Indian paintbrush and lavender-blue lupine. She smiled at the flowers, the abundance of food, the laughter of children, reveling in the disembodied joy of small things: to build a fire, pick berries, feed her family, do all that was necessary each day. At that moment, she thought perhaps these days were the best portion of her life, so content was she. Like a bee on a flower, a bird on a breeze, a fish in a current. To live abundant. To be as meant to be. And her heart was good.

On their trek back to the Bitterroots, they grazed their horses in meadows floating in gold dust, the pollen of goldenrod and wild sunflowers. In early morning, yellow-breasted meadowlarks with black-chevroned chests perched regimental in the prairie grass, whistling their reveille.

Women from many villages assembled in upland meadows—Weippe Prairie and Camas Prairie, an ancestral gathering place—to pick grub-white mulberries so abundant they filled large baskets woven from hemp, bear grass, and corn husks. With practiced hands, they also dug camas bulbs from the prairie soil. Generations toiled together, and young girls were given their first *tuk'es*, a long digging tool crafted of wood, bone, or stone, to honor their growing womanhood and new responsibility in feeding the tribe. It was a special day for a girl, a baptism into her new status.

The daylong work was laced with talk and laughter about families, romances, children, tribal events. They floated about the vast purple meadows, moiling among the roots, unearthing tubers like gnarled scepters of the soil. The rich smell of humus and uncoiling roots emanated from the earth's flesh.

At night, after a day of labor, mothers with babies retired to their tipis, safe in suckling darkness under furs. The rest of the women sat around the campfire, peeling the bulbs' tough skins with stone blades as they sang. Digging bulbs was backbreaking work and an honored tradition, a mainstay of the Nimiipuu's toil to amass sustenance for winter. The roots remained plentiful even as the buffalo and salmon diminished under the white man's onslaught.

Camas root gathering was also a time for women to share their handicraft in beading, weaving, and tanning. Nimiipuu women had become especially admired for their beadwork. Clothing and everyday goods, even weapons and warhorses, bore their exquisite work.

Among the skilled beaders in the Wallowa tribe was a man named Bird Stepping, who did exceptional work and was a "two-spirit," so called because he seemed both male and female. The Nimiipuu believed, as did most Indian cultures, that two-spirits had a special link to the spirit world and drew strength from both sexes. They often attained the status of shaman or medicine man or woman by virtue of their dual identities.

There were two-spirits among the Nimiipuu and many among the Crow. A Crow two-spirit called Woman Chief had become a warrior chieftain of sixty lodges in her village. As a child, Flying Horse had seen Woman Chief during the intertribal buffalo hunt on the plains. Woman Chief gave her hope that she could perhaps do the things that she yearned for: riding and hunting and being a warrior.

Flying Horse did not like to dig camas or pick berries or tan hides. She was clumsy at weaving bear grass and even worse at beading. But her mother would not listen and ignored her sulking empty-heartedness while performing such tasks. But Tall Tree noticed.

Autumn was coming soon, when the salmon would run and their legend retold. For thousands of years—long before they learned to hunt buffalo with their Plains brethren—the Nez Perce relied on salmon for their survival. The kingly fish leapt like a spangled mantle up the river to die in the waters of their birth while their fingerling spawn journeyed downstream to the ocean, a cross stream of birth and death. This was the time of spearfishing for the Nimiipuu. At dark, drumming and chanting pulsed on the shore as spear hunters launched canoes with big torches at the bows. The fires burned in mackled reflection on the obsidian water, and the fish came to the flames like moths. Spears—mere elongated glints in the torchlight—sang through the night air. Over the labored hours, an entire season's sustenance would be heaved into the boats.

Flying Horse loved this time and was swept up in the excitement. On the sly, her father asked if she would like to come with him on the boats. Her face shone with eagerness. She was on the lake amid the throng before her mother knew where her daughter had gone.

As her father had suspected, Flying Horse was a natural hunter; he let her spear the salmon and pull the heavy, thrashing fish into the boat. She did this for many hours and did not tire. Even the men on the boat marveled at the girl's strength. They marveled, too, at Tall Tree's curious permissiveness in allowing his daughter such an honor. But their boat landed a record catch that night, so they were not wont to complain of a girl spear hunter among them.

The next morning, Flying Horse hugged her father affectionately, for she knew that he would suffer the wrath of her mother. He smiled with pride at his strong daughter and put his arm around her shoulders, which ached from the arduous night.

Tall Tree asked his daughter if she remembered the night several years before when they had seen trumpeter swans on Lake Wallowa during a full moon. Indeed, she could not forget that magical night and thought of it often—the night air fluid with the feral sounds of the forest, the singsong of crickets, and lapping water. The moon slid among the clouds, its light gently washing upon the water's surface. The great white birds floated like ivory frigates on a sea of silver, and Flying Horse gasped at their beauty.

She remembered a swan rising from the water. With extended, swooping movements, she dipped her head and body beneath the water, then spread her graceful wings, still submerged. Rising from the surface, droplets like sprays of diamonds danced across the surface. Finally, she embraced the air to glide just inches above the lake.

"You are like the swan, my daughter. Strong and beautiful and tough. The swan carries a heavy burden in her beauty, but she is strong enough to glide over *and* beneath the water with grace."

They walked with each other in silence, understanding thick between them.

TWENTY

SOILED DOVES

WHEN RANSOM first walked the streets of San Francisco, he felt as if he had *arrived.* Since leaving his homeland across the ocean, he carried a feeling of *hiraeth*, a Welsh word that could not be translated in English exactly but which meant a void in the soul, a longing. For Ransom, it was perhaps an elegiac yearning for home, for rootedness, for belonging. It seemed San Francisco filled all those needs.

He settled—as much as a restless soul can—in the young city. His small investments, mostly in the stock market and railroads, yielded revenue. He continued to gamble, but only with calculated risk. He rented a small suite at a hotel that afforded him the amenities he sought as a gentleman of moderate means.

Though he had finally found some comfort of the body and soul, he still had dreams of Bronwyn, nightmares of that day at the castle ruins, of her being dragged away, or of her strangely deserting him to marry another, sometimes even her rapist. He had tired of his sexual forays and liquor-induced lusts, lush in the velvet night but fetid in the rude morning light, like embalmed passion. His desire for women became more a yearning of the heart than the flesh.

Now only occasionally was he taken by a woman's charms. He was a curiosity to women and a favorite of the local prostitutes, whom he was more likely to take for buggy rides than to bed and paid either way.

He liked to show up on a sunny Sunday afternoon and take several of the women who were not otherwise occupied out for a picnic. They would laze in a meadow, like fresh laundry wind-strewn upon the grass. The women talked or read aloud—those who could—or French braided each other's hair. Ransom would pretend to sleep with his hat over his face. But he eavesdropped on their saucy banter and feminine giggling.

They would loosen their stays and take off their high-topped boots and sometimes their layers of petticoats, feigning modesty and threatening to scold Ransom if he dared peek, then chortle at their bawdy irony.

Ransom was genuinely interested in their stories. Some had suffered terrible hardships as orphans or abandoned children, had run away from drunkard fathers, escaped grinding poverty, crushing factory work, or unspeakable sexual abuse he could only guess at. They inevitably landed in the sole profession that welcomed them unconditionally and promised them a bed. They were, in the end, only able to keep clothes on their back by taking them off, only able to keep the wolf from the door by welcoming him into their boudoir.

As their youth and beauty faded, they faced a downward spiral to degradation, disease, and death. The final stop was the dreaded cribs: small cells open to the street for any and all manner of men. Squalid and rat infested, each dark room contained only a cot on which the woman performed her work sixteen hours a day until she succumbed to disease, beatings, murder, or suicide.

Given the grim fate that awaited most, Ransom marveled how the women could laugh and cavort and flirt with such abandon. *But then*, he thought, *hope is the flower of youth, and denial its nectar.*

The women were not self-pitying nor looking for sympathy. In fact, they always seemed perplexed that Ransom should find their stories interesting. They accepted their lives nonchalantly, although sometimes their dark memories, long dormant but roiling deep with reptilian menace in their heads, conjured powerful feelings.

When their voices quivered and their lashes moistened with emotion, Ransom would pat their hand and say, "Now, now, you're better off far away from all that!" and then they would ride in silence for a while, his hand warm and comforting.

Ransom often visited Madam Chernov's, a bordello of some stature and impeccable style. It was there he made an extraordinary discovery.

Sitting alone in a side parlor cosseted behind swagged curtains, he was reading an advertisement in the *San Francisco Bay Chronicle* about a new invention for avoiding being buried alive. A phobia had swept the country, first fueled by accounts of gravely ill Civil War soldiers being buried alive. Then the Victorian neurosis was set aflame by Edgar Allen Poe's "The Cask of Amontillado," a terrifying tale of live internment published in *Godey's Lady's Book.* Now hundreds of new inventions claimed to protect against the ghastly mishap.

Ransom was reading about "The Improved Coffin with Hatch," Patent No. 81,437, when he was interrupted by the rustling of skirts in the adjoining music room. He leaned forward in the wingback chair to look past the curtain. A woman sat at the piano and fanned out her sheet music.

She had luxuriant hair the color of oxblood—enhanced, Ransom guessed, with henna from the druggist (for he had been privy to some of the beauty secrets of prostitutes while eavesdropping during his picnic outings). Her creamy complexion and peach-blossom cheeks untouched by rouge, her magnolia neck, her deliberate manner all bespoke a cultured demeanor.

She hummed under her breath, then began playing. The piece was an old English ballad Ransom recognized. She sang to her own accompaniment in a sweet soprano with a quivering vibrato.

Ransom sat with the newspaper in his lap and absorbed the tremulous strains. Her voice brought to mind his mother's, sweet and fluttering above the chorus in the church choir. When he began absentmindedly humming along, the woman cast a sideward glance and realized that she was not alone.

"I didn't mean to startle you," he said when she had finished the piece. "You sing beautifully, and I haven't heard that tune for so long. Won't you please continue?"

She smiled accommodatingly and dipped her head in appreciation, then turned back to the piano. With ivory fingers upon the keys, she found her place in the sheet music and began with easy confidence, leaning into the keyboard as if her entire body were absorbing the music through her hands. When she had played the last chord, there was a moment of silence as she searched for another favorite to play.

"Do you know 'All Through the Night'?" Ransom asked. It was a beautiful Welsh lullaby.

She smiled. "Yes!" She began to play the tune by heart, and at the end of a running chord, she found her pitch and softly began the first high note of the song: "Sleep my child and peace attend thee." Her voice soared with the piano.

With the second verse, he stood behind her, joining her in a deep baritone so soft and melancholy it melted her heart.

Slowly, tenuously at first, the two voices found each other, commingled, then ascended in harmony. "Soft the drowsy hours are creeping, Hills and vales in slumber sleeping." Their voices floated about the piano notes like two meadowlarks fluttering, flirting, then gliding in synchrony.

They closed the song, both sharing the same drawn-out, intimate note, and the woman felt herself flush at the sensuous silence that followed. Ransom took her hand, lifting her fingertips to his lips. "Thank you for that pleasure, madam," he said, relinquishing her hand as his eyes met hers. Then he picked up his hat and left the parlor.

TWENTY ONE

A FERN UNFURLED

SYLVIA DANCING had not grown up with opulent silks and satins, with classical music or coiffed hair. In fact, her childhood had been austere, crushing. She was the daughter of a minister whose sharp-angled righteousness and finite planes of truth went unsoftened by any charitable contours. His wrath was the very power of his faith.

As the eldest of eight children, she felt his harsh theology most acutely. She wore the yoke of his scourge with quiet tolerance, but in the inner recesses of her soul, a small, hard core of rebellion took seed. As her father's tyranny tightened around her, the seed flourished like a tender fern unfurling in a dark and rocky place.

She was fourteen when she realized a deeper reality than she had been born into—the reality that she did not love her father. In fact, she hated him. She despised his godling airs and counterfeit piety and wondered why parishioners were so gripped by his magnetism.

This realization split open a chasm in the landscape of her being, which, heretofore, had been sanguine in its habitual acceptance of things as they were. Her conscience became a minefield of emotions—guilt and anger, relief and loss, but, most of all, hope—until she reached the solid ground of certainty and a dream of escape.

On her sixteenth birthday, without warning or farewell and in the deep of night, she left her home forever and boarded a train to New York City. There she found a textile factory and began using her sewing skills to eke out a livelihood. In the squalor of the sweatshop and her shabby tenement room, she recreated herself. She started with her birth name, Sarah Danville, which she changed to Sylvia Dancing. She thought her new name beautiful, even lyrical, and it represented that which her father held in adamant disfavor: dancing, expressiveness, flamboyance.

She gathered about her all she could salvage from her former life. She took a tally of those things as a child might count coins from a piggy bank. She had a good education, including a solid knowledge of literature and mathematics. Through her father, she had developed a disciplined mind and frugal ways. The only true talent Sylvia recognized in herself was her musical ability; she had a fine soprano voice and had played the organ in her father's church since she was young. Indeed, it was the only means of self-expression she had been allowed.

Her mother had taught her sewing, embroidery, knitting, and quilting. The church ladies once praised her exquisite needlecraft: "Why, Sarah! Your work is lovely! God has truly blessed you as a seamstress. Beautiful!"

This pleased her, but she had soon pushed the perimeters of what the devout ladies considered pious dress.

Sylvia's impulse was to embellish, and when she perused the pages of *Godey's Lady's Book*, she saw fashions of such exquisite decoration and colors that she felt as if she had opened the gates of paradise. These, *these* were wonderful! But in expressing her enthusiasm to her mother concerning such fashions, she was met with the steely gaze of disapproval. *Godey's*, she was informed, was not proper entertainment for a young girl of Christian deportment, and Sylvia was forbidden to read it again.

But she did read it again. In fact, again and again. She hid issues under her trundle and relished their taboo pages as an adolescent boy coveted girlie postcards.

The pages inspired her profoundly, and she unwittingly pushed the bounds of her own attire. Pleats a little too snug, enhancing her slender waist and budding breasts. A yoke of a dress cut a smidge below her collarbone. Even lace, generally used as modest edging, ever so slightly intimated sensuousness.

The infractions were minuscule but bothered Sylvia's mother. She complained to her husband: "I have noticed Sarah's needlework is becoming too fancy. So much lace and embroidery! And did you see how tight her bodice was today?"

It was with surprise and a sense of betrayal that Mrs. Danville regarded her husband's failure to recognize Sylvia's malfeasance. "Now, Mother. Do not fret. She is pious and abiding in all other matters. We cannot fault her for her beauty and talent. And I do not think God faults her either." So Sylvia continued to sneak her bewitching stitchery past her mother. But her heart ached with forbidden notions of feathers and spangles and embroidery and ruffles of which she could never partake.

After her escape to New York, she began to explore the interiors of her unexpressed self. She sculpted the contours of her new life with skill and spirit, determined to make something of herself, to have nice things and the freedom to enjoy them.

Hope propelled the gilded chariot of her dreams, but it lurched and pitched in the bog of reality. Her first job was in a glove factory, but she had not bargained for the backbreaking work, long hours, and appalling conditions. After nearly two years, she felt the drudgery eating her alive. Her dingy room with gas stains on the torn wallpaper closed in on her as her father's domination had.

One day at the factory, Sylvia shared her despair with the young woman working next to her. The girl had similar aspirations and offered that she had decided to become a nanny with a wealthy family out west. "I read there's a shortage of women in California. Any female with gumption enough to go can find a rich husband in a wink!" she pronounced with authority. "I saw so many ads for nannies in San Francisco. They interview girls in New York and pay their passage west."

The idea seemed to have merit, and Sylvia's spiraling despair brought a feeling of finality she feared she would never escape if she did not act soon.

She would need references, her friend told her, which could be easily forged if one had no previous nanny experience. Desperation took the edge off Sylvia's guilt. She found herself composing a fictious reference out of whole cloth that spoke glowingly of her character and dependability. Her "reference" was a Mrs. Lewis Saufer, a banker's wife whose family had moved to Chicago and who begged her to join them. However—and here the lie took on especially elaborate dimensions—she stayed behind to care for her sick father, who had recently died.

Sylvia soon landed an interview with a family bound for San Francisco. She put on the nicest of her three dresses, freshly pressed, and oiled her hair to a sheen before the mottled old mirror above her dressing table. She flashed an uncharacteristic smile at the image and was startled by its beauty. She was ready. On her way to the interview, she guiltlessly fastened in her hair flowers picked from a storefront flower box. She had written an entire letter of lies. Purloined pansies paled in comparison.

Sylvia recounted her sad story to the kindly woman and added, casting her eyes downward in manufactured grief, "I have nothing left here, since my father passed. Nothing but sadness. I want to start a new life in California," she said. "I just *adore* children. When I saw your ad, I was so excited."

The charade worked beautifully. The woman asked how soon she could start. Sylvia was on her way.

On the train west, she had occasion to meet an interesting old couple. Burton and Erma Kay Yale had traveled an entertainment circuit for twenty years, back and forth from New York to Chicago to San Francisco. Their song-and-dance show of popular minstrels consisted of songs about California and gold miners and pioneers going west, invariable crowd-pleasers that fed off the gold and land fever sweeping the country.

Sylvia hungered to hear about California, and the Yales obliged with stories of the theater, popular divas, and scandalous love affairs. Sylvia confided to Erma Kay that her nanny position was only a means to an end, that she hoped to land gainful employment, perhaps as a seamstress, in San Francisco. Erma Kay said seamstresses were in demand, which heartened Sylvia. In fact, Erma Kay volunteered, "I may know of a position with an old friend of mine, a former diva named Madam Chernov. Perhaps you have heard of her."

No, but she would be very interested indeed to meet Madam Chernov. Erma Kay wrote a letter of introduction for Sylvia and drew a crude map of the Pike Street area of San Francisco, with a star indicating where Madam Chernov lived.

What Erma Kay had failed to mention, but which became obvious upon Sylvia's arrival at Madam Chernov's establishment, was that it was a brothel, albeit lavish and elegant. Sylvia introduced herself and presented the letter of introduction from Erma Kay.

"I need a dressmaker with flair," Madam Chernov said to Sylvia, looking her over and noting the details of her dress. "Someone who can really dress my girls in style. My salon is known for style. But the dressmaking shops around here are robbing me blind! I can barely afford to keep clothes on my girls."

As she related her woes to Sylvia, Madam's "girls," dressed in such finery as Sylvia had never seen, strolled about the chandeliered lobby and the grand staircase in a palace of velvet dreams not quite their own, arm in arm with gentleman companions.

Madam herself was dressed in silver-gray Shantung watered silk, tailored exquisitely to her form. Sylvia was intoxicated by the lavish decor and well-coifed courtesans. Here she could create the fashions she'd dreamed about in *Godey's*! The next day, she appeared at the bordello doors with her valise and all her earthly belongings, ready to begin work.

TWENTY TWO

MODESTY REDRESSED

WHEN MEN initially caught sight of Sylvia Dancing, their first impression was one of wonder that such a refined creature could be found in a brothel, even Madam's. She was different from the other girls: educated, cultured, demure, elegant. *Ironic*, she mused, *that my girlhood dreams of fashion would come true in a bordello!* She felt an odd pang of vindication—a Pyrrhic victory, perhaps, but a stylish one, over her father's puritanical parsimony.

She became so adept at tailoring that some of the wealthy women of Huntington Park had gotten wind of her talents—how this happened without the knowledge of their husbands' philandering she did not know. One matron had unabashedly sent her a letter requesting her services.

Madam flatly refused Sylvia's request to do outside work. "You are my employee, and I provide lodging. You came to me from a New York slum. I'll thank you to show some gratitude!" Over a year's time, tensions had grown between the two. Madam Chernov marveled at the talents of this quiet girl Erma Kay had sent to her and was thrilled by the dresses she produced for a fraction of the cost the city's finest dressmakers had charged. But Sylvia's sophistication and small but growing notoriety galled the territorial madam.

It also vexed Madam that her customers inquired about Sylvia's availability for activities other than tailoring and she could not accommodate them and reap the profits. She had talked to Sylvia about working for her in other capacities, but Sylvia curtly answered: "My talent is in dressing others, not *undressing* myself."

It was customary for prostitutes to pay for their own dresses. Madam Chernov had required that the dresses the girls purchased be approved by her. This ensured her impeccable style *and* her markup—a source of resentment for the girls.

After Sylvia was hired, the girls saw a way to finagle themselves out from under Madam Chernov's thumb. When they started wearing Sylvia's opulent creations without her approval, Madam felt her control slipping. She was further enraged when a new girl who wished to curry Madam's favor divulged that Sylvia was designing dresses for the girls at far less than she charged Madam. This, Sylvia felt, was only fair since their budgets were far more limited. But the increasingly cross madam disagreed.

Within two years, Madam had started calling Sylvia her "tailoring tart" or "stitching wench" in front of customers to humiliate her and requesting arbitrary alterations for which Sylvia was not compensated. Sylvia knew it would be only a matter of time before she was out the door, so she devised a plan for her own timely departure. She saved her money like a miser and each day counted closer the time when she would be able to leave Madam Chernov's.

Her plan of escape was richly embroidered. She had already purchased her own sewing machine (the one she was using had been purchased by Madam, and she was required to pay rental for its use). Her plan required saving enough money to rent a small place and buy sufficient supplies to get her started as a seamstress. During her visits to tailors and seamstresses under the guise of a potential customer, she had taken diligent notes on charges and costs of materials. Her calculations encouraged her, and she had already acquired several wealthy clients surreptitiously.

Some of Madam's wealthiest and most refined clients would approach Sylvia with social invitations, no doubt enticements offered with the prospect of garnering future favors of a more intimate nature: "My dear, could I take you to dinner at Cliff House Restaurant? The ocean view overlooking the bluffs is simply stunning! Quite something. Have you been there?" or "Miss Dancing, have you been to the new California Theatre on Bush Street? It is quite magnificent! You really must see it."

She accepted some offers, for she thirsted for more culture, but with the caveat that she was not in the market for other entertainments. Sylvia's quiet integrity and refinement inspired trust, and she found that her gentlemen companions confided in her things they did not tell their own wives—tales of business dealings, lost gambles, fears, even childhood dreams.

These wealthy men, some of them city fathers and prominent politicians, showered Sylvia with gifts, either out of genuine affection or in hopes she would change her mind. She stuffed her pride deep in the back of her mind and the money deep in a drawer. When other girls went drinking or shopping, she sewed or read the classics or played the piano in the small parlor and sang softly to herself. Sometimes patrons stood quietly outside the parlor, puffing on their cigars and soaking up the mellifluous soprano strains.

A week after Sylvia met the mysterious man in the piano parlor, she saw him again. But on this occasion, Ransom made his presence immediately known, walking up to her and bowing in greeting. "I hope I haven't startled you *this* time," he said with a broad smile.

Ransom asked Sylvia if she might have dinner with him, a request that elicited a pleased but somewhat discombobulated expression. "I would enjoy that very much, but, ah, are you aware that I work for Mrs. Chernov *only* as a dressmaker?"

Ransom got her meaning quickly: "Yes, yes, I'm aware. I would very much like to see some of your creations."

"Well, as a matter of fact, you've seen *many* of them. The girls here wear them," she said with a sly smile.

Since first meeting Ransom, she had asked the girls about his background. They mentioned his odd practice of taking them on picnics or carriage rides and paying them for their time, without further requests. This had intrigued Sylvia and strangely excited her.

Ransom and Sylvia went out to dinner several days later and quickly took to one another. Two gentle souls who had been brutalized too long by misadventure, they found solace and genuine enjoyment in each other's company.

They talked of many things. He was pleased to meet a woman who not only could read but also was well read. Both had read Mark Twain's short story "The Celebrated Frog of Calaveras County." Ransom had read Jules Verne's adventure novel *Twenty Thousand Leagues Under the Sea*, and Sylvia had just finished Lewis Carroll's *Alice in Wonderland.* "A strange book but so fanciful, if you care for that sort of thing," she offered. Both had read about Leo Tolstoy's masterpiece, *War and Peace*, causing a stir on the East Coast, but neither felt inclined to tackle the massive tome.

They shared their stories of how they had arrived in San Francisco, each editing out the unsavory details of their past, like forging references or killing a man. Each commiserated with the other's experiences of New York factory work.

Sylvia asked about Ransom's boxing—a blood sport she detested, she was quick to admit, but, playing to his masculinity, she conceded: "It must require a great deal of toughness and skill."

Ransom did not acknowledge her grudging compliment. He was more concerned she thought him loutish. He countered that he no longer boxed but that it was not just a sport of blood and toughness but also required strategy, analysis of one's opponent, and, most of all, an artful defense. But skepticism clouded her face, so he quickly changed the topic, not wanting to mar an otherwise harmonious evening.

Ransom dreamed of Bronwyn that night. But this time, Bronwyn came to him, kissed him on the forehead, and touched his cheek. Then she turned away into the Welsh mist, leaving behind the nostalgia-sweetened smell of humus and bracken and moss.

The next day, Ransom sent a note to Sylvia, thanking her for the pleasure of her company and requesting her presence for an evening at the theater a week hence.

Their meetings soon became regular and much-anticipated engagements. Before long, they were meeting weekly, much to the dismay of Madam Chernov and her girls, for his time with Sylvia was time and money taken away from them. Their evenings were of a genteel nature and usually included dinner, the theater, or a stroll in Huntington Park. He often asked Sylvia to play the piano in the parlor, too, and they would sing duets. Ransom had taken Sylvia on a picnic to the country, but this communion with nature had few similarities to his countryside forays with brothel girls. No lying in the grass with loosened corsets and bare feet and exposed calves. No unpinning of chignons and letting down of luxuriant tresses.

Instead, they talked or meandered the park or read aloud to each other. Sylvia recited Dante Gabriel Rossetti's popular sonnet "The House of Life." Rossetti had burst upon the literary scene after exhuming the unpublished poems he'd buried in sorrow with his dead wife.

Such gentle pursuits with Sylvia pleased Ransom, and he expected no more. Sylvia had been cloistered and notions of romance curbed. She had never even had a beau to speak of. (The rotund industry barons and crotchety old bankers who courted her at Madam's hardly qualified.) Her vicarious education at the brothel may have yielded instruction regarding matters of the flesh but little of the heart.

One night after dinner, Sylvia requested Ransom stop the buggy *behind* Madam Chernov's. When he helped her out of the carriage, she deflected his goodbye kiss. Instead, she kissed *him* on the forehead and touched his cheek. Then she took his hand and led him up the narrow back stairs, a secret passageway specifically designed for discreet comings and goings. He followed her like a lamb, but his heart beat like a lion's. When she unlocked her door and pulled him into her room, he asked her softly: "Are you sure?" But he could see that her eyes were bright with yearning.

TWENTY THREE

FROM THE EARTH RISING

FREDERICK'S BUSINESS expanded so quickly that he had become nearly well-to-do. He installed a handsome sign—*Cortland Photography Studio*—in green script with a red drop shadow skipping across a yellow background. He hired a young woman to keep books and wait on customers and Willie's orphan boy, Chester, for deliveries and schlepping equipment.

Frederick had made a name for himself in the postcard industry. Victorians were hungry to experience the West and viewed postcards through stereopticons in their parlors. He also photographed for survey teams scouring western lands for development. He received a telegraph from William Henry Jackson, America's foremost wilderness photographer, inquiring if Frederick could join a survey for the Yellowstone region. The federal government had hired Jackson and a geologist named Ferdinand Hayden to document the Yellowstone area for the nation's first national park.

This was an exciting prospect. The Nez Perce had shown him their sacred places around the Yellowstone River. It was a land of phantasmagoric legend, with geologic formations that defied the eyes: waterfalls and geysers and moiling waters among rock striated with dazzling colors. For years, trappers and Indian scouts had told of the region's wonders, which seemed incredible beyond belief.

Jackson's partner, Ferdinand Hayden, approached geology and surveying with religious zeal as "man's destiny," the means to "a beautiful plan for the physical development of our continent." He was a small man so wired with energy that the Indians called him Man-Who-Picks-Up-Stones-Running. His pronouncements about Yellowstone seemed exaggerated, but his photographs bore out his words.

As reports and photographs revealed the geographic superlatives of the area, the press waxed poetic about man's rightful dominion over the earth—that God intended the untamed land to teach man about His ineffable plan and the earth's resources for human use.

A year before Hayden's survey, Nathaniel Langford, a leader in a previous Yellowstone expedition, wrote in *Scribner's Monthly*:

> [Yellowstone] possesses adaptabilities for the highest display of artificial culture, amid the greatest wonders of Nature the world affords. . . . [T]he march of civil improvement will reclaim this delightful solitude and garnish it with the attractions of cultivated taste and refinement.

Frederick read these accounts with creeping chagrin, wincing at what would surely result in loss of Native sacred land. The survey was the master plan for settling the West. It would give Manifest Destiny *teeth*. But it was the opportunity of a lifetime. How could Frederick not accept? It took him only minutes to answer Hayden's telegraphed request.

The expedition launched a month later, trekking along narrow mountain trails, through rocky valleys, and inside caves under waterfalls. Each day, Jackson loaded up his fat little mule, Hypo, named for the hyposulfite in darkroom chemistry. He led the way, Frederick following with Elmer, and the other mules—loaded with plates, cameras, chemicals, and tripods—trailing behind.

Frederick captured a buffalo amid the swirling mists. Its dark dignity coalesced with the strange beauty of the land. It seemed a part of it. Frederick thought the image would make a fine postcard. Just as he predicted, it sold extraordinarily well.

The survey, completed in 1872, was published with great fanfare in *Scribner's Monthly*. The same year, Congress declared the area Yellowstone National Park, the world's first national park "established for the benefit and enjoyment of the people."

Frederick was grateful for the experience. But he could not squelch a scuttling guilt that the natural beauty of the land the Nez Perce had shown him would soon be overrun. And he had led the invasion.

Joseph and Ollokot rode alongside a grove of birch saplings, slim and straight as tapers, standing white against green foliage and the Wallowa Mountains. They were returning from hunting stag and had bagged a huge buck, which they draped over a packhorse. But its rack was so large that it dragged on the ground, so they severed the head at the neck, drained the blood, and tied it to the top of the horse's load. The head bobbed with the horse's movement and looked puzzled, as if its body had been rearranged and it no longer remembered how to run, so far from its ennobled stance high upon the ridge.

The brothers watered their horses at the shore of Wallowa Lake and soaked up its glassen surface. Like a blue mirage of longing, it reflected dreamy, snowcapped mountains and alpine forests bristling at its edge.

The tribe swam in its waters, hunted game in the woods, and raced horses in the meadow. Of the eighty or so Nez Perce villages spread across the Columbia Plateau, Joseph and Ollokot felt the jeweled Wallowa was the most beautiful spot of all. They believed they were predestined to live and die in this land, as the salmon died in the land of their birth. They believed that Mother Earth was provider of all and all life returned to her. To disrupt this order was to dishonor her and to scatter the people's seed and spirit to the wind. Thusly the people had lived prosperously for millennia.

But ancient Nimiipuu shamans had foretold of vast change, so when new ways and new people visited their lands, they did not fear to embrace what seemed prudent and discard what did not. They had welcomed the horse two centuries before and developed a superb horse culture. They welcomed Lewis and Clark, and the trappers and pioneers after them, and became vigorous trading partners and held pride in their peaceful relations with whites.

When whites pervaded their lands and spread disease, more than half the Nimiipuu died, and for the first time in thousands of years, they feared for their future. Whites seemed strangely immune to diseases that killed Natives. The Nez Perce thought perhaps the whites' holy book protected them, so in the 1830s, they sent a group of headmen across the continent to St. Louis to explore the powerful medicine of the Bible.

What followed was a further scourge upon the people: a schism cleaved the Nez Perce, some adopting Christian ways, others not. Young Joseph and Tuekakas had been baptized as Christians and tried to adopt Christian ways. But they ultimately abandoned Christianity, saying whites taught people to argue about God. They wanted no part of the bickering. "Two ears are worth ten tongues," young Joseph said.

Joseph remembered the day his father lost his faith. While riding home, Tuekakas—his heart ragged—tore up the 1855 white treaty that promised the Nez Perce their land. He also tore up the prized possession he had carried with him for decades: a Gospel of Matthew from his Christian baptism. The words and religion of the whites, he said, no longer held honor.

Young Joseph longed for the days before the whites had come—when his peoples' hearts were united and strong, when the lands were free to roam, the children healthy, the buffalo abundant. He recalled with bittersweet reverie the sojourns of his youth to buffalo country. They would feast and dance and play games and race horses and tell stories. And the children played stick games in the meadows or sat by the campfires at night and listened to the adventures of elders and warriors. But now his heart-listening was troubled, full of noise. He could not shut his ears and hear his soul.

Joseph and Ollokot moved on along the Yellowstone River. Whites called the area "Wonderland" for its beauty and bizarre geologic formations. The white press claimed Indians were afraid of Yellowstone, believing the geysers and hot springs gushed from hell. But in fact, the Nimiipuu believed the land was sacred and called it "unfinished by god." They basked in this land alive with spirits: drifting mists and bubbling bogs, rocky shorelines striped with brilliant reds, oranges, and yellows. The erupting waters rose from the earth's soul. The hot steam was its life's breath. They beseeched the volitant spirits. They danced and chanted and prayed for buffalo and for courage, for peace and a good life. From the earth rising came beneficence and strength, and they gave thanks for its bounty.

But they would not long have the land to themselves. Whites

would build a massive log hotel with sprawling wings near Mammoth Hot Springs in 1883, blocking the ancient Nez Perce path to buffalo country. Modernity thrust itself upon the wilderness like a monolithic totem rising suddenly from the ground, as if sharded from a seismic shift.

TWENTY FOUR

ASHES OF ROSES

ONE DAY, RANSOM surprised Sylvia with a buggy ride to Nob Hill, a fashionable district where industry barons were building mansions at a feverish pace. They passed block after block of resplendent estates rising ostentatiously from treeless new lawns surrounded by filigreed iron fencing. Ransom turned down a side street and stopped the buggy before a row of townhouses, Italianate with elegant pillars flanking double doors. He stepped down from the buggy and reached up for Sylvia.

Sylvia beheld Ransom with a stunned gaze. "Where are we going?"

"To see how our betters live," he said, guiding her toward the door. Curiously, he had a key. They walked into rooms sumptuously appointed, walls papered in de rigueur William Morris designs. In the back parlor, Sylvia noticed a sewing machine just like hers, as well as bodice forms and bolts of laces and silks. *Godey's Lady Book*, *La Mode Illustrée*, and *Harper's Bazaar* were fanned out on a coffee table.

"Do you think this would be enough to get started?" Ransom asked matter-of-factly.

She stared at him, confused. "What do you mean?"

"Would you be comfortable starting a business here?" he clarified.

Incredulity swept over her face like shadows of clouds across a landscape. Her wide eyes scanned the room in disbelief.

"Ransom, I couldn't afford rent for a *closet* here!"

"Never mind the rent. Would you be comfortable here?" he insisted.

She seemed at a loss: "It's a palace. More than I could even dream!"

"Well, good. Then it's settled," he said with finality and coaxed her toward another room. "Come, my dear. There's more to see."

The adjacent bedroom was well appointed with a large bed and carved walnut headboard taller than Ransom. He pulled Sylvia over to a closet door and opened it.

"I took the liberty of having your clothes unpacked in this closet. I hope you don't mind. I thought this would be the most logical place, since you'll be dressing, and *undressing*, in this room." He looked at her with a mischievous smile, and his eyes dropped to her bosom. He brushed his fingertip lightly across the cleavage nestled in her elaborate lace ruffles.

She shook her head. "I am baffled. Whatever do you mean?"

"Sylvia, I won this townhouse and a played-out silver mine in poker several days ago. A cocky young rooster didn't know what to do with all his money. He didn't know much about poker, either! So, here it is. And here we are. I'd like you to have it.

"I can't think of a better use of the place," he continued. "You can set up your dressmaking shop here. It's in close proximity to all the mucketymucks you'll be serving." Ransom stood in front of her with his arms outstretched to her shoulders. "Besides, I was getting annoyed having to share you with old man Harrington, that decrepit old sot. Now I have you all to myself." He grinned slyly. "Of course, my only stipulation will be that I'll be your regular tenant whenever I'm in town."

"Oh, that's the *only* stipulation?" she countered teasingly.

Ransom smiled a boyish grin. "You'll be repaying me in more generous ways, I'll wager. In fact, you can start *now*!" He lunged at her playfully, gathering her up in his arms and slinging her onto the bed in a flurry of petticoats and gleeful giggles.

He pounced on top of her, sank his face into her ruffled bosom, and growled playfully. She shrieked and squirmed under his weight, then wrapped her arms around his head of black hair and kissed him.

"Ransom Fallon. Fate smiled upon me the day I met you." She looked at him with eyes as sparkling as a meadow pond in spring. "You are too good."

"You deserve it, Sylvia. You are *too good* for Madam. I'll not tolerate you wasting your life at that place. You're going to start your own business, and I'm going to help you do it. I have no doubt you'll be an excellent investment."

Ransom rolled over and crossed his arms behind his head. "Besides, I had a helluva lot of fun planning this. I'm quite proud of myself." He smiled, his eyes traveling over the room, pleased with what he saw. "My only regret is that you weren't there to see Madam's face when I told her that you were moving out of her establishment. My God, she had a fit!" He smiled at this thought, puffing up with satisfaction at the scene.

"She hated to lose you." He turned his affectionate gaze to her. "You little strumpet."

Sylvia was indeed a good investment. She proved a quick study regarding not only the people end of business but financials as well. Ransom taught her to keep books, and together they drew up a budget and projections for how much income she needed to survive comfortably.

Thanks to Madam Chernov's clientele, she had ready-made customers. Competing madams began coming to her, anxious to reap the benefits of Madam Chernov's loss. Sylvia's business grew quickly, and she hired an Irish lacemaker and seamstress named Molly Mulligan. Irish girls were known for their exquisite lacework, and Sylvia felt lucky to have found the young woman.

It was not long before Sylvia landed an elite client from Nob Hill. Mrs. Morris Winston was the wife of a lumber baron. Sylvia designed for her a dress of lavender damask with shimmering brocade, spending tedious evenings stitching silver filigree to the cuffs and collar with Molly. The full skirt draped swags of fabric with silver lamé rosettes to dazzling effect. The dress complemented to perfection the diamond-and-amethyst earbobs and necklace Mrs. Winston planned to wear to the ball.

During the final fitting, Mrs. Winston glowed as she looked in the mirror. She seemed to grow in stature as she swelled with pride and looked regal despite her rotundity. Mrs. Winston's dress would turn heads. She was a feather in Sylvia's cap and her ticket to San Francisco's aristocracy.

Soon, she was dressing the wives of men who had sought to *un*dress her not so long ago. It mattered not that she had worked in a house of flesh. In fact, it enhanced her reputation, for it was deliciously scandalous. She became the secret weapon her clients used in the battle of vanities.

Sylvia meticulously prepared for her appointments with these women, careful to stage each with all the accoutrements of success. She wore her own loveliest dresses, knitted her hair in a handsome coiffure, and her greeting room was appointed with fresh flowers, fancy tea cakes, and the most recent editions of *Godey's* and *La Mode Illustrée*. She also displayed on fitting forms her creations in progress for other wealthy matrons, whose names she dropped casually.

Molly was a godsend. Sylvia had found her unemployed and sitting on a park bench, making bobbin lace on her little lap pillow. Sylvia stopped to admire the lace and asked if she had other sewing skills as well, to which the girl laughed and replied: "Madam, me fingers 'er nimble with thimble and machine, as well."

Indeed, Molly's sewing was every bit as fine as her lace making. With Molly's power of embellishment, Sylvia began incorporating lace into her dresses. Sylvia hired another girl for Molly to train when she could no longer keep up with demand.

In the evenings, the two women sat by the fire in the parlor, Sylvia doing handwork or poring over fashion magazines for ideas while Molly sat in the stuffed chair with her half-moon pillow of emerald velvet in her lap. On it lay dozens of beautiful little bobbins, the tools of her trade, splayed out from threads radiating from a vortex of pins at the center. Her hands flew deftly, rhythmically, intertwining the threads, the bobbins clicking in a musical cadence like chimes. Ever so slowly, an intricate design took shape within the cluster of pins.

The process seemed magical to Sylvia. Once, she had asked Molly how on earth she could remember the correct sequence for each bobbin. Molly laughed. "Tere's no rememberin' to it. Ya don't tink; ya just do. Tinkin' is dangerous, me dear mum always said!"

Molly's lace making was instinctual, born of memory in her fingers from generations of lace makers. Some of Molly's bobbins were 100 years old, sterling silver, painted porcelain, carved walnut.

Sylvia also hired a young French girl named Francoise to greet customers when Sylvia was busy. Sylvia liked the idea of having a French woman in her shop; Paris was the haute couture capital of the world. She encouraged Francoise to pepper her language with French terms. Customers were absolutely taken with her. Sylvia consulted Francoise often about French pronunciation and intonation so that she could fortify her own deft affectation with the language of couture.

Sylvia's evangelical father had taught her that language was power. Now she put that lesson to use for her own capitalist endeavors rather than saving souls. Many of San Francisco's wealthy were East Coast educated with an attendant affectation in speech. Such speech was used as a blunt object over the working class as surely as the police used batons on the skulls of union rioters. Sylvia was acutely aware of the power. Her humble domain as seamstress—she preferred "haute couturiere"—was as exclusive as the estates of her rich patrons.

Her salon brimmed with the loveliest fabrics in the richest hues. Dupioni silks in ashes of roses and bleu celeste, crepe de chine in Mikado yellow, damasks in shimmering celadon. Sylvia had learned the fine art of presentation when enticing clients. Silk was not just silk but rather Chinese Dupioni or Japanese crepe de chine. Pink was no longer pink but amaranth of opalescence, or ashes of roses, or Imperial coralline. These words rolled lusciously from her lips like fine liquors and intoxicated her by their potency. And her clients as well.

Once, Ransom pointed out her mischievous affectation, more bemusedly than accusingly. She laughed and said, "I'm only beating them at their own game, *mon cher.*"

Her customers would not admit ignorance so did not question Sylvia's choices of fabric or color or style, even though they often did not understand her lavish descriptions.

Only once did a customer call her on her charade. Mrs. Sherman Granville was a matriarch of an enormous lumber fortune, and her presence was towering both in flesh and in spirit. She was a straight-talking, no-nonsense woman with no patience for the pretensions of the wealthy class she so resented being a part of.

Sylvia proceeded cautiously with the formidable Mrs. Granville, having heard stories about her terseness. When the dowager sat silently—

presumably patiently—listening to Sylvia, she gained confidence and began to pitch in her grandiloquent style a most stylish and, as it happened, expensive dress.

"May I suggest, Mrs. Granville, a fitted jacket in silk jacquard, lapis in color, accented with covered buttons and piping in heliotrope. A jabot of contrasting heliotrope crepe de chine would be, ah, so *tres beau.* And the skirt would be draped in lovely scallops with silk rosettes. And a chapeau swathed in lapis crepe de chine accented with contrasting heliotrope and repeating rosettes. A mother-of-pearl brooch with ostrich feather plumage set at a rakish angle would be most handsome, Mrs. Granville."

Mrs. Granville pursed her lips and puffed up her already ample bosom. "You'll kindly talk English, madam, or you shall not get one red cent of mine. All your pretty words don't mean a hill of beans to me! Heliotrope, chapeau! My land! You should be a politician, child, with such a facility for language."

Sylvia smiled, unflustered by the miffed matron's outburst, then proceeded, in plain English, to describe her vision of Mrs. Granville's new dress.

Upon hearing the unembellished spiel, Mrs. Granville said simply: "That will be adequate. When will it be done?" That was Sylvia's first session with Mrs. Granville. But when she came for the final fitting, Sylvia noticed the grumpy dowager had a slight, uneven smile as she looked in the mirror.

"Well, my dear, you've managed the impossible! You've made this tough old buffalo presentable. Congratulations. The Ladies of the Bay Society will be sufficiently clucking." She chuckled deliciously at this thought.

Before exiting, she slapped a $10 tip in Sylvia's hand. "My husband said you were in a whorehouse before you started this business. You've got moxie, madam. I'll say that for you. And talent. You're a right smart capitalist."

TWENTY FIVE

SIREN SONG

MORE THAN A YEAR had passed since Ransom had witnessed the mountain-lake siren in the saloon. His visit to Spotted Horse to investigate his winnings had revealed the mine to be a ramshackle affair and a disappointment, and he wasn't anxious to go back into a mine shaft, even if it was his own. But one day, Sylvia reminded him that he really should investigate more.

So, Ransom packed up his horse with saddlebags, satchel, and bedroll for the long trek. The direct route through Nevada Territory to Idaho covered desert, so he opted for a longer, more hospitable route up the beautiful San Joaquin Valley, through Oregon, then Idaho Territory. It was rugged landscape, with forests of gargantuan trees shrouding the mountainsides. In some places, rocks piled up in fantastic geologic carnage as if the guts of the earth had heaved forth. One early morning, he rode along a ridge overlooking a vast river valley. The tops of bristled pines pierced the mist below like sharp quills through a bed of floss.

When he finally rode into Spotted Horse after nearly three weeks in the saddle, he was immediately struck by how much the town had grown. He had arrived during a furious thunderstorm, and the streets were channels of muck. He was wet and cold and needed a hot bath and shave and his clothes laundered.

That evening, sitting in the saloon, Frederick welcomed him back to Spotted Horse. When Willie McGee walked into the Rusty Spur, Frederick uttered under his breath, "Here comes the evening's entertainment."

"Hands off yer cocks and pull up yer socks!" Willie bellowed. "The mud's deep as Hades out there, like tryin' to walk with a dog fuckin' yer leg!"

For all his banter, Willie was not a bad gambler, and he and Ransom took the bulk of the winnings that night. During the game, Frederick said, "Ransom, you should stop by and I'll shoot your portrait. I have those new backdrops from San Francisco."

Ransom showed up cleanly shaven the next morning at Frederick's studio, his black hair pomaded, his suit jacket newly pressed, looking the quintessential gentleman.

Frederick pulled out a backdrop of a Victorian mansion in the distance with trees and craggy terrain in the foreground. It captured the paradoxical contrast between genteel wealth and frontier ruggedness, both realms holding ubiquitous but illusive charm for romance-drenched Victorians. Frederick propped a tree stump in front of the canvas and gave Ransom a Henry rifle to set rakishly on the stump, then handed him a Derringer pistol. "Here, stuff this in your waistband." He directed Ransom to cast his eyes pensively toward an imaginary horizon. "Now look out beyond, like you're looking at your vast estate."

Ransom sent the portrait to Sylvia with a letter joking that he hoped she wouldn't forget him while he toiled out in the wilderness. He imagined her unwrapping the picture and admiring it, then setting it on her mantle. He smiled at the thought.

Ransom's mine was a half day's ride from Spotted Horse. Along the way, his Thoroughbred flicked its ears back and forth constantly and flared its nostrils, taking in the smells of the wild. When the stallion suddenly stopped and whinnied a deep, quivering clarion call, Ransom followed the animal's intent gaze. Across the mountain pass was a cloud of dust: a herd of wild horses.

"Sorry, old boy." He patted the horse's neck. "I know it's tempting."

They traveled along a mountain trail through trees and meadows, then made their way over a ridge and through a mountain pass at dusk. Ligaments of sunlight streamed through the clouds like ribboned fire, gilding the mountain ridges.

Beyond was a small farm nestled in a meadow. Under a grove of trees, his horse nibbled the feathered tops of the tall grass as he walked. Ransom gazed down the hillside at the curious sight of a woman sitting in a chair in front of the cabin. In her lap was a rabbit she stroked methodically. Behind her stood an old man brushing her long, golden hair with sweeping, gentle strokes. Ransom stopped his horse and leaned on the saddle horn. He heard the old man's lilting Irish brogue as he talked to the woman, perhaps telling her one of his many tall tales. Intermittently, she would laugh, her mouth slightly curled in amusement.

After what seemed a long soliloquy—properly embellished, to be sure—the man put down the brush and began plaiting her hair in a long French braid. *How did he learn such a womanly task?* Ransom wondered. But his mind quickly dredged an answer, revisiting a memory long forgotten, of an English estate not far from his Welsh village. Ransom remembered the stable boys plaiting the tails of fine harness horses with red ribbons. No doubt the old man had been plaiting hair of horse *and* human for a good many years.

Ransom's eyes wandered over the woman and rested on her face. A wave of realization hit him: the chimera at the mountain lake and later in the saloon! His stallion stopped munching, grass hanging from its mouth, sensing a sudden tenseness in its rider.

This, then, was where the lovely lake nymph resided! Hidden away like a fairy-tale princess in an isolated wilderness cabin like Rapunzel—with an old, gnarled man, no less.

Her laughter wafted up the hill as if to entice, and without hesitation, Ransom nudged his mount down the slope toward the cabin. The old man and woman did not see Ransom until he was among the outbuildings of the homestead.

"Could I trouble you for some water?" Ransom called out, and the old man turned and raised his hand in greeting.

"To be sure, it's hot today. You're welcome to a drink, be it water or whiskey." The bandy-legged Irishman shuffled toward the horse and rider. "Ah, you sit a fine animal! Rare to see a Thoroughbred in these parts!"

"Well, I bought him in San Francisco," answered Ransom. He dismounted and shook the old man's hand, but his eyes rested on the young woman standing with the rabbit in her arms. She wore brown, canvas miner's pants cinched with a leather belt and a white cotton blouse rolled up at the sleeves, the same attire she'd worn in the saloon. Then he remembered the lake scene, and his eyes took a visual tally of curves underneath clothing until her blue eyes arrested his reverie.

"My name is Ransom Fallon. I'm passing through on my way up the mountain to the McGregor mine."

"Aye, I know it. Will ya stay for supper? We're as hungry for news as you are for a home-cooked meal!" the old man offered. "Me name's Seamus. This is me daughter, Sorrel."

She nodded, meeting his eyes, not a hint of feminine shyness nor coyness in her gaze.

Ransom felt oddly challenged by her directness.

"Thanks, but I won't put you out for a meal, miss," Ransom answered.

Seamus laughed. "Sorry to disappoint you, young man, but if you're expectin' a *woman*'s home cooking, your luck's run out. 'Tis cursed I am for not teachin' her to cook." The old man feigned regret, but the young woman took the old man's arm, beaming.

"I'm the lucky one, and you'll be too, Mr. Fallon, if you stay for supper. My da is the best cook—man or woman—this side of the Bitterroots. There's chicken and dumplings in the kettle, and fresh strawberries and cream for dessert, so you're in for a treat. I'll go set the table." She set the rabbit down in a pen, her golden hair burnished by the setting sun. The long braid the old man had so deftly plaited dangled down to her belted waist.

"You can wash up at the pump out back. I'll take care of yer horse," the old man offered, taking the reins. "Come now, beauty. You fine thing," he murmured to the horse admiringly.

Ransom sauntered to the pump, rolling up his sleeves as he walked and taking in the tidy farmstead with its sturdy, rough-hewn fences, horses grazing in the meadow.

The plank barn looked to have been built recently, and the cabin was stone and set partially into the side of the hill, not unlike many of the homes Ransom had left behind in Wales. The cabin looked a bit like a dwarf's cottage, with flower boxes and flowered curtains. Ransom wondered if the homey touches were feminine flourishes or if the old man was homemaker as well as cook.

Ransom pumped the handle, and the well water from thirty feet below began its hollow churn, gurgling in the pipe. He smelled the sweet spring water as it gushed out of the spout in a silvery braid and stuck his head in the cool stream, running his hand through glistening black hair. It felt damned good.

His mind wandered back to Sylvia, but the sun-kissed mirage of the lake nymph washed over her image. He felt the beginning pangs of adventure surge within. In his younger sexual forays, he had relished the adventure of walking into a brothel, meeting a woman, of learning her nature. But this. *This* was luscious serendipity. Who would have imagined such a beauty cloistered in this isolated wilderness?

He had not had this feeling for years. He felt settled, fulfilled with Sylvia, his wanderlust happily sated. So this sudden resurgence of concupiscence surprised him, even privately embarrassed him. But it excited him nonetheless. He gulped several mouthfuls of water, brushed the dust off his hat, then headed toward the cabin.

TWENTY SIX

SWEET-SMELLING STRAW

THE SAVORY SMELL of chicken soup filled Ransom's senses. He realized he was famished. Over a crackling fire in the stone fireplace hung a kettle. Within, succulent shreds of chicken meat floated in simmering broth. Seamus dropped dollops of dough into the golden broth, and the ragged meteors rolled and puffed. Sorrel placed a warm loaf of bread on the table with freshly churned butter, then bowls of fresh strawberries and fresh cream.

From atop a shelf, Sorrel retrieved two tin cups and an empty jelly jar, along with an unlabeled whiskey bottle, the contents of which Ransom could only guess. Probably moonshine or some derelict effort at distillation. Sorrel grasped the bottle with strong, brown hands and uncorked it as her eyes caught his. Her crooked smile was part amusement, part challenge, as if the drink she'd uncorked would take its measure of the man.

"You are a drinking man, Mr. Fallon?" she asked and filled his tin cup with whiskey before he could answer. All three sat down, and Ransom raised his cup: "To the hosts."

The woman nodded, smiling. Seamus downed the tin cup in galloping gulps. Sorrel followed just as lustily, the rich amber liquor in her jelly jar disappearing down her throat. Ransom took in a secret breath of courage and likewise slugged down the liquor, then waited for a vile kickback. But he was pleasantly surprised. It was not bad.

He smiled with a look of pleasant incredulity. Ransom knew good Irish whiskey and good Scotch bourbon, and this was more than passable. He set the tin cup down: "Damn, that's good. I haven't had whiskey that smooth since San Francisco."

"Aye, that's a good lad!" Seamus beamed. "I knew ya had good taste."

The old man picked up his knife and fork and turned double-fisted to the serious business of supper. The sounds of intent appetites and resolute eating, of tin scraping tin, of tearing bread and chewing, filled the room. The three ate ravenously and did not speak. Finally, his plate empty and hunger sated, Seamus reached for more bread and turned to the traveler.

"What might ya be doin' out in the middle of nowhere, Mr. Fallon? You bein' a cultured man on a fine horse in the middle of this raw land."

"I acquired the deed to the old McGregor place. It's supposed to be near here. Like as not, it's played out. But I thought I'd take a look."

They talked for some time about claims in the area that had and had not yielded, about homesteaders and a brief history of how Seamus and Sorrel had come to settle in the valley.

Ransom listened intently and humored the old man, for he liked Seamus. Sorrel said little, except to occasionally interject good-humored chiding or editing of the old man's exaggerations. Ransom noted her easy manner, unfettered by feminine pretense. She shoved her plate away and rested her arms on the table, then drank more whiskey, showing no signs of its effect. Finally, she rose and excused herself to check a mare in foal.

Seamus cleared the table and scrubbed the dishes, talking all the while. Ransom leaned back against the wall, stretched his legs, and settled in for an hour of listening to stories spanning many years and many lands. Seamus was an interesting old codger, like many Ransom remembered in his childhood village. They were the keepers of the tales worth remembering—and many that were not.

Seamus was pent up with a world of remembering and a hankering for an audience more receptive than a young woman who had heard it all and had more important work to do. The old man soaked in the luxury of his new listener. Finally, Seamus came around to the subject of Sorrel, and Ransom's attention, which had started to wane, was rekindled.

"She's a beautiful lass, to be sure," said Seamus, "and the men once flocked around her like eager tomcats. But they got discouraged. She's an independent soul. Takes care of this farm just like a man. But here she is, this fresh young peach, with a core hard as iron. I worry she won't never find a man and I'll die and she'll have no one." Seamus shook his downcast head over his whiskey. It occurred to Ransom that the wily old man was making a stab at matchmaking, since all the local beaux had been thwarted.

"But God knows she can take care of herself," he continued. "And better than any man. Still, this is no life for a single woman in this untamed land. Such a waste."

The old man's voice trailed off as his thoughts pooled in drunken remorse. Ransom cleared his throat, then stood up. "If you don't mind, I believe I'll bed down in the barn. I appreciate the meal and hospitality."

Ransom found his horse unsaddled and let out in the paddock, his saddle and bedroll inside the barn. He was untying the roll when he heard the shrill whinny of a horse in the next stall. He peered over to see Sorrel settled next to a pregnant mare sleek with sweat and obviously agitated. Sorrel looked up.

"She's having trouble. Her water broke four hours ago, but the foal isn't coming. I'm afraid it might be dead."

"Is there a horse doctor around here I could get?" Ransom asked.

She shook her head. "I know what to do. But I need help."

Ransom nodded and opened the stall door. He took off his jacket, then knelt down by the mare's head. "Tell me what to do."

"Just hold her head and don't let her thrash around or get up. I'm going to try and reach inside and see if I can feel the foal."

He took the mare's halter and began stroking her neck, then nodded to Sorrel to proceed. She rolled up her sleeve above the elbow and, lifting the mare's tail, slowly began to push her hand and her arm into the mare's womb.

The mare's eyes rolled back in panic, the whites flashing. She thrashed her hind legs out, but then was still. Sorrel pushed inward slowly, her eyes cast up toward the loft, her brows knitted in concentration. Her arm was consumed past the elbow, and she tried twisting the angle, groping for a tiny hoof or a muzzle, anything she could find.

"Ah," she gasped. "I can feel the shoulder . . . but the foal's breach." She moved her hand inside the mare. She felt the foal shift and kick slightly. "He's still alive. He's moving."

She tried to move her hand down the foal's shoulder to his front legs, but her arm was not long enough. She could reach no further. She shook her head, discouraged, her chin resting on the mare's rump. "He's at an angle. I can't reach him." She sighed and pulled her arm out gently. She took a rag and wiped off her arm but did not look at Ransom.

"Here, let me try," he said, unbuttoning his shirtsleeve and pushing it up his forearm. "You'll have to tell me what to do."

He traded places with Sorrel and began to navigate under her direction.

He could feel the colt's neck and withers, and then, further down, its chest and upper leg.

"Try to get his front legs outstretched so you can pull him out that way," Sorrel instructed calmly. Ransom grasped the foal's upper leg, and it began to squirm.

"He's kicking."

"That's good," Sorrel said. "He still has some strength."

Ransom ran his hand down the slender leg and cupped a tiny hoof. He grasped it. As he pulled gently, he felt the other hoof strike his arm. He opened his hand and grabbed both front hooves. The foal struggled to break away, but he held fast.

"I have both front legs now," Ransom said, and he began pulling.

The mare grunted and heaved in pain and kicked out her legs. Ransom pulled the slender limbs through the birth canal, but it was slow going and difficult work. The mare was exhausted and her contractions weak. Finally, Ransom tugged the two little hooves outside the mare. Sorrel got up and gripped one of the legs. Together, they coaxed the foal's legs, then his head out. Sorrel cleared the birth sac from the foal's muzzle to breathe, and the foal flailed and struggled its way toward life.

It lay in the straw in a film of blood and the white birthing sac. Its twisted, gray umbilical cord, ropy and streaked, meandered atop the straw from the mother to the foal's belly. The foal's wet ribcage heaved, its lungs filling with air. Sorrel pulled the birthing sac off its limbs and body and took a knife and cut the umbilical cord several inches from its belly. Then she began rubbing the foal down with a rag.

"Oh, what a fine little one you are!" Sorrel purred. She beamed at Ransom. "Thank you. You saved his life. He and the mare would have died if you hadn't been here. I couldn't have done it by myself."

Ransom rubbed his weary, blood-streaked arm with a rag and leaned back against the stall, exhausted. "Glad to be of service. I had no idea I'd have to work as a midwife for my supper." He smiled.

She leaned her shoulders back against the barn boards, tired but relieved. There were streaks of dirt and blood on her face, and an unruly wisp of blond hair coiled down the side of her cheek in voluptuous untidiness. A slow, drowsy smile crossed her face like a sunrise, and Ransom noticed again her cerulean eyes. Even in his exhaustion, he longed to reach across the sea of straw, golden and sweet smelling but impossibly vast in its intimacy, to stroke the swell of her cheek.

TWENTY SEVEN

CLAP OF CONDOR WINGS

RANSOM'S IDAHO MINE, only several miles from Sorrel's farm, was in a sorry state, with rickety timbers and a dilapidated shack built on a stream. Ransom purchased two mules and hired two men to begin cutting timbers on the mountainside. They would hitch a mule to each log and drag them down to the stream's edge.

The mules were named Grant and Lee, the horse trader said as he rode away. Ransom thought he'd caught a smirk on the man's face. Now Ransom understood the joke, and the joke was on him.

Grant, a short, obstinate brown mule, was strong as a young ox but took affront to the existence of Lee, a handsome white mule that disliked work and disliked Grant even more. The mules feuded all day long and exchanged nips, bites, and lateral, one-legged kicks each time they crossed paths on the narrow mountain trail. They provided fine entertainment for the two roustabouts-turned-loggers. Ransom noted ruefully the inverse proportion between the amount of guffawing and chortling and the work that got done.

In the meantime, Ransom explored the mine with a dog-eared map as limp and dirty as an old kid glove. The map was poorly rendered and his progress slow, picking through narrow passages and correcting the map by flickering lamplight. Occasionally, he chiseled rock to examine formations of iron ore, quartz, and pyrite. Where those formations were evident, silver was not an unlikely companion. But there was a crude miner's saying: "A mine is like a woman. Don't be fooled by a come-hither smile. Either way, you pay!"

It was ironic that he was once again digging inside the earth. But *this* was different. This was *his* earth. He wasn't risking his life for a meager wage or another man's fortune. *In fact*, Ransom thought wistfully, *I'm not getting any wage at all.* If the mine turned out to be only a romantic diversion, so be it. It had led him to Sorrel. That was reward enough.

It occurred to him that the mine was also a valid excuse for spending time in Idaho Territory. Sylvia would not question his long absences. This thought instantly yielded a vein of guilt in his upright fiber. He realized he missed Sylvia.

Nevertheless, having a mine was exciting.

Gold and silver fever was sweeping the country. First, the California Gold Rush of '49. Then, in 1861, gold was discovered on Nez Perce lands in

Idaho Territory. Finally, gold would be discovered in 1874 on the Sioux Reservation in the Black Hills. Miners panned gold dust through screen as effortlessly as sunlight through gauze. Treaties were violated, Native lands overrun. The march westward in the name of gold and silver, in the name of land, in the name of Manifest Destiny, was unstoppable. The Bismarck *Tribune* wrote:

> As the Christian looks forward with hope and faith to the land of pure delight, so the miner looks forward to a region of fabulous wealth, where the rills repose on beds of gold and the rocks are studded with precious metal. The time has come when the entire army could not much longer keep the country from being over-run by the invincible white man—the hardy pioneer.

The Black Hills discovery in 1874 would be quickly followed by government efforts to keep Indians in check. General George Armstrong Custer led an expedition to establish a fort. He had won celebrity as "America's most celebrated Indian fighter" after the 1868 slaughter of Cheyenne chief Black Kettle's village on the Washita.

Custer's Black Hills Expedition was grand: a thousand horse soldiers, a hundred covered wagons, howitzer cannonades, and enough munitions to mow down the entire Sioux nation. Custer was in his element, leading a force that spread out behind his horse as far as the eye could see. With his typical melodramatic flair and eye for publicity, he took three newspaper reporters and a photographer on his trek.

The golden-haired general ordered a rococo display of regalia extravagant even for him: a sixteen-piece brass band mounted on white horses, the musicians dressed in scarlet tunics with shiny brass buttons and red, ostrich-plumed hats. The band provided an air of pomp in the western wilds of Indian country. With such armorial trappings, his entourage was reported in style.

In August 1874, Custer's men discovered a deposit of gold so propitious that they returned to camp covered in gold dust. The discovery reverberated between the two coasts like the clap of condor wings echoing against steep canyon walls. Newspapers heralded the finding with great fanfare and argued that any Indian rights could not stand in the way of progress and God's ultimate plan. Frederick read with chilling unease the *Chicago Inter Ocean's* unabashed stance regarding gold in the Black Hills:

> Pleasant as be the pastures of Indian children and the slopes that hold the bones of their dead, they must leave the land. There is gold in the hills, and the white man desires to take possession of it. The Indian is but an episode in the advance of the Caucasian. He must decrease that newcomers may grow in wealth. Happy for him the day when the last of his tribe shall fold his blankets around his shrunken limbs, and take his final sleep, to waken in the eyes of the Great Spirit.

The Bismarck *Tribune* echoed the sentiment:

> This is God's country. He peopled it with red men, and planted it with wild grasses, then permitted the white man to gain a foothold. As the wild grasses disappear and white clover gains a footing, so the Indian will disappear before the advances of the white man. Their prayers, their entreaties cannot change the law of Nature; cannot arrest the causes which are carrying the Indian to his ultimate destiny—extinction.

After the discovery of gold in the Black Hills, President Grant would order prospectors to be allowed onto the reservation.

William Tecumseh Sherman was Grant's top brass of the Indian campaigns. His scorched-earth policy in the Civil War had forced the South to her knees. He intended to bring the Indians to their knees as well. Hated and feared, his likeness compared to a vulture with scrofula,

Sherman made the transition from ruthless wartime general to ruthless Indian fighter seamlessly. Grant's order pleased Sherman. He wrote in a memorandum that if prospectors should find gold on the Sioux's protected land, "I understand that the President and the Interior Department will wink at it."

Custer predicted what would happen. In characteristic appreciation for his formidable red foes and with remorse at what would surely end in the loss of their civilizations, he wrote privately to his wife:

> If I were an Indian, I think I would greatly prefer to cast my lot among the free open plains, rather than submit to the reservation, there to be a recipient of the blessed benefits of civilization, with its vices thrown in without stint or measure.

But in a more public proclamation, Custer posted an achingly honest dispatch to the *New York World* about his new command, with a prophetic twist:

> We are goading the Indians to madness by invading their hallowed grounds and throwing open to them a terrible revenge whose cost would far outweigh any scientific or political benefit possible to be extracted from such an expedition.

TWENTY EIGHT

SUMAC DREAMS

IN THE YEARS since Sorrel and Seamus had first homesteaded in Idaho Territory, they procured a small band of brood mares: a mustang, an Arabian, two grade Thoroughbreds, a Blackfoot Indian paint, and two Appaloosas they had received in trade from local Nez Perce. They also had two Percheron draft horses—Bett, a mare, and Brute, a gelding—for farm work. Seamus and Sorrel both knew horseflesh. They bred their mares to a local Thoroughbred-Arab stallion, red as bloodstone, with a fiery spirit. The mares had yielded a foal a year and showed a melding of their parents with the stamina and speed needed for the US Cavalry, their primary buyer.

During her forays hunting or looking for stray cattle, Sorrel occasionally came upon wild horses, and she spotted a paint mare she hoped to capture. One day, she found the band grazing in a meadow and inched closer. She rode a mustang mare, fleet and sure-footed, though too rawboned to be called handsome. She thought her horse fast enough to keep up with the herd.

The stallion spotted her immediately and trotted with head upright and tail aflare. He nipped and kicked at the mares, gathering them jealously. As she approached, he pawed and reared, baring his teeth, then savaged the mares into motion. Like a gathering whirlwind, the herd surged down the valley.

Sorrel's mustang, fired by her instinct to run with the herd, skimmed across the grass, the trees a blur. Sorrel's eyes watered from the wind in her face. She was exhilarated and felt the same buoyancy in her mustang, whose churning legs ate up the ground and spit it out again. The band stampeded down a ravine and across a shallow river, water exploding in a fusillade beneath their hooves. Sorrel's horse plunged into the spray, close on their heels.

A wall of thrashing horseflesh tore up the canyon. Sorrel marveled that her game little steed did not tire. They gained the summit, her mustang flanking the trailing mares. Hitting flat ground, shedding the drag of gravity, the herd raced forward, but the mustang stayed with them.

Then Sorrel beheld—across the stampede, through the din of dust—a horse and rider! The two riders ran abreast like bookends on a quaking shelf as the stallion urged the herd down a steep, rocky incline to shake his pursuers. *The wily old sot!* Sorrel thought. The riders pulled up at the precipice. Their horses reared and threw their heads, their frenzied energy pooling at the cliff's edge.

The other rider was a Nez Perce woman on a striking Appaloosa. The women looked at each other, and Sorrel shrugged, as if admitting the stallion had duped them. The Indian woman smiled. They turned back and rode side by side, resting their winded mounts.

The woman said something in Nimiipuu, then followed in halting English: "Follow many time. *T'o t . . . s'a min.*" She struggled for English words. "Smart . . . chief horse."

"Yes, smart." Sorrel nodded. She motioned to the woman's spotted horse, bigger than her own. "Strong!" she said, then thumped her fist to her heart.

The Indian woman beamed and nodded. "Yes." Pointing to Sorrel's scruffy little mustang, she pounded her chest twice, then said slowly, "Small . . . but . . . big." And Sorrel smiled.

The Nez Perce woman was tall and coltish, like Sorrel, her hands and body angular and strong, her manner muscular. They wanted to say much, but the language barrier yoked their enthusiasm. They walked their horses along the plateau in silence. Then Sorrel pointed to herself and pointed north in the direction of her farm. Sorrel wanted to show her that she had horses of her own. They rode through several valleys, crossed a river, and climbed a rise. Then Sorrel pointed down a hillside at her brood mares grazing in the meadow. The woman smiled at the foals gamboling and bucking in youthful bombast.

They leaned over the rail, the sun beginning to cast long shadows. Sorrel pointed to herself: "Sorrel," she said. "Sorrel." The woman nodded, then pointed to herself and spoke a lyrical stream of consonants and breathy vowels. She smiled at Sorrel's worried look, then concentrated to say in English: "Flying Horse."

"Flying Horse," Sorrel repeated, relieved.

Several days later, Flying Horse appeared on the ridge above the farm, and Seamus pointed her out. Sorrel grabbed the nearest horse and galloped bareback up the hill. Flying Horse wanted Sorrel to come with her. Although she had work to do, she obliged. They rode for a couple of hours to a vast valley filled with horses. Many were paints or spotted Appaloosas.

They passed through the herd, horses leisurely parting for the two. Sorrel was in paradise, so many horses beyond her imagining. As her skilled eye cataloged their lines, she saw that many were fine animals, with strong conformations and well-formed heads.

The two women rode to a holding corral of cut aspen poles. Inside, colts separated from their mothers whinnied pathetically, flustered, churning up dust. Flying Horse pointed to them, then to her own lap and made a sharp chopping gesture. Sorrel saw that the weanlings were little stud colts to be castrated. She nodded her understanding.

Sorrel and Seamus had heard that the Nez Perce, unlike other tribes, practiced selective breeding, castrating all but their finest male horses. Their husbandry techniques were so superior, Meriwether Lewis noted in his journals, that horses gelded by the Nez Perce recovered quickly with none of the swelling or oozing infections attendant with traditional white methods.

Beyond a brace of trees, two young men held a colt to the ground. The process was smoothly orchestrated and took only minutes. The little colt trotted away, stiff legged and indignant, his hind legs swiping high at his groin irritation. Once he was away from the mean men, he nuzzled the violated area and walked around for the rest of the afternoon with black balm smeared on his nose, neighing plaintively to his emasculated friends. The colts were looking for their manhood, the men quipped, which Flying Horse conveyed in a mix of sign language and English. Sorrel laughed.

Sorrel vowed to have them geld her own stock. In the past, she had hired a local doctor, and the process had been a bloody mess.

Sorrel and Flying Horse became easy friends. Although they did not understand each other's spoken language, subliminal understanding was thick, like mother's milk between suckling twins. Their strongest bond was their love of horses. Their skills on horseback rivaled any warrior or soldier. They moved in concert with the animal, as a tree with the wind. Both possessed a precocious physical courage uncommon in girls of either culture. Mothers discouraged such brazenness, which might intimidate prospective husbands. And to be husbandless was to be shamed.

But Flying Horse and Sorrel did not wish to be married and saw no shame in being unattached. The shame, in fact, was in being dependent, beholden to men and shackled to domesticity. They found solace in each other's company, a growing kinship that both whites and Indians gossiped was more than friendship. Disgruntled braves whose attentions had been rebuffed or ignored by Flying Horse grumbled that she was a "two-spirit," that she liked women better than men. Flying Horse knew they said this, for her own mother told her so.

Not long after meeting Flying Horse, Sorrel discovered a magical place, a broken-down cabin amid riotous vegetation. The sun coaxed from the gnarled and neglected apple trees clusters of red orbs, fruits of labor from long ago, from beggared dreams and hardscrabble hopes. Behind a collapsed barn, hidden among weeds, was a pocked stone slab with an iron manacle corroded to a rusty rind. Once used for slaughtering, the slab exuded a strange displacement, as if it had silently absorbed the shrill screams of the beasts killed there.

Sorrel picked an apple and plopped down in the grass to bask in the morning. The cabin was cloaked in sumac and vines boasting clusters of unripe grapes compressed with promise.

The first white settlers had built the cabin forty years before. A solitary glass window had miraculously survived the decades, the only nod to civility—a luxury, perhaps, for the woman of the house, facing south to let in the sun. Sorrel stepped inside. Crickets quieted. Dust floated. The smell of old wood and forgotten space filled her nostrils. The floorboards, brocaded in moss and gray lichen, were punky as rotten squash. Sumac flared across the glass, backlit by the sun, a transparent damask of red-veined green and yellow. *Like a kaleidoscope*, she thought.

Grapevine tendrils meandered aimlessly. The place was lovely in its uprooted yearning. Sorrel knew the measure of devotion required to carve a home out of wilderness.

Sorrel shared her discovery with Flying Horse, who admired the glass window. But then her spine stiffened and her eyes widened at something on the floor. Sorrel followed her horrified gaze to a frog skeleton draped in desiccated skin. It had probably wandered into the cabin and then, unable to find its way out, fossilized in its desperation. Flying Horse turned abruptly and ran from the cabin.

Sorrel was stunned at her friend's baffling departure. Outside the cabin, Flying Horse pulled a pouch from inside her tunic. Sorrel recognized it as an Indian birth amulet for a baby's umbilical cord. It held strong medicine for the child. The amulet was exquisitely beaded in greens and yellows. Now Sorrel understood. Flying Horse's sacred symbol was a frog.

Sorrel touched the amulet. "Beautiful, beautiful," she repeated. She pointed to the cabin and shook her head. She crossed her fists stridently over her chest as if to say: "You are strong! You will live long!"

But Flying Horse was distressed. She could not shake the augury of her own death. Sorrel did not know how to assuage her friend. She took a knife from the sheath on Flying Horse's belt. Holding her own hand out to Flying Horse, she cut a slit. Little fjords of blood spread across her palm. She took Flying Horse's hand and cut the same small gash. They grasped each other's palms, wound to wound, their blood intermingling. They locked gazes. Flying Horse's lips curled slightly at the edges, like a leaf wafting in a breeze. And her heart was strong.

TWENTY NINE

WILD AT HEART

RANSOM HAD NOT SEEN Sorrel Lanning since he had offered his midwife services in delivering her foal. Thoughts of her trickled into his waking hours at the mine and into his dreams at night, as water summons thirst.

He decided he would ride to her farm under the ruse of asking her help in finding his mule, which had run off. Since he planned to arrive at dinnertime, he hoped to get a meal from Seamus, too. Seamus waved a greeting from the porch as Ransom rode down the slope.

"Good lad, just in time for dinner. Come, come in. Just hatched a good batch of whiskey, so you're right on time!" Seamus chuckled. When

Ransom walked through the door, Sorrel smiled at him brightly, and he was encouraged.

"Mr. Fallon! Good to see you! Have you come to see how your foal is doing? Here, have a seat." She pulled out a chair and reached for the whiskey jug on the shelf.

Ransom scanned Sorrel's form as her back was turned. He averted his gaze and caught Seamus's eye, who had an amused smile on his face and gave Ransom a passing wink, as if to say, "I know why you're here!"

They sat down to a meal of roast venison, corn meal, and fresh garden beans. Ransom had been eating mostly pinto beans and bacon and was ravenous for home cooking. They talked and ate and drank Seamus's brew while the fire in the hearth crackled and leapt.

Ransom basked in the home comforts and found himself longing for a woman's company. He asked Sorrel if he could see her colt, and she was pleased by the request. They walked out together toward the barn.

"Do you ever see the wild horses?" he inquired.

"Oh, yes! They water up at the mountain lake. I can always tell when they're near. The mares squeal and snort," she said.

"I don't want to impose, but I was wondering if you might be able to help me find them? One of my mules ran off with them. I'd like to try to get him back if I can," Ransom said. A wave of guilty pleasure sprangled through him.

"I'd be glad to," she answered. "I've chased them before. There's a paint mare in that band I'd like to have. She'd be a good brood mare. But that stallion is a smart one."

Ransom could see Sorrel was excited by his suggestion, but not for the same reasons he was, certainly. He felt his anticipation grow. He stepped behind the stall door to hide his excitement as heat ran down his torso and up his legs.

Two days later, Ransom met Sorrel at her farm in early morning. After they'd had a cup of coffee, Sorrel packed apples and sandwiches Seamus had prepared for them. Both brought coiled lariats in hopes of catching the mule. They rode up the valley wall toward the lake, a mile away. It was big country. Only if they were lucky would they catch a glimpse of the band, and only if they were *very* lucky would they get close enough to give chase.

As Sorrel took the lead down a rocky incline, Ransom's eyes moved over her contours. The wide leather belt wrapped around her waist seemed as sensuous to him as any corset he had ever unlaced. He longed to put his hands about her torso. Her hips fanned out gently, slender almost like a man's, to buttocks rounded in the saddle like the bottom of a pear. His eyes settled on that tiny triangular darkness in the middle where the saddle seat did not meet her cleaved flesh. As she rocked back and forth with the horse's careful steps, his gaze finally wandered to her long thighs, strong sinew stanchions over the saddle's leather.

Sorrel wore a white shirt rolled to the elbows with no undergarment. She was utterly unaware of her allure as her breasts, rounded as honeydew, swayed under her blouse, backlit by the sun. Ransom caught their silhouette through the cotton, the suspended curve of cupped flesh. Thus, he fathomed her beauty in a state of festering bliss, swelling hard against his saddle seat, his heart beating like a tempest of lusts inside his chest.

They rode for an hour over rocky terrain, through cedar forests and open meadows.

Ransom asked Sorrel about her farm and her horses, about their breeding and training. He was genuinely interested, and Sorrel's passion poured out easy and ebullient. Perhaps she had been so isolated that she never had a chance to talk about the things she loved with anyone but Seamus.

Sorrel asked Ransom about his own background. He talked of Wales and how beautiful it was, like the country they rode in, rugged and magical. When he said "magical," he noticed her ever-so-slight surprise.

"You sound like Seamus," she said, smiling. She understood him, and that pleased him.

Sorrel spotted dust rising from the river bottom above the trees.

"I think we've found them," she said. They nudged their horses into a canter down the gentle slope. They were downwind from the herd and hidden among the rocks and trees. Sure enough, Ransom's gray mule was among them. They decided to run the herd toward an open meadow to pick out the mule. They readied their lariats and spurred their mounts, breaking out of the trees at a dead run. The stallion immediately caught sight of them and screamed a warning to his herd. The mule, not having the speed of the other animals, fell to the back of the pack.

Ransom and Sorrel headed for him like a pair of tandem rodeo riders. Sorrel landed her lariat square on the mule's churning head, but Ransom's lasso landed fallow on his rump and fell to the ground. Just as Sorrel was about to wrap the rope around her saddle horn and pull in the mule, her mare veered sharply, and a low-hanging branch smote Sorrel's face and sent her somersaulting out of the saddle. She skidded across the rough ground until her leg hit a tree root.

Sorrel's mare balked, white eyed, and then, realizing that she was riderless, continued on at a full gallop, following her instinct and the stampeding herd. Ransom reined in his horse to a rearing stop and jumped off. Touching Sorrel's shoulder, he asked urgently if she was hurt.

"We had him," she snarled impatiently, "until I got thrown!"

"Don't worry about my mule. Are you hurt?" he insisted.

She tried to stand, waving him away, but her leg throbbed inside her boot.

"Goddamn it! My ankle!" she said, wondering if it was broken.

"Let's get the boot off before it swells," Ransom said. He picked up her foot before she could resist. He could tell it was painful getting the boot off, but she gritted her teeth and suppressed a wince. A doctor—or at least Seamus—would have to tend to it.

"We'll have to ride my horse home," Ransom said. "I'll catch your mare later." He put her boot into his saddlebag and turned to her. She had already blushed embarrassment at his touch. Now, seeing that he would have to help her walk and get in the saddle, she desperately looked for a handhold and struggled to stand on her own.

Without warning, he leaned down and scooped her up in his arms. He wanted to stand there and soak her in, absorb her weight into his arms, his chest, touch her skin underneath its cloth, and not let her go. But he could feel her body tensed in embarrassment.

"You can't walk on that ankle," he said matter-of-factly. He carried her to his horse and lifted her up into the saddle sideways. Then he mounted and lifted her more comfortably to sit in his lap sidesaddle with her hurt leg over the saddle horn.

"I suggest you put your arm around my neck. We wouldn't want you to fall off again, now, would we?" he said.

She caught his eyebrow rising with a hint of slyness. She stewed in her dependency as he put both of his arms around her, took the reins in his hands, and gathered her against his chest. She resented her predicament, and she resented Ransom. Yet his touch struck a wildness in her.

He felt her resistance but relished it. He had discovered her weakness. This Amazon who did not cower from Comanche, cougar, or copperhead was in fact a coward in matters of the heart. Renegade Sioux could send a thousand arrows hissing through the air, and she would not back down, but if Cupid slung but one gentle barb from his passion-filled quiver, she ran for the hills. This realization was honeyed ammunition for his embattled heart. He longed for her, even defiant in his arms.

THIRTY

FROM SOULS OF GREAT BEASTS

IT WAS THE TIME of burnished leaves and animal coats thickening, of Chinook winds laced with chill. Chief Joseph and his Wallowa Lake tribe had traveled to the plains in a great gathering with the Crow to begin the autumn buffalo hunt. For some moons now, the buffalo had been harder to find, the herds much smaller. Scouts rode farther to spot herds, and holy men saw fewer buffalo in their visions. The dancing and entreaties of headmen became more rigorous.

Flying Horse loved the buffalo-calling dance: dancers wore buffalo heads with great manes draped behind them. They carried elaborate shields or painted spears, enacting bulls fighting and herds running. The people's chanting pulsed through the air like the whisper of arrows. When the exhausted dancers collapsed—for a buffalo mantle weighed that of a stag—men and women ceremonially skinned and butchered them. From a young age, Flying Horse joined her mother and aunts in the ritual.

Medicine men held up parts of the buffalo to call the spirits: horns, hooves, hearts, tails, scrotums. From the souls of the great beasts came strength and sustenance. And the people gave thanks.

Since she was little, Flying Horse had watched her mother and other tribeswomen butcher buffalo. Sings Like Lark would slit the underbelly from chest to groin and open the bloody-fleshed cavity, revealing the complicated engine of the beast—heart, lungs, kidneys, liver. She pulled all from the cavity, along with the steaming intestines and stomachs. Occasionally, she felt hard balls within a stomach: rare "buffalo stones" from buffalo licking themselves like cats. To find one was strong medicine. On one of these occasions, she gave Flying Horse the knife to cut open the stomach. When her daughter pulled out two balls as big as her mother's fists, all the women laughed and clapped.

The women would then pull the mighty mantle from the animal's body, revealing massive pink and white muscles, mounded like boulders and striated with sinew. The process always amazed Flying Horse. The hunt meant survival through winter and was a crucible for hunters and their buffalo horses. One animal could feed 100 people.

Flying Horse's father, Tall Tree, belonged to the Buffalo Society. She longed to know the exhilaration of the hunt. But many braves would be against a woman joining. It was tradition: men hunted, women butchered. But butchering held no romance, no danger. Her father had allowed her to spearfish with the men; why could she not hunt buffalo too?

She secretly decided to join the hunt, no matter the consequences. Woman Chief of the Crow had proven herself first on the buffalo hunt, and Flying Horse vowed this for herself.

The buffalo-calling dance the night before the hunt whirled with strong spirits. During the excitement, Flying Horse slunk away to a woods where her horse, a big bay mare, was hobbled and a cache of war paint and weapons hidden.

She had admired a Crow hunter and his mount, both painted completely blue with white dots like a blue-streaked man-beast studded with driving hail. She and her horse would not be blue but red, and their markings not hail but thunder.

From a bladder, she smeared red paint, iron oxide, and pussy willow buds ground in bear grease over the bay's body. In the moonlight, she looked like a blood-soaked chimera.

Crimson scrawled across the dawn sky. The valley came alive. Dogs barked. Children rubbed their eyes. Women bustled over boiling pots, loaded litters, dismantled tipis. Hunters painted their ponies with nature's brightest hues, embellished by trinkets, feathers, and beads.

Flying Horse disappeared into the woods where her horse waited. She pulled from an otter bag rawhide clothes, men's clothes—a tunic and leggings dyed red. She wrapped a rawhide strip tightly over her breasts to hide her sex, then donned the crimson buckskin. With bow and arrow quiver slung across her back, she mounted her mare to become a blood-red centaur.

They trotted to a vast swath of prairie descending to a river basin where thousands of buffalo watered. Hunters rode along the opposite bluff a mile away. Their tiny silhouettes were beautiful to her, like cave paintings against rose-colored stone.

The riders began the attack. The buffalo roiled, and dust billowed above them as they stampeded along the valley. Her horse plunged down the slope. At a dead run, they came upon a Crow on a big black-and-white paint, his legs churning like pistons. The horse ran an arm's length from a bull, the hunter's bow and arrow pulled taut for release.

He aimed behind the left shoulder, at the beast's heart. At close range, a well-placed arrow could sink to the hilt. To down a buffalo with one arrow was most honorable. And most dangerous. The Crow shot his arrow true, and it sank deep into the animal. The bull grunted, stumbling to its knees. Its long horns spiked into the ground, catapulting the one-ton body into a spectacular somersault.

Flying Horse had never seen such a sight. Her mare passed the brave and now was running along the herd in the middle of a whirlwind. Ahead, Flying Horse saw a blur. A rare, old, white bull! She nudged her steed, pulling up along the beast's massive body. She had not realized she'd already pulled an arrow from her quiver and strung the bow! For an instant, doubt pierced her heart. But she must not think, only *feel* the true aim of her arrow, feel the clean kill.

She let her arrow fly, and the bowstring sang. The arrow sank behind the shoulder, but the bull kept running. For an instant, Flying Horse's heart skipped. Bitter recriminations flooded her head. The bull thundered on, then stumbled several more paces in a zigzag spiral before falling in front of horse and rider.

Her horse's instincts were faster than her own. She lunged high into the air and soared over the careening beast. Flying Horse felt as if they were flying. She had made her first kill, and her brave mare had run as a seasoned buffalo horse!

A Nez Perce brave rode on her heels, his bow aimed at a large cow. His arrow sliced deep, leaving two tufts of feathers like a deadly butterfly landing on the beast. The goliath fell instantly, her bearded chin skidding along the ground until her hindquarters collapsed.

The herd dispersed in all directions, scattering into gullies and woods. Riders pulled up their mounts. The hunters talking spiritedly. Who had killed the white bull? The Nez Perce brave who had been behind Flying Horse greeted her. "You made a fine kill, friend!"

She could only nod back at him. "You are Nez Perce?" he asked. She nodded again.

"What is your name?"

She knew now she must talk, and her spine stiffened in resolve. To reveal her womanhood might blacken her name, her family name. But there was no help for it.

"My name is Flying Horse, daughter of Tall Tree, a great hunter of the Buffalo Society, the Wallowa clan."

The brave did not speak for a moment. Flying Horse gulped hard and braced herself for his ridicule. Or worse, his laughter. But his reaction surprised her. "Yes. I know of Tall Tree. He is a brave hunter, as is his daughter. My name is Fire Bear. We must return to our kills and partake of their courage."

Both turned their horses around and started back to the downed buffalo dotting the prairie. By now, other buffalo hunters were gathering around this new hunter who had killed the white buffalo. They galloped up in boisterous congratulations, slapping the hunter on the back and yelling victorious chants. They asked the hunter what his name was, but the rider was strangely mute. Finally, Fire Bear spoke: "This great hunter is Flying Horse, daughter of Tall Tree of the Wallowa clan."

The gathering riders were stunned. Then an angry brave bellowed: "A woman! This is not allowed!"

Fire Bear spoke again. "Who says a woman cannot hunt buffalo? I know of no law."

By now, the riders had reached the body of the white buffalo. Fire Bear dismounted and pulled a knife from his leggings. He cut a slit in the animal's abdomen, and steam rose in the crisp morning air. He felt inside the warm guts for the liver, then cut it out and walked to Flying Horse, holding it up in both hands, his forearms bloody to the elbows. The liver was the color of oxblood, smooth and gelatinous, and shaped like a small cavalry saddle. It was the custom to eat the raw liver from a kill, for it promoted strength and strong heart.

"Partake of your victory," he ordered.

Flying Horse leaned down, grasped the hot liver, and ripped savage mouthfuls, defiantly eyeing the men. The meat was liquid soft and slimy, its taste sour and grassy. She concentrated to swallow; to retch would show her weakness and bring derision.

Some reeled their horses away in disgust. Fire Bear remained at Flying Horse's feet. "Do not mind them," he said. "Your heart is strong. But you know this already."

News of the strange woman hunter soon spread throughout the Nez Perce and Crow encampments. As Flying Horse rode into camp, onlookers parted, murmuring, some in awe, some in anger. She knew she must face her father in front of all the tribe. Her heart shrank. *What if Father is ashamed?* The horror that he might cast her out stabbed through her mind. She rode through a hostile gauntlet to her father standing beside her mother. His face was granite, raw-cut, inscrutable. She longed for his love, his pride in her.

She jumped off her horse and handed the liver to her father. For an agonizing instant, she feared he would not take it and her humiliation would be beyond redemption. His face was hard. But then the corner of his mouth wafted upward. His eyes softened in pride. He reached out and took the liver.

He slowly bit into it and swallowed. Then he held it high and said: "Behold Flying Horse, my daughter, a great hunter. Though she be a woman, she honors me with her bravery. And she brings much meat for our people. This is an honorable thing."

Flying Horse felt suddenly faint. She was no longer a great hunter but instead a little girl, her father's daughter. She wanted to hug him, but she stood still before him. He smiled down at her, and pride was full in his visage. But under his breath he whispered: "Now, brave hunter, you must answer to your mother. Her wrath is much greater than that of a white bull!"

THIRTY ONE

MANIFEST DESTINY

A BUFFALO HUNT of a different sort would be covered by the national press on the western Nebraska plains. George Armstrong Custer was instructed by the US State Department to host a Russian dignitary, Grand Duke Alexis, on a hunt. Custer had just finished his 1874 Black Hills Expedition, and newspapers across the nation and their readers ate up his flamboyant stories.

Buffalo hunting had become so de rigueur that the US government treated foreign dignitaries to a taste of the western frontier with sponsored bison excursions. Custer was grand marshal of the hunt, and Buffalo

Bill Cody served as chief scout. Both were renowned as the West's most dashing heroes: Cody was America's leading buffalo killer, Custer America's premier Indian killer.

The press flocked to the orchestrated event. Frederick would be there with a cadre of other photographers, including the British photographer William Illingworth, hired by Custer's Black Hills Expedition. Frederick and the Englishman bonded quickly over frontier tales.

The honorary first kill was reserved for the guest, but the grand duke was a terrible shot. Custer and Cody were flummoxed as to how to give the duke his victorious kill. Buffalo Bill finally put the grand duke on his own horse, Buckskin Joe, and gave the rotund Russian his ornately engraved rifle he called Lucretia. Cody led the duke up beside a buffalo so he could shoot the animal point-blank, finally downing it. All sighed with relief when the myopic duke finally hit his target.

Custer had a special treat planned for the hunt's last day. They would pretend the buffalo were Indians and charge them, yelling, "Get 'em boys! Kill those redskins!" When they were done, fifty "Indians" lay dead on the prairie. Alexis made several kills and kissed Custer exuberantly. It was the last charge against "redskins" that Custer would survive.

Frenzied media coverage spurred the mania for buffalo hunting as a means to fast money. Promoters touted buffalo hunters as "businessmen with rifles":

> If you have a gun, can ride a horse and shoot straight, you can make more than the President of the United States! That's right! There's 100 million buffalo in the West that need killing for industry and we need good men who can do the job!

Train travelers could not resist the mystique of a buffalo hunt on the frontier. When a herd was sighted, a prickly spine of rifles out the windows discharged a horrific noise, leaving a fog of smoke. Thousands of buffalo were left to rot in the sun for mere seconds of thrill seeking.

All things buffalo became the rage—robes, mounted buffalo heads, buttons, combs, knife handles, ink pots made from buffalo hooves. Women even wore collars, cuffs, and hand muffs of buffalo fur.

Buffalo extinction was the official solution to "the Indian problem." General Sherman urged General Sheridan in 1868: "I invite all the sportsmen of England and America for a grand buffalo hunt and make one grand sweep of them all." And Colonel Richard Dodge famously wrote: "Every buffalo dead is an Indian gone."

Homesteaders and bone-picking crews hired by carbon works made a living harvesting buffalo bones on the plains. And a booming industry made hooves into fertilizer.

Not all Americans reveled in the hunt. Some famous buffalo hunters were publicly remorseful. Famous buffalo "runner" Frank Mayer later opined in his popular book *The Buffalo Harvest*:

> Maybe we runners served our purpose in helping abolish the buffalo. Maybe it was our ruthless harvesting of them, which telescoped the control of the Indian by a decade or more. Or maybe I'm just rationalizing. Maybe we were just a greedy lot that wanted to get ours, and to hell with posterity, the buffalo, or anyone else, just so we kept our scalps and filled our money pouches. I think maybe that is the way it was.

After rancorous political wrangling, Congress passed a bill in 1874 deeming it illegal to kill buffalo that could not be used for food. But President Grant refused to sign it. Buffalo hunting had destroyed the big northern and southern herds and now moved into protected Indian land. The bill resurfaced in 1876, but that summer, the Battle of the Little Bighorn brought anything smelling of Indian support to a grinding halt.

For Indian tribes across the continent, prairies once brimming with buffalo became Golgothas of rotting flesh, scenes so vile as to insult the sun. The rivers ran red, the ground matted in blood. The 100 million buffalo that once roamed the plains from one horizon to the other were exterminated with such wonton mindlessness that eventually only 1,000 remained.

As the buffalo waned, so too did tribal ways. An Indian fable spread among the nations and came to be chanted in mournful song by medicine men and whispered to children as bedtime stories. Frederick had heard Nez Perce parents tell the story. Draped in allusion, lyrical as a poem, it told of the disappearing sacred buffalo in words their hearts could abide, for the truth was too hard.

It went: "The buffalo saw that their day was over and they could no longer protect the people of the plains. The last of the great herd gathered to make council. One red dawn, when the morning mist was still floating upon the land, the leader walked to the side of a great mountain, and the mountain opened up. Inside, the world was green and good, the rivers deep and clear, no longer red. The wild plums were blossoming, the pink buds were many and fragrant and pleasing to the eye. Into this world of beauty, the last buffalo walked and was never seen again."

THIRTY TWO

DARK LUSTER

LATER, FREDERICK would be entertained by William Illingworth's stories of Custer and his Black Hills Expedition. Illingworth told of a Cheyenne shaman named Medicine Arrow who smoked the peace pipe with Custer. Medicine Arrow guarded powerful sacred medicine given to the Cheyenne by a deity. It contained four sacred arrows and the scalps from five enemy tribes: Crow, Ute, Shoshone, Pawnee, and Blackfeet.

Custer told Medicine Arrow that he had not come to make war, but the medicine man was skeptical; to show his distrust, he tapped ashes on Custer's boot. He warned Custer that if he did not keep his promise of peace and fought again, the Everywhere Spirit would rain death down upon him and all his men.

That was not the only omen, Illingworth recounted. Custer's chronicles in the *New York World* mentioned a comet near the Big Dipper that upset his Arikara guides. They believed it showed divine displeasure and conjured the spirits of dead braves to join the Sioux warpath.

Only days later, Custer's entourage witnessed a falcon chasing a passenger pigeon. This excited the staff zoologist, who believed them to be extinct. The pigeon landed underneath the belly of a grazing horse and hid from the falcon. Bloody Knife, Custer's Cree scout, was troubled by this strange prairie drama, for it carried ill portent.

There was one other omen that haunted Bloody Knife. As a warrior, Custer had achieved much, but as a hunter, he had yet to kill his first grizzly. On the Black Hills Expedition, he vowed to do this. His opportunity finally came when Bloody Knife spotted a big male watering near the river. The bear was very old, with brittle, worn claws, stubs for teeth, and his coat ragged with scars. Custer shot the beast, but it lumbered away toward the nearby timber. Bloody Knife, afraid the general would not get his prize, fired into the animal multiple times, finally downing him.

Custer was jubilant. He immediately wrote to Elizabeth: "I have reached the highest rung on the hunter's ladder of fame. I have killed my grizzly!"

Bloody Knife knew the bear was not a grizzly at all but instead an old cinnamon bear. But he allowed his boss to bask in the victory of the kill. He was used to his grandiosity.

Custer ordered the men to heave the animal onto its belly for a more dramatic picture. When they did this, the blood from its multiple wounds sprayed upward, splattering Custer's fringed rawhide tunic. Another speck hit Bloody Knife square in the forehead, and the spray traced a perfect line across his neck.

This was bad medicine, Bloody Knife said. The bear's spirit had sent a parting portent. Bloody Knife ran to the river to wash the blood, but he could not erase the dark luster of its stain.

"Bloody Knife is a surly, impertinent sort," Illingworth told Frederick. "He always grumbled to a fellow Cree scout in their native tongue the same words. I was curious and asked that scout what he was always saying. You know what that Cree told me? He said: 'Yellow Hair can't hit tent from inside!' "

THIRTY THREE

SAVAGE SEDUCTION

CORNELIUS BLADES was the most despised man in Spotted Horse. Women walked across the street to avoid him, ushering their children away in haste. Men drifted from him when he entered the saloon. As a once successful slave trader in the South, he was used to being ostracized.

When the war ended slavery—at least, of African blacks—he found his skills transferred profitably to the Oriental trade. He slid into his new role as smoothly as a fat bull snake down a rat hole.

His small, sharp eyes were knifepoints of savagery set in fleshy sockets, his skin cobbled with acne. His thinning pate of pomaded hair was slicked back like the feathers of a stewed crow. His sagging jowls smiled rarely and then only deviously, made more grotesque by lips peeled back to reveal rotten stumps of teeth.

He lived in a ramshackle cabin on a windswept homestead with his wife, Katherine, a twig of a woman made even smaller by the bulk of her husband's cruelty. Word was that she had come from a wealthy plantation family in Alabama. At least, that was what her husband liked to claim in the saloon when intoxicated and surly.

"By God! I brought her down from her high horse!" He'd slam his fist down on the bar counter, slurring his words, his eyes bleary. "That bitch and her holier-than-thou old man thought they're better'n me! But they ain't!

"Near kilt 'er ole man that she had to marry me! The fuckin ole sot! Yeah, I said 'had ta.' She *had ta* marry me. She was in the family way! Thought she was too good to lay with me. But she did. She did lay with me." He remembered the deed with sly relish. And his drinking companions felt somehow that it had not been by choice that she had lain with such a man.

One day, only a couple of weeks after Blades and his wife had moved to Idaho, Katherine came to town for supplies. Sorrel saw her at the general store and noted her timid demeanor, so shoved back in her own private world that discourse with the outside world was no longer possible. Katherine purchased flour and other sundries, then walked out of the store, hunched from the weight of her abandoned hope.

Mr. Marston turned to Sorrel and said, "That poor woman. She has some mighty mean bruises. I hate to think what her life must be with the likes of him." He shook his head in despair and resumed stocking his shelves.

On her return home, Blades exploded in anger that she had not gotten his pouch tobacco, which he had failed to tell her he needed. His fingers curled around her arms. He wanted to punish her, insignificant as she was—like a prairie mouse to a mudland viper. And he very well might have killed her had it not been for a noise outside. He grabbed his rifle and ran through the door. She felt a wave of regret that he had not finished her. She longed for peace but knew not how to bring it herself, so meek had she become.

She could no longer remember the girl of her youth, who had been spirited and laughed and had beaux. She did not remember the garden parties and the soirees and the fine dresses. She no longer remembered how she had even come to be with this man who was her husband.

Nor did she remember that he had not always been so deplorable in his person. He once had a suave side, although the bedrock of his character had always been sinister. In his youth, he had moved among gentry with some charm and propriety. But he always sensed their distaste of him, for he dealt in flesh. They themselves owned flesh, and they needed him, yet they did not want the association to be known. This hypocrisy galled him.

It was understood that daughters of his customers were off limits. Any time he attempted, no matter how charming, to approach a young lady, she excused herself with the haste of a woman taken with nausea. He aspired to become gentry, for his earnings were comely enough to buy the trappings, but he was denied access to young women of status. He was particularly taken by the petite young Katherine, whose daddy was a big plantation owner and heavy buyer of slaves. Blades was devastated when she politely rejected him. But he would not accept rejection. He would have her.

Katherine had loved soirees. She still had a daguerreotype from her last garden party before her unhappy marriage—a joyful photograph with her closest friends posed at a long table. Katherine's younger brother held a large mirror, framing her for the camera. She looked at the portrait often in the beginning of her marriage but now could not bear to see it. Her reflection seemed a specter, an illusion, not even herself.

It was the day after that photograph was taken that Blades came to Katherine in the woods. He surprised her from behind some trees but approached with a friendly greeting. She had always been able to extricate herself from him at parties, but when she tried to excuse herself, saying she needed to get home for dinner, he grabbed her horse's reins.

"Now, now, I know you are shy," he said softly, "but, please. I just want to talk for a bit. That's all. Please don't be afraid. Here, let me help you down. Let's just stroll for a bit. Then I'll get you home."

He took her firmly by her waist and pulled her from her horse, then made a bow toward the path, gesturing to her to proceed: "Shall we?"

He tried to make conversation with this woman he so utterly desired, but while words came out of her mouth, she did not seem to be talking to him. She avoided his gaze, glanced back at her horse often, and was nervous. Her disinterest pricked his conceit, and he lost his temper.

"How have I affronted you?" he barked. "You think you're too good for me?" He resolved to put her in her place and pinned her against a tree. "All I want is a little kiss, and then you can leave. That's all. It's a small request, but perhaps too great a one to give to the likes of me! Is that it?"

"No, no," she said in a trembling voice, her face stark as a stripped tendon. She could see in his face something she had never seen, and it terrified her. She tried to break away, to run, but he threw her on the ground and then . . .

But she didn't want to think about it. She could not think about it. When it was over, he laughed over her face, breathless from his terrible exertion. Then he stood over her, his pride hanging between his legs, glistening with the slime of his seed, his crepe-skinned scrotum waggling like a turkey wattle, all in plain view. He gathered his genitals in his hands and, stuffing them into his fly, poked in his britches casually as he smiled down at her.

Then, suddenly, he was a consummate gentleman again. He pulled her up and brushed her off and rearranged her ruffles and hair. He took her hand, and they walked slowly back to the horses. Before giving her the reins, he turned to her: "I'll wager a five-pound note my seed is in you. I'm such a fertile rascal. I've gotten more nigger wenches with child than I can count. But don't worry. If a baby comes, I'll marry you. And we'll be happy, won't we, Katherine?" Then he gave her the reins and slapped her horse's rounded haunches. "Home to Daddy!"

Katherine told no one of her terrible secret. But two months later, it was clear that the seed of Cornelius Blades was in fact within her. Her monthlies had not come, and her stays became tight. She could tell no one, for the truth was too awful to share. She wanted to die, to get rid of the baby, but there was no one she could turn to who knew about such things. She had plenty of beaux, even one close to proposing, but there was no time for proper courtship. Her shame would be known too soon.

There were no options—save one, and it was worse than death: She sent a letter to Blades. She would marry him, but only if they left to go west. She did not want to disgrace her family's good name.

Blades sent an immediate reply by messenger. Yes, he would marry her and tell her father he planned to take his daughter west. "In fact, my love," he wrote, "I have lucrative business prospects out west. So, this is all quite fortuitous." His savage seduction was complete. Katherine's future had been set like an iron trap.

Only one person suspected the truth: Katherine's mammy, Tilda. The night before her hasty wedding and departure, Tilda took her "little girl" by the shoulders: "Ah don' know what he done to you, chile. But when de' baby come, there be no need to stay wid 'im. You come back home where you be safe, and ole Tilda can take care of you and your chile. Now, don' you forget what yer mammy tell you, sugar plum."

Katherine cried in Tilda's arms until she finally fell asleep. The old black woman took from around her neck a rawhide necklace with a tiny cloth pouch. Inside were some tiny chicken bones, charmed pebbles, and a pinch of ashes from a funeral pyre—a voodoo necklace her grandmother had given her years before. It was all she could give Katherine as protection against a man and a future Tilda feared would ravage her little girl.

THIRTY FOUR

CREATURE COMFORTS

THE SOFT, BLUE vagueness before dawn collected itself. Pink fringed the horizon, and mist lingered along the tree rows of the Lanning farm. A robin perched on a pitchfork left upright in the garden.

Buttoning up her coat in the crisp, spring mountain air, Sorrel came out of the cabin and made her way to the barn to milk the cow. She didn't see him until she came out again to feed the chicken, and there he was: an old, yellow dog. He had moseyed onto the farm but kept his distance, lying with his head between his front paws. When Sorrel saw him, she thought, *Here comes trouble. A rapscallion that probably kills chickens and steals eggs and runs cattle and absconds with whatever else he can*. She'd have to scare him off the place.

But when she walked up to the cabin, hauling a wooden bucket of milk warm from the cow, the dog sat up on bony haunches with gentlemanly composure. He looked at her patiently with soft eyes that seemed to say he'd be mighty grateful for any scraps she could spare—if it wasn't an inconvenience. He wasn't begging exactly. Rather, his look was one of entreaty, humble but dignified. She was impressed with his manners, especially since he was very thin and hungry.

She wished she could give him food and then he'd be on his way. But wild dogs were incorrigible. She didn't want a worthless scavenger lingering on the farm.

She stomped her foot and yelled at the dog. He backed off, then turned tail with hangdog resignation. But he seemed to know her heart wasn't in it. He turned around and lay down again, his head resting on his paws.

In the hayloft, she stopped working long enough to sneak another look at him and knew she was going to offer him something and the consequences be damned. Seamus would chide her as a softy, but she knew he would secretly feed the dog if she didn't. After her chores, she cut some smoked beef from the smokehouse, then poured fresh cow's milk in a tin. She placed the meat and milk on a tree stump, then stepped back and called the dog.

"Come here, you old gentleman. I know you're hungry," she called out. The dog lifted his head, and his ears perked forward. But now he was the distrustful one, for he had learned that kindness was sometimes a trap. He whimpered but did not move. She went into the house, and the dog crept slowly up to the food, then wolfed it ravenously.

Day by day, the dog gained confidence. But it took weeks before he finally accepted food out of her hand. He became her constant companion, following several paces behind in the field, the barn, along the fence line. Lying down patiently while she cleaned the plow, fixed a fence, or dug a posthole. Never was there a missing chicken or egg or morsel of meat that wasn't given to him freely.

Sorrel called him "old gentleman." For want of a better name, it stuck. He melted into the small family, and now they were a threesome.

He began sleeping on the rag rug in front of the dry sink, then advanced to the foot of her bed, then finally *atop* the bed at her feet. Ever so gradually, he worked his way up toward her, curling up first in the crook of her knees, then against her back, and finally getting as close as he could, his head resting on her clavicle. He curled up like a comfortable old shoe, with compliant familiarity and sturdy devotion, assuming the shape of his mistress.

Sorrel found solace in his warm presence and the soft velvet of this muzzle against her neck. Even though he smelled bad and snored and sometimes growled and his legs churned in his dog dreams, she thought him far less troublesome than any husband.

Each night, she and the old dog would make their nightly rounds—bed down the livestock, latch the chicken coop door, blow out the barn lantern. Then they would crawl into bed, and Sorrel would press her face into his fur, still cold and fluffed from the night chill and smelling distinctly of dog. She loved the ritual.

One morning, after she had let Old Gentleman out for his morning constitutional, he stood outside the door and whimpered. Sorrel opened it nervously, afraid to find him wounded from another fight with a raccoon or badger. Instead, he stood perfectly intact, save a pained expression in his doleful eyes. He looked embarrassed; his furrowed brows, gray at the temple, seemed to acknowledge that he knew he had been bad but there was no help for it.

In his mouth was a tiny newborn kitten, a yellow ball of fur with its pink face and paws curled up like a shrimp, its eyes still not open to the world. The dog held the kitten gently in his mouth and released it in her hands without looking.

"What have you found, you old yellow dog?" she scolded gently, wondering if this was all that was left of the litter and if Old Gentleman had been the culprit or the savior. She fashioned a tiny bed of rags inside a tin pan and laid the kitten near the warmth of the stove. The kitten was only hours old and would have to be fed from a makeshift nipple. Sorrel could think of nothing that would work until she remembered the hog intestine casings inside the smokehouse. She scraped the meat from inside the intestine and pricked a tiny hole in the casing. She spooned in milk, frothy and sweet and still warm from the cow, then bound the end with string.

Old Gentleman rose with interest to watch the process. Instinctively, the kitten's tiny sandpaper tongue began working, sopping the milk. Old Gentleman took to licking the kitten's body while it nursed and then licked its mouth clean after it was done. They became inseparable friends. Sorrel was touched by Old Gentleman's maternal caring and felt guilty she had ever suspected him.

She told Seamus she didn't know what to name the kitten and that a man with his gift for blarney was more qualified than she for the task, a comment he accepted as a compliment. To be sure, Seamus put considerable thought into the charge. He considered the heralded names of ancient Irish chieftains and mythological creatures and leaders of the little people. But in the end, he hearkened back to his yellow-mopped little brother in Ireland who had died of consumption and malnutrition in the famine. The raggedy little kitten had the same coloring and would be named Charlie.

Charlie the cat fared much better than Seamus's baby brother. He grew into a big tiger tom with a long, fluffy coat that seemed superfluous on a frontier farm where function held a knife's edge over form. He was a Lothario among scruffy barn cats, and he wore his pretty-boy machismo with a haughty nonchalance. Aside from his constant companion, Old Gentleman, he preferred the company of people in general and Sorrel in particular.

Together, the big yellow dog and the big yellow cat would follow

Sorrel around the farm as she did her chores. The only activity that enticed Charlie remotely was milking the cow, for the warm milk emanated a mammary sweetness. During milking, he sat atop the stall door like a barn Sphinx and purred in feline reverie.

He could tell from the pitch of the squirting milk when the pail was nearly full. He would suddenly open his eyes as if a dinner bell had rung in his head and drop down next to the pail, ready for a spurt of milk. Sorrel then grasped the long teat, soft and pink white like the inside of a rabbit's ear, and squeezed a milky stream straight into his mouth.

Old Gentleman came too for his turn. He tried to lap up the frothy stream, and the milk splattered in his eyes and on his forehead. Charlie licked off whatever Old Gentleman could not reach with his own tongue, and the yellow dog sat obediently with his eyes closed until the cat was done. It was a comfortable symbiosis between barnyard buddies. Old Gentleman did not realize, nor would he have cared, that Charlie got the better part of the deal.

At night, the two retired to Sorrel's bed and waited for her. The old dog would cozy up to Sorrel's front and Charlie inside Old Gentleman's belly like nesting dolls, all coiled in each other's warmth.

THIRTY FIVE

TWO SPIRITS

THE SPRINGTIME after Flying Horse's first buffalo hunt, she showed up at Sorrel's farm one day, beaming. She had something special to share. She helped Sorrel with chores, feeding the horses, and throwing corn to the chickens, thinking it an odd thing to repeat work that Nature would do on her own. She wondered at the white propensity for dominion over Nature. But she helped, for her heart was big, and she was anxious to share her surprise.

When they arrived at Flying Horse's village, they rode through a huge horse herd on the mountainside to a little clearing. There, among the trees, was a spotted mare with two foals. The women knelt in the grass, petting the two foals, little stud colts blanketed in spots like inkblots splattered upon a page. They were sassy and insistent for milk and squealed and nipped at each other to get the best suckling position for their mother's teats. Sorrel finally positioned one on each side of the mare to quell the commotion. Flying Horse and Sorrel laughed; now they could talk in peace.

They dropped into the grass and watched the mare and her babies. They were beautiful, beautiful, Sorrel kept saying, and Flying Horse understood her admiration.

Flying Horse finally cleared her throat and turned to Sorrel: "*Ayi*, sister, we are same like baby *sik'em*. Yes?" Flying Horse pointed to the twin foals.

Sorrel smiled: "Yes!"

Flying Horse began again: "Gift to you. One for you, one for me."

Sorrel's eyes went wide with surprise. She shook her head slowly, then more adamantly as the thought sank in. "This is too great a gift. He should stay with you, Nimiipuu."

Flying Horse smiled. "You Nimiipuu too!"

Sorrel smiled as well and finally nodded agreement; to resist such generosity would be insulting. They sat in the meadow, talking of how they would train the foals together and how strong they would become, for both parents were fleet and brave of heart. Sorrel stood to leave and pulled Flying Horse to her feet. They embraced.

"Qe'ciyéw'yew', ayi," Sorrel said. "Thank you, sister."

Sorrel kissed Flying Horse, her lips lingering tentatively in gratitude and in desire.

As a student of human nature, particularly woman's nature, Ransom was curious about Sorrel's lack of interest in men and wondered if perhaps her friendship with Flying Horse was more than platonic. He had a fascination for the subtle vernacular of female emotion. *Much more complicated,* he thought, *than that of males, who are, basically, simple creatures.*

He had known of love affairs between prostitutes. Perhaps their work exposed them to the worst instincts of men, thereby marking the male gender untrustworthy. Or their libertine sensibilities had spilled out beyond traditional mores.

He asked Sylvia about his observations once, though their language was veiled in cryptic Victorian parlance. She thought, then answered that perhaps ladies of pleasure felt a sisterhood in their strife, similar to what the Welsh or Irish felt against the British. They found security in that loyalty, and it filled many needs. For some of them, perhaps it was their natural inclination, she added. Farm animals and dogs show that kind of behavior. Why not humans? she suggested. And finally, where would a woman of the night find a man that would truly love her, tainted as she was? It was natural to turn to each other for love.

Ransom marveled at Sylvia's reasoning and thought perhaps she had previously pondered the question as well.

When Sorrel arrived back at her farm that evening, Ransom was there, already seated at the table and on his second cup of whiskey. He could feel the whiskey, and he liked the feeling.

He greeted Sorrel. "You're not limping. Your ankle's healed?"

"It's fine," she said, waving it off, then quickly changed the subject. "How's your mine? Are you a silver tycoon yet?" she teased.

He laughed. "Far from it. I caught my mule finally. Now I have a pair of mules that fight and a couple of good-for-nothing drifters who sleep on the job. They're not much help. But I'll give it a try for a while. A mine isn't for the impatient."

"Smart man. A philosopher," Seamus piped up. "You'll be needing more pocheem for tinkin' like dat." The little Irishman filled up Ransom's cup a third time. They ate dinner and talked more about the mine and town gossip. And then Sorrel mentioned that her Nez Perce friend had given her a fine Appaloosa foal. She did not know how she could ever repay such a gift, for this colt was of their finest bloodstock.

Ransom sat sipping his whiskey, pondering their friendship. A fine-blooded horse was the most generous gift a Nez Perce could bestow. Whatever their relationship, it would not deter him. He would somehow insinuate himself into her life, through stealth or charm or ingenious means—certainly through the old man, who had his own plans for foisting Ransom on Sorrel. Seamus, bless him, interrupted his musing to put thought into action.

"Sorrel, sweet, why don't you show Mr. Fallon your fine new foals. He's a good judge of horseflesh. He appreciates such tings."

"Yes, I'd like that," Ransom chimed in, grateful for Seamus's finagling and anxious to be alone with Sorrel. He followed Sorrel out the door, followed by Old Gentleman, then Charlie. Seamus watched them leave and smiled to himself—a trio of doting males following an unwitting goddess.

THIRTY SIX

CLOVEN TONGUES OF FIRE

ON HIS WAY TO San Francisco, Frederick boarded a steamboat on the Columbia River to Portland, from which he witnessed breathtaking terrain: plunging gorges, rushing rivers, mountains blanketed with trees so gargantuan it seemed God had created them on the scale of giants rather than men. Ligaments of light cast rays through mystic colonnades like temples. Rain mizzled gentle from vaulted canopies. Frederick understood why Indians honored the forests as divine and the trees as great totems reaching to the heavens.

From the steamboat he saw many lumber camps, and a new world opened to him. The titan trees and the men who cut them down made for dramatic photographs. On his return trip, Frederick stopped to photograph a camp. Lumberjacks eagerly posed for him atop stumps as big as cabins, with long, two-man saws called "misery whips," for the saws took measure of men's capacity for pain.

Virgin forests were invaded by lumberjacks and bullwhackers by the thousands, and tent towns grew common as toadstools on old stumps. Once-serene glens echoed with chopping and sawing and bullwhips and the eerie crackle of thousand-year-old trees tipping on trunks hacked down to threads of life. Frederick was haunted by the slow, searing pops that soared to a scream, then shattered, as towering trees crashed to the forest floor.

Then teams of twenty oxen or draft horses pulled the massive columns on skids oiled with bear grease to chutes called flumes. The trees bulleted down mountainsides to rivers.

Rivers were so choked with wood shavings that salmon in their annual journeys upstream flopped in nothing but sawdust, eyes bulging, gasping at their bewildering fate. Mountains once cloaked in forests were denuded to ghettoes of stumps, bald as a mangy bear.

Jacks laid bets on the ages of the giants they felled but wondered privately at destroying a thing that had been alive for thousands of years, since Jesus Christ himself had walked the earth. Frederick had read that naturalists now believed some of the primordial conifers were 5,000 years old and older. The magnificent trees seemed like gnarled old men rooted in stony ground, watching silently while modernity rampaged toward them. He wondered at the ravages visited upon the land and its native inhabitants and could not countenance that what took nature eons to create was torn asunder so recklessly by man.

For thousands of years, in autumn, Nez Perce youth set out into the forests on vision quests to seek their spirit forces, called *wyakins.* Boys and girls were sent alone beyond their childhood wanderings and familiar terrain. They fasted and contemplated the world and opened themselves to listenings of the earth. Eventually, they were visited by the spirit of an animal or other natural sign that became the spirit seeker's namesake. And they absorbed the bedrock being of that wyakin.

Many wyakins were inspired by animals: Crazy Horse, Sitting Bull, Bird Alighting. Others came from the mundane: Red Moccasin Tops, Whittling, Black Kettle. Still others came from the land and sky: Man-on-a-Cloud, Rainbow, Thunder Rolling from the Mountain. Some names were inspired from battle visions: Bloody Chief, Plenty Coups, Five Wounds.

Wyakins were not without a sense of humor. Some youngsters came back with names like Man Afraid of His Horse, Big Mouth, Bad Smell, Lost in Trees, One Who Steps in *Coopaw.*

Fire Bear was eleven summers when he was sent into the forests. He was small for his age, but strong. He walked for days, sleeping in caves and hollows, making a nest of fallen evergreen needles. That summer had been singularly dry with punishing heat. The trees had suffered. The forest floor was carpeted in a duff of needles, soft and nutmeg in color.

Several days into his spirit search, Fire Bear smelled the subtle but unmistakable whiff of smoke. The air was heavy, and the light had a strange, stunted quality. The sunset was blood red, the reddest he'd ever seen, and he knew its terrible beauty came from the sunlight sifting through the detritus of massive fire. Fire Bear did not know how far off the flames were, but in the gathering darkness, he saw a shadowy tableau of animals moving through the forest.

The moon was dull through a gauze of smoke. Animals increased in numbers, stags and caribou and bear and cougar and fox and porcupine and badger. They walked listlessly through the trees like haunts with no purpose, unnaturally close, their fear of each other supplanted by a fear much greater.

Fire Bear made his way east with the exodus of beasts. He mourned the huge trees rooted in harm's way. The largest might survive the onslaught, though scarred and stripped.

He traveled all night, and as dawn's blush collected through the screen of trees, he noted the forest's strange silence, no lively cacophony welcoming the morn. A haze hung below the forest canopy like dreary netting. The morning light bore through the forest in horizontal rays, weighty bars of smoke suspended in the air.

He reached an opening and saw a red glow spreading in the western sky, festering flesh around an erupting boil. Now the cavalcade of wildlife seemed surreal. Fire Bear had heard from elders about great fires that devastated entire mountains, stopped only by great rivers wide enough the fires could not jump. It was an ancient parable on an elemental scale: fire against water, their opposing natures clashing in spectacular struggle. Fire Bear was now many days into unfamiliar ground and hoped to come upon a lake or river soon as his only refuge. He heard sounds he did not recognize—cracking, booming; low, haunting moans, caterwauls akin to an owl or bobcat but sustained in an arcing pitch of terror.

He believed the trees were burning with such heat that sap now sizzled inside, as camas bulbs over a campfire hissed, then burst. But the sounds seemed to come from spirits rather than anything of the earth. Perhaps it was death rending their wood torsos of flesh, leaving them keening in searing lament. With that thought, his heart beat in quickening panic, for how could his small, inconsequential soul survive if those of such sovereign giants could not?

He wondered if this was the sign of his wyakin. But he did not feel a cleansing catharsis—only a dull, thrumming fear. His mind could not process the magnitude of the threat. So he regarded the mélange with odd detachment, his perception extruded through a sieve of disbelief.

The boy reached a mountain ridge. Below, along the deep cleft of the valley floor, he saw a ribbon of pink silver, dawn's light reflecting the meandering course of a river. In the west, ominous black effluvia spread across the sky.

He hurried his pace but stumbled in exhaustion. A crushing weight seemed to squeeze his lungs. He swallowed hard, his parched throat gravelly as a river bed in drought. Lurching down the mountain slope, gravity pulled him faster than his weary legs could run, and he collapsed over rocks and a jumble of fallen tree limbs. The mountainside was a sullied stampede of wildlife in such motley variety it resembled a dream.

A family of skunks scuttled across the forest floor, the kits crying and mewling pathetically after their harried mother. For an instant, Fire Bear yearned for his own mother to keep him safe. But he quickly drove the thought away, ashamed and afraid of his fear. A stag bound past in broken stride. Its back leg hung at the hock joint by ropy tendons and rags of flesh, the hoof dangling in grotesque spasms.

A blond cougar slunk on the ground, camouflaged by a shawl of soot on its back, barely visible but for its pale underbelly. It snarled a snappish growl and peered back at the phantom fire with eyes slitted in fear.

Now Fire Bear could see, across the slope to the north, cloven tongues of fire leaping above the trees. He momentarily felt a wave of relief that the wind came from the southeast, *against* the fire. But his heart shuttered when he realized that the air whipping the trees was not wind at all but rather the voracious vacuum of fire sucking up air in its path. The inferno pulled at him and the forest animals with murderous lust. Fire Bear beheld a diorama of creatures canted in effort against the wind, skeletal silhouettes quivering before the flaming backdrop of heat. The fire's roar was deafening, their effort frantic mime against a wall of sound.

The avalanche of beasts pitched down the slope toward the river. Suddenly, steps away, a fireball plunged alongside him. He could not believe his eyes, for the fireball was a huge grizzly, his fur aflame. The acrid stench of burning hair and flesh filled the boy's nostrils.

Together, bear and boy plunged into the water. The bear hit the river with a pitiful moan. A rush of flames and steam rose in a hiss. Fire licked the glimmering surface before the river extinguished it in churning bubbles.

The bear did not surface for several seconds, and Fire Bear wondered if it was drowning, too maimed to swim. Finally, its nose and ears popped up, then its head with patches of raw flesh and burnt, stubbled hair.

The bear moaned again in agony and relief. He swam in circles, as did all the creatures in the water, a roiling soup of beasts with a boy among them. The boy felt more beast than human and was grateful for their company.

This, then, was his vision, his wyakin. His namesake was to be Fire Bear, a spirit born of fire and survival. Later, elders would shake their heads in amazement that this sprite of a boy should be visited by such powerful medicine. It was a wyakin that would bring him great respect and a wide berth in the tribe's regard. It was a wyakin that would help him in the face of great danger.

THIRTY SEVEN

GILDED GRANITE

SORREL HAD MADE few acquaintances with local women, but she was immediately drawn to Gert Houston, whom she'd met at Marston's General Store. Gert was a middle-aged woman who ranched by herself. Tragedy had molded her into varying textures of toughness and tenderness. She smoked a corncob pipe and cursed like a teamster but, in the same breath, said babies were proof that God hadn't given up on mankind. The only feminine trappings she claimed were quilting and gardening. She did both exquisitely.

She was an independent soul with unorthodox notions, yet she was well tolerated—in fact, loved and respected. A group of steadfast quilting ladies had taken her into their fold, although they were often shocked by her language.

Gert had built a life on the rubble of loss but mortared with doggedness. She had lost her family in a Shoshone attack, the cabin burned and with it her babies in their cradles. Her husband, John, was struck down in the field while plowing. Had she not been picking berries for a pie in the woods, she would have been killed too. As it was, she lived with a terrible guilt that she had not been there to comfort her babies in their terror, to be with her husband in his final moments on earth.

Her feelings, she knew, were irrational, and her closest friends told her so, trying in every meager way they could to eradicate her guilt. But Gert would carry the guilt forever. It was part of her, like the scars of burned flesh.

All she had left was a garden and a graveyard. But from both, she found comfort. Three solitary crosses kept her company in her loneliness, though she could not abide the mounds of dirt: firstly because of what was under them, and secondly because dirt unplanted cried out for life. She gathered wildflowers by the armload that she transplanted atop each mound, carrying on one-way conversations with her loved ones beneath. There was no one to overhear the conversations and wonder at her sanity, save the birds and prairie dogs, who held no judgments.

She whispered to her little one deep in the ground: "Eliza, my beautiful, sweet girl. Pink hyacinths. Don't they smell so good?" And she remembered the fresh, sweet smell of her baby when she stuck her face in her tummy to tickle her.

Later that spring: "Here, Jacob. Blue lupine for my darling boy." As she watered the flowers, she smiled, reminded of an occasion when she had been changing his diaper and an arc had spouted from his little winkie right into her face. "What a little Dickens you were, Jacob! You rascal."

She transformed the mounds into oases of affection. Somehow the wooden crosses seemed grateful for the company. In spring, the mounds became effusions of shooting star and crocus and trillium and fairy slipper. In midsummer, filmy-petaled poppies, like slender, disheveled ladies in floppy hats, riffled in the breeze in a scarlet chorus. Autumn welcomed honeysuckle and pussytoes and paintbrush and mule's ear. The prairie winds sifted through the blooms, scrawling their wildflower scents on the air and bringing memories of her family.

Gert had always wanted roses, and the quilting ladies combined their pennies to order a rose bush from the Sears & Roebuck Catalog. She planted it at the foot of John's grave, where it flourished, yielding copious clusters of ivory buds like dollops of whipped cream.

Adjacent to the graveyard was her garden. As the graveyard had taken away, so the garden gave back. The regiment of vegetables kept her company, and she talked to them as she talked to her family beneath the dirt.

She collected buckboards of livestock manure from the neighbors as happily as if she were carting wagonloads of gold nuggets. When she forked the virgin prairie, the proud sod relinquished only monstrous anvils of dirt. Gert longed for the soft, moist crumble of soil that made seeds happy. She toiled and cursed and toiled some more, vowing to break down the soil before it broke her.

Her vegetable seeds were obliged to show their appreciation: tomatoes, eggplants, peppers—fleshy, bright jewels of her labor, their skin sleek and taut. She gloried in their morning sheens, dappled with dew, fresh and eager. Later in the season, the cabbages appeared like plump ballroom belles in petticoated petals, preening their flounces in rank and file. Gert loved the cabbages best.

Gert had always worn her father's antique gold watch on a chatelaine around her skirt waist. It was her constant companion, though she no longer needed to prepare John's dinner or wash diapers or raise her babies from their naps. Now it simply ticked to ease the terrible silence and to move time forward lest it stand still, dicing the day into a salad of familiar tasks. From these simple daily chores from dawn to dusk, Gert found comfort and solace, perhaps even sanity.

The lone woman learned to become self-sufficient because she would not be beholden to others who had experienced their own considerable challenges. She learned to hunt, and her shooting became a matter of pride. She could hit a prairie dog at 100 yards, a fair shot by anyone's measure. When a wildcat developed a nasty habit of killing her chickens, she hid in the coop all night until the rapscallion showed up for dinner. She broke him of the habit permanently.

She learned to fix fences and mend her cabin chinking, daubing a mixture of mud and hog hair she prepared herself. She had few heads of cattle but decided they needed branding and enlisted the help of two of the quilt ladies. They agreed only on the condition that their assistance be in holding the ropes from a distance and not actually putting brand to the poor creatures' hides, for they were sure they would faint. Gert plowed and gathered wood and dug postholes. She worked to forget, and she worked to remember.

She tried to stop herself, tried to divert, squelch, stymie her awful tidal thoughts. But they washed over her, as inevitable as the ocean lapping upon the gritted sands of her memory, over and over and over again. Her mind would lead her to the lonely plot of ground where John's strapping, six-foot form and shy, dimpled smile lay, John and her two babies. She wondered how much of John was left, how much of her babies with their once-pink bodies, pudgy and buoyant with baby fat, remained in the cold, dark earth.

She had read once about the funeral pyres the Hindus of India built for their dead. She thought how much easier, how much more dignified this parting of the body was than elemental decay, the slow dismemberment and eating away. Such decimation of beauty she could not abide. Her mind harangued her with such thoughts until she feared she would go mad.

How could God give her such a severe gift? Her life, but with nothing left to hold her to earth? Images of John's dissembled flesh dogged her, woke her at night. Her grief butted up to despair. She could not navigate through her loss. Escape seemed her only path.

She could hang herself from a barn rafter with John's rough hemp rope. Or shoot herself with John's double-barrel Avery shotgun. Or slice her wrists with John's big Bowie knife. But, somehow, the part of John she loved most reminded her why they had come to this homestead, why she must continue—so that his death and the deaths of their babies would not be in vain.

So one day she made an uneasy truce with life and decided to live. All the while, the knife, the rope, and the gun sat sanguine, taunting. But she made peace with them, too. The tools John had used in life she befriended. She imagined his touch was still in them, the grip of his strong hands clutching them, like an Atlas grip on her desire. And she held fast, for him.

THIRTY EIGHT

COMMERCE OF NEED

MORE THAN TWENTY YEARS after Gert had lost her family, she got a new neighbor only a couple of miles from her farm on a long-abandoned homestead. Bull Bamrick grew up in Tennessee on a tobacco and cotton plantation his grandfather had homesteaded forty-five years earlier. He had married late in life and lived halcyon days with his wife, Elizabeth. Like his father, he hoped to have a house full of boys with whom he would go hunting and fishing.

But the war came, and his plans became vagabond dreams, lost to a world that no longer existed. At the end of the war, Bull found himself a ragged, ex-Confederate colonel at the carnage of Vicksburg, facing a 500-mile slog back through the broken South.

He returned to a plantation in ashes, the slaves gone, carpetbaggers squatting in the big house, and his wife and child dead. Bull stumbled to the family cemetery where a half century of Bamricks were buried. He fell to his knees before two new mounds of dirt, caressing the soft earth, and began to cry. The tears ran down his cheeks and onto the red dirt, tiny opals shimmering atop the soil. These rough-cut jewels of his raw grief were all he had left to give his dead wife.

He went west, like many Southerners. Not for gain or for a new life. He simply followed the human flowage, like blood from a wound that, with nothing to hold it in, spills out to places unbidden. He did not know where he was going or when he'd get there.

The mountains had spoken to him and become his only geography of hope. The rolling swells at the foot of Idaho's mountains were like great breasts of moss, green and nurturing, so much like Tennessee that his heart ached.

In a copse of trees, he found a small cemetery overgrown with brambles. One upright stone bore the names of a woman and baby who had died together in childbirth. The graves gave him strange comfort, as if surrogates for his own wife and child.

He decided, on the spot, that this would be his new home. He stood in front of the plots, removed his hat, and introduced himself. They could take care of each other, he offered. Nearby was a stream and rolling hills blanketed in buffalo grass and wild clover and camas flowers he thought would be excellent grazing for cattle. On the banks of the stream, he would build a cabin.

When Gert heard that she had a new neighbor, she wrapped a slab of salt pork in burlap from her smokehouse and gathered some of her produce and saddled Sally the mule to welcome the new arrival. She found him chopping aspen poles for the corral fence.

"Well, howdy." Gert held out her hand. "I heard I had a new neighbor and brought you a welcome basket. Ain't much. Some salt pork and garden vegetables. I ain't much of a cook. Didn't think it'd be kindly to foist my burnt corn muffins on you quite yet."

Bull laughed and introduced himself. They talked about their farms and the land and quickly discovered that each had lost family. Gert said she was lucky—"if you can call it that"—to have her family buried close.

"You're welcome to visit anytime," she said. "I got plenty of farm tools and a plow." She wanted to say more but found no words.

Two weeks later, Bull saw Gert again at the general store in Spotted Horse, and they greeted each other like old friends. Gert invited Bull over for dinner two nights hence: "I don't know if you're ready for my cooking. But seein' as how you made it this far, you must have a pretty strong constitution. You can probably survive an assault on your stomach."

"I'd be much obliged for a home-cooked meal. It's been nigh six years since I've had one," he said. "Anyone's cooking would be better than the Confederate Army's. You needn't worry about impressing me."

Gert spoke the truth. She was *not* a cook. Her coffee was the consistency of pine tar, and her flapjacks had the tensile strength of manhole covers. But the sausage she had put up in her smokehouse was as savory as the thick bacon he remembered from his plantation. She made scrambled eggs suspended in freshly churned butter, and she had fresh cantaloupe from her garden. She sat at the table, wiping her hands on the front of her apron. "Sorry to serve you breakfast for supper," she said. "It's my only meal that's edible."

Bull ate voraciously, slyly saving the flapjacks for last so they wouldn't taint his palliative experience. Gert's feminine inadequacy didn't vex Bull, for he found her company refreshing and a balm to his lonely heart.

Gert pulled out a pipe and offered him a similar one filled with a Nez

Perce tobacco concoction. They sat together in high-back cane rocking chairs, smoking, talking, and Gert sewing quilt blocks.

Gert talked about business and politics, cattle and crops, the weather and the railroad and Indian troubles. She was a breed of woman he had never known, and he guessed that she had been forged as much by the prairie as by her own God-given nature. For the first time since he had knelt upon his wife's grave, he felt perhaps he might find relief from despair.

Marston's General Store was the scene of another accidental meeting. There, Magnolia Man-Happy encountered Willie buying canned peaches in a back aisle. Magnolia was new to Spotted Horse. She'd been a black slave mammy in Alabama before the war and had built a small prostitution business for herself with three young black women from her home plantation. They had traveled west after the war with the plan to go to Oregon. But winter came, and Magnolia and her girls got waylaid in Spotted Horse. She decided there was enough business to stay.

The big black woman waddled up to him and tapped him on the shoulder. "Mistuh Willie, folks say you hep that fool Clarence Forester and those po' orphan babies south of town. You good, even if yo' mouf bad. That what I think," she began. "I new in town and I needs a home fo' my mule, Lester. But I wanna pay in black molasses, not greenbacks, if'n you catch my meaning. What you say, Mistuh Willie?"

For once in his life, Willie was speechless and rubbed his whiskers, contemplating Magnolia's ample person. Then he blurted out without the benefit of thought: "How's a bastard find the keyhole in all that?" He looked at her up and down.

But Magnolia was unfazed. "You get on top of big Magnolia, and I do the rest. Don't you worry none. Maybe it been so long you forgot how!"

Willie privately admitted Magnolia might have a point. "How many pokes?" he asked.

"One a week and oats for my Lester," Magnolia shot back.

"Well, damn me. I'd not fuck Cleopatra for a week's oats."

"If'n you can get it up for two, my ass is the blackest!" Magnolia challenged.

"Ya 'ave a deal, madam!"

Willie wondered if his shillelagh could stand up even once a week. But he smirked to himself at the thought of sitting atop Magnolia's chocolate mountain of flesh. He was willing to give it a try.

THIRTY NINE

LONG SQUASH, ROUND MELONS

IT WAS FALL. The season of harvest. The canted light and clarity in the crisp air gave the illusion of nearness. Squirrels and prairie dogs cached nuts. Spotted Horse was having its annual autumn social. It was a busy time for Frederick, photographing proud gardeners with produce, quilts, and sleek, fatted livestock. Folks brought wagons brimming with vegetables and fruits, chickens and pigs, and canned goods, all for bartering. They laid out their wares on quilts on the grass or tablecloths of red gingham or, for the poorer folks, burlap bags or flour sacks.

The social was a gardeners' showcase, a time to cluck over others' produce and bask secretly over one's own. Folks set out their earthly rainbow—orange carrots, red tomatoes, green peppers, purple eggplant—glistening with children's polishing. Turban squash streaked scarlet, green, and gold like silken headdresses of Turkish princes. Long squash and round melons, mated in contrast like garden parables in a guiltless Eden.

Eliza Klineck glanced across the lawn to see her apple-cheeked son chasing a girl while holding a long zucchini at his crotch. They were both laughing gleefully, and adults were giggling, too, their shoulders up about their ears to hide their amusement, their hands over rounded mouths, trying to admonish but unable to muster the sternness. Eliza was horrified, then relieved when another mother turned crimson as her own son packed two melons chest-high under his shirt. The two mothers caught each other blushing and burst out laughing, then shrugged in resignation.

Children hugged kingly watermelons and pumpkins, rotund in their colorful raiment. Boys challenged each other to contests of strength, grunting to lift the fleshy boulders. Other children, squealing, spilled out like bright beads on the lawn.

The local Nez Perce came bearing their own offerings—sweet oppah bread, roasted camas bulbs, and baskets of huckleberries, blueberries, and walnuts. They brought luxuriant pelts and exquisite needlework. There were woven baskets big as washtubs and diminutive as teacups. The white women flocked to the baskets—always handy on homesteads for hanging laundry, collecting hens' eggs, and the many other womanly chores.

Nez Perce women coveted calico cotton and pretty buttons and traded eagerly for such finery. A Nez Perce chief paid US currency for candied apples for his children, and a white farmer traded shotgun cartridges for smoked venison. Despite barriers of language, exchanges flowed freely, lubricated by handshakes and friendly smiles.

Willie McGee and his barbershop buddies were knotted around the pumpkin competition, making wagers on which was the heaviest as the orange behemoths were hoisted onto scales. Willie placed his money on a misshapen, obese pumpkin that looked as if it had begun to melt, spreading its gelatinous-looking heft along the ground. Remas Hartland had bet on a fine pumpkin, very large, plump, and perfectly globular, while Floyd Hawkins swore his choice would outdo them all: tall, ovoid, and tilting like the tower of Pisa but with a squiggly, pig-tail stem on top.

"My pumpkin'll win, or I'll shit cinders on main street and smile doing it!" Willie vowed. When it won by four ounces, he slapped his thigh and guffawed heartily and motioned to his friends to fork over the loot. Floyd grumbled, "Age before wisdom," but should have known better than to taunt his lightning-lipped adversary.

"Pearls before swine, my good friend!" Willie quipped, chuckling.

Frederick was busy photographing prizewinners, who clutched their produce under broad grins: a little boy sitting atop a monstrous pumpkin; children playing among watermelon scattered on the ground; and a little girl in a dress posing proudly in front of her father's produce stacked on makeshift shelving.

At the other end of the festival was a large gathering and much excitement as adults paired up for the gunnysack race. Young men and women strategically placed themselves by those with whom they hoped to share a sack. Ransom had tipped the announcer to let him know when the competition would begin and made sure that he was talking to Seamus and Sorrel during the announcement. They had been admiring some horses, and the ruse seemed completely innocent.

As young men and women rushed for gunnysacks, Ransom grabbed Sorrel's arm firmly and hauled her through the crowd: "Be my partner, Miss Lanning! Come on! We have to hurry!" Through the jostling and excited voices, her protestations were lost, and she found herself stepping into a huge feed sack with him.

He took her arm and placed it around his middle and put his arm tightly around her waist. Then, looking ahead, he coached her: "I believe there is some strategy required in this game. We have to work together, or we'll end up on the ground. When I say jump, we'll jump together. We have to get a rhythm down."

She stared at him, then down at the huge gunnysack they shared and could not believe her predicament. But when the pistol cracked, she came to her senses, and everyone was off, bounding across the field like sentient sacks of potatoes. Immediately, pairs collided or collapsed in mounds of giggles.

Sorrel felt Ransom's arm lifting her with each jump, and she felt a rush at the authority of his strength. She clung desperately to his torso with her right arm to stay upright, the muscles over his ribcage and abdomen rippling and flexing with each effort. She was surprised by this new sensation and found herself suddenly irritated that she must concentrate on the very public effort of staying upright when she was filled with private want.

But neither had sufficient focus for the nuances of the competition when their minds were elsewhere. Sorrel jumped too soon in her discombobulation and threw them both off balance. As they went hurtling toward the ground, Ransom pulled her close, and she landed on top of him, his mouth against her cheek. His lips wisped her skin in a barely perceptible kiss. She struggled against him to get upright, but the burlap bag impeded her movement, and she fell back on him in her effort. He pulled her tight against him, his breath hot on her face, and whispered, "You are beautiful even in a gunny sack." He held her for just a moment as she strained for escape, then released her.

Exuberant onlookers bordered the course like laundry flapping on a clothesline. Frederick had rushed to the finish and was busy setting up his camera and tripod to photograph the winners. Only two pairs remained upright in the end; piles of burlap-clad partners lay strewn about the field, struggling and laughing.

Ransom rose to help Sorrel from the gunnysack. She tried to resist him without revealing to spectators that she'd been an unwilling participant—in fact, a captive of Ransom's artifice. "You are very clever, Mr. Fallon," she said through gritted teeth, "but also very clumsy!" As she stepped out of the sack, she pushed him, still standing in the bag, and he crashed to the ground, where she left him struggling to extricate himself.

"Oh, pardon me! Do you need help?" She smiled down at him. Her slapstick brought new waves of laughter, and Ransom laughed too at her comical rebuff. But it had not escaped the throng that Ransom Fallon managed to maneuver the reticent young woman into a gunnysack with him. That was, indeed, the closest any man had ever come in proximity to Sorrel's comely form.

FORTY

ECHOES OF STONE

DURING SPAWNING time, after the Nez Perce caught their fill of salmon, they sat on limestone cliffs and watched the fish swim a deadly gauntlet of grizzlies waiting in the rapids.

The Indians marveled at the ways bears caught fish. Most chose the rapids, but others found more ingenious methods. They were extraordinarily dexterous, even with massive paws and six-inch claws curved like whalebone. Some bears foraged along the shoreline for mussels and clams, breaking open shells with the delicacy of sterling fork tines.

Often, younger adult males had neither the patience nor social status to gain a strategic position in the rapids, so they lumbered through the shallows of salmon with much bombast. But the fish, wily and skittish, evaded such clumsy hunters. The bears often came up empty-pawed, roaring their frustration.

Some snorkeled for fish in calm shallows with their faces underwater, eyes open. Their rounded ears remained above water, for bears instinctually like to keep their ears dry. On the shallow, pebbled river bottom were dead fish or those ailing, so exhausted they could barely keep their bodies righted.

Mother bears with cubs in tow often hunted at the places their mothers had hunted. While they waited patiently for opportunity, their cubs bobbed in the water like furry corks or romped on the shoreline, sometimes sliding down mud runs, entangled in play. Mother bears fed their thrashing catches to their little ones. But younger cubs often preferred batting the tails or pouncing playfully on the big fish to the more serious task of tearing flesh.

Sometimes bears caught pregnant female salmon, their bellies bulging with eggs to spurt in a pebbled nest at the river bottom. This was a special treat for cubs. They would watch their mother hold the fish on a flat rock and press down on the fish's bloated abdomen until scarlet-colored, jellied eggs squirted out in a globular pile. The family would feast on the flat rock of eggs, relishing them like a platter of caviar.

Most amazing of all were bears that had overcome their fear of wet ears and actually dove for their food. The Natives regarded these diving bears as special spirits.

Once, when Fire Bear was about sixteen summers, he swam out to spy on the diving bears. The water was crystal clear, and Fire Bear could see the rocky bottom even in its deepest depths. He swam underneath the water and hid behind a curtain of water plants undulating with the current. A bear bobbed on the surface, treading water.

The grizzly dove, and Fire Bear's heart leapt at its surprising gracefulness. Twenty feet down the bear swam, lips peeled back, long incisors glinting in the watered sunlight. The bear's eyes were wide open, scanning the bottom. He went directly to a fish prostrate on the bottom, four feet long and barely alive.

The bear wrapped his jaw over the salmon, the fish having nary the energy to protest. In a dreamy and languid arc of billowing fur, the grizzly pushed off the river bottom and returned to the surface with his prize.

The water's surface was a rippling crystal membrane, and Fire Bear saw the rocky cliff above and tree foliage like liquid emeralds parsed in kaleidoscopic refraction. For the rest of his days, he remembered the experience and sometimes touched his necklace of grizzly bear teeth, wondering if the teeth had belonged to an extraordinary diving bear that had braved the deep bottoms.

After Flying Horse met Fire Bear on the buffalo hunt, she thought of him often. She felt a strange freedom in being championed by a man who understood her strangeness and accepted it. She had not intimidated him. *Rather*, she thought, *he admired me*. She had not thought this reaction possible from any man other than her father.

The son of a medicine man of a neighboring village, Fire Bear was quiet and well liked. He was of average height but stocky and strong. In games of hand combat or bow and arrow, he excelled. But he had not a warring spirit and thought more of tending the tribe's stock or planting, though other young men saw little honor in it. He possessed a rare courage to walk a separate path from others. He did not join the other braves in berating Flying Horse after the buffalo hunt. He stood by her side. His friends elbowed him and chided him playfully that he desired the one who did not desire men. He said nothing. But he thought of her often as well.

They would meet again during the autumn festival where neighboring tribes gathered. He had been in a bow-and-arrow competition but had not been doing well. He saw Flying Horse watching on the sidelines and extended his bow to her, a gesture that stunned and dismayed the other competitors.

"Here. You try," he offered. She stepped forward and took his bow. She shot the arrow true, but the braves only waved her off in disgust. Fire Bear regretted his words, wanted them to retreat back into his mouth, sorry for the embarrassment they had caused her.

Several days later, he met her in a camas meadow after seeing her shoot a rabbit. He complimented her on her keen aim. When she smiled brightly, he was once again smitten. After that, he found himself riding often to the same meadow, in hopes of meeting her. Once, he was sure he had seen her on her horse among the trees, but she slinked away.

Flying Horse did not know in her heart if she could have feelings for Fire Bear the way she did for Sorrel. This troubled her, for she knew the easier path led to marriage with a brave and away from Sorrel.

Her mother somehow understood and had counseled her that Fire Bear was tolerant and honorable and understood Flying Horse. She added that he was strong enough and respected enough that he could withstand the ridicule of having a "different" wife, that he would indulge her different ways. Flying Horse knew that what her mother said was wise and true, and she thought about it hard.

It was for this reason that, one morning while riding through the camas meadow, she found herself holding her horse in place when she saw Fire Bear advancing, rather than escaping into the trees. When he realized that she was holding her ground, he smiled slightly and held his hand up in greeting.

"Ah, you do not run away. Is your horse's leg broken?" he said.

She smiled at his joke: "His leg is strong. And his heart has found courage today."

"Courage is good," Fire Bear replied. They both sat astride their horses for a moment in silence, gazing out at the expanse of blooming camas. Then Fire Bear said: "I am riding to the river to see if the salmon are coming soon. Can you ride with me?"

Flying Horse smiled and nodded. That was the first of many morning rides together. Their growing pleasure in each other's company was palpable. Flying Horse began to feel she could do this thing required of her as a woman.

While they were riding in the foothills one morning, dark clouds gathered, and thunder grumbled. The grass trembled under the ominous sky. Flying Horse and Fire Bear came to the mouth of a cave. The air inside was cool, and the moss-covered stone dripped and echoed off the wet walls. They sat together on a rocky cliff, sheltered from the deluge, their legs dangling. Lightning ricocheted across the sky, and rain pattered gently on the leaves.

Finally, Flying Horse broached the question that had been dogging her since first meeting Fire Bear: "You are not troubled by my strange ways, as are other men?"

Fire Bear smiled and did not speak for a moment. "If you are strange, it is a strangeness I like. You are strange like the diving bears. They go where others fear to go. You are strange the way my mother was strange. You have her bravery. And my father loved her for it."

He did not look at her but held his gaze on the valley below. The thrumming rain formed rivulets that swelled and finally tumbled over scarp and crag, leaving the rock gleaming and speckled in aqueous sheen.

They returned to camp after the thunderstorm had run its impetuous course and the sun had returned, falling in drapes of light from billowed clouds. Approaching Flying Horse's village, they saw the fires smoking meat and clay pots steaming, filled with sweet camas root. The savory aroma of roasting buffalo meat wafted with the wind, and they both realized how hungry they were.

Flying Horse's mother noticed the difference in her daughter right away. There was a calm in her eyes, a comfortable acquiescence in her shoulders as she rode into camp with Fire Bear. Sings Like Lark turned to her husband and motioned with her eyes toward their daughter.

"Flying Horse has found love," she whispered. He peered at his daughter, trying to decipher what clues his wife had noticed so readily. He frowned.

"How do you know this?" he said, almost accusingly. "I see no difference."

"There is a difference." Sings Like Lark nodded. "Fire Bear will come to you soon."

Tall Tree did not know how his wife knew these things, but he had learned from experience not to question her pronouncements. He was relieved that his daughter with strange ways would be betrothed, and to a man he considered worthy.

FORTY ONE

BROKEN HOOFBEATS

THE TOWN'S HARVEST festival culminated in a horse race. Inevitably, the men—white, Indian, black, Chinese—moved to the outskirts of the celebration to begin wagering. They brought prized possessions to ante: guns, bows, smoking pipes, saddles, drinking flasks, buckskin shirts.

Sometimes, oddities of particular masculine utility required explanation across cultures; a white farmer demonstrated to a chief how a shaving cup and brush with a straight edge worked and lathered up his chin. The Indian laughed, for the Nez Perce did not have facial hair. Nevertheless, the fancy cup and brush interested him. He mimicked the farmer's demonstration, and all his red cohorts laughed at the suds on his face. But then they were anxious to try the ritual themselves.

A brave showed a white cavalry officer the efficiency of a Nez Perce ram-horn bow. Coveted by many local tribes, a Nez Perce bow was a highly engineered hunting weapon, steamed and straightened and secured with glue from salmon skin and sturgeon blood. An arrow shot by such a bow could drive completely through the loin of a buffalo.

The booty was spread out and assiduously examined. Then the horses were brought out—sleek, prancing animals that hungered to soak up their own speed. A cavalry officer with a handlebar mustache brought his chestnut Thoroughbred stallion, long-boned, every ligament built for running. It danced and threw its elegant head and circled its handler in unruly impatience.

A Nez Perce brave brought a black Appaloosa mare with a blanket of spots across her haunches. She stood demurely, ears flicking back and forth as if annoyed by the bombast of the rowdy stallions around her. Beautifully composed, smallish but sleek, the mare had powerful haunches and did not suffer fools. When a nearby horse knocked into her, she bared her teeth and bit him.

A Nez Perce paint stallion was led toward the crowd. He was monstrous and magnificent, and a hush fell as the men admired the animal. The stallion inspired a flurry of betting, and odds went up propitiously in his favor.

The last horse was Flying Horse's big bare mare she had ridden in the buffalo hunt. The Nez Perce men knew how fast the animal was, but the whites, skeptical of a woman rider, cast their bets against her. Fire Bear bet his prize bow on Flying Horse. He smiled up at her and told her she'd better win or he wouldn't be able to hunt anymore and would have to go hungry. She smiled at his joke: "My mare will run much faster knowing your bow is at stake!"

Seven horses stood at a line drawn in the dirt with a stick. The course was flat except for a gentle dip near the fringe of the forest and was marked by several trees and boulders, around which the competitors would gallop for the return to the finish line. The horses reared and pawed and threw their heads in anticipation. The gun went off.

The steeds exploded like sparks from struck flint. They ripped past the crowd, horses and riders jostling for position. Flying Horse and her horse were clogged in the middle. She held her horse back so as not to ride up the backside of the mount in front. The mare was frantic to run, her speed pooling up like floodwaters before a dam break. Flying Horse maneuvered around a slower bay and let her horse go. She felt the sweet press of acceleration as they passed two horses. The field rounded the bend past the trees and boulders and straightened for the homestretch.

The horses stampeded toward the finish line, a cloud of dust behind them. Near the end of the straightaway, the legs of the two leading horses tangled, and a mass of hooves and hair and hocks catapulted into the dirt, half-ton animals colliding, grunting, their underbellies like great tumbling barrels. One mount alighted from the fray, riderless and frantic. The other, the chestnut, lay struggling, thrashing his legs, the whites of his eyes rolling in terror.

The two riders struggled to their feet. The cavalry officer with the handlebar mustache saw immediately that his horse's foreleg had broken. He sat in the dirt beside the animal to calm it, rubbing its elegant neck and talking soothingly in its ear. But there was no help for it, and the officer's eyes pooled with tears.

The men gathered over the horse splayed on the ground and shook their heads. The cavalry officer coaxed the chestnut to stand on its three legs. It had carried him across the country. They had survived the Battle of Gettysburg and wars with the Sioux. He had even taught the horse to lie down in battle as a bulwark for him to shoot from behind. A gallant animal, a friend through adversity.

He led his horse hobbling toward the woods, its broken foreleg hanging forlorn. They disappeared into the trees. The sharp discharge of a revolver echoed.

The big paint was declared the victor, but it was a hollow honor. The gamblers collected their booty with none of the usual braggadocio. Flying Horse had been behind the two colliding horses and a nose ahead of the paint but had veered sharply to avoid the calamity and lost her lead.

Fire Bear ran to her: "You are not hurt?" he asked, concern written in his dark face.

"No. I am fine," she said flatly, perturbed he thought her fragile. "Your bow is lost."

"No matter," he answered. "You are not, and that brings me happiness."

Flying Horse understood that Fire Bear's intentions were that of an aspiring husband. Like a willow branch dipping in a river and leaving a gentle wake, so Fire Bear's touch quickened something within Flying Horse. And her heart was good.

FORTY TWO

OF HUMAN BONDAGE

CORNELIUS BLADES had not lied to his new wife. He did have urgent business out west. Through his associations in the slave trade before the war, he had made some business connections in Idaho and San Francisco that he felt would make him rich again.

His business in black slaves had dwindled to nothing during the war. Not only were most plantation owners off fighting, but it had also become difficult to keep slaves under lock and key, and the social structure had broken down so utterly that many escaped to the North, and there was no one to stop them. The Northern blockades, too, had shut down shipments of human cargo from Jamaica and Africa. Slave traders suddenly found themselves with no livelihood.

But the Oriental slave trade in California was booming. There were few regulations—at least, that were enforced—and new money flowed as auspiciously as grapes budding in Napa Valley's neophyte vineyards.

He would go west and ply his trade in San Francisco and the gold-mining fields. The business principles were essentially the same, and he congratulated himself that he'd been savvy enough to diversify before the war. The transition had already proven lucrative for him and, in many ways, far less problematic than dealing in black flesh.

For the most part, Chinese women brought to America were docile as newborn fawns, partly because their culture demanded it, partly because they came without families, and partly because they had no language skills, education, or survival skills from which to draw any semblance of defense. Chinese girls were raised in a culture as narrowly circumscribed as their tightly bound feet.

Many Chinese woman bore as a mark of their womanhood "lily" feet, a condition in which the toes were broken, then bound tightly as young girls. Growth was impaired to little more than stubs, rendering women barely able to walk. The feet were soaked in a concoction of herbs and warm animal blood so the necrotic flesh fell away and did not turn to gangrene. This strange vestige of Chinese femininity served Blades's own purposes exquisitely, for it greatly reduced his prisoners' mobility. *They didn't need goddamn feet for the work they did, anyway,* he mused.

Most of the Chinese girls had been kidnapped from their homelands or sold as infants, sometimes by their own fathers. They were raised by a concubine or a duenna until they were of a saleable age. Blades hired an old Portuguese duenna to manage his girls. He felt she was sometimes too easy on them. But she said: "Honey goes further than vinegar with girls. And I've never lost a girl in my care." That was proof enough for Blades of her efficiency, so he allowed her to do as she would.

Blades had been introduced to the Chinese slave trade in New York's

Chinatown. He purchased several young Chinese girls from a tong in a New York port. Through the tong, Blades had brokered an agreement with a Chinese lumber baron in Boise, who wanted to purchase girls as servants.

In South Dakota, en route to Idaho, he traded three of the girls for the title to a small gold mine near Spotted Horse. He thought he'd gotten the better deal, as the girls had lesions on their legs and torsos, the beginning signs of syphilis. He wanted to unload them before they lost their worth. Thus he launched his new career dealing in yellow flesh, transporting human cargo like insentient urns to become mere vessels for the pleasure of men.

While Ransom was in San Francisco, newspapers were on fire with exposés about the Chinese slave trade, exposing details so shocking that growing crusades of churchwomen were incited to march into tong districts to rescue enslaved Chinese women.

The articles recounted how girls, some as young as six, were transported on Chinese clipper ships to San Francisco, where they were taken to a joss house in St. Louis Alley, stripped naked, and examined by brothel owners or agents for wealthy men. They could be purchased for prices that ranged from $200 to $2,000.

The most beautiful girls were sold as mistresses. The next rung down went to elite parlor houses. Most other girls went to the brothels and opium dens of tong masters in Chinatown districts. Some were sold to brothel caravans that rolled from mining camp to mining camp or traveled along the routes of cattle drives or railroad crews. Medicine shows and theater troupes also offered tents of pleasure.

Many ended up in the notorious cribs, open to the street, with barred windows through which they beckoned customers for twenty-five cents.

They could not refuse a customer, no matter how ghastly, no matter what venereal disease might have eaten up his flesh. In the cribs, hell yawned to receive the putrid masses, the women themselves already deep within its abyss.

Ransom read a lurid article in the *Alta California* about San Francisco's sirocco of sin:

> Every city on earth has its crime and degradation, its moral cancer, the lower hell, the maelstrom of vice and iniquity—from whence those who enter cannot escape. . . . [T]he Barbary Coast . . . is strewn with the wrecks of humanity. . . These poor creatures are all slaves, bought in China. . . . [C]hances of escaping kidnapping, beatings, prostitution, and slavery, are very slim indeed.

The article related the myriad horrors prostitutes must endure, the worst saved for last:

> We enter a room, dimly lit. . . . Stretched on the floor of this foul-smelling den are four miserable wretches, the victims of the most fearful and loathsome disease with which the vengeance of God has cursed sinful humanity. . . [T]he women lie dying, by inches, a slow, lingering, horrible death. One lifts from a face a cloth. In place of mouth, lips, cheeks and nose, we see a horrible cavity, the eating away of the flesh, the bare bones exposed, the grinning effigy of death's head. We rush from the room.

It had been two years since Frederick had visited San Francisco and purchased his secret box from the old Chinese man in Chinatown. Since then, Chinese clients—mostly families who worked in the laundry at Spotted Horse—had started coming to his studio. He thought he might return to the store to look for Chinese items for props. His business was booming, and he could well afford these small investments, for Oriental wares were inexpensive.

But he had an ulterior motive for visiting the store. He had an idea for a photograph that would inspire his Chinese clientele and be a good seller in the postcard market.

He walked into the store, surrounded by a cacophony of gewgaws and trinkets piled so high that he felt they might topple down around him. Two small twin girls, probably the old man's granddaughters, huddled behind the glass counter. The twins were maybe four or five years old. They held small Oriental dolls dressed in shiny fabric and giggled as they crouched behind the counter.

Frederick greeted the old man and indicated his tripod and the camera he carried with him. "I would like to photograph your little girls," he said to the old man. The man frowned and shook his head strenuously in refusal. Frederick had heard that the Chinese were superstitious about photography, that some thought it robbed their souls.

"I can pay good money," said Frederick.

The old man looked hard at Frederick. "How much?"

"Five dollars?" Frederick answered. The old man's eyes popped. He nodded abruptly.

Frederick set up his tripod and camera in the back of the store and motioned for the girls to stand side by side. Their faces shone clean and pure against the clutter, striking in their identical perfection. It was unnatural, wondrous. He was thrilled to capture such rare, strange replication—their skin like porcelain, their lips puckered rose buds. Black hair, pulled back sleek and taut, framed their round faces. Their eyes seemed sleepy in abeyance. They wore pink satin tunics with black slippers and held identical dolls in diminutive hands. Their innocence hurt his heart.

He took three photographs. As he left the store, his thoughts led him to Cornelius Blades and the gossip that Blades dealt in Oriental girls. This had been the subject of much conjecture in Spotted Horse. He didn't want to think about it. But the harder he tried to resist, the more these forbidden thoughts harangued him.

He thought of the black lacquer box where he kept his secret photographs. He reasoned it was innocent enough, but somehow he felt complicit, guilty, as if he were keeping the women themselves captive in the jewel box. And he wondered at himself, at the strange nature of human bondage—at what deep, devious impulse drove men to desire, to dominate other human beings, especially women.

Wasn't he a good man, a kind man? Yet even he felt the impulse to possess, albeit in the private reaches of his own heart.

FORTY THREE

BESEECH THE EARTH

GERT HOUSTON rose in the middle of her garden and placed a hand on her aching back. She'd been hoeing and spreading cow manure in the soil for hours, and her bones told her they'd had enough. The sun hung low in the western sky, casting the tea-stained light of autumn, slightly melancholy. She cherished these little pockets of time when she could simply bask in the languor of the moment, gazing out on the meadow, the breeze wisping her hair, until the rigors of survival closed in upon her and crowded out the luxury of her brief daydream.

After dinner, she stoked up the fire and sat in her rocking chair, darning socks, quilting, knitting a winter scarf. It was during these times that her mind wandered back to memories of John plowing bare chested with the traces over his shoulders. Giving his sweat and labor to the land, beseeching the earth to give back to him.

Though it had been nigh three decades, she still thought of him daily. She wondered if the memories came out of force of habit or still-sedulous sorrow. No matter. The memories visited as unceasing as rooster calls in morning and cricket song at night. She was swaddled in his essence.

Then Bull had arrived, as broken as she. A man who knew how to live with ghosts, who had borne the unbearable and come out the far end of despair. They found easy company in each other. Gert was seven years Bull's senior, but their sorrows seemed weighted the same in time's affliction. Both weathered beyond their years, the volatile juices of youth having dried up, what was left was something quieter, but lasting. Youthful intimacies were unexplored in a world of what-might-have-beens.

She loved Bull—not as she had John, but she found that despite her years of loneliness, there was still a place in her heart for affection, even love. She knew this place existed because of a dream she had of Bull in his youth. She reconstituted him in her imagination: his barrel-chested physique, now thickened with age; his sly, youthful smile, now troughed by years; and twinkling eyes, now enshrined in nests of wrinkles. In her dream, she had been young too, and they embraced as ardent lovers. She awoke refreshed. The aura stayed with her all day, and she found herself smiling.

Their occasional meetings at the general store or socials soon ripened into friendship. Then a deeper affection slinked in, like a mouse when the door's ajar. They were courting as surely as a turkey cock preens before a willing hen, but they didn't know it. Not until Beulah Nattingly blurted out to Gert that they were "made for each other. Everyone can see that plain as day" did Gert realize that she was part of a couple again. Gert looked at Beulah incredulously.

"Don't you tell me, Gert Houston, that you don't know. We all see it. If'n you don't have the sense of a peahen to see what's happenin', we're jus' gonna have to plan the wedding ourselves! We already have the flowers picked out, and Florence Evans is going to design an arbor. No use tryin' to get out of it!"

Bull was given the same lecture by husbands motivated by the prodding of their insistent wives rather than any romantic notions. Their message to Bull was more along the lines of "Bull, Beulah says you better propose to Gert soon. I sure as hell wish you'd get it over with, just to get Beulah off my back! She and those damn ladies are in a tizzy about all this. They got it all planned, down to what nightdress you're wearin' on your honeymoon. So, I'd say you're in a tight spot, my friend. Doesn't look like there's a way out, 'ceptin' to just get hitched."

And so it went. One evening, Bull rode to Gert's farm on his big chestnut gelding, got off, and knocked at the door, a knot of resolve in his throat. Gert answered puffing on her corncob pipe, and Bull proposed right then and there. Slick as a whistle, quick as a wink, they were engaged.

The announcement let loose a flood of feminine energy. Wives planned the wedding, and husbands drank in the pub as unimpeded bachelors for weeks following. The quilting ladies gathered autumn flowers from their gardens by the armloads, trundling them in wheelbarrows and buckboards: sunflowers and asters, mule's ear and lupine, cornflowers and Indian paintbrush.

Florence Evans brought a wooden arbor in her wagon and placed it on the front walk to the church. The ladies commenced twining sunflowers and purple asters in the latticework. Urns brimmed with reds, lavenders, and yellows, boasting dramatic fountains of buffalo grass at the center. Little girls tied ribbons around clutches of purple cornflowers and scarlet paintbrush at the end of each pew.

Gert had little say about her wedding gown; it had already been planned by Sarah Taunton, who thought ecru muslin a nice choice. Gert stood for hours while a knot of ladies busied themselves attaching lace and pinning and arguing and repinning the dress *just so*.

Frederick set up his camera outside for a wedding portrait near the arbor. As the townspeople gathered from all directions, pouring into the church, they marveled at an amazing sight: surrounding the perimeter of the church, perched on milkweed and purple-headed thistles, were thousands of monarch butterflies gathering for their long migration south for the winter. Gert loved the big orange butterflies, their wings delicate as stained glass but constitutions tough as tigers. They looked like bright-orange bunting along the edges of the church lawn.

The church was filled to overflowing. Gert had insisted the entire town be invited. All the quilting ladies and their husbands and children came. Capurnia and Honey Boy came with their children. Even Magnolia and Lillian Bordeaux, the town's dueling madams, seated themselves discreetly at the back of the church. They caused bonnets to turn and necks to crane and lips to flap and a buzz of disapproval to spread from pew to pew. The two madams smirked at each other and enjoyed the scandal.

Willie McGee and his barbershop bachelor buddies sat together in a pew, sticking out like a line of stunted kernels on an otherwise well-formed ear of corn. Willie, as usual, could not be trusted to behave with propriety. It being a wedding, Willie shared the only bit of marital advice he could conjure: "Me pappy always said, 'Don't marry a woman with big hands. Makes your pecker look small.'" Then, rubbing his chin, he added: "Looks like Bull's in trouble." His quip caused the old men to snicker until Mrs. Thornton, her spectacles down on the tip of her hawk nose, turned a searing look of reprimand their way.

Sorrel and Seamus came, and Ransom—back from San Francisco—had arrived too. He had not been inside a church since his youth in Wales and attended now only to see Sorrel. He sat across the aisle and slightly behind her so he could admire her without notice.

Sorrel's hair aroused in him something unbidden. He wanted to bury his face in the explosive profusion of prairie-wheat gold, wrap it around his throat. She wore her dungarees and white shirt. *She probably doesn't own a dress*, he thought. He noticed her strong, tanned hands, her cut-up knuckles and calloused palms; how odd they seemed alongside the proper hymnals and the sea of ruffles and bonnets and sashes of the ladies. She was a virago, sinewy and lithe, with a wildness that seemed electric to him even as she sat quietly in a church pew.

As the organ blazed the opening chords of the wedding march, reverberating through the pews, the congregation rose. Gert walked down the aisle, beaming as bright as a sunflower. Bull stood smiling at the altar. All felt the rightness of the union, the joy of something meant to be, and they smiled too.

But Ransom's mind was elsewhere. He was like a schoolboy smitten with adolescent ardor, albeit privately embarrassed by his own obsession. Even as the preacher recited the liturgy, he thought of her pressed against him in the gunnysack race. He imagined chasing her across the prairie grass and wrestling her to the ground, just to feel her strength. Where other women seemed as fragile China dolls, she was a totem. Where they had porcelain curves, she was carved earthy, as the plow cuts humus under sod. She was of the earth, with a raw, unrealized beauty he lusted for the way a farmer lusts for rich ground.

FORTY FOUR

WILDERNESS OF DESIRE

RANSOM WAS INSIDE his mine, chinking away at a vein of granite flecked with mica and pyrite, when he felt a sudden shudder in the floor. He knew instinctively that terrifying tremble, like the earth exhaling before some great effort. He dashed for the entrance. A curtain of dirt rained down from the ceiling beam, nearly cutting off the light. His mind tore through a gauntlet of regret and irony that he should die this way. That the terror of his youth should finally enshroud him, destroy him. *God damn it! You fool!*

The beam was coming down in a slow, groaning surrender. It hung diagonally in midair, like a guillotine blade. He felt its crushing weight skin his back. But he gloried in the pain, was exhilarated by it, for the punishing beam was *behind* him. An explosion catapulted him through the air and outside the mine entrance. He lay stunned, head resting in the crook of his arm, loving the earth and remembering the men of his youth who had not been so lucky, who had found themselves on the other side of a cave-in.

When he finally rose, his back felt raw, excoriated. His fingertips found the warm ooze of blood beneath his ripped shirt, the roughness of abraded, broken flesh. He did not feel pain. The adrenaline of near death brought a strange freedom from feeling.

If I can ride, I might seek out the nursing assistance of the comely Miss Lanning. He could not have come up with a more convenient excuse. Even a woman of her tough fiber would feel sympathy for such a wounded man. Mounting his horse gingerly, he felt both guilty and giddy about the prospect of an intimate interaction with Sorrel.

When he rode into the Lanning farm, Seamus was there to greet him with his customary heartiness until he noticed Ransom's pained expression and blood-streaked clothes.

"What the blazes, man! Did ya take a trip to hell witout dyin' first!"

Ransom winced as he dismounted his horse. Now the pain was coming. "The devil damn near got me. There was a cave-in."

"Well now, lad. We'll fix you up. There'll be whiskey involved, I'm sure you're sorry to hear," Seamus chuckled. "Come into the house. I'm as good at nursin' men as horses—"

Ransom stopped and turned to Seamus, stiff as a cardboard cutout. He uttered in a low tone intended only for Seamus's ears: "Uh, Seamus, I was, uh, hoping for perhaps a woman's nursin', if you get my meaning?"

Seamus winked. "Well, bless ya, lad. I'm ashamed I didn't tink of it meself. I must say, I'm impressed by the measures you're willin' to take to see me daughter," he laughed. "You're a dedicated man!" The two conspirators walked into the cabin, and Seamus announced excitedly that Ransom had escaped death and was hurt bad.

"Darlin', can you nurse Mr. Fallon and fix 'im up? I'll ride to get the doctor," Seamus said. "Sure as the devil, his ribs are broken."

Sorrel stared at Ransom in alarm, then gathered some rags and retrieved the whiskey bottle.

"Sit here, Mr. Fallon. Here, have some of Da's whiskey. It'll cut the pain." She hurried outside to fill a pail of water from the pump. Back inside, she winced at the ripped flesh and blood that had clotted in great gouts at the surface of the deeper cuts.

"You'll need to take off your shirt. Here, I'll help you," she said gently. He unbuttoned his shirt and did not look up at her, afraid his eyes might expose his secret. He flinched as he bent his arm backward to pull off the long sleeve, and she helped him slowly, grimacing as she pulled the shirt from the serrated flesh. She glanced at his shoulders and chest rippling with muscle, and it occurred to her that she had not seen a man's body in any degree of undress since she was a girl. She felt suddenly uneasy but did not know why, surprised and a little sheepish at the intimacy she felt in the simple warmth of his shirt.

Ransom noticed her discomfiture and the slight blush of her cheeks. His gaze lingered as he tried to decipher her thoughts, and her skin prickled as her own eyes skittered from his gaze. She busied herself with a washcloth.

"Sit on the bench," she ordered, and was surprised at the curtness of her voice.

"You are a stern nurse for a wounded man." He smirked and looked her boldly in the eye. He recognized what she perhaps did not, that her rebuffs came from her attraction—not aversion—to him. He felt the urge to take her by the shoulders and kiss her hard. Instead, he smiled internally, then crossed his big forearms over his chest and succumbed to her less-than-tender nursing.

"Well, I don't think you're going to die," she said. Her voice softened.

"This will hurt." She took a deep breath, then touched the wet cloth to a gash, strangely thrilled at the touch of him.

Ransom's back was knotted in thick musculature she had seen only in fighters who made their living by the rigorous use and abuse of their bodies. She was surprised to see such a physique in a man she thought to be cultured.

"Were you a boxer?" she blurted.

"Why do you ask?"

"Well," she stammered, at once embarrassed that she had acknowledged his body. "You're built like a boxer," she answered flatly.

"As a matter of fact, I was a boxer," he said, pretending not to notice her blushing. "How do you know what a boxer looks like?"

"My da used to take me to boxing rings when I was little," she answered.

Ransom stared at her incredulously. This was a tantalizing clue to her mysterious persona, explaining perhaps her unvarnished demeanor.

"Seamus took you to boxing rings?"

"No. My real da, before he died," she said, then was silent, remembering the terrible beatings she'd seen men take, some refusing to fall but too weak to shield themselves from blow after bloody blow.

The experience wasn't all terrible. The men ringside would pinch her cheeks and talk to her in gentle, high-pitched voices. She hated and loved the spectacle, mesmerized by the gladiators inside the ring meting out punishment with their bare knuckles. Her mind had registered each blow, assessed its force, sought clues about the physical fortitude of the man who had sustained it. It was a kind of brutal geometry she seemed to understand instinctually. But she could not abide the barbarism of onlookers who reveled in such public suffering. It seemed unspeakable voyeurism. Eventually, Seamus convinced Patrick to leave Sorrel at Mrs. McGillicuddy's and spare his small daughter the horror of watching men being beaten to a pulp. One had died in front of her.

"I don't like boxing," she said. Agitated now, she pressed clumsily on his back, and he winced.

"I grew up in a poor mining village. There weren't many ways to make money. Boxing was better money than working the mines, and a damn sight more humane. When I came to New York, the money was even better."

But he stopped, seeing now that Sorrel was lost in her own dark thoughts. He sat in silence, regretting that what he had hoped would be an opportunity to win Sorrel's affection had instead driven her back again.

Ransom had broken some ribs, the doctor said, and a few gashes required stitches. The doctor asked for Sorrel's help in bandaging Ransom, then told him he should rest his bones and allow his wounds to heal up.

"You're a lucky man, Mr. Fallon," the doctor pronounced, "but I s'pose you already know that."

But Ransom did not feel lucky. After he was bandaged, Sorrel announced she had chores and walked out the door, lost to him again.

Ransom thought this was as good a time as any to return to San Francisco to see Sylvia. He was in no condition to work his mine. His back and ribs were smarting—his feelings, too—from Sorrel's rebuff. Sylvia's soft touch and heart would do him good. Although guilt crept into his eagerness to see her, he missed her immensely.

When she greeted him at her door in surprise, her shining smile warmed him. They talked hungrily, Sylvia giving Ransom an update of her clients, Ransom telling Sylvia of the mine, the town, of the characters he had met. They dined at a nearby restaurant that night and, plied with wine and good food, bedded with as much exuberance as Ransom could muster with his wounds.

Sylvia compensated for the restraint his pain induced with an ardor that surprised him. She smothered him in feathered kisses from forehead to toes, purring to him to be still and not move an inch as she showered him with her pent-up affections. She sidled and curved about him like cream intermingling with honey, in silken caresses that both melted him and girded his desire.

Exhausted, happy, they finally lay in the big feather bed in content embrace and fell asleep cocooned like downy milkweed within a velvet pod. Sylvia did not tell Ransom that her heart had ached for his return. She did not tell him that she had waited each day for his letters to arrive and had hoped each time she peered out her front window that she would see him tying his horse to the ringed post. Something within kept her from pouring out her heart, but what she had not said in words she said in hungry embrace. She knew now that she loved him, and he knew now the depth of her love.

Lying with his sinewed arms around Sylvia, Ransom wanted to protect her, to be with her, to love her. As his mind coursed about the shadowed room and over the wispy silhouette of her hair and soft, parted cleft of her lips, he wondered why on God's green earth he had ever left this woman for a damned mine. Self-reproach pressed on his chest like an anvil. Was his love as double-faced as a poker card—the king of hearts, whose visage laid down from either angle looked earnest?

There seemed within him a wandering flame that had not even the constancy to follow the breeze of its own contentment but flickered in an errant current. Like a dark zephyr in a cave, its pulse came from some far-off portal, rushing through the black toward a distant promise of paradise.

Ransom basked in his time with Sylvia and especially enjoyed evenings sitting with her in the parlor. He sat in the big wingback chair by the fireplace, his long legs crossed, smoking cigarettes he rolled himself. He read by the light of the nearby hurricane lamp while Sylvia hand-stitched a dress bodice or sketched designs.

He occasionally commented on his reading and was secretly pleased when Sylvia replied intelligently on a political issue or a literary work. *What an amazing woman!* he thought. A talented and astute businesswoman who had the intellectual and spiritual depth he had so admired in his mother. To think he had found Sylvia in a brothel!

And that thought brought him to another realization of equal fascination: that he had found another singularly rare woman, vastly different from Sylvia, in the middle of nowhere in the mountains of Idaho.

As Ransom stared at the pages of his book and the kerosene lamp in Sylvia's parlor flickered, he remembered a stormy night when he had ridden out onto the range with Sorrel to find a missing calf. The sky thundered in collapsing violence, and rain buffeted them in sheets. The horses picked their way down a mountainside until they came to an abrupt precipice illuminated by a jagged streak of lightning. Sorrel urged her horse over the edge undaunted. Ransom realized in that instant that her fearlessness was greater than his own tinsel courage, and he was too awed and ashamed by this fact to admire her for it. He spurred his horse savagely over the cliff, and together man and mount lurched down the abyss.

The calf was at the bottom of the canyon, bawling shrilly. With anger that surprised him, he pushed Sorrel aside and gathered the panicked calf in his arms and up onto his saddle.

Ransom shivered as he recalled that night, even though Sylvia's parlor glowed with quiet warmth from the hearth's fire and the soft light of the kerosene lamps. He was grateful for the gentle comforts Sylvia provided him. But at the memory of Sorrel, at the memory of her touch, blood surged down his torso and thighs and pulsed under the book cradled in his lap. He knew that as soon as he was mended, he would return to Sorrel and the wilderness of his desire.

FORTY FIVE

OF WIND & FIRE

IT WAS THE TIME of year the Nez Perce called Hopelul, when the earth unfurled its vestments of colors before she was blanched in frosty slumber. The fall trees were bejeweled, sumac and wild grapevine splashed red, giant thistle nodded shaggy purple heads. Pink fireweed and scarlet Indian paintbrush washed meadows in dazzling pigment.

Spotted Horse was abuzz with talk of the big Nez Perce endurance horse race. It was an annual event-turned-festival held in fall and a gambling extravaganza open to all contenders. Legendary among the Indian nations of the Great Plains and the Pacific Northwest and whites from the far reaches of western territories, the race was the ultimate test of horse and rider; it covered 100 miles of the earth's most dangerous terrain between the rising and setting of the sun.

Many had died on the course—from nature's treachery and from man's. Stakes were heightened by rivalries between tribes, between ex-Confederates and ex-Federals, by Old World rivalries that had immigrated to the frontier.

Talk of the race dominated the poker game at the Rusty Spur. Rumor was that James Slickum—the banker—and Cornelius Blades were bringing in a ringer, a racehorse from San Francisco. And the ex-Confederate Bull Bamrick and the ex-Federal Red Stryker would both be in the race. They had fought at Vicksburg on opposite sides. Folks liked to play up the rivalry, even if Bull and Red did not.

Lubricated by liquor, conversation ricocheted from topic to topic until finally returning to the horse race. They discussed the nuances of gambling on an event wrought with such vagaries. Hard to wager, they philosophized, since luck had more bearing on the outcome than speed and stamina. It was a crapshoot, a free-for-all, risky business all around.

Thor Lundquist enumerated the most dangerous sections of the race: "There's the Devil's Spine, and Hell's Spittoon and the Ridges. Remember when the leaders fell off that cliff at the Ridges? Hell of a thing! Lost a ton on that race. 'Bout anything can happen."

But Willie, a hopeless gambler who would bet on where his piss might land on a flat rock if nothing else presented itself, hoped for a big win. "I'd like to break even this week," he quipped. "I need the money."

As of late, Willie's buddies at the poker table and barbershop had noticed a change in him. His mouth wasn't as sharp, and he seemed distracted. They had seen him driving Magnolia in his buckboard and teased him that he "must be gettin' some brown sugar."

"Likely to smother in it," Willie quipped. "Boobies big as watermelons. Hardly know where to start!" His poker mates waited for more lurid details, but Willie clammed up.

"Well, tell us, man! What's it like fucking a big nigger woman?" the blacksmith, Buck Hanson, demanded.

"Like swimmin' in chocolate," Willie answered tamely, then waved them off. "I gotta feed the horses." He bolted from the table, leaving his friends flummoxed at his uncharacteristic reticence. He *had* been swimming in chocolate, and he was surprised that, after the first clumsy couplings with Magnolia, he had found comfort in her company. He even started sleeping the night with her, waking to her mountain of dark, warm flesh with a sweet feeling that life was not all hard.

They both had tough veneers and sharp tongues that at first ground against each other like unmatched cogs. But flesh on flesh in the darkness of a feather bed seemed to soften their edges, and their shared loquacity finally loosened their brittle notions and joined them in a curious congress.

In the wee hours, Willie talked about his hard childhood in Ireland, of watching his mother die of tuberculosis and starvation, then leaving his family behind or else risk starving himself. Magnolia spoke of her childhood in Georgia in cryptic words. She had grown up a slave, he knew. But when she told him her mother was beaten to death by an overseer in front of her very eyes and those of all the slaves, Willie blurted: "Why didn't someone kill the son of a bitch?"

Magnolia looked at him hard. "What you think, dummy? I was *a slave*! We all was. They woulda kilt us. We got no choice. No more'n you when the rich folk take your land an' burn yo home an' starve yo momma."

An epiphany of sorts seeped into Willie's jaded old brain, like a deep wound reopened. He never supposed he had anything in common with Magnolia. But he suddenly realized they were the same, both crushed under the heels of oppressors. His family held no more power than Magnolia's had in protecting themselves.

Following this revelation, he was loading milk jugs and canned goods in his buckboard to take to the orphans south of town one day when Magnolia waved at him and yelled, "Hold on!" She waddled with a gunnysack of produce over to his wagon. "The Weavers live on the way. I go wit' you an' give 'em some food too. They bad off and five chillen to feed."

The Weavers were a black family, but Willie saw now that they all needed help, skin color be damned. He helped her hefty form up onto the buckboard, placing both hands on her broad, skirted backside for the final push.

"You gettin' fresh with me, Mist Willie!" she laughed. "I charge you extra for dat."

"You gonna wear me out, Miss Maggie," he said. "But I'll die happy."

The wiry little Irishman climbed up beside the black woman twice his size, and they rode away side by side on the buckboard, smiling.

The horse race and festival involved heavy horse trading, and horses blanketed the nearby mountainsides and meadows. There was feasting and dancing and drumming and peace-pipe smoking with kinnikinnick—a mixture of willow bark, sumac leaves, sage, tobacco, and marrow from buffalo bones. Kinnikinnick held spiritual power of the buffalo and brought a feeling of well-being. Its smoke drifted over the camp and induced storytelling and friendship and the sharing of news about deaths, births, hunts, battles, troubles with whites. Campfires blazed with longing, the spirits of dead wood glowed in the coals, and hearts reminisced.

Mothers, daughters, grandmothers worked together to prepare the feast. Savory smells wafted through the village: buffalo meat, venison, salmon, eel, and wild turkey were skewered and roasted. Red and white women traded favorite dishes. Indian women tried fried chicken, cherry pie, and pumpkin bread; white women tried oppah sweet bread, turtle soup, and roasted eel. Sings Like Lark sampled Beulah Nattingly's peach cobbler. Gert tried Grey Fawn's pemmican and was pleasantly surprised. It was like beef jerky but made of dried buffalo meat and berries. Grey Fawn wrapped several strips in dried corn husks tied with grass for Gert to take home. And she was much obliged.

The festival culminated in the big horse race. A stunning Nez Perce Appaloosa was the prize. Professional gamblers flocked to the race. Cavalrymen, their horses seasoned and battle-tested, came to compete against the redskins they had tried to kill in the past. The Nez Perce demanded that all come in peace; but once the race began, treachery out in the wilderness could not be checked. Riders had been clubbed, horses tripped, saddles and bridles sabotaged, hapless riders dragged over rough ground in gruesome deaths. The race was legendary not only in purse and pride but in peril as well.

Victorian families hungry for spectacle came from as far as Portland, Missoula, and Helena. Tourists crowded to the most dangerous points on the course where injuries or deaths were likely. They came in buckboards, surreys, and buggies with black bonnets ribbed like bat wings and faintly sinister. Eager onlookers brought picnic baskets and games for the children and fiddles to dance the hours away while they waited for the riders.

A scout tore into a camp, yelling that the riders were coming. All rushed to the best vantage point. Riders thundered past on magnificent chargers, leaping a cliff, fording rapids, plunging down a bluff, scrambling on narrow paths over a thousand-foot drop.

Men and horses died with increasing frequency each year. The frontier competition captured the imagination of the country. Western newspapers as far away as San Francisco, Salt Lake City, and Seattle reported on the infamous race with hair-raising accounts. Dramas of rivalries, especially between Indians and the US Cavalry, were played up, and villains and heroes depicted with literary verve.

The Portland *Oregonian* telegraphed Frederick to hire him for the event. He had already planned to photograph the race but was glad to be financed for his effort. Before the race, Frederick took portraits of the mounts and their riders. Bull posed on his leggy Thoroughbred gelding.

Crooked Hawk, a Nez Perce brave, sat atop his chestnut-spotted Appaloosa, and a Blackfoot chief on a big paint.

Frederick photographed Sorrel and Flying Horse on their young twin stallions, not even three years old yet: Flying Horse's Alla, Nimiipuu for "fire," and Sorrel's Dagda, named after the mightiest of Gaelic gods. The only women in the race, they made for a great postcard and a fascinating newspaper story. There were Arabians and mustangs and one black cowboy on a bay Morgan. Frederick had more subjects than he could manage and worked from sunup to sundown.

Flying Horse had become recognized by her people as a gifted horse doctor and shaman. She had shown much eagerness to learn all she could from Nimiipuu elders. They shared with her their powders and salves and liquids made from native plants or animals and their chants and brave-heart songs to protect strength and courage.

Flying Horse rubbed the horses with hot poultices of crushed wild geranium to soothe muscles. She crushed an exudate of horseradish to rub on sore tendons and prepared a concoction from wild clematis as a stimulant and restorative.

On Zaanasq, the eve of the horse race, leaden clouds scudded across the sky, barbs of lightning flashed, and thunder rumbled like distant kettledrums. But for all the sky's bluster, the weather soon subsided. Flying Horse and Sorrel sighed with relief, for the course would be even more perilous if wet or muddy.

Late into the night, they sat beside a small fire along the rippling river as frogs trilled in the meadow. The fire crackled, and reflections danced across their faces. They were comfortable in long silences. Flying Horse cleared her throat. "Sister, I have words." She haltingly shared her encounters with Fire Bear, how she had resisted his interest. "But it is the way of the world. It is what is expected of me. And what life is there for us?" she whispered over the fire.

"Yes," Sorrel said. "I understand. I have this experience too. A white man. I did not like it at first. I thought of you. I wanted to run away. My heart was confused." They were silent for a long time.

Flying Horse poked the dying fire and turned to Sorrel.

"There is more," she said, then hesitated and did not speak, as if she could not say the words. "The Nimiipuu world is leaving. The whites want our land. You know this. They say we must go to a reservation. We cannot do this. We must fight. But we cannot win against so many. Nimiipuu talk of Canada. Sitting Bull is there." Flying Horse's eyes were dark and disconsolate. Sorrel touched her hand in sorrow. She knew Flying Horse's hard words were true.

They did not sleep but drank in their time together in the velvet dark. Their horses, imperious in the moonlight, sensed the coming challenge and awaited the dawn.

FORTY SIX

RIDE THE DEVIL'S SPINE

THE NEXT MORNING, a tiny silhouette of horse and rider galloped across the blushing horizon as if rousing dawn's flames. The rider blew a whistle made from a golden eagle's ulna wing bone, its strains echoing down the vast meadow.

More than 100 horses and their riders gathered at the starting line. A Shoshone rode bareback on an albino with ghostly, ice-blue eyes. The rider was bare chested, dressed in breechcloth and leggings, man and horse both daubed in war paint. A Sioux brave arrived on a small blue roan mustang so skittish that the rider could barely contain the animal in its own skin.

The ex-Union soldier, Red Stryker, rode a flashy, sorrel Arabian mare with a flaxen mane and tail. She threw her elegant head, anxious to run. Bull Bamrick sat his Thoroughbred chestnut gelding, a gift from a Confederate officer who'd lost his legs at the Battle of

Champion Hill. The two men nodded to each other. Theirs was a soldierly bond, although adversarial. They had never talked to each other but knew the other had fought at Vicksburg. They wondered how close their fates—and bullets—had crossed on that battlefield.

There were many Nez Perce riders, some with Appaloosas or paints, others less showy. Flying Horse and Sorrel rode their leopard-spotted stallions, both very young in a race that favored older, seasoned horses with strengthened lungs and hearts and tested temperaments.

The horses stood as if in a skirmish line in battle, rearing and wheeling, eyes rolling, their haunches and necks already lathered in sweat. At the crack of the starting gun, the wall of horses burst like a cavalry charge.

A Blackfoot's big paint gathered into an arc, then extended his magnificence. He weighed more than a half ton, with fire in his veins and legs like iron pistons. He pulled to the lead. Bull Bamrick's Thoroughbred was only a nose behind, its muscles rippling under skin so fine that it outlined arteries like tributaries on a map. The animal was bred for blazing speed at shorter distances. Bull hoped its blue-blood heart would not bleed out later in the thin air of the mountains.

The Nez Perce Appaloosas had been fired by the crucible of the buffalo hunt, not just animals of speed but also fearless and tough. Arabians, too, were desert horses, with scorching stamina and spirit. Bedouins believed God had breathed a handful of wind to create them. All ran under a vast, sheltering sky, spreading out into a basin carpeted in purple camas like frigates plunging through waves of an azure sea. Their hooves rose high in the tall camas, manes and tails flaring in wind-combed pinions.

Soon, the speed slackened to a measured gallop. The Blackfoot's paint, Bull's Thoroughbred, and the Sioux's roan mustang ran abreast, eclipsing each other in surging strides. Flying Horse and Alla rode on their heels, stride for stride.

Cornelius Blades was atop a powerful Thoroughbred, its coat of molten silver mottled as if by raindrops. Blades had purchased the dappled creature in San Francisco in partnership with the banker, Slickum. The horse had impressive eastern bloodlines and had won several stakes races. Slickum thought the animal a good investment as a racehorse and breeding stud.

But the stallion was truculent and bad tempered and nearly impossible to control. Blades tried whipping the horse into submission but only drove the stallion into a frenzied rage. The horse threw its head from the Spanish spade bit in its mouth, a demonic thing based on the leverage of cruelty, with a metal piece gouging the roof of its mouth when the bit was pulled.

Sorrel was in the middle of the pack, biding her time, when she noticed that Blades's gray was bleeding. Ropes of saliva-foamed blood trailed from its open mouth as it frantically tried to ease the pain. Blades cursed the animal's unruliness and beat it mercilessly about the head so that the horse could hardly think about the business of running.

The pack thundered down a wooded slope. It emptied into a worn path skirting a cliff above a river. The pack strung out on the narrow trail, and it was here that the gray stallion turned its mind from running to ridding its back of the scourge with cudgel and cruel hands. The path was bordered by a precipitous drop to the river, obscured by trees and brambles. The horse ran against trees to unseat its rider and unhinged Blades's legs. Instinctively, the animal sensed opportunity. It stopped abruptly and reared, pawing so high that he nearly fell backward.

Blades went flying over the cliff and fell through the underbrush below. The drop was considerable, and Sorrel heard Blades tumbling through the gauntlet, tree limbs and brambles cracking and snapping. His fall was punctuated by descending vulgarities, then, finally, a splash. After some seconds, the enraged rider surfaced in the river below, sputtering threats of killing "that son-of-a-bitchin' stallion."

Sorrel did not want to lose time by stopping, but she could not abide such cruelty to a horse. She quickly dismounted and caught the gray's reins, ungirthed the saddle, and pulled the savage bit from its mouth. She threw both over the cliff, where they dropped for a spell until snagging on branches. She waved her arms at the stallion, but he needed no urging.

With silver tail arched and ears pricked toward the mountains, he bolted away like quicksilver.

She leapt on Dagda to catch the pack. It had ebbed out into a broad plateau that came to the foot of a mountain. Horses and riders began a rocky climb that folded back on itself in steep switchbacks—a grueling incline of 3,000 vertical feet in four miles. The horses toiled up the mountainside, their heads and necks pumping, ribs heaving in labored breath. Endurance pitted against gravity, lungs gasping for thin air. The mountain began to take its measure, dashing the coursers against the rocks of their own limitations.

The mountain route was studded with boulders and an alpine carpet of scruffy vegetation. The air was crisp and thin, and tatters of mist lingered in rocky gulches. Higher still they climbed, above the tree line and into a raw loneliness. Cornices of snow lay in the hollows, and the horses kicked up crystals like fairy dust.

The exhausted animals began to string out. The Shoshone on the albino and a Nez Perce on a black Appaloosa mare were isolated on the trail. The Shoshone smiled, but the Nez Perce saw too late his dark intention. The Shoshone pulled a knife from his calf scabbard and struck the other on the head, knocking him backward off his horse, then quickly jumped off, grabbed the man's topknot, and sliced off a fist-sized patch of scalp, leaving the exposed skull gleaming white like an eggshell. The Shoshone hastily chanted coup over his dazed enemy, then alit on his horse and was gone. The ambush took only seconds.

The race had been long and lawless, effort now wrung from sheer stamina. The riders approached high country, and the trail became more treacherous. It zigzagged through large shards of stone, opening to vistas with plunging chasms so forbidding as to make one's hair stand on end. Rivers in distant valleys appeared as mere ribbons.

The Sioux on the roan mustang and Red Stryker on his sorrel Arabian caught up with the Shoshone. A pack of seven or eight horses lagged several hundred feet behind them. The roan mustang was a scrappy piece of work, lean and gritty, small boned but bighearted. Challenge was clear in its dark eyes. The Sioux let him run, for the horse hungered for its own speed.

One of the most dangerous junctures in the race approached: The Widow's Gap was a six-foot expanse between two cliffs, below it a thousand-foot drop, a gaping maw of hell.

Mounts were exhausted after climbing the rough trail and had little distance to accelerate for the leap. Riders spread out cautiously, none trusting the others while negotiating the plunge. The leaders cleared the fissure in a cascade of horseflesh. Then came the second throng.

A Kutenai bareback on a glimmering copper bay with a mane of black obsidian came around the curve and leapt valiantly. But in exhaustion, one of its hind hooves missed the brink of the cliff, and gravity pulled the animal down like a savage predator. The horse drew strength from parts unknown and clawed at the cliff ledge with its front hooves, its neck and shoulders pumping up and down like an iron derrick, its mane like raven wings lashing the air. But the rider was dead weight, clutching the animal around its neck. Gravity finally sucked the beast and its burden over the cliff, its front hooves dragging trenches in the dirt before disappearing over the edge.

Flying Horse's heart pounded, for she had been following the horse and rider for several miles. Alla cleared the gap directly after the doomed pair. Flying Horse's hands trembled and became clammy. She could not calm her racing heart or drive the image from her mind.

An hour after Widow's Gap, Sorrel pulled up beside Flying Horse. They were relieved to see each other. They loped for a piece across a sprawling prairie, rocking in the pitch and yaw of their horses' canters, the sound of hoofbeats rhythmic as prayer.

Together they made steady time and caught up with the lead group of riders. The course turned down a gentle slope to a mountain stream.

The two women laughed as their horses thundered across the pebbled shallows, shooting geysers under their hooves. Some riders allowed their mounts to drink, but only a little; too much water when a horse was hot could twist its guts with painful cramping.

They eased the pace to rest their mounts and basked in the calm of the landscape while they could. Several more miles would bring them to the most treacherous part of the race: the Devil's Spine, where a cleft of stone loomed like Satan's anvil, jutting to a sheer vertical drop.

There, Flying Horse and Sorrel took their horses wide from the glut of horses and lurched over the edge and down the escarpment—half falling, half flying, hooves barely touching the earth. The declivity was so steep that the horses' haunches dragged on the rocks. Front hooves struggled desperately for footing. Sorrel saw the eyes of riders and beasts alike rolling in terror, riders flapping their arms frantically, looking for handholds where there were none.

Alla and Dagda found impossible footing halfway down the slope. Others hurtled in spectacular somersaults. A heap of animals and riders collected at the bottom, struggling to escape being crushed, and those still descending scrambled to avoid the writhing pile. A thicket of spectators gasped and cringed at the carnage. Here Frederick and other photographers had set up their cameras.

Bull Bamrick's sleek Thoroughbred had dropped back in the pack, its endurance playing out. As man and animal skidded down the embankment, Bull spotted Red Stryker crumpled at the bottom, his Arabian on the ground, thrashing in struggle. Bull's horse hit the bottom upright but frantic. Bull leapt off his horse and grabbed Red by his collar, afraid to look up at what might be crashing down upon them. He dragged the man away from the melee.

He did not know why he helped this man who very well might have tried to kill him at Vicksburg. But he knew Stryker to be a good man and thought he would have done the same for him. The red-haired Stryker stirred slightly, then opened his cornflower-blue eyes to find himself in the old Confederate's arms. Bull smiled a wry, crooked smile that they, two old cavalry foes, should end up this way.

Two horses lay at the bottom of the cliff, their legs broken. One rider had been crushed and was unconscious. Another had broken his neck in the fall, his head cocked at an impossible angle, glazed eyes still open.

Sorrel and Flying Horse tried to avoid the mayhem, lurching in unison, a free-falling ledge of flesh. Dagda's legs spread out in all directions, his neck distended and looking for a landing. But the big paint knocked him in midair, and Sorrel hurtled sideways. Dagda landed on jagged rocks, and Sorrel felt a sharp hoof strike her shoulder with such force she thought surely it had broken. But she felt no pain. Adrenaline screamed through her veins like filament on fire, cauterizing all but her instinct to survive.

Dagda struggled to his feet and lunged helter-skelter from the mass. Sorrel frantically extricated herself, her shoulder covered in blood. She looked up to see that Flying Horse and Alla had cleared the melee and were galloping away. Relief rushed through her that Flying Horse was safe.

The last big bend in the race curved around a huge dome of granite called the Buffalo Hump. The lead racers tore around the hump and picked up speed, the horses sensing the finish. They ran through a brace of towering cottonwood trees and then over a ridge. Below them stretched a mile of sweeping prairie. The chargers unleashed newfound speed.

Flying Horse held lightning in her hands. Her heart ached at her horse's great heart. There were five horses running abreast, their noses as close as a chariot team bound in harness. The Shoshone on the albino lashed his horse, and its ears pinned back, white muzzle stretched out, nostrils flaring red like breathing fire.

Beside the albino, the big paint coiled and uncoiled in sweeping strides. The Blackfoot crouched low over the pumping withers of his piebald catapult. The Sioux's little roan mustang was like a child's pony next to the huge paint, but its compact body flattened close to the ground like a missile and nosed ahead.

Beside the mustang was a cavalry officer on his black Arab stallion. The mustang and the black ran neck and neck—and then Flying Horse saw the cavalry officer pull something from his belt. He leaned down toward the mustang's churning front hooves and stuck a short-barreled shotgun between its legs. The game little horse hurtled toward the earth, launching its rider and then rolling full force over the Sioux, leaving him crumpled on the plains.

There were four horses left now, like the Four Horsemen of the Apocalypse, gathering up the ground and flinging it behind them. Flying Horse leaned forward and felt the sweet press of acceleration. How could her horse have more to give? He drank up the wind and went after the black Arabian. His body arched, gathered, then exploded in sprawling release. He gained on the Arab, whose ears rotated back at the approaching marauder. Flying Horse clung to her horse, loose as water, melting into his motion, all else falling away.

The finish line banner loomed ahead. Crowds of people mottled in colors and moiling motion yelled and screamed. But Flying Horse heard nothing, felt nothing but the churning of her horse and her own beating heart. Alla stretched out in one last supreme effort and nosed ahead of the black.

FORTY SEVEN

PAVANE OF PASSION

RANSOM CUT huge oak beams for his mine entrance, the old ones having so inhospitably collapsed on him weeks before. Ransom asked Sorrel's help. She arrived early in the morning, and they toiled for several hours, using his mules and pulleys. Once the job was complete, Sorrel said she had to get back for chores. Ransom said he'd ride back with her since he had to go to town anyway. They rode side by side, talking of Gert and Bull's wedding, Ransom's mine, and the Nez Perce horse race in which Sorrel had narrowly escaped with her life.

"That was a nasty fall you took at the Devil's Spine. Amazing you weren't hurt worse," he said. "If I hadn't broken my ribs, I'd have been in the race. My horse has speed."

They approached a trail through a swampy area he had ridden many times. A devious plan occurred to him.

"How about a little race?" he said.

Sorrel quickly agreed. Dagda had been well tested against other horses.

Ransom suggested a wager.

Sorrel, still game, smiled: "Sure, what do you have in mind?"

Ransom gave her a contemplative look. It was now or never.

"Well," he said, "you know the Carltons are having a big barn dance. How about if you lose, you go to the Carlton dance with me? *And* you wear a dress? I've never seen you in a dress."

Sorrel frowned at his sudden courtly overture.

"Mr. Fallon, you are being forward. I don't dance, and I don't have a dress," she answered with distinct archness in her tone.

"Oh, come now. It's a simple wager. Are you afraid you'll lose?" he countered, hoping she would take the bait.

"Of course not!" she shot back. "My horse is a prairie horse. He'll run your Thoroughbred into the ground."

"Then you have nothing to fear. Let's bet on it. If I lose, I won't ask again."

She winced internally, for she realized—to her surprise—that she didn't want him to give up on her. But a part of her was afraid. She suddenly resented the dilemma. *What the hell!* She had confidence in Dagda. And it would be satisfying to put this presumptuous man in his place. She couldn't help herself.

"Alright!" Sorrel said. "You've got yourself a deal!" With that, she spurred Dagda, and he plunged forward. Ransom was quick behind her.

As a seasoned gambler, Ransom had learned some simple lessons in life. One was to weigh the odds before putting down a heavy bet. The other was to know the terrain. He knew that there was only a narrow ridge of solid ground through the mushy swamp of duckweed and burdock. His plan was to take the hidden high ground while Sorrel bogged down in the soft marsh bottom.

Both horses charged down the slope and into the tall grass. Ransom's horse followed the spine of hard ground by habit. Just as Ransom planned, Sorrel's horse sank hock-deep in mud. Dagda labored, kicking up huge clods like errant cannonballs. Seeing that Ransom's horse was on solid ground, Sorrel reined her mount up behind the tall Thoroughbred but had lost valuable time. Dagda remained weighed down by swamp muck. They gained on Ransom's stallion but not quickly enough. Ransom's Thoroughbred won by a diminishing nose.

They had barely pulled up their horses when Sorrel said accusingly: "Well, I don't suppose you knew that was a bog, did you?"

Ransom smiled and shrugged. But he was honest. "How else would I ever get you to go to a dance with me?"

"That's a dirty trick if I ever saw one!" Sorrel complained.

"Are you reneging on your bet?" he challenged. But before she could answer, he offered, "I'll teach you how to dance. It's not hard. And I'll get you a dress."

Sorrel's jaw dropped. *Buying me a dress! How dare he.*

He ignored her incredulity. "I'll drop it by tomorrow. And I'll pick you up for the dance Saturday night at six," he said; then he reined his horse back toward his mine.

"I thought you were going to town," Sorrel blurted.

"Nope. My work here is done." He smirked, looking her full in the eyes, and she understood that she had been thoroughly bamboozled by Ransom Fallon: professional gambler, surreptitious suitor, and dirty rotten sneak.

Ransom had gone to great lengths with the ruse, even putting thought into what dress she might wear. While in San Francisco, he had asked Sylvia her dress size under the guise of buying her one, saying she shouldn't have to make all her own clothes. With this information, he deduced Sorrel's size. She was taller by several inches than Sylvia, slimmer in the hips, broader shouldered.

He purchased a dress he thought might fit and that she would not find horribly frou-frou, a French term to describe a frilly fashion. It was periwinkle silk, simple lines with a fitted waist. It had a sweeping décolletage that Ransom imagined would sheathe her breasts sensuously but tastefully enough to fulfill the requirements of her modesty and his own salacious tastes. The dress was elegant and unfussy and, he thought, befitting Sorrel's style if she ever chose to have one.

Ransom dropped the dress off at Sorrel's cabin the next day, setting the paper-wrapped parcel in Seamus's arms when he answered the door and telling him it was a dress for Sorrel. Seamus laughed heartily at this joke. "Aye, lad. That's a fine one! And did ya bring a gown of gold for me? 'Twould be worn as much!"

Ransom chuckled. Then he asked if Sorrel had told Seamus about the little wager they'd made. Ransom explained what had transpired and that she would be going to the dance with him Saturday night. Seamus rubbed his chin, impressed at Ransom's cunning.

"You're a sly one, me boy! Never thought I'd see this day. But, mind, bringin' the dress and puttin' it on her are two different tings entirely!"

When Sorrel came into the house from work in the field, Seamus mentioned nonchalantly that Ransom had brought a package for her. Then, prudently, he said he needed to go to town for supplies and wouldn't be back for several hours. Once Seamus was gone, Sorrel sat at the table and poured herself a whiskey. She sat for a bit with the shot glass in her hand, as if it were an old friend and she needed the company. Then she downed it, walked over to the package, and tore away the wrapping.

Sorrel had not had a dress since she was little, when her real father was alive. She touched the silk and felt the folds in her hands and admired the sheen of the fabric. It was beautiful. There was something sensual in the fact that Ransom had chosen such a dress for her.

She took off her work clothes and slipped it on. She had no undergarments. The dress fit, albeit a bit snug. She gazed down at her form and felt her body's contours inside the silk. She grabbed Seamus's shaving mirror. It had been so long since she had looked at herself in a mirror. Occasionally she saw her rippling image in the trough when she watered the horses or in a pail of water when she leaned over to wash her face by the pump. But she rarely saw herself. She examined the image in the mirror closely, her eyes, her hair, her breasts. She wondered what Ransom saw when he looked at her. A little spark of self-awareness took hold. And she knew he was beginning to unravel the hard knot of her resolve.

All week long, Sorrel worked feverishly on the farm. As she chopped wood, forked hay, and fixed fences, thoughts of Ransom washed over her, unannounced and insistent. She wondered at her agitation, a roiling of emotions she did not understand. Irritation, embarrassment, nervousness. Even fear. *Yes, fear*, she admitted. She was afraid. *How did it happen*, she wondered, *that this man has insinuated himself into my thoughts and I am helpless to shut him out?* It was as if her body had embraced what her mind sought to deny. He was both the sickness and the cure.

From the long desert of her desire wafted a faint wisp, a sea breeze of coming rain. Like the Sphinx with its secrets, her passion had been long buried. Now it trickled up, the birth of an oasis, her thirst both parched and quenched by this man she denied.

But it was vexing to her. She was not used to serving compulsion. It impeded what, in the past, had been clear, unobstructed focus: her love of horses, her dream to build the farm, her entrenchment in hard work and the farm's demands.

What was even more troubling to Sorrel—what hovered over her, dark as gathering clouds, although she had not sorted it out in any conscious fashion—was her knowledge that romance and the conclusion to romance, marriage, seemed the end of freedom, tantamount to imprisonment. Marriage required a woman to be disassembled, diminished. Yet women accepted this with eager acquiescence. Indeed, many a woman *manufactured* her own diminishment to make her mate seem larger than he was.

Sorrel could think of few married women who maintained their independence. Gert was outspoken and self-reliant and had been a widow so long that no matrimonial vows could decree her servitude. But she was a rarity.

So, Sorrel denied her desire, because acknowledging it was inconvenient, and acting upon it inconceivable. She simply chopped wood, dug holes, and hammered shingles more vigorously than ever.

Ransom showed up at six o'clock Saturday night and found Sorrel in the barn, forking hay furiously. But she had on the blue silk dress, and she was ravishing. His gray eyes devoured her, even the angry, downcast eyes that avoided him. His practiced gaze affirmed a thrilling discovery: she had on no undergarments or corset. The silk traveled over her contours, pressing insistently upon her flesh, taut about her full breasts, which spilled from the low scoop of the neckline as she leaned over. He felt like a schoolboy seeing a woman's breasts for the first time, surprised at his swelling titillation. He took his hat off and held it below his belt.

The shimmering silk wrapped around her slender, ligamented waist and skimmed down the soft swell of her hips, flaring into folds and swirls of fabric about her feet. Ransom saw that she wore her rough farm boots. She—or Seamus—had apparently tried to clean and polish the boots, although they were worn and tired. His heart ached at her utter lack of knowledge concerning women's fashion. He had forgotten to get her shoes, and of course she had nothing appropriate for a dance, ornamentation being superfluous to her character.

Her body was like a blue urn skimmed with fire, the silk electric as she moved about the barn. He could nearly feel his fingertips along her ribs, her waist, her hips, so intensely did he want to touch her.

"You look lovely, Sorrel," he said, but she did not acknowledge his compliment.

"I'll be done in a moment," she replied curtly. "Seamus says to go inside and have a drink with him while you wait."

Seamus welcomed him with much fawning.

"Ransom, me lad, come in, come in. You'll be needin' a drink for this job, I'll wager. Sorrel's mad as a bumblebee in a cowpie," Seamus chortled, his shoulders shrugged up around his ears in delight. "How you ever got a dress on her is one of those wonders of the firmament! I've been feedin' her whiskey to lighten her mood, but it's not taken off the edge. She's sharp as a scythe ready for cuttin', me boy. So steady as ya go."

Seamus poured Ransom a tall drink, and they settled down to wait for Sorrel. When she came through the door, her sapphirine eyes blazed like diadems, her high cheeks like tea roses. She was more beautiful than ever. Seamus had French braided her hair, and the effect enshrined her face like a crisp, gleaming jewel. Ransom did not know if it was the whiskey or the dress or her beauty or her burning wrath that gave her such radiance, but it smote him full force, like a galleon broadsided in a storm, leaving him unloosed in his churning passions.

"Well, let's get this over with," Sorrel announced curtly, wrestling within the iron cage of her own self-consciousness.

Sorrel struggled to pull her flowing skirts up to mount Dagda. She sighed heavily in exasperation as she tugged the folds of blue fabric over the saddle and down about her legs. They set out for town, five miles away. She rode as if she were on her way to the guillotine, her spine ramrod straight and visage like a block of ice.

He pulled up his horse. "You look like you're riding to your execution. Is this really that horrible for you?" he asked.

She looked at him sharply. "Isn't it enough that I'm going to this goddamn dance! Do I have to like it too? Did you really think that putting a dress on me would solve everything? I've never even been to a dance. I'll be the laughingstock of the entire town. I feel like a fool!"

"Alright, let's not go to the dance. The last thing I want to do is embarrass you, Sorrel. But I would still like to teach you to dance," he said. "Let's go to the flat rock up the trail."

He led the way, and she followed in sullen silence. They dismounted and tied the horses. He took her wrist and pulled her up the path, feeling the strain of her resistance in the sinew and bones in her arm. But he did not let go. He raised her right hand in his and took her left hand and placed it on his shoulder.

"This is the correct position," he said. "Now I'll teach you a simple box step. Just follow my feet." He began slowly, in a purely didactic tone. He counted as they stepped. It reminded him of a delicate dance of the Middle Ages he had read about in the tales of King Arthur as a child. A slow, stately pavane of controlled passion.

But he wanted to pick Sorrel up and swirl her about in a wild waltz. He wanted to embrace her and kiss her madly and engulf her in his desire. Instead, he held her hand lightly and encouraged her with all the self-control he could muster.

"Since we don't have any music, I'll hum the rhythm," he said. He began in his low, melodic baritone, stepping slowly and rhythmically. He felt a loosening in her stiffness. But then she stepped on his foot and quickly pushed him away, her humiliation blanching her face as stark as stripped bone.

"I can't do this! I'm ridiculous!" she stammered and dashed away. He ran after her, catching her by the arm, but she wheeled and flung a fist at him. He ducked and grabbed her around the waist. Together they tumbled down the hill into the grass, where he pinned her, his weight crushing, his face so close she could not avoid his demanding eyes.

"Look at me!" he ordered, and she twisted in an effort to turn her face away. She gritted her teeth and wrung her wrists in his iron grip. But there was no place to go. Her eyes flashed like blue ice, watery but with the sharp fixity of diamonds, before she slammed them shut. She hated him.

For an eternity, it seemed, they lay in the middle of the meadow under a public sky, their most private feelings laid bare. Ransom was horrified, and he despaired at his stupidity. He had humiliated her in a way she would never tolerate. Pigheaded and arrogant, he had misread her. She wanted no part of him. She wanted only to be left alone.

He opened his mouth to say he was sorry, that he was a fool. But suddenly he felt, reverberating deep from Sorrel's chest, the beginnings of laughter.

My God! she thought. *How did I get in such an absurd predicament?* She then considered Ransom's suave demeanor. Surely *he* had never been in such an uncomely situation. Surely *he* had never been greeted with fists during a romantic advance!

An ironic laugh spilled out of her. Her chest surged with relief—relief that finally, *finally*, she did not need to feel the agonizing self-consciousness she always felt with him, the taut violin string of sexual tension. Her heart had mutinied and freed her.

Her laughter came, too, from the intrinsic humor of their predicament: he atop her and she prostrate and red-faced and veritably sputtering and hissing. And finally, her laughter was born of genuine joy; despite her resolute efforts, love had come to her. Ransom had outlasted her rebuffs, had persevered through repeated rejections. She was happy. And her laughter came rolling now from deep within her, though she could barely catch her breath under his weight.

Ransom was puzzled. But he felt Sorrel's body soften, no longer resisting him. And when she opened her eyes, they were full of longing, relief. She was laughing at herself. Not at him. Ransom began to laugh as well, and he rolled off her and onto his back. They lay together under the sky, their laughter skipping across the feathered tips of buffalo grass.

"Oh, you are a fool, Ransom Fallon, to want such a woman!" she gasped.

"That, my dear, has already been established." He rolled to his side. "Now do I at least get a kiss for my considerable effort?"

She stopped laughing, but a nervous smile remained. "I'm afraid you'll be horribly disappointed. You see . . ." And her spine stiffened again with discomfiture. But she did not shrink from his gaze: "I have never kissed a man."

Without skipping a beat, he replied, refusing to acknowledge her self-consciousness. "You're resourceful. Improvise."

He expected her to squirm, to look away. But he underestimated her. He saw now the same determination she'd mustered for other challenges. She gulped a breath of courage. She put her arms around his neck. She lifted her lips to his. She kept her eyes open, as if to observe in his eyes any disappointment.

He searched her eyes for the same clues, but all he saw was an earnestness that touched him. She *did* want him. He smiled and she smiled and she kissed him.

"You see," she said. "I told you. I'm sure I'm exceedingly boring for a professional like you."

"On the contrary, my dear. It's an excellent start. But thank you for acknowledging my considerable expertise." He leaned down and pressed his lips to her forehead ever so gently, then continued, "If you follow my instruction diligently and with a great deal of practice, you can become an expert like me."

She laughed at his feigned arrogance, and he kissed her again in earnest. She followed his lead. From that point on, no courage was needed. Her heart pounded from new use, and she felt urgent with desire.

For an instant, she remembered Flying Horse—her body, her bronze skin, her embrace. But her mind quickly leapt beyond, to the memory of two badgers she had once seen mating on the bank of a stream, wildly rolling and biting and tumbling in a sexual frenzy. Now *she* was a badger, a bear, a lioness. Her passion had been earthbound, plodding, unsure. But now it was unleashed.

FORTY EIGHT

OLD TRUTHS TRODDEN

JOSEPH AND his Wallowa tribe had seen much the last ten winters. The prophecy that the Nimiipuu would face vast change unfolded before his eyes and under his leadership. They understood they had no choice but to live with whites. But in the spring of 1872, when the tribe moved from their winter home deep in the protected canyons of the Snake River up to the Wallowa Valley, where the tribe's cattle and huge horse herds had rich summer grazing, Joseph found settlers marking out homesteads and building cabins.

He approached them on his horse. In broken English and Chinook trade jargon widely used between whites and Indians, Joseph spoke gently but firmly: "White friends, this valley is our ancestral land. We have lived here for many generations. You cannot live here. It has been decreed by your own government in Washington."

But the settlers answered that the land was now opened to them and they had registered their claims in the federal land office in La Grande. Joseph had learned from his father that white government had many chiefs that often spoke different words. Joseph knew that the area congressman returned to La Grande for the whites' Fourth of July parade and festivities. The leaders of the town often invited area tribes to ride in the parade. So, Joseph and Ollokot rode 100 miles west to La Grande to meet with the congressman.

The congressman and the Indian superintendent met with Chief Joseph. They honored the peace-loving Nez Perce, they said, but this was an issue for Washington, and they did not have the power to help him. A La Grande newspaper reporter wrote that "although the Nez Perce chief was most impressive and honorable, his efforts were in vain, for it is in the nature of things that this beautiful Valley will be settled immediately."

Riding home, Joseph told his brother, the words bitter on his lips: "Words cannot stop an avalanche."

The Nimiipuu began an uneasy coexistence with white settlers in their beautiful valley. One of the first settlers was a man named Wells McNall. He was as short and wiry as he was loud and bellicose, often drunk and quarrelsome, each quality worsened by the other. He was a known Indian hater, and friendly whites had counseled the Nimiipuu to avoid him. "He is a devil looking for trouble," they warned.

One day in June 1876, Fire Bear went hunting for deer with his friends Wind Blowing and Eskamus. Wind Blowing shot a doe and hung it from a tree, away from predators, while they continued to hunt. On their return, Wind Blowing was climbing the tree to release the deer when two white men thundered into the clearing and yanked their horses to a stop. The Indians recognized the smaller rider as McNall.

"Where'd you hide our horses, you sons o' bitches?" McNall yelled as he dismounted his horse. He saw Wind Blowing's rifle leaning against a tree and grabbed it. The other rider, Alexander Findley, aimed his rifle at the Nez Perce.

"We know nothing of your horses," Fire Bear answered.

Wind Blowing climbed down from the tree. He said in broken English but in a measured tone: "We no steal horses."

"We'll see about that!" McNall challenged and goaded Wind Blowing with the rifle. Wind Blowing grabbed the mouth of the rifle and tore it from McNall. But McNall rushed him, and they fell to the ground, wrestling.

"Shoot 'im, goddamn it!" McNall yelled at Findley. Findley fired, and Wind Blowing went limp; a wound from his back spurted blood. The white men jumped on their horses and galloped away.

Fire Bear and Eskamus carried Wind Blowing's body back to the village and laid him before Chief Joseph. The people amassed around them, sobbing and caressing Wind Blowing's face. Joseph did not speak. He looked down at his dead friend, his eyes hard but moist in quiet sorrow.

Joseph and Ollokot knew there would be hard reckoning. But they were not without powerful white friends. They met with the area Indian agent at Lapwai, who wrote General Oliver Howard, commander of the US Army's Department of the Columbia, that the white settlers Findley and McNall had committed "willful, deliberate murder."

Howard, too, was sympathetic to the Nez Perce. A Civil War officer who had lost his right arm, he was devoutly religious and nicknamed "Old Prayer Book" by his troops. Wood had been very critical of President Grant's decision to revoke the treaty with the Nez Perce and open the entire valley to whites, an order Wood called "a blunder, if not a crime."

Howard sent his assistant adjutant, Major Henry Clay Wood, a lawyer, to Lapwai to oversee the talks. Joseph and Ollokot were joined by the old chief and shaman Toohoolhoolzote and nearly forty other Nez Perce headmen.

Joseph told the major that Wind Blowing had been much respected by his tribe, that he had been peace loving and the white who had killed him was a known Indian hater. He said:

> Wind Blowing's life has been taken in the Wallowa Valley, and the earth is drinking up his blood. The valley is more sacred to me than ever, for it also holds the bones of my father. From this time forward, whites must go from the valley forever.

Furthermore, Joseph wanted the two white men tried for murder.

Wood was deeply touched by the quiet dignity and restraint of the tall chief. He said he would do his best to present their story to General Oliver Howard, who was going to Washington to recommend to the president of the United States a settlement with the Nez Perce in the Wallowa Valley. But Joseph and the Nimiipuu had been disappointed many times before by whites.

"It makes my heart sick when I remember all the good words and all the broken promises," Joseph said to his brother.

Early in 1877, despite General Howard's advocacy, Washington exonerated Findley and McNall and demanded the Nez Perce move onto a reservation only a sliver the size of their ancestral land. They had until May to move their people and livestock to the reservation.

Joseph was stunned. He and Toohoolhoolzote tried one more time to meet with Howard. But he was intractable now that official decisions had been made. Toohoolhoolzote spoke strong words: "The earth is my mother. I never sold this land, and I will never give up the land of my ancestors. It is part of my body. What person pretends to divide the land and tell me where I must live?"

Howard bellowed back: "I am that person! Twenty times over you repeat the earth is your mother and the land is sacred. You say God created the earth complete, and it should not be disturbed by man! That white improvements are crimes! Let me hear no more! I demand you come to business at once! You will move to the reservation, or we will force you to move!"

Joseph knew the long-feared day of reckoning had come. Howard had "shown them the rifle." They must surrender or fight. The old truths had been trodden over; the oracles of ancient prophets were coming true in his lifetime.

The nation's 100th anniversary, bloodied by Custer's defeat, fired a fierce verve for vengeance. The Nez Perce now fell squarely in the crosshairs of the nation's wrath. Joseph and Ollokot rode back in silence over hills and meadows they'd played in as boys, as had their father and father's father and their ancestors 16,000 years before that. All lost. They came to a burned forest, the mountainside covered by a thin blanket of snow helpless to hide the fire's devastation. Gnarled trees stood like skeletons against an oyster sky, bleak and bald as a vulture skull. The charnel ground seemed to Joseph the very texture of despair.

FORTY NINE

POUND OF FLESH

FREDERICK HAD KNOWN Wind Blowing, knew his gentleness, and mourned his death. He understood the young man's death meant a breaking point for the Nez Perce. He felt acutely the irony of his own situation, watching the demise of the Nez Perce culture as he profited from the rise of his own white civilization. The nation was ablaze with celebrations of the nation's 100th birthday, and he was busy photographing patriotic parades and centennials.

The young country was full of itself, profiteers made money hand over fist, and the common man brimmed with hope for fast money, free land, and a new life. Frederick himself was thriving.

Even the Indian wars had been going reasonably well. Custer had massacred Black Kettle's Cheyenne village in Oklahoma territory. The red Natives had been largely subdued in the West but for several Nez Perce chiefs who still refused to move to reservations. Manifest Destiny was bearing fruit. The West was being conquered, and fireworks burst in celebration from coast to coast.

Fireworks of a less celebratory sort were amassing on the banks of the Little Bighorn River in southern Montana territory, as 15,000 Cheyenne, Blackfeet, and Sioux—the Hunkpapa, Oglala, Miniconjoux, and the Sans Arc—gathered. It was the largest concentration of North American Indians in history.

The Sioux chief Sitting Bull danced the sacred Sun Dance and slashed his arm in sacrifice. He had a vision that the white army would come, but the soldiers' horses were upside down, and soldiers tumbled to the ground. Oglala chiefs Crazy Horse and Low Dog and Hunkpapa chiefs Gall and Rain-in-the-Face had joined him.

Brigadier General Alfred Terry was camped on the Yellowstone. His Arikara scouts reported that Sitting Bull was upstream. Terry summoned Colonel Gibbon to move up the Yellowstone and block the Bighorn River at its mouth. Custer and his Seventh Cavalry were to attack Sitting Bull's camp from the south and drive the Lakota toward Gibbon. The plan was to surround the camp and annihilate Sitting Bull and his people once and for all.

On arrival, Custer thought his best strategy was a surprise attack, and he did not wait for Terry. But the surprise would be on Custer. The carnage took less than thirty minutes, a cataclysm compressed into a speck of time. Custer and all his battalion—more than 250 men—were killed. Custer's body would be found two days later by General Terry, along with hundreds of bodies sprawled on the ground like shadows with no source. Shoals of black crows gathered on their terrible perches, pecking out eyeballs and leaving withered holes gazing at the sky.

Custer himself was found stripped naked and propped in a sitting position. He had been shot in the left temple and the chest. There were two other wounds that were particularly symbolic: two Cheyenne women had found Custer's body and pushed awls in each of his ears to improve his hearing, for he had not listened to the chiefs when he smoked the peace pipe with them a season before. They had told him that if he should ever break his peace promise and fight the Cheyenne again, the Everywhere Spirit would destroy him.

The Sioux and Cheyenne *had* exacted their pound of flesh. The victory heartened the few non-treaty tribes still resisting the white juggernaut. But it brought dread to their hearts, too. They feared the hardened resolve of the white man in the wake of the terrible carnage.

Months after the battle, a military expedition headed by General Sheridan's younger brother Captain Michael Sheridan was sent to the Little Bighorn to exhume the bodies of the fallen officers for proper reburial. A photographer named John H. Fouch was with the expedition and telegraphed Frederick to request his help photographing the battlefield. Frederick was anxious to see the battlefield after reading so much about the debacle in the newspapers.

Within a mile of the battlefield, Frederick and Fouch smelled the stench of hundreds of dead horses in various degrees of decomposition. Their carcasses were like bony huts, dry hides draping skeletons like coconut hulls. There were many human bones, too, scattered by scavengers with a randomness that held no regard for the sacred or the dead.

Frederick and Fouch busied themselves setting up their equipment. As the expedition began disinterring bodies for proper reburial, an Army sergeant found a macabre trophy under a corpse. A soldier had fallen on a Cheyenne warrior whose shield bore an oval patch of cured human skin, its outer edges laced with sinew and stretched to its full expanse. The skin bore a tattoo depicting a unicorn, a lion, and a coat of arms flanked by British Union Jack flags. Frederick immediately recognized the tattoo as the coat of arms of Eton College in England. Years before, he had seen photographs of the mutilated body of Frederick Wyllyams, a British citizen and Eton graduate who had been killed by Sioux and Cheyenne nine years before the Little Bighorn.

Through a spectacular fluke of fate, Wyllyams's body was found by a fellow Eton graduate, Dr. William Bell, who had come west to study the native Indians for the Ethnological Society of Great Britain. Bell knew that the missing patch of skin on Wyllyams's right arm had been an Eton tattoo because he had the same tattoo on his arm. Now before Frederick's very eyes was that same tattoo *in the flesh*.

Not far from Custer's corpse, his faithful Thoroughbred had been buried. Vic had carried Custer from Bull Run to Black Kettle's annihilation and, finally, to the Little Bighorn. Unlike most of the cavalry horses, the animal had been buried in respect for Custer.

Two captains, Homer Wheeler and John Bourke, were disinterring Vic. Frederick could not surmise why they were disturbing the poor beast. Then it became clear. One of the men pulled from his saddle a surgeon's saw and climbed down into the grave. He began sawing off Vic's right front hoof at the fetlock. The two men took turns sawing for quite some time, cursing and sweating, but finally removed all four of Vic's hooves.

"What are you doing with those?" Frederick finally asked.

"Inkstands," Wheeler answered. "We're gonna make inkstands outa 'em. And they'll fetch a pretty penny."

Wheeler put two of the hooves in an empty King Arthur flour sack. Frederick's mother had always used that brand for baking. Frederick was appalled.

But the captain's efforts were ill fated. Only a month later, Wheeler would lose his precious hooves in a poker game to an Ohio baker turned soldier. Sergeant Henry Raichel of the 7th Cavalry, Company K, was soon after killed in the Nez Perce War, the flour sack hanging from his pommel. Frederick would see the same flour sack on the saddle of a Nez Perce boy riding from the Bear Paw battlefield. The boy marveled: *surely, these were the hooves of a mighty warhorse and held strong-heart medicine.*

FIFTY

WORLDS APART

IT HAD BEEN only a couple of days since Ransom had stormed the ramparts of Sorrel's shuttered heart. He rode to the farm to find Seamus out feeding chickens. Seamus had noticed a change in Sorrel after the evening of the dance. He didn't wait for Ransom's pretense for visiting.

"Sorrel's up at the lake, *Mr. Fallon*," Seamus enunciated, his Irish brogue carving around his name. Ransom knew the old man had been onto him all along. Seamus added, an ever-so-slight Irish wryness in his inflection, "I think she'd be takin' a bath right about now, if I'm not mistakin'."

Ransom smiled, grateful, and spurred his horse into a gallop up the slope. Seamus chuckled to himself, pleased as a pig in mud with the knowledge that a man might have finally broken through his daughter's brittle shell—and a man fine as Ransom Fallon. He began singing "The Wild Rover" in full lung to the chickens.

The water glinted like a bed of diamonds as Ransom walked to the edge of the rocks.

"Hello, Sorrel," he said in a low voice viscous as thick cream.

Sorrel's eyes flashed in surprise. She was submerged in water to her neck, her arms suddenly wrapped in urgent modesty about her breasts. Ransom saw her undulating form beneath the water. Her face was beautiful, her golden lion's mane wet and flattened in golden crimps down her back, swept away from her face, her empyrean eyes as translucent as water. Her lips, sculpted crescents of flesh, were so slopingly sensuous his heart ached.

Ransom stood on a large rock and began taking off his boots. Sorrel wanted to run, but she was embarrassed to show her backside, so she backed away, still hugging her nakedness.

He pulled his shirt over his head, then unbuttoned his pants, letting them pool at his feet, and stood at his full manhood, She felt a strange fullness in her chest that spread down her torso with an effulgence that sapped her breath. He dove into the pool, his body slicing through the water toward her, like a torpedo crashing through her thinly veiled battlements. Her chest pulsed and her soul expanded, opened as if to welcome the onslaught, a mutiny within her own resistance.

He reached her underwater and rose before her, his arms encircling her, first around her legs, then hips, then back. His face rose above hers in a cascade of water. Before she could react, his mouth was on hers and his arms around her shoulders, his body flat against hers.

She struggled against the sheer power of his embrace, for her instinct was to resist such strident physicality no matter the source. But she found herself melding into the energy of his passion, devouring it, then giving it back again.

Behind her, a slender waterfall cast its jeweled strand down the wall of stone and roused in Ransom a rush of memories—the mists of Wales, its rivers tumbling to a sea of mythic spirits. All swept him away to this end. He was the torrent, she the sea, intermingling into an ocean of flame.

Ransom had returned to Sylvia in San Francisco several times since first discovering Sorrel. He knew it was only a matter of time before Sylvia noticed that something was vying for his heart's attention, so intuitive were her powers of observation. Perhaps she had already noticed his distraction. She would sometimes ask brightly what he was thinking about. He wondered if her curiosity was laced with jealousy or fear of imagined trysts. And it pained him that he should cause such a worthy woman heartache.

But deceit itself seemed a kind of foreplay, weighted with guilt and also titillation, his secret heightening his seduction. His wandering want felt fresh, like a child's thing. And he fell into Sylvia's arms willingly, giving his alias heart to her.

Sylvia *had* detected something in Ransom. Now she gazed at the bed and the expanse of sheet between them. It seemed desolate like a frozen ocean, even as the air, self-consciously intimate, remained charged with their intermingled exertion. She wanted to reach out and pull back the wisp of hair from over Ransom's brow as he slept and touch his cheek. But he was beyond her reach, an intimate stranger, distant as marble.

She knew that something had come between them, but she had already resolved to settle for what remained of his heart, so in love was she. She had come to love him too much, and now a terrible yearning punished her, as if her love had been trapped by its own device but had not the heart for freedom.

He left the next day and kissed her goodbye. A normal kiss, warm and affectionate. But he held her an instant longer than he might have in the past. And he said to her, "You know, I don't deserve you, Sylvia."

She saw through his transparent admission of unworthiness, could see his guilt as clearly as through glass. He realized this and was saddened. He admired her. He appreciated her. He enjoyed her company. In fact, he loved her. He could not simply discard her.

Ransom knew of men who maintained—with varying degrees of diligence—multiple romances, even marriages. There were those who traveled with purpose, as the cattle drivers, surveyors, and steamboat captains, and there were those who wandered purposeless: drifters, outlaws, gamblers. The free-for-all, rough-and-tumble of the frontier fit hand and glove with infidelity.

Ransom was no angel, but he was essentially honest. Save for his first romance with Bronwyn, he'd never been in love until Sylvia. His sexual forays had been of the body, not of the heart. He had hurt no one. In fact, his courtesan bedfellows had seemed happier for the association. And he went on his merry way, unencumbered, unentangled.

Since setting up Sylvia's townhouse, Ransom had not shared a bed with another woman. He had felt no inclination. His desire was only for her. That is, until Sorrel.

Although he loved Sylvia, he could not resist Sorrel. Whereas his love for Sylvia was like a gentle rain, soaking, soft, sustaining, Sorrel had caught him like a thunderstorm on the open prairie, punishing and inescapable. No more could he run from his compulsion than from the sky above him. He knew he would go back to her.

In fall 1876, Fire Bear and Flying Horse were married under a beautiful waterfall where Nez Perce had married for thousands of years. Frederick asked Fire Bear if he might photograph their mountain wedding, and Fire Bear assented as long as it was from a distance. It was a sacred ceremony, he said, to be shared with only family and the tribe. Frederick set his tripod and camera so that the spectacular waterfall was their backdrop. It fell like a necklace strung gracefully down the rocky bosom of the mountain, pooling in a froth of lace.

Sorrel stood behind Frederick and watched the marriage from this far vantage. Flying Horse nodded her appreciation. Crisp Chinook winds braided themselves into late-fall breezes. A lip of ice formed at the shallow shoreline of the river, edging out into deeper waters, following the cold.

Farther up the mountains, winter had set in. Saddles of snow lay upon the withers of the peaks, and craggy, granite faces of mountains jutted out like gargoyles.

Members of the Wallowa and Camas Meadows tribes, the family and friends of the bride and groom, stood about the cliff and the hills below to witness the wedding. There was drumming and chanting, and a shaman raised a beautiful ceremonial headdress of two swans, their graceful necks intertwined. The headdress was symbolic of lasting love and loyalty, for swans mated for life and were caring, careful parents. When the bride and groom donned the swan headdresses, they made for a magnificent vision. Frederick hoped he had properly captured the image, for he had never seen such an elaborate wedding couple.

Flying Horse did not see Sorrel for many days after her wedding with Fire Bear. She rode through two mountain passes and many meadows before she passed over a ridge and looked down on Sorrel's farm. She waited there while the stallion grazed the tops of the prairie grass. When Sorrel emerged from the house and noticed Flying Horse at the top of the hill, she waved, and Flying Horse pointed in the direction of the mountain lake. Sorrel nodded, and Flying Horse turned her horse away.

The mountain lake was only a mile up into the hills. Flying Horse waited on a boulder in the water, her usual place. Sorrel thundered up the path on her horse and galloped into the shallows, right up to the boulder, where she jumped off with great bombast. She splashed all over Flying Horse, as she had done so many times before. Flying Horse laughed, and they splashed each other in childish glee, laughing and yelling, each in her own language. When they were breathless and completely wet, they slumped on the boulder together, smiling broadly and panting.

Sorrel touched Flying Horse's arm. "You are married now!"

Flying Horse nodded and smiled. She paused, and a fish jumped as if to break the silence. They began to talk with energy, piecing together words from both languages like a free-form scrap quilt, connecting loose ends with sign language and headshaking in affirmation or negation. They talked of horses, salmon spearing, the buffalo hunt. Their talk turned to news of violence between whites and Indians, and their mood faded to solemnity.

They sat hugging their ankles and resting chins on their knees and were silent for a spell. The water was cold, and their teeth now chattered.

In labored English, Flying Horse began: "Darkness coming for my people." She put her fist over her chest, then extended her arm toward the mountains: "Our land no longer ours. Whites take even government land. No stop." She spit the words out like too much dill weed.

Sorrel knew this was true. She knew the Nez Perce had no place to go.

Flying Horse sighed. "Earth old dog with too many fleas. Too many *white* fleas!" She pointed to Sorrel accusingly but then smiled. Sorrel returned it wistfully.

"No. You no flea. You dragonfly," Flying Horse corrected, and Sorrel knew this was a compliment. The Nez Perce and other plateau tribes admired dragonflies and believed them to be sacred bearers of good fortune.

Then Flying Horse cast her eyes downward and was silent. Finally, she choked out hard words. She might never see Sorrel again. The US government had ordered the Nez Perce to a reservation and they must go or fight. Her voice got very low. She had had dreams, as others had, that her tribe would ride far into the mountains and find much hardship.

They were solemn and silent, and Sorrel took her hand.

Finally, Sorrel said brightly, "I have a wedding gift for you!" She took a rifle case from the pommel of her saddle and turned back to her friend, outstretching her arms. The rifle was an 1866 Winchester "Yellow Boy" repeating rifle in a beautifully beaded rawhide case. Seamus had bought it from a Kutenai. A Shoshone scalp and fingers hung from the rawhide. The Shoshone, Sorrel knew, were enemies of the Nez Perce.

"Use it, my sister. It will give you strength in battle."

The gift was bittersweet and freighted with portent. *How could my friendship with Flying Horse have come to this? A wedding gift of a gun to my dear friend to defend herself and her family from whites.*

Flying Horse touched the beaded case, then pulled the gleaming Yellow Boy from its sheath, running her fingers across the polished brass receiver that gave the gun its name.

Sorrel turned and took a flour sack full of cartridges from her saddle horn. She had purchased ten boxes of Henry .44 caliber rimfire cartridges at Marston's General Store. The sack held enough for 150 shots. Sorrel took the gun from Flying Horse and showed her how to load the rifle from the brass loading gate, slipping the cartridges into the long metal tube that held fifteen. She shut the gate and cocked the lever-action brass handle, then handed the gun back to Flying Horse.

"Aim at that rock." She pointed. "It shoots true."

Flying Horse settled the gun into the cradle of her arm and lined up the sights. The two women had played at target practice many times. Sorrel knew Flying Horse had exquisite aim. The Nez Perce woman shot off the tip of the rock 300 feet away and turned to Sorrel, beaming.

Their smiles faded as they hugged each other goodbye. Their embrace held years of yearning, a lifetime beyond touch, hope beyond harm. They knew they would never see each other again. They knew the Nimiipuu faced a struggle for their very existence—that they would not go to a reservation but could not defeat the whites, whose numbers were like fish in the ocean. Their only hope was to escape beyond the "Medicine Line," the Canadian border, where Sitting Bull had found refuge after the Little Big Horn.

That night, in sheets crisp and white as the moon, Sorrel awoke to a hazy dream unsettling in its residue. She walked out into the cool night air, restless, unable to sleep, and feared for her friend.

FIFTY ONE

FOOTFALLS UNDER A FULL MOON

SPRING 1877 came to the Bitterroots, and the mountains heaved off winter. Scaffoldings of snow collapsed down slopes as swollen rivers thrashed in their banks. Buds tight as baby fists opened, and meadows unfurled carpets of purple camas and white crocus.

It was May. The non-treaty Nez Perce refused to move to the reservation. Seven chiefs, Chief Joseph among them, chose Camas Prairie as the location to round up the Nimiipuu tribes' many thousands of horses and cattle and bring their people together. Here they would visit their sacred places one last time, for there were many sites that held spirits and powerful medicine, places where the earth cradled the bones of their loved ones or marked births, marriages, divine wyakin quests.

The people wept at their leaving, at the breaking of spiritual bonds that should never be broken with the land. Hearts were full of fury, too. Ollokot had counseled angry young braves that the white numbers were too great; they would never stop coming, and although Nimiipuu hearts were strong, their numbers were small. Young warriors knew not what to do with their fury.

One such young man, named Wahlitits—Shore Crossing—had much vengeance in his heart. A white settler had killed his father, Eagle Robe, the previous year and gone unpunished. Wahlitits vowed to find the settler and kill him. Along with two friends, Swan Necklace and Red Moccasin Tops, Wahlitits searched for the man but could not find him, so they killed three other settlers who hated Indians.

Whites formed a vigilante posse against the Nez Perce, and young Nimiipuu warriors gathered a war party of their own. Killings on both sides ensued. Any hope of peace unraveled along a broken path of vengeance.

Chief Joseph knew General Howard would punish the entire tribe for the violence ignited by the three young men. He also knew the elders could no longer control the hearts of their young warriors, who had seen too much injustice go unanswered. War was now inevitable.

Joseph and the other chiefs moved the people and herds to White Bird Canyon to better defend themselves when the soldiers came. The canyon was a verdant declivity of undulating swells nestled between mountains, with rich grazing and sheltering folds. Nez Perce scouts reconnoitered the

US Army forces and returned to White Bird Canyon with troubling news. Cavalry troops at double the Nez Perce's strength were coming.

The Nimiipuu under the non-treaty chiefs mobilized. The milling blanket of humanity arrived weary from riding many days from their villages and traversing treacherous rivers and jagged land. As they surged laboriously down the valley, Joseph's heart was sick. His people seemed like a swarm of horseflies bristling over an open wound. But the wound was their own.

Joseph directed the people to set up camp at the bottom of the canyon, at a bend in the Salmon River. At dusk, he sat on his stallion, overlooking the valley. The flickering lights of campfires reflected off tipis and the somber faces around them. Shamans and medicine men and warriors danced the dance of war, drums and brave-heart chanting echoing between the valley walls.

Joseph's blood burned with the hollow words, promises broken, injustices unpunished. As a leader, he had smothered the fires in his heart, but now it seemed impossible to avoid the reckoning: better to die a proud warrior than to live under white dominion. Tyranny was mangling the spirit of his people. To lose their land was to lose themselves. The dreamer war dance now dominated their rituals with such vehement abandon it seemed not to resemble those of Joseph's youth. His heart was heavy. The faith of their forebears seemed a distant illusion.

His father's deathbed prediction haunted him in his waking hours—and in fitful sleep: "A few years more and the white men will be all around you. They have their eyes on this land. You must stop your ears when asked to sign a treaty to sell your home." Now his people were refugees with no home.

Women pottered about busily, wrapping food bundles and filling bladders with water for the warriors to take into the hills. They ground herbs on stones for poultices and salves; the pungent smell of sage, rosemary, and lavender wafted through the village. They stuffed the medicines, as well as willow bark and wild ginger for painkillers, in hide bags.

Sings Like Lark packed pemmican, venison jerky, and fry bread with elderberry jam for Tall Tree. And she made a beaded necklace for him to wear, braided with her own hair.

Memories of family, good times, their homeland visited the people with sharp longing. Their voices were soft, solemn. Fear and hope and sadness were palpable, diffused into the tasks of preparing for battle, as shock shunts out the unthinkable and focuses only on the familiar.

The drums and chanting had quieted, and the fires had been doused. All tried to sleep. But near midnight, as a pocked moon hung in the obsidian night, there came a shivering howl of a coyote: a Nez Perce scout signaling that Perry's companies had arrived under cover of darkness and were positioned at the summit of the canyon. They would most probably attack at dawn.

In the dark, wives kissed their husbands, mothers kissed their sons, and the warriors mounted quietly and headed up into the hills. Flying Horse kissed Fire Bear and handed him the Kutenai rifle and the bag of cartridges Sorrel had given her. "Use my gun, husband. It holds powerful medicine. And know I am there fighting beside you."

They had agreed that she would stay behind to help protect the elders and children and serve as a runner for fresh horses and ammunition to warriors.

The women watched the warriors leave, a mass of steeled resolve under a blue moon.

The war ponies lunged up the valley wall, then fanned out. The silhouetted braves showed the breadth of their power in the moonlight and put hope in the women's hearts.

Joseph's brother, Ollokot, led a band of warriors. He sat calmly, cloaked in brilliant color and lethal patience. His horse snorted from the climb, white eyed and throwing its head. The warrior took in the panorama bathed below in lunar blue. A prairie breeze caught the eagle feathers in his hair, brushed his stern cheekbone. He felt the roughness of the rawhide shank in his fingers. His long thighs clasped the ribcage of his horse. Together, mount and man breathed in the night air. The warriors split into two groups on each side of the valley. They would wait among the rolling hills until dawn, then flank the soldiers as they advanced.

A couple of miles beyond the canyon, white soldiers were sleepless too. They passed the hours cleaning their guns or writing letters or last wills in handwriting jagged and spurred as barbed wire. One mended a brass button hanging by threads and admired his handiwork, the buttons now standing at attention in tight rank and file.

Braves sat tufting arrow feathers or tightening bowstrings, cleaning guns, sharpening axe blades with flint. Fire Bear took Flying Horse's Winchester rifle out of its beaded parfleche. He had shot it before, but he was used to his own Henry rifle, so he practiced loading cartridges into the loading gate.

Chief Joseph held counsel with the other chiefs. They wanted to tell the captain that they did not want to fight if they were allowed to continue on to buffalo country. They decided to approach Perry with a flag of truce at dawn, requesting to leave the land in peace. In the meantime, however, the warriors hid up in the hills, waiting to see the commander's response.

At the sun's first sliver of light, meadowlarks called from dew-laden hills. A vermilion smear spread across the eastern horizon. Nez Perce scouts spied Perry's command as it began the four-mile descent into White Bird Canyon. The canyon still lay in darkness, but the Nimiipuu were anxious to show Perry there was no need for battle. As the companies approached, their advance quickened. Many civilian volunteers had joined the two companies and outnumbered Nez Perce warriors two to one.

When they saw the group of six Nez Perce approach with a white flag, some volunteers let loose a deadly volley. A Nez Perce sharpshooter killed Perry's bugler, who rode at the commander's side. This hampered the commander's orders and caused disarray among the troops. Meanwhile, the eager civilian volunteers were already galloping toward the camp to attack the women and children. The warriors exploded out of the hills and cut down the volunteers and their horses.

When the shooting started, Flying Horse grabbed Fire Bear's Henry rifle and cartridges and snuck off into the rocks above the camp and waited, anxious for the soldiers to come within range.

Perry tried to deploy his troops, but Ollokot, with Fire Bear at his side, led an attack on the company's right flank. The wall of warriors plunged into the seething blanket of steel. Some warriors carried tomahawks or war axes, gripping the grooved familiarity with exhilarating weight, ready to crush, cleave, and gut. Some had ram-horn bows and their own distinctively marked arrows. Some had rifles—Springfield carbines or old, cumbersome, muzzle-loading muskets traded from fur traders many years before. Only the chiefs and best marksmen had coveted 1873 Winchesters with fifteen-round cartridges, or Spencers that could shoot fourteen shots per minute without reloading. Flying Horse was grateful to Sorrel for the beautiful Winchester that now protected Fire Bear and her people.

Whatever their weapons, the Nez Perce had become fabled among white soldiers for their marksmanship, both as sharpshooters and on horseback. Some dismounted at a full gallop, positioning themselves behind trees and rocks. Others had already taken places in breastworks dug with rifle butts or axe handles. Still others clasped their mounts with iron-hard thighs, their arms cradling rifles, steadying their eyes between sight and bead on chosen targets. And there were ample targets—bluecoats riding upright, frantically grappling for ammunition or reloading their rifles.

Nez Perce braves were also adept at riding on the sides of their horses at a full gallop, a feat that required tremendous leg strength. Shielded by the horse, a rider could shoot either over the animal's withers or under its neck.

The Nez Perce killed with single-minded efficiency. They did not scalp or desecrate bodies or molest women prisoners but were fearsome fighters on the battlefield, often working in deadly concert with their brethren in hand-to-hand combat.

At one point, Swan Necklace lodged his axe deep in the chest of a bluecoat but could not extract it. He found himself with no weapon, facing an oncoming soldier with a Springfield rifle. He slammed aside the barrel as it discharged and sank his teeth into the soldier's neck. They scuffled about like a two-headed hydra. The soldier tried in vain to hit the Indian with the butt of his gun. In one vicious rip, Swan Necklace tore at the soldier's neck, unleashing a sparkling ruby geyser, spattering nearby soldiers and Indians as the two twirled to the ground in a ghastly pas de deux of death.

Perry's ranks by now were in complete chaos, more than a third killed or wounded, the rest scattered up the canyon walls. The Nez Perce had lost no warriors.

The Nez Perce left the white dead unmolested but scoured the battlefield for supplies, collecting sixty-three rifles and numerous pistols, cartridges, horses, and pack mules.

The next day, two more groups of Nez Perce joined the embattled band. War chiefs and heralded warriors Five Wounds and Rainbow returned with their buffalo-hunting parties from Montana, along with their entire villages of families.

The chiefs held quick council and decided to head for high country, for they knew their victory would bring Howard's wrath upon them in full force. They packed hastily, a thousand footfalls under a full moon, and left behind a river choked with the bodies of white soldiers. The purling water stumbled and tripped about the grotesque flotsam, spreading scarlet stain beyond the gore.

FIFTY TWO

MILK OF HUMAN KINDNESS

SOME TEN MILES NORTH of White Bird Canyon, Mrs. Porter, a farm woman, sat on the stool in the barnyard as eager baby pigs clamored and squealed about her knees, hungry for milk from a big nursing bottle. She had fashioned the makeshift bottle from her husband's empty hair tonic after the sow had died of swine cholera. Mrs. Porter feared the pink babies would be lost, so virulent was the fever. She'd lost four in a litter of nine and considered herself lucky.

Now the little ones were robust. Their tiny corkscrew tails wiggled and waggled in eagerness as they nuzzled her knees. She marveled at nature's caprice in putting tiny, ridiculous curlicue tails on such portly bodies, but that was the charm of pigs. She picked up the runt of the litter first and fed him before the others got their turns. Left on his own, he would get barely any sucks at the bottle and would not survive. The entire process was one of squealing, poking, snorting, jostling, and sloppy, impassioned sucking. But she enjoyed the enthusiasm of the babies and watching them grow strong.

She was just finishing up with the last piglet when she glanced up and saw two Nez Perce riding up her farm lane. She had traded with the Nez Perce for twenty years—for riding horses and mules, baskets, and wild rice and berries. She had reaped much from their friendship during a hard childbirth when Sings Like Lark had come to help her. That child was now six years old, and she often thought the little boy would not be with them had it not been for the Indians.

She recognized Tall Tree and Sings Like Lark. She stood, wiped her hands on her apron, and walked toward them, waving a broad welcome. She had heard about their troubles in recent days and was distraught that it had come to such a bad end, knowing the Nez Perce to be peace loving and prudent.

"Hello, Missuz Porter," Tall Tree said slowly, enunciating clearly. Over the years, he had learned enough English to barter with settlers.

"*Ta'cmeeywi*, Tall Tree," she said, bidding them good morning in their own tongue.

They talked for a short while, and Mrs. Porter acknowledged her sadness about their predicament. She had thought she might see them one last time before their flight, for they liked to buy her pies and sweet rolls.

But they had not come for baked goods. Tall Tree asked haltingly for any cloth she could sell. They could pay in US currency, he said. Sings Like Lark looked at Mrs. Porter hard: "For bandages."

She welcomed the two Nimiipuu in the house and asked them to sit at her table. She gave them some cinnamon rolls, which she knew Tall Tree relished. While they ate, she gathered supplies for them: a basket of fresh potatoes, beans, and carrots; a pail of milk, which they poured into two buffalo bladders; and two chickens tied by their legs and hanging upside down, cawing softly as if sedated. She also had a bolt of calico fabric for curtains. "Will this do?" she asked. Sings Like Lark smiled faintly and nodded.

Tall Tree began counting out money on the table for payment. But Mrs. Porter pushed the money back to him, shaking her head.

"You need now for your children," she said.

Tall Tree shook his head; he would not take her charity. But she took Sings Like Lark's hand and touched Tall Tree's shoulder. She pointed out the window at her little son running in the barnyard. She patted her heart and pointed to them, then put the money firmly back in Tall Trees hands.

Mrs. Porter hugged Sings Like Lark before she mounted, then patted her own chest again to express that she cared for them and wished them safekeeping. They smiled and turned their horses to go.

"Oh, wait!" she yelled. She ran in the house and came out with a paper bag. Inside were a dozen cinnamon rolls. Tall Tree laughed.

"For the children. Now, don't you eat them all, Tall Tree!" she chided the big man playfully, shaking her finger at him.

All three laughed. But when they waved a final goodbye, grief laced their smiles. Mrs. Porter feared for her old friends and knew she might never see them again. The milk of human kindness dried up mighty quick when Indian troubles heated up among settlers. She wondered how many whites would forget the goodwill of their red-skinned neighbors when they stood to gain Nez Perce land.

Frederick read newspaper accounts of the Nez Perce flight, and his mother sent clippings from Missouri as well. As he read, his mind filled in raw details. Winter was coming.

Frederick gazed at the images he had taken of Joseph and Ollokot. Of Nimiipuu children. Of the wedding of Flying Horse and Fire Bear. Life flattened to photographs. He felt their sorrow—and his own culpability—engraved upon each page.

The stunning defeat of the US Army at White Bird Canyon had taken place on the one-year anniversary of Custer's last stand, and newspaper headlines blared with indignation and horror from coast to coast. How could "red savages" defeat a modern army with modern weapons, scientific strategies, and well-equipped soldiers? The military was just as surprised by Nez Perce strength and strategies. General Shanks reported to newspapers:

> Joseph's party was thoroughly disciplined; they rode at full gallop along the mountain side in steady formation with perfect precision, galloped into line, reined to a sudden halt, and dismounted with as much system as regulars.

The troops quickly came to realize that the Nez Perce were far better riders than themselves and skilled marksmen. The Nez Perce horses, too, were superior. Not only did they possess great speed and phenomenal stamina, but they had been trained to stand quietly by their riders during battle and did not flinch even at heavy artillery.

Furthermore, the Army had underestimated the Nimiipuu's ability to negotiate rugged terrain and raging rivers, even with hundreds of families and thousands of horses in tow. The Nez Perce had crossed the swollen Salmon and Snake Rivers during spring thaw when the rivers were at their swiftest and most deadly. Pulling travois and carrying heavy packs, children, elderly, and wounded, the horses churned hard in the roiling currents. Men and women swam beside the horses so as not to tax the laboring animals further. Yet the tribe had not lost one tribe member or horse.

When the cavalry tried to cross the frothing river, they struggled for nearly an entire day and then finally rode two days out of their way to find a better place to cross. Meanwhile, young braves stood on the other bank, taunting the soldiers to come after them. When attempting the Salmon, the drill was the same. Sergeant McCarthy wrote:

> We were in a bad fix. We could not cross like the Indians. [Swimming] the river was a failure. A raft was a failure also. How the whole tribe of Indians with horses, women, papooses, etc. got across was a puzzle. We didn't have the engineering skills to cross.

Newspapers began to lionize Chief Joseph, giving him the sobriquet "the Red Napoleon." Headlines blared in monstrous black letters the humiliating defeats of the Army and the brilliance of the Nez Perce. It was, after all, the quintessential American story: the underdog victorious in the face of insurmountable circumstances. Americans, ironically, wanted to believe that the wild West—recently domesticated by the railroad, telegraph, and telephone—was still untamed, that the "noble red savage" still drew great primal power from the wilderness and the mysteries of the human spirit.

This was not the same old story of white against Indian; the Nez Perce tribe had the longest history of unbroken friendship with whites on the continent. The Nimiipuu were a civilized and sophisticated breed of red man, honorable and formidable foes. But for all their peaceful ways, they were remarkable warriors. General Howard even conceded to newspaper reporters, "They fought as well as any troops I ever saw."

Chief Joseph himself had the unmistakable stature of a leader. His massive six-foot, three-inch frame, handsome face, and noble manner commanded respect from all who met him. He was eloquent in what he did *not* say, his quiet dignity unprofaned by speech. When he spoke, his words of moderation, peace, and justice resonated with Americans as those of a wise and prudent man.

The fact was, however, that several chiefs shared the credit for the success at White Bird Canyon. The Nez Perce were a remarkably democratic people, and warriors and chiefs of individual bands had autonomy. Braves took initiative to free the enemy's hobbled horses, commandeer mule trains of artillery, and rout sharpshooters. This concept was lost on the US military and American newspapers. The white military was based on iron structure and inflexible strategies, not pliant, instinctual, *individual* abilities.

Admiration of their opponents' fighting ability notwithstanding, the two leading generals in the US Army, Sherman and Sheridan, maintained that the Nez Perce must be crushed. Both were veterans of the Civil War who had employed strategies of utter annihilation. They subscribed to this strategy for their red enemy as well. They faced not only an Indian uprising that threatened to spread to conquered tribes but also a national public relations debacle.

After White Bird Canyon, General Oliver Howard was ordered to capture and punish the perpetrators of the uprising. He quickly assembled a force of 250 well-armed men, two Gatling guns, a mountain howitzer, and a pack train with enough ammunition to blow the Nez Perce into Dakota territory, should he ever catch up to them. In the meantime, Howard had gotten a report that a previously peaceful Nez Perce chief, Looking Glass, planned to join Joseph. Like Joseph, he had attempted in every way possible to remain peaceful with the whites and avoid war.

Looking Glass's villages were nestled along the middle fork of the

Clearwater River in a beautiful valley cultivated in corn, potatoes, squash, and melons. There were milk cows and livestock penned in neat rail fences and a herd of over 800 horses.

Captain Stephen G. Whipple wanted a surprise attack on one of these villages at dawn but didn't arrive until late morning. The troops thundering down the mountain valley gave the village time to flee, but only with the clothes on their back. They left behind their tipis and possessions, smoke still curling from breakfast campfires. Whipple's troops killed a mother and children, trampled the gardens and tipis, confiscated the cattle and 700 horses, and ate meat still roasting over fires.

A soldier sampling stew noticed a hand protruding piteously like a broken tree branch from the nearby stream. He walked down the gravelly shoal of the riverbank and found water coursing through the tresses of an Indian woman, her black hair commingling with the river grasses along the bank. Flumes of red joined the current from a tiny, dark hole in the woman's back.

The soldier followed her outstretched hand, its fingers reaching desperately under the water. Nestled among rocks stippled with sunlight was the body of her baby, rocking gently in the current. Its big eyes looked up through the water at the soldier like earnest acorns, a little hand waggling back and forth as if to wave goodbye in its watery grave. The soldier, unnerved by their grisly work, stumbled quickly away.

Looking Glass and his village soon joined forces with Joseph. After three battles with the Nez Perce in only three weeks, the US military had not fared well: sixty-three soldiers dead, not one Nez Perce warrior lost. The Nez Perce were making a mockery of the US military, and Americans lapped up the David and Goliath battle.

FIFTY THREE

A GOOD DAY TO DIE

WHEN LOOKING GLASS and other chiefs joined Joseph, the Nez Perce had five consolidated bands numbering about 750 people, including 200 warriors, and 3,000 horses. They headed east to the ancient Lolo Trail through the mountains, then over the Continental Divide into buffalo country. At the south fork of the Clearwater River, they pitched hundreds of tipis. Steep, rocky bluffs flanked the river, its bed grassy and strewn with large boulders.

Howard's scouts spotted the Nez Perce camp, and the general, now freshly supplied, forced a march to the Clearwater. They reached the bluffs in early morning, and the big cannon and guns were set up overlooking the camp but out of sight. As dawn broke, Nez Perce scouts sighted them, and the village burst into frantic activity like a nest of ants just provoked. Warriors yelled and grabbed cartridge belts and jumped on horses. Women snatched up children and supplies, running for the hills.

Flying Horse and Fire Bear ran from their lodge, hastily gathering guns and ammunition. Fire Bear, stripped to the waist, threw two cartridge belts across his chest, then embraced Flying Horse goodbye. Flying Horse had once again been asked to stay and protect the village, but this time she would not remain behind.

At White Bird Canyon, at the far flanks of the battlefield and close enough to the women and children to render aid when necessary, she had sat as a lone sharpshooter and picked off soldiers. When night had fallen and the Nez Perce collected all of the guns and ammunition, she slunk across the field and sliced off brass buttons, epaulettes, and medals from soldiers. She had fleeting thoughts of slicing an ear or finger, for such mementos would strike horror in white soldiers. But it was not the Nimiipuu way. Although white soldiers often mutilated and took souvenirs of flesh from native dead, Nez Perce chiefs forbid such practices.

Flying Horse rode back with her booty. She sewed brass buttons across her tunic and epaulets and two medals from an officer's tunic in the same fashion the officer had worn them.

After Fire Bear left that morning at Clearwater, she rode Alla into the woods. There, she braided her hair, and tied in eagle feathers, notched and painted in the Plains custom, to symbolize kills of the enemy. She had four. A good showing for any warrior. She painted her face and Alla's head and haunches. Finally, she donned her tunic and two cartridge belts across her chest, with Fire Bear's Henry rifle in a holster across her back.

She leapt atop her horse and wheeled him toward the mountain pass but was alarmed to see Fire Bear sitting atop his war pony at the edge of the woods. His countenance was inscrutable. She walked her horse up to him silently.

"I must do this," she said. "Is it not dishonor for an eagle to die a rabbit's death?"

Fire Bear's eyes were sad but proud. "I have always known this," he said, "that you are an eagle in a woman's body."

He took his thumb and smudged war paint from his chest to rub red marks on her cheekbones. He studied his handiwork on her strong face, and the ends of his mouth curled up—not in a smile but in a grimace of irony that Flying Horse understood. This was their strange destiny.

"Hokahey, sister warrior, hokahey," Fire Bear said, reciting words the Nez Perce had adopted from their Sioux enemy. It meant "Today is a good day to die."

Together they wheeled their horses toward a high bluff and made their way up the rocky incline to join the other warriors.

Howard ordered the assault. Howitzer shells burst into the valley below, but the bluffs were so steep and the trajectory of the big gun so high that shells burst fallow beyond the camp.

The Indians knew that the troops could not descend such a steep declivity and would have to ride another mile downstream before making an attack. Toohoolhoolzote gathered a group of sharpshooters and raced up the river, forded the deep current, and galloped up a wooded slope. They took cover behind craggy outcrops and waited for the attacking column to begin its descent. The Nez Perce fire was withering, reducing the column to chaos on the slope of the crumbling clay bank.

In the meantime, another group of warriors led by Ollokot had galloped to the opposite end of the soldiers' forces. Fire Bear and Flying Horse were part of this cadre. When Ollokot noticed Flying Horse riding with the warriors, he nodded silently to her in affirmation. They had ridden up the far bluffs to attack the force's rear. But before their very eyes stood Howard's pack train of ammunition. The warriors charged. The soldiers, caught off guard, milled in a frenzy, scrambling to create a skirmish line as they grappled with their guns and struggled to push cartridges into gun barrels or attach bayonets.

The braves were only fifty yards away when the troops began firing. The Nez Perce reined their horses behind rocks and into the trees. Flying Horse spotted mules tethered to the north of the soldiers. She thought she could sneak behind the rocks and cut their ropes. She told Fire Bear what she was doing, and before he could stop her, she was slinking behind the rocks. He ran after her. At least he could give her cover.

By now the smoke between the warriors and the skirmish line hung thick, and Flying Horse used it to her advantage. Crawling to within twenty-five feet of the mules, who reared and brayed pitifully, she scuttled into the herd through the carbine roar. Fire Bear was behind her among the rock, the acrid, metallic smell of gunpowder smoke searing his lungs.

He glimpsed her cutting the animals' ropes. They stampeded. She grabbed a passing mule, and it dragged her out of camp. By now the soldiers had spotted her, and they shot into the melee, downing some of the beasts. Fire Bear drew their fire as Flying Horse made her escape. When she reached the rocks, she released the frenzied mule, and Fire Bear pulled her behind cover. She had freed more than a dozen pack animals loaded with supplies and ammunition.

Howard had been forced to regroup on a small plateau. Now his army was surrounded by Nez Perce in a small area. The high cliffs they had sought to make their stronghold now imprisoned them.

Chief Toohoolhoolzote had fire in his heart from the strong words with General Howard at Fort Lapwai. Although his bones were old, his heart was like a young man's, fresh with rancor. He wanted revenge. The old chief and twenty of his best warriors plunged across the river and then up the steep bluff, surprising the batteries of the big guns from their flanks. Toohoolhoolzote killed the first two soldiers, and his warriors let loose a deadly enfilade that destroyed one battery and crippled the others. More Nimiipuu joined the warriors on the bluff. There the attacking army suffered its heaviest losses.

Howard ordered his soldiers to dig rifle pits to repel a siege on their own forces. The Nez Perce maintained control of the river, and the soldiers suffered with no water as the blistering July sun beat down on the battlefield. Howard ordered several charges to regain control of the river but was handily repulsed.

Nimiipuu women spent the day carrying water to the warriors, an arduous job since they had to work their way far beyond the soldiers' rifle range. Sings Like Lark and the other women built stone breastworks, piling rocks to provide cover for sharpshooters. They placed willow branches across the top to shade eyes and hide gun barrels and gathered clumps of grass for braves to wear on their heads as camouflage.

The women dismantled the camp, too, and piled supplies on travois in haste. But they were forced to abandon nearly eighty tipis that lay within the soldiers' gunsights, all of which held caches of buffalo robes, food, cherished possessions, and sacred ancestral treasures.

The warriors laid siege to Howard's men for nearly thirty hours, giving the camp enough time to escape and make their way to the Lolo Trail. They left behind a field of carnage. Despite the surprise attack and soldier strength twice that of the Nimiipuu, US Army casualties were four times that of the Indians. And the Nez Perce had entrapped the superior force with sophisticated battle tactics the whites had never seen. Still, it was a Pyrrhic victory; the Nimiipuu had lost many supplies and were in full retreat.

Howard's troops, exhausted from lack of water and the long siege, buried their dead and nursed their wounded. Howard allowed his troops to rest. The Indians had taken all arms and ammunition, but the troops pillaged the remaining tipis, then burned the village to the ground.

While Flying Horse and her tribe fought for survival, Sorrel and Seamus had fallen ill. Seamus had influenza and a high fever. His old bones ached as if the marrow were being sucked from them, and his shriveled body, racked by convulsions of nausea, seemed as if it might fall apart. Sorrel had no fever, and her nausea subsided as morning wore on.

Ransom arrived at the farm to find both sick and stayed to nurse them as best he could. Alarmed at Seamus's deteriorating condition, he got the doctor. As soon as Doc Farnsworth entered the cabin with his black bag and glanced at Seamus, a shadow of concern darkened his face. Their friendship had long been marked by playful insults. The doctor tried to rally his humor now and told Seamus he looked even worse than usual.

Seamus managed a dry smile: "At least I have an excuse."

The doctor put his hand on Seamus's forehead. The old man was burning up and had lost a great deal of weight. He told Seamus he must try to drink water: "No whiskey, Seamus. That'll make you worse, though I know you won't believe me."

He gave Seamus a teaspoon of castor oil, which caused the little Irishman to curse: "Damn, Doc, you'd give a dying man that swill and make me suffer so? Not even a chaser of whiskey to wash it down?"

"Ah, now, Seamus. If you had your druthers, you'd cut your ice cream with whiskey!" the doctor joked. He selected two other medicines: subnitrate of bismuth for the vomiting and five-grain Dover's powder for diarrhea. After he gave doses of each to Seamus, he handed the bottles to Ransom with instructions for administering them later. He patted Seamus on the shoulder, reminding him, "Bed rest and lots of fluids for you, Seamus. And no whiskey."

"Well, if this goddamn influenza doesn't kill me, you will, sure as hell," Seamus quipped, but it was all he could do to deliver his parting shot when his chest fell with fatigue.

Doctor Farnsworth turned to Sorrel next and commented on how healthy she looked. He asked about her symptoms and felt her forehead. Then he asked Ransom to step outside for a moment. The doctor turned to Sorrel and asked if she could be pregnant. Her eyes flared in surprise, and a sudden blush stained her cheeks and neck a bright pink.

The doctor smiled. Seamus chuckled raspily from his bed. Even in his sickness, his face seemed to shine with a new smile.

"Saints be praised. I'm going to be a grandfather! And Ransom a father!"

"The morning sickness will pass soon enough, Miz Lanning. Congratulations," the doctor told Sorrel. Then he went outside to tell Ransom both good news and bad news: he was to be a father, but Seamus was very ill, and Farnsworth feared the worst.

Sorrel and Ransom were married two days later. They asked Gert and Bull to be their witnesses, and Gert brought some flowers from her garden for Sorrel's bouquet. Sorrel wore the blue dress Ransom had gotten her for the dance. Frederick was there too, to photograph the bride and groom.

Sorrel had asked that a family picture be taken with Seamus. But he was too weak to get out of bed, so Ransom carried him outside and put him in a rocking chair. Ransom and Sorrel stood behind him. Old Gentleman and Charlie sat watching as if they felt left out, so Sorrel called to Old Gentleman to lie at their feet, and Charlie sat beside the old dog.

It was a fine family portrait, Frederick exclaimed. But he saw Seamus slumping in the chair as if wilting and rushed to get the shot.

Seamus had gotten his wish—none too soon, he chided Ransom wanly: "You took your sweet time, young man!"

Ransom smiled. "Well, your daughter was exceedingly uncooperative. I thought she would *never* notice how charming I am!"

"Stubborn Irish," Seamus chuckled, but then a racking cough shook his frame.

That night, Seamus asked Sorrel for a shot of whiskey to celebrate. She and Ransom exchanged a look of anguish as she went to the cupboard for the jug, for neither saw a need to deprive an old man of whiskey in his last hours.

Sorrel spent her wedding night at Seamus's bedside. His breathing was labored and his fever punishing. Pink glowed through the windows at the hint of dawn, and she looked down at her adopted father.

He was a man full of days. A life that spanned oceans. Loves that spanned continents.

He was restless. Half conscious, he looked up at Sorrel longingly. "Glorious tings I've seen." His words were sluggish and his brogue heavy as potatoes, as if returning to the tongue of his youth, the land of his childhood. "The shores of Donegal . . . Lady Liberty . . . the legs of a grand Thoroughbred."

He licked his crusted lips, trying to wet them for more words. He lifted his gnarled hand to Sorrel's cheek. "You remember them for me, sweet?" She nodded, her eyes filling, releasing rivulets down her cheek.

"Aw, darlin'. 'Tis a fearful ting to love. Painful . . . but . . . beautiful. You are my joy," he murmured, his mouth curling into a gentle smile. "We had a fine life, child." He squeezed her hand.

Then he looked beyond her, at the window, his old eyes sparking as if with a ray from heaven, a spreading radiance in the wake of a departing soul. He closed his weary eyes, and his chest rose and fell, then was still.

FIFTY FOUR

HANDFUL OF STARS

RANSOM SHOWED up at her doorstep Sunday morning. An odd time, Sylvia noted, since he had always arrived on Friday afternoon so they could spend the weekend dining and talking and lovemaking. She felt the foreboding as soon as she opened the door, and her heart dropped like an anchor into a dark sea. His eyes seemed as blank sockets, his large frame like a shadow skulking on its own visage.

"Hello, Sylvia," Ransom said softly, holding his hat in his hands. She did not embrace him, and he was gratified that she was so intuitive.

"Hello, Ransom," she said with unsure words. "Please, come in. You're just in time for breakfast." She led him to the sunroom and left to get an additional cup and saucer. She poured him a cup of coffee. He hid his eyes from her searching glance.

To fill the strained silence, she told him that she had gotten a wonderful new client from Knob Hill. "Mrs. Cunningham, the wife of a large vineyard owner," she added.

He smiled emptily with counterfeit joy. "That's wonderful, Sylvia. I always knew you were a natural businesswoman." As she talked, his admiration for her made his chest ache, for he fathomed the depth of her brave heart, making conversation until he was ready to tell her his news. In mid-sentence, he took her hand and kissed it, then held it to his cheek with interminable sadness, soaking up the finality of their love.

He did not seem able to say the words, but his eyes presaged what his lips could not utter. Finally, she said them for him: "I know that you are not coming back, Ransom." Her words came arduously, like the intimate undressing of grief. Somehow, she felt maybe she could stand it if she spoke the end rather than hearing it from him.

Ransom's thoughts were hollowed out. He said little except that he loved her and would always love her. That he respected her and admired her and felt lucky to have had her in his life. He said he hoped she believed him. She answered that she did.

She took the tip of her forefinger and ventured across the tundra of emotion between them to touch the vein in his hand. She pressed down softly on the bulging bluish flesh, noting the gentle resistance of the blood flow within, the thin casing of life pulsing, meandering like an underground stream. And she yearned to flow with it, to wend her way back to his heart.

Ransom embraced Sylvia for a long time. As he turned to leave, the sunlight filled his eyes. *Gypsy eyes*, Sylvia thought, *beautiful eyes*. Now they were pools of molten silver, moist with sorrow.

As he walked out the door, panic gripped her chest, her heart falling in pieces, dismantled. He had been her constellation, her handful of stars. Now he left only an abyss of abandoned love.

The door closed behind him. She plastered her body flat against it, as if to soak up all that was left of him. Then, sobbing, she crumpled to the floor like a broken promise.

Sorrel collapsed exhausted in the bed; newly made, its sheets were cool and taut. The scent of the sun and prairie breezes in which they'd been hung to dry permeated their threads and sweetened them. Along with the scent of fresh-cut clover and horses in the barn, these smells were her favorites. In them was something that quieted her heart.

Ransom was in San Francisco, taking care of business and getting some of his personal belongings to bring back with him to the farm. He would be returning that night, and she realized how much she missed him.

Her stomach was swollen like a mare's belly, and she thought about how Ransom had helped her deliver the foal. She had never imagined herself being pregnant and having a child, although she had been midwife to many baby animals. She was nervous about mothering a human baby, but Gert assured her there was nothing to it.

The baby's arrival was only weeks away. Gert had become a regular visitor to the farm, giving Sorrel advice on what she would need. Diapers, of course, and baby clothes and a little tub to wash the baby in and a cradle. Sorrel had quipped to Ransom that she thought Gert was enjoying her pregnancy more that she was. But Sorrel was glad to oblige her, for Gert was a generous soul and, having lost two babies in her life, deserved whatever vicarious enjoyment she might derive from Sorrel's condition.

Gert had become a conduit for the local ladies' doting. They were not comfortable with Sorrel, but when accompanied by Gert, they brought used baby clothes and bottles and diapers and rattles and more advice than Sorrel could absorb. Gert trafficked the women's enthusiasm.

As the birthing time drew closer, visitors brought foodstuffs, knowing Sorrel's legendary lack of cooking skills and taking pity on Ransom. The pantry brimmed with canned peaches and jerked beef, dried apples and smoked ham, potatoes and other produce.

When the baby came—on schedule—she popped out "quick as a whistle on a summer day," Gert said.

"You sure make good babies," Gert added.

Gert told the quilting ladies that Sorrel was as natural a mother as an old sow suckling a dozen little ones, a comparison that made the ladies blush and shush Gert. "Well, it's true!" Gert said. "All her husbandry with horses and critters and such sure paid off. Let's just hope the child doesn't end up walking on all fours."

The baby, named Ella after Gert's middle name, was good natured and healthy. But then, Gert never expected Sorrel would have a finicky or colicky baby. What amazed Gert was Ransom's fatherly instincts. For such a big man, she expected him to be fumble fingered and coarse with the pink little being. But he was tender and sensitive, could change diapers nimbly, and when bathing little Ella made her giggle and sputter in delight.

He was in love with his daughter and would not be separated from her even when Sorrel breast-fed. He watched as Sorrel cradled Ella below her rounded, swollen breasts. The baby's little rosebud mouth wrapped around Sorrel's nipple, hungrily sucking the milk, like liquid serenity. When Sorrel switched Ella to her other breast, he loved the way her nipple, wet and glistening, retained the shape of Ella's mouth, as if proud in its own fulfillment.

Ransom had made a cradle of pinewood varnished a bright golden brown. Gert cautioned him not to make it too small so she wouldn't grow out of it quickly. It was big enough that Charlie could cuddle with little Ella as she slept, and the velvet engine of his purr lulled her to sleep.

Old Gentleman at first whined and felt left out. He'd put his paw up on the cradle's edge, contemplating squeezing in with Charlie and the baby. But he inevitably thought better of it and slumped on the floor next to the cradle with a resigned grunt. At night, he still slept curled beside Sorrel. Charlie, being independently minded and arbitrary as cats are, sometimes remained with Ella and sometimes slept nested with Old Gentleman.

Charlie took on some strange habits after Ella was born. He liked to collect her little socks from her bassinet and bring them into the cradle with her. Perhaps, since Sorrel would not let him bring in field mice he had caught as gifts, the balled-up baby socks were a close enough approximation. When Sorrel got up in the morning, Charlie would be curled up beside Ella, a mound of baby socks lying at the foot of her cradle from a busy night stalking socks.

Old Gentleman was attentive to Ella too. As she grew, he was her ever-faithful friend, a bond reinforced by food dropped during meals, accidentally and on purpose. As she got older, she liked to sit at the table barefooted and place morsels of food on her toes. Old Gentleman and Charlie would sit licking the tiny scraps from her pinkies as she giggled.

Summer mornings, before Ransom rode to his mine, he sat on the front lawn with Ella while Sorrel did chores. Ella loved the arbor of blue morning glories Seamus had constructed from saplings and sticks. He had cherished the flowers that looked like fanciful silk bugles of garden sprites—or "the little people," as Seamus called them. Ella imagined little fairies living in the morning glories, a fancy that was encouraged by Ransom's colorful descriptions of the little people he had spied and that Ella had just missed seeing. After a particularly ornate tale, Sorrel accused Ransom of inheriting Seamus's gift for blarney.

Ella inherited her mother's love of the outdoors and a propensity for creatures and nature. And like her mother, she showed a disdain for dresses. Sorrel saw no reason why she should wear them and dressed Ella in overalls. Ransom did not object, except to say that Ella should wear dresses for special occasions and not wait, like her mother did, until she was a grown woman.

Ella's favorite secret place was the far edge of the meadow under three towering elms that stood in a row, their trunks thick as locomotive engines and as powerful in their upright steadfastness. She called them the three sisters and spent hours at their rutted bases, collecting seeds and pods and pretty rocks and arrowheads among their whorled roots. She found comfort in them save one thing: the middle "sister" had, among the limbs and leaves, a huge, gnarled burl on her trunk. It was as grotesque as the severed hog head Ella had seen once in the refuse pile after butchering day.

Ella studied the burl often in morbid fascination and felt a muddle of emotions—fear, distrust, and pity for the sister that bore such disfigurement within her leafy tresses. Ella was four when she brought her father to her secret place. He sat with her under the tree. They relaxed there for a while and then, sheepishly, as if she felt guilty for sharing the tree's awful secret, she told him something was wrong with the tree.

"That means the tree is strong, Ella," he said. "It's a scar where bugs attacked her. But she was healthy and strong. She didn't let the bugs hurt her. Her bark surrounded the bugs and buried them so they couldn't escape. She killed the bugs. It's like she ate them."

Ella was taken with the drama. The burl became a noble scar, a knobby medallion of the tree's toughness, and Ella came to admire the middle sister most.

One morning when Ella was five, Sorrel was filing a mare's hoof in the barn when she heard a shrill scream in the paddock. Ella had found her baby rabbit dead in the grass, its little torso crushed flat, its eyes bulging in surprise. An earthen halo encircled it in the dirt, the telltale impression of a draft horseshoe.

Ella blamed the Percheron horses, Betty and Brute. She did not know which was the culprit and so viewed both with suspicion. Ransom found the little girl in the paddock scolding them sternly.

Sorrel helped Ella wrap the baby rabbit in lettuce leaves and tie the bundle in twine like a little mummy in shimmering jade silk. Sorrel suggested that Ella draw a picture to bury with the bunny. Ella devoted much of her morning preparing the tribute, which included a pencil drawing of herself holding the rabbit.

Ella suggested the burial be next to Seamus. She insisted that Betty and Brute attend the funeral: "They will be ashamed when they see what they did." So, the parents stood at the tiny burial alongside the two guilty draft horses as Ella pronounced that they were very sorry for their sins and would never step on a bunny again. Sorrel told Ransom she should be lucky to have such a fine funeral.

Ransom asked Frederick to take a family portrait in front of the cabin. Afterwards, Ransom insisted that he stay for dinner. Ella was excited to have a new audience with whom to share her collection, which included pods, cones, a hummingbird nest, a weasel skull, and insect hulls, all carefully collected in a cigar box. In it was an item like a tiny red pine tree. She explained in professorial detail that it was the tongue of a pileated woodpecker, that the bird stuck it in tree holes to snag juicy grubs and bugs.

Ransom had bought a large book with color botanical plates in San Francisco for Ella. She absorbed the pages voraciously and learned to recite their Latin names with academic verve.

After dinner, as Frederick was leaving on his horse with pack mule in tow, he happened upon Ella in the meadow, oblivious to his presence, engrossed in a one-way colloquy with a large oak tree. She was presenting a strange insect skeleton and other oddities, her singsong child's voice babbling like a small brook over rocks, happy in its own unfettered momentum. Frederick smiled as he passed, grateful to the oak—far wiser than himself, he was sure, and patient in its attentiveness.

FIFTY FIVE

SUN OF BIG TROUBLE

BY AUGUST 1877, the Nimiipuu had been in flight for three months since leaving their ancestral home on the shores of Wallowa Lake. They had traveled 600 miles through the world's most rugged land and fought three major battles. The white army had suffered heavy casualties: nearly eighty soldiers, including fifty dead. The Nez Perce had sustained only four dead—women and children—and eight wounded. Still, the tribe was weary, the children sick, the horses footsore from the rough terrain and relentless pace. The Nez Perce had lost a fifth of their herd but still had 2,500 horses.

The band arrived at the Big Hole basin at the fork of the Bitterroot and Big Hole Rivers. It was a good place to hunt and gather food for the coming winter and rebuild the strength of the people. After humiliating defeats, General Howard did not pursue the Nez Perce on their path along the spine of the Continental Divide.

Flying Horse awoke to the distant memory of a dream, of nocturnal drums, thrusting stone, and flashing steel, of hurried footfalls on ancient trails. She awoke gasping, the acrid smell of blood in her nostrils. Fire Bear kissed her and asked sleepily what was troubling her. He had taken to calling her *bi-bi*, a term of endearment. He used the name now and stroked her hair.

"I cannot sleep," she told him. "I am going out for some cool air. I'll be back soon." She returned his kiss. She stepped into the night air, wrapped her deerskin tightly around her, and listened to the night sounds—the river's flow, the snort of a horse on the hillside, a wolf howl.

All was calm. Yet her heart was not quiet. A cold breeze swept up, leaves swirling about her, and the wind hissed in the rocks like spirit warnings. A shudder scuttled down her spine as a scream seared the air. A violent flurry of feathers in a nearby tree, the final struggle of an owl in the talons of a hawk.

At dawn, Flying Horse went to the shaman Toohoolhoolzote and told him of her terrible imaginings and the death of the owl in the talons of the hawk. He looked gravely to the mountains and after a solemn quiet said: "We must ask the aid of the spirits and the mountains for protection, child. There will be great struggle. Many will die, but some will find freedom in the land to the north. I know this to be true." Then he looked to the ground and sank into silence. His own night dreams had been a sludge of twisted struggle, and his spirit power withered in despair. The deaths he'd seen in his vision were many, and one of them was his own.

Another shaman, Pile of Clouds, had awakened in a cold sweat, low voices in his head beseeching him to move quickly through the country of the Big Hole. The next morning, he pleaded with the chiefs at council: "Death is on our trail! My medicine told me to move on. Death is approaching us! We must hurry through this country. There will be tears in our eyes."

Perhaps the shamans had sensed the vibrations of the telegraph wires pulsing treachery against the Nimiipuu through the mountains. General Howard *was* telegraphing Colonel John Gibbon to march on the Nez Perce from the east with six companies, a wagon train of ammunition, two howitzers, and many citizen volunteers. From the west, Howard would meet Gibbon at the Big Hole where Joseph's people were camped. The utmost haste was adjured, for they had a chance to surprise the refugees and crush them.

Despite the shamans' protestations, Chief Looking Glass argued that the people and horses were exhausted and needed rest. It was hard to resist the bounty of the basin and its tranquil charms after so much suffering and with winter soon ahead. The Big Hole was an idyllic crescent of brooks, flowers, and grasses fringed by a rocky cordillera with forest-clad slopes beyond. A vast village of tipis was set up along the banks. Nearby thickets of alder, willow, and pine provided excellent lodge poles. The streams teemed with fish, the prairie with antelope. The herd cropped rich grass.

A majority of the council decided to rest for a day. They had outdistanced Howard's troops by at least two days, and scouts reported that there were no troops anywhere in the area. The Nimiipuu reposed. They played games. Women cooked feasts. Little girls set up tiny doll tipis. Boys fought mock battles.

That night, there was joyful drumming and chanting. Braves reenacted their exploits on the battlefields of the last three moons. Medicine men chanted prayers of thanks for Nimiipuu victories. The shaman White Eagle wore a spectacular bird-beast headdress festooned with feathers, bones, and primal oddments that flowed and jerked as he danced. He called upon the war-soaked spirits of those who had died and asked for strength and courage, for freedom from the white man.

The warrior Yellow Wolf rode into camp on his magnificent warhorse. He wore the headdress of a wolf with a cascading bonnet of eagle feathers and a painted shield bedecked with black-tipped ermine tails. The village was awed by the sight of such a fine warrior.

All danced to drums and chants, unaware that from the hills and ridges, several hundred soldiers watched, marveling at the strange tableau of shadows gyrating in the glow of the flickering firelight. The soldiers had converged from east and west, marching hard to make a surprise attack.

After the camp was finally quiet, about 2 a.m., the crouching soldiers made their move down the gullies and ravines and across streams to get in close proximity for a dawn charge on the slumbering tribe. As the troops looked down upon placid white tipis, smoke wisping lazily from their tops, they knew they would be attacking a village of mostly women and children. What were the orders regarding civilians? Colonel Gibbon answered simply: "No prisoners." *No quarter given. Kill them all.* Among the women and children were warriors who had defeated them at every turn. The end justified the means.

Dawn gilded the mountains as an elderly Indian rode out to the horse herd. A rifle report echoed against the hills. Horse and rider were cut down, and soldiers swept down the slopes in a furious fusillade on hundreds of sleeping families. Every soldier had been issued a Springfield rifle, a revolver, and ninety rounds of ammunition.

The storm of bullets ripped through the air, slashing lodges, cutting down Nimiipuu wholesale as they were disgorged from their tipis. Entire families collapsed in heaps. The basin was thick with smoke and the dawn riven with the deafening rake of bullets.

The village exploded in confusion, women yelling, men shooting, babies crying. Warriors stripped for battle and others naked in their haste and wearing only cartridge belts loaded their guns as they ran. Women rushed from tipis, carrying papooses and dragging little children toward thickets, riverbanks, or rocks.

The soldiers were already at close range, some using rifles, others revolvers. So heavy was the discharge that soldiers were powder burned in the heavy smoke. The refugees running from the lodges made easy targets. They scrambled, crawling, holding close to the earth as if seeking her protection. Women were struck down, their babies screaming and clutching their mothers. An old woman cried medicine songs above her fallen warrior son amid horrific gunfire. The sun of big trouble had come and cast the shadow of anguish upon the Nez Perce.

FIFTY SIX

BLEEDING EDGE OF A SHAMAN DREAM

FLYING HORSE and Fire Bear had been sleeping naked under mountain-lion skins, melting in the warmth of each other's touch and the lushness of the soft furs, when two bullets pierced the hide of their tipi. Fire Bear pulled on his breechclout and Flying Horse a deerskin dress. Under cover of the furs, they scurried to the pine thicket and flattened to the ground behind rocks. Man and woman leveled their rifles in unison and took aim at the attacking bluecoats.

Soon Tall Tree and Sings Like Lark came scrambling behind the rocks beside Flying Horse. Tall Tree held her mother up as her legs dragged on the ground. Sings Like Lark had been shot in the left breast; her hide tunic was soaked in blood. Flying Horse wiped her hand across the dress and uncovered the small hole in the hide. She took her knife and cut the hole bigger, then noticed blood trickling in runnels underneath her mother. She gently lifted her mother on her side and cut the back of the tunic with her knife. Under the flap, her mother's back bore a large, ragged hole as if gnawed by wolves.

Her mother was still conscious, and Flying Horse tried to smile down at her, but desperation darkened her face. "I know it hurts, but it is not so bad."

Her mother recognized her daughter's well-meaning deception and gathered a broken smile. "I am glad, my brave daughter, that you have strong medicine in your heart. I am proud of you beyond words," she said. She did not want to die without her daughter knowing this, that Sings Like Lark was not embarrassed by Flying Horse's different nature.

"I will get mud for the wound," Flying Horse said. She grabbed a handful of thick clay and marsh grasses from the nearby riverbank and made a poultice to stop the bleeding. Sings Like Lark barely winced at her daughter's ministrations. Flying Horse made a pillow of grass for her mother's head and covering her with furs to keep shock and cold from her body. She kissed her mother's forehead. "I must fight."

"Yes! Fight, daughter!" Sings Like Lark answered, vehement.

Lieutenant James H. Bradley and his company had first assaulted the village from its left flank near Ruby Creek. An aspiring writer, Bradley had already distinguished himself in the national press as the officer who first discovered Custer and his fallen men at the Little Bighorn. Newspapers published his riveting dispatches about the gruesome discovery and battles with the Nez Perce. He had penned a book and, eager for glory, saw this as an opportunity for a dramatic firsthand account. But his book would not be published. As he led the charge against the village, he was shot and killed outright by a Nez Perce sharpshooter.

Meanwhile, Captain William Logan's soldiers crossed the stream in a heaving tangle. The Nimiipuu sought cover in a grove of willows and let loose a fury of gunfire. Here a great number of soldiers died. Among the willows were Wahlitits and his pregnant wife, Telnayas. She matched her husband well, spirited and brave like him.

Wahlitits and Red Moccasin Top were the brash young braves who had killed three Indian-hating whites and brought down an avalanche on their people. They had fought in battle many times and survived unscathed but for bullet grazes.

Hidden in the thicket, Wahlitits told his wife she must try to escape, but a bullet ripped through her tunic, and blood gushed from her abdomen. She was seven months pregnant and screamed for her baby. Wahlitits hugged her desperately and yelled to the other warriors that his wife was wounded.

Directly across the creek bank, Captain Logan stood holding the revolver with which he had shot Telnayas. Wahlitits exploded from the willows to avenge his wife, but the officer fired again, killing Wahlitits instantly. Telnayas leapt to her fallen husband and wrenched the smoking Enfield from his grip. She fired point-blank at Logan's forehead, and the back of his head exploded in chunks of blood, brains, and skull. Logan's men answered with a furious volley that tore through her body and swollen abdomen. She fell across her husband.

Nearby, Rainbow, Red Moccasin Top, and Bird Alighting fired from the willows. They were very close to the soldiers' trenches, under scorching gunfire. Rainbow downed two soldiers when Red Moccasin Top was hit. Bird Alighting ran to him.

"I am done! I will not live! Go!" Red Moccasin Top uttered in a gurgling grunt, for he had been shot in the neck, his wampum necklace severed by the bullet. He would die soon but saw Rainbow killed first as the wounded Bird Alighting dragged him from the gunfire.

Helping Another, the wife of Wounded Head, lay in the tall grassy riverbank among the willows. She held her little girl tight in her arms and tried to cover her with her body. But willow twigs fell like hail above her head under the enfilade of bullets. The little girl yelped, then went limp, eyes still wide. Helping Another screamed and sank her sobbing face into her dead child's chest.

Yellow Wolf had run from his tipi with only his *kop-luts* war club. He came upon a wounded bluecoat crawling like a drunken man. He clubbed him and grabbed the soldier's Springfield rifle and cartridge belt. Then he saw the dead man's mouth was open, his teeth falling out. Yellow Wolf picked up the odd teeth—made by man, not the Creator. *How strange the ways of whites*, he thought.

Within twenty minutes, the soldiers had captured the village. The ground was littered with Nez Perce dead and many more dead and wounded in the rushes and woods. The soldiers were ordered to set all lodges ablaze. But, wet with dew, few ignited.

Surviving Nimiipuu hid in the surrounding grasses and ridges. After the initial shock of the charge, their blood burned like fire, and they began a bold onslaught. Soon the soldiers found the tables turned and were surrounded by the victims they had attacked while sleeping. Colonel Gibbon frantically ordered a retreat into the hills.

With the soldiers in hot retreat, Flying Horse turned to her mother under the furs. Sings Like Lark's eyes were closed, her hands crossed on her chest as if in prayer. Flying Horse leaned down to feel the heat of her breath, but there was none. She had died while her family fought beside her. Flying Horse placed her head on Sings Like Lark's clasped hands and began to weep. Tall Tree slumped beside his daughter, tears running down his face. Then he looked to the sky and the Great Creator and bellowed his anguish from his cleaved heart.

The Nez Perce returned to grisly carnage. As the troops retreated up the rocky hills, wails of grief rose behind them as families discovered their dead. Even the battle-hardened Colonel Gibbon could hardly bear the sound as he huddled in the trenches with his men. Later he told *Harper's Weekly*,

> Few of us will ever forget the wail of mingled grief, rage and horror from the camp when the Indians returned to find their slaughtered warriors, women and children.

Nearly ninety Nimiipuu had been killed, sixty-five of them women and children. Respected chiefs and warriors—Rainbow, Five Wounds, Wahlitits, Red Moccasin Top—were dead.

The whites sustained heavy casualties too: thirty-one dead, including three officers, and thirty-eight wounded. The once pristine stream was now stained scarlet with the blood of Indian and white.

Even in their grief, the Nez Perce began digging graves, tearing down lodges, and packing horses. Nimiipuu warriors kept the soldiers immobilized in the hills and under siege while the village below buried their dead and regrouped after the slaughter.

The soldiers hiding in the hills had neither food nor water and were cruelly parched. Some soldiers had at their disposal the dead cavalry horse of Lieutenant Charles Woodruff. After two days without water or food, they ate its flesh raw as they could not start fires that would attract Nez Perce sharpshooters.

On the second day, when the sun was highest in the sky, Nez Perce braves overran the soldiers manning the twelve-pound mountain howitzer. They dismantled the big gun and absconded with a mule train carrying over 2,000 rounds of ammunition for Springfield rifles. This was a considerable windfall, in addition to the many rifles gathered on the battlefield. Most Nez Perce warriors did not have white soldiers' lethal repeating rifles. This had heavily tipped the odds in white favor.

Late in the afternoon, Gibbon's bivouacked troops noticed a huge cloud of billowing black smoke. The Nez Perce had set the mountainside on fire, and a strong wind fed the inferno, ushering it up the hillside toward the soldiers. Smoke roiled and orange flames leapt twenty feet high. Surrounded on all sides, Gibbon issued a battle cry: "If the worst comes, men, charge through the fire and send them to a hotter place than they have given us!"

The soldiers watched the wall of flames gallop nearer and nearer. The thick smoke began to suffocate them. Just as they were about to burn to death, the wind shifted, and the fire turned back on itself and its own blackened embers, then died. The men cheered wildly amid coughing and choking.

The Nez Perce dismantled the village and packed their belongings in great haste. Joseph and the other chiefs believed General Howard was quick on the heels of Colonel Gibbon, which indeed he was. When Howard arrived the next morning at ten, he was disappointed to find Joseph and the Nez Perce long gone.

Colonel Gibbon, sitting under a makeshift shelter of pine boughs, greeted the general. "Hard to believe those Indians rallied after such a surprise attack and made such a fight," the colonel marveled. Gibbon's men were seasoned veterans of the Civil War and Indian campaigns. All agreed the battle had been the hardest fighting they'd ever seen. Newspapers widely quoted General Howard's praise of his opponent:

> Joseph gathered his warriors, recovered lost ground, and recaptured his numerous herd of ponies, which had been cut off by Gibbon's men, buried most of their dead, and made good his retreat before my forces arrived the next morning. Few military commanders could have recovered after so fearful a surprise.

But Joseph did not praise himself or the other Nez Perce chieftains. He grieved such terrible losses. His own wife, mother of his three-month-old baby, was wounded. He blamed himself for her suffering as she lay in the travois being dragged along the rough ground. They had been arrogant in their victories, had not heeded omens sent to them. The bleeding edge of a shaman's dream came to them like a knife blade to their throats. It had been a fatal mistake.

FIFTY SEVEN

EYE OF THE NEEDLE

THE QUILTING LADIES were beside themselves. At the general store, Gert had seen Katherine Blades so hunched over and bruised that she could barely walk.

"It's a crime to sit by and watch that son of a bitch slowly kill her," Gert said. "We have to get her out of there!" She had promised Mrs. McGill she wouldn't curse at their quilt gatherings, but Mrs. McGill knew better than to admonish Gert on this particular occasion. Her eyes were hard as burnished steel, her resolve as unyielding.

"Where would she live?" Mrs. Denton asked. "I can't take her. I have five children." The other women mulled the question, bent over their quilt blocks.

Mrs. Miller, a steadfast and outspoken Christian, believed it wasn't right to take a wife from a man, no matter how horrible the man, and rip asunder what had been promised in God's name. But her conviction wilted before Gert's wrath.

Helga Stoneburner cleared her throat to speak. Gert had brought the eccentric recluse to a gathering one day without the approval of the other quilting ladies. But they had come to accept the old woman, as they had Gert.

"Well, my Helmut's been gone for over a year now," Helga began, her enunciation slushing through her toothless gums. "I need help on the farm, and I could use the company. Katherine can stay with me."

"Cornelius Blades will come after you," Mrs. Miller warned.

"He'll have to argue with my dogs and my shotgun," Helga answered, unbothered.

"That's right good of you, Helga," Gert said with strident appreciation. "We can all share our produce with you and take up an offering at the church. Or I'll go door-to-door and wring it out of everyone who calls herself a Christian."

Gert's iron eyes landed squarely on Mrs. Miller. Her threat was none too veiled. The ladies quickly volunteered their garden produce and smoked meats lest Gert publicly challenge them to perform their Christian duty.

"Alright. It's settled. Katherine will stay with Helga. Now we have to figure out how we're gonna get Katherine away from that demon from hell. I can take my buckboard. Who's gonna go with me?" Gert stood up and looked about the room. No takers. The ladies crouched intently over their quilt blocks, her ire burning the tops of their bowed heads.

"Well, I never saw such mealy-mouthed mollycoddles," she thundered with her hands on her hips. Mrs. McGill was at least relieved that Gert hadn't inserted any obscenities in her remonstrance. But her relief was short lived.

"Well, goddamn it! I'll go ask Sorrel. She'll go with me!" she declared righteously.

The next day, the Sabbath, Gert appeared at Sorrel's front door and told her what she intended to do. Gert had her buckboard and her rifle. Just as she supposed, Sorrel went to get her shotgun—better for short range—and told Ransom matter-of-factly that she and Gert were going to take Katherine Blades out from her misery.

Ransom gently suggested that he go instead, but Sorrel said that Katherine wasn't likely to trust the likes of any man after what she'd been through. No, she said. This is something that women have to do. Ransom knew it was no use to argue with Sorrel.

Sorrel and Gert arrived at the farm to find seemingly no one there. They walked up to the board porch, and Sorrel cocked her shotgun and nodded at Gert to knock. But no one answered. Gert called out Katherine's name.

They opened the door cautiously, slowly walked in, and peered into the shabby interior. They were trespassing, but the point seemed moot. They were coming to take a man's wife from him. Gert heard a shuffle. She pulled a curtain back under a cupboard to find Katherine cowering in a fetal position.

"Katherine," Gert said gently. "We've come to take you out of here."

She stared up at Gert, terrified.

"He'll kill me if I go," she croaked.

"He'll kill you if you don't. Besides, we'll protect you. Now come along and help us gather your things." Gert pulled the tiny woman to a standing position in the light.

Gert and Sorrel glanced at each other and felt waves of guilt lurch down their chests. Why had they waited so long to come to this woman's rescue? Her face, once blushed and peach smooth, was now corrugated with scars. They were horrified at her deteriorated condition. A keloid flap of flesh ran down the outside of her left eye, partially covering it, obviously a wound that had healed without a doctor or sutures. Her neck was blotched a violent pastiche of purple, and her right cheek had a fresh red welt on it.

Gert went to the dresser drawer and looked for Katherine's clothes, but there was little to find—some old torn petticoats, a dress so threadbare Gert thought it hardly qualified as a rag. In another drawer, she found Katherine's cotton wedding dress. She laid it out on the bed, which had no sheets, only old mattress ticking stained with blood and grime.

Katherine looked at the dress blankly. It seemed like a snake's discarded skin, a gossamer tunnel from her past. She looked at the door, then back at the shabby husk of her life with Cornelius Blades draped on the bed.

In a hunched shuffle, Katherine went to the corner of the room and knelt down. She pushed in a floorboard. From beneath it she pulled the necklace her mammy had given her for protection. Then she stood up.

"There is nothing else I want," she mumbled, drawing from the faint fumes of courage left at the bottom of her soul. "I'm ready."

Outside, she stopped suddenly. "I need to do something," she said meekly. She walked around the back of the outhouse. There, in an unkempt row, were six small mounds. All were overgrown with weeds, saving one mounded with fresh dirt. She bowed her head, her lower lip quivering, her eyes welling. Then, she turned away and walked to Gert's buckboard.

After the Nez Perce's devastating losses at Big Hole, the blood of young warriors boiled. Most of the casualties had been children, and the chiefs could no longer quell their rage. Several young men went on a rampage, killing four whites at a ranch house, then, several miles further, two more whites.

The Indian tribe moved west, crossing the Continental Divide once again at Bannock Pass. They camped several miles from a stockade where white settlers were sheltered. White Bird and Looking Glass assured the whites there would be no trouble as long as the Nez Perce were allowed to pass through the valley. But an advance guard of angry renegade warriors discovered a wagon train of freighters and killed five whites. Two Chinese cooks were left unharmed; the warriors had no quarrel with their race. They confiscated supplies, mules, and horses and burned the wagons.

Chief Joseph's people were now 1,200 miles from their homeland, a savage world away from the shores of the blue Wallowa Lake. They had traveled over terrain as varied as the earth could offer, from welcoming camas prairies to the plunging Hell's Canyon, from snow-peaked mountains to wind-sculpted sand bluffs. But the terrain ahead of them would be the most challenging yet for the exhausted people and their horse herd.

They had been on the run for months, had fought ten battles against superior forces sometimes ten times their number and outwitted them, winning all but the battle of the Big Hole.

When Chief Joseph and his tribe came to the Lolo Pass and the Bitterroot River, they had to make a choice that could mean their very existence. They could go north toward Canada, only 250 miles away but through dangerous Flathead country and past Fort Missoula. Even worse, the Flathead had allied themselves with the US Army. Or they could go south—a much longer route—along old ancestral trails familiar to them that ran along the Continental Divide toward Yellowstone territory. From there they would turn east to buffalo country and the land of their old allies, the Crow.

After considerable counsel, the chieftains decided they were not ready to risk going through such treacherous territory to reach Canada. Instead, they would go to the land of the Crow. With powerful allies, they hoped to live in peace on the isolated plains of Montana.

They traveled along the spine for nigh 500 miles before reaching the land of yellow stone, where for generations of summers they had rested en route to Crow buffalo country. But recently, the US government had confiscated the land and their most sacred places for the country's first national park.

A massive offensive was being planned by General William Tecumseh Sherman himself, to surround the Nez Perce from all directions at Yellowstone. Sherman had come to Montana, one newspaper wrote, to put things right, once and for all:

> The lion in him has been roused by the defiant progress of the Nez Perce. By personal attention General Sherman has raised up an army on all four sides of Joseph. We wait hopefully for news that the Nez Perce have been struck hard and fatally. They are too brave and dangerous a foe to escape.

Sherman had devised a strategy to corral the Nez Perce in a valley with no means of escape. Colonel Samuel Sturgis and six companies of the Seventh Cavalry had been ordered by Sherman to block Clark Fork on the east where it expanded from deadfall canyon walls to a broad plain. Five companies from Colonel Merritt's cavalry regiment were dispatched south of Clarks Fork on the Stinking Water River. Ten more companies waited in reserve on the Little Wind River, farther south. And General Howard was coming from the west. All officers were crusty veterans from the Civil War and Indians wars.

But Colonel Sturgis, a veteran officer who had lost his son at the Battle of the Little Big Horn just a year before, hated all Indians with consuming vengeance. Vowing revenge, he had taken over Custer's Seventh Cavalry. He grew impatient waiting at Clarks Fork, and when his scouts spied the Indians on the trail to the Stinking Water, he believed the Nez Perce had decided on a different route. Sturgis salivated with the taste of vindication. He moved his troops quickly in pursuit of the renegades.

Sturgis had fallen for Chief Joseph's brilliant ruse. A group of warriors with a herd of horses as a decoy postured as the main body of the Nez Perce caravan. The warriors had traveled over some of the land's most spectacularly rugged terrain along the rim above the plummeting Clarks Fork Canyon, crossed Dead Indian Hill, then continued on to the

Stinking Water. At daybreak, the warriors made a great stir of dust, tying sagebrush to the horses' tails and milling the animals to create a cloud. The lure worked, drawing Sturgis's columns toward the decoys and away from the mouth of the canyon, leaving it unguarded. Meanwhile, the main mass of nearly 700 Nez Perce and their herd of 2,500 horses slunk through a slender chasm of rock to escape, directly under the noses of General Howard and Colonel Sturgis.

The Nez Perce plan was daring, for it required funneling an immense crush of people and livestock through a plunging slit so narrow that two horses could not fit abreast, like threading a stampede through the eye of a needle. Horses and humans lurched down the depths of the defile, dropping a sheer thousand feet in a quarter of a mile. Howard's aide-de-camp, Lieutenant C. E. S. Wood, described the passage to newspapers as "like going through a gigantic dark railroad tunnel."

By the time Sturgis and Howard realized they were on a wild goose chase, their forces had quagmired in terrain barely passable for a mountain goat. The Army horses and mules fell on the steep trail and clogged the passage. Howard told newspapers he "had to admire the quick wit of Indians who had the hardihood to break such an impassable route."

FIFTY EIGHT

TWO WORLDS COLLIDING

THE SACRED LANDS of Yellowstone had become the de rigueur playground of wealthy white Victorians. Since the area had been declared a national park five years before, they flocked to the park sporting formal attire, ornate walking canes, and frilled umbrellas. Roadways had been built to accommodate fine buggies and wagonloads of gawkers. The parkland that Frederick had helped survey for the government now yielded a lucrative income in tourism photography for him and for hundreds of vendors who flooded the area, selling trinkets and doodads.

The previous month, George Cowan, a former US marshal and prominent attorney from Helena, had contacted Frederick to photograph his family vacationing in Yellowstone. They had a party of nine and had been assured by General Sherman, who had been a tourist at the park just days before, that they would be safe from the renegade Nez Perce. Frederick told the party that he himself had met Chief Joseph and that he and his people were honorable and friendly. George and his wife, Emma, were impressed that the photographer had met the famous chief the entire nation had been reading about with rapt curiosity. They took comfort in his reassurances.

Frederick took the party to the big geyser, the bubbling mud pots, the Yellowstone Falls, his subjects awestruck by the spectacular geological spectacles.

After spending several days with the party, he packed up his mule and horse and left their campsite at the lower Geyser Basin to head northwest, back to Spotted Horse. It was a two-week journey through rough country. Mr. Cowan had made it worth his while.

But a darkening guilt consumed Frederick. He practically *felt* the noose of the white world tightening around Chief Joseph's neck, and he had helped tie the rope. Now he was photographing tourists in the secret places the Nez Perce had held sacred for thousands of years, places they had shown *him* just years before.

He was thinking exactly these thoughts when he noticed a party of Indian scouts led by a white soldier riding over a ridge. They galloped up to him, the white man introducing himself as Stanton G. Fisher, a scout for General Howard. The Indians with him looked to be Bannock, deadly enemies of the Nez Perce. Stanton explained that General Howard was in hot pursuit of the Nez Perce from the west and that the Indians were on a rampage and had killed some tourists. Frederick could not believe his ears. The scout asked Frederick if he had seen the tourists, and he blurted out that he'd been with them at the lower Geyser Basin several days before. Fisher thanked him, and the company galloped off in that direction.

Frederick immediately regretted aiding the white scout and was even more chagrined when he read in the *Helena Weekly Herald* that Fisher and his Bannock scouts had caught up to the rear guard of the Nez Perce warriors and engaged in a gun battle. The newspaper quoted Fisher about his difficult climb up the 10,000-foot mountain elevation:

> It was the roughest country I ever passed through. Every foot obstructed with fallen timber and huge boulders of granite. I cannot fathom how an entire tribe and their horse herds could have possibly traversed such terrain.

To Frederick's consternation, some young Nez Perce renegade warriors *had* killed tourists in Yellowstone. But Chief Joseph, Frederick read, intervened and saved the hostages—the Cowan family Frederick had just photographed days before! Emma Cowan and her family had been spared and reunited with her husband, George, who had been grazed in the head but survived. Frederick was haunted by the episode and lamented his dilemma, lodged between his own white race and the Nimiipuu people he had come to love.

Looking Glass rode east into Montana ahead of the Nez Perce refugees to ask the aid of the Crow. Nimiipuu warriors had helped the Crow fight the Sioux, and Looking Glass counted on their help now during the Nez Perce's greatest time of need. But to his shock and incredulity, the Crow told him they could not welcome them to their land, that to do so would bring white wrath upon them. In fact, some young Crow braves had even taken up arms with whites and were serving as scouts. Any hopes of finding refuge in their ancestral buffalo country were dashed, and bitter disillusionment corroded Nimiipuu hearts.

Despite the many miles and tribulations since leaving their homeland, Joseph's desire had continued to arc back to his beloved Wallowa Valley. But all his hopes were now vanquished. After counsel, Joseph chose the only course left: north to Canada to join Sitting Bull. But the trek would be hard.

Two days later, at Canyon Creek, Sturgis caught up to the Nez Perce. Anxious to redeem himself after his embarrassing blunder, he had rushed to join Howard's forces and took on the task of chasing down the Nez Perce. With 400 men, his columns traveled sixty miles in one day through rain and cold to overcome the elusive tribe.

The next morning at dawn, 150 Crow warriors caught up with Sturgis's column. They were "gaudily arrayed in war costume, but more eager for Nez Perce ponies than for Nez Perce blood," the colonel told the newspapers. The Crow were fierce warriors and had fresh, battle-seasoned horses. They would be valuable allies in the war against the Nez Perce.

Now Sturgis believed he could stop the Nez Perce Indians within the towering walls of the canyon before they made their way up the narrow ravine to the plains. His forces pressed the rear guard of the Nez Perce cavalcade hard. But the warriors formed a defensive line across the rear. They had a large number of wounded, some in travois that slowed the pace.

The Nez Perce sharpshooting abilities held the soldiers and Crow in check with murderous fire. Other contingents of Nimiipuu warriors rode up the rimrock cliffs and let loose a blistering assault on the enemy below.

The Crow ran skirmishes against the Nez Perce rear guard to stampede the horses they protected so vigilantly. Nez Perce warriors had fought with the Crow against the Sioux several winters before, so both were familiar with the other's guerilla tactics. In fact, the Crow were far more successful in inflicting casualties than Sturgis's men.

Ollokot and Yellow Wolf were riding together through a rocky gulch. Yellow Wolf turned to Ollokot: "Do you know, I saw two Crow riding against us who played with us as youth in buffalo country!"

Ollokot confirmed he had seen them too, and their hearts were on fire with bitterness at the betrayal. But they had not seen older warriors and were heartened those men valued the long friendship with the Nez Perce and had not taken up arms against them. Ollokot and Yellow Wolf dismounted and took cover in a fissure in the rocks. They saw one of the Crow they recognized riding his horse among the rocks.

"I will kill that dog!" Yellow Wolf resolved. Fueled by vengeance with a ragged edge of recklessness, Yellow Wolf took off, half crawling, half running, along the rocks and gullies. When he was near enough to get a bead on the enemy warrior, he yelled out: "I am Yellow Wolf of the Nez Perce, friend!" He shot the Crow in the skull, dead.

Yellow Wolf drew a barrage of Crow fire and took a flesh wound to his thigh. But his heart was big with anger, and he did not feel his wound. He was glad he had killed the Crow traitor. He jumped upon his horse and wheeled around just as his mount took a gunshot wound to its neck, grazing its mane. It was a fast horse, even faster when fired by the adrenaline of panic, and man and horse charged out of the maelstrom, leaving his playmate-turned-enemy dead behind him.

Flying Horse and Fire Bear stayed with the rear guard as they moved up the ravines. The smoke from the discharging carbines lingered so thick that they had to wait for pockets of air to spot the positions of their enemies. Flying Horse spied a group of Crow riding hard in a gully below her.

They galloped past her unseen, and she urged Alla after them at a full gallop. She gained on them and leveled her Winchester, hoping that when they rode out of the gulch, she would surprise them from behind.

She shot a Crow off his horse and fired again, hitting a horse in the shoulder, sending it crashing on top of its rider. By now a Crow had seen her, but she was at an advantage being behind them. She shot again, hitting a warrior off his horse. She aimed at the lead horse, hoping to bring it down. But several Crow bullets zinged past her, ripping a flesh wound in her arm. Another Crow fell as Fire Bear thwarted the last enemy rider.

Fire Bear galloped up to her, his face dark. "Flying Horse, your father is hurt!"

Together they galloped back to the milling thicket of refugees. Tall Tree had been fighting alongside other warriors at the rear guard, and a Crow bullet had hit him in the abdomen. It was a bad wound, bleeding profusely and very painful. Tall Tree was still conscious but fading fast. Flying Horse jumped off her horse and ran to her father.

"There is nothing you can do, daughter. Go fight," he whispered. "They need you."

Flying Horse looked at Fire Bear and nodded at him to go fight. But she stayed with her father, afraid he might die without her at his side. His abdomen was hemorrhaging great gouts of blood and emitted the rank smell of torn and damaged intestines. The Indians recognized the odor as coming death, for it spread poison throughout the body.

Flying Horse pushed Tall Tree gently on his side, afraid of what she would see. The rifle slug had ripped a huge hole of mangled flesh; shattered bone and torn intestines bulged from Tall Tree's back. In the white man's genius for designing killing devices, the new rifled bullet expanded out in ragged flanges on impact and spiraled through flesh, ripping and twisting with devastating efficiency.

Flying Horse ran to a pack animal and pulled from it a buffalo robe and her mother's pouches of herbs. She dragged her father on the robe back behind a boulder to dress the wound and tore a swath of Mrs. Porter's calico fabric for bandages. She worked fast to mend her father's wound as best she could so he could ride. Her heart ached, wishing her mother were still alive, for Sings Like Lark was a natural healer and would have patched up her father more gently. Flying Horse made a poultice from creek water with a concoction of ground chamomile, witch hazel, and yarrow. Chamomile helped prevent infection and pain. Witch hazel and yarrow checked hemorrhaging.

She poured water on the wound to clean it, removed embedded fragments of the lead bullet, and stuffed the poultice into the wound, then wrapped the calico around her father's torso. By now he was fading in and out of consciousness, and Flying Horse raced against her fear.

Finally, she took a horn spoon and mixed ground willow bark, mugwort, and chamomile with water. She lifted Tall Tree and coaxed him to drink the potion for his pain. Flying Horse grabbed a horse with a special high-backed saddle that had belonged to a Crow warrior killed by Nez Perce. The saddles were used to transport the badly wounded because traveling with travois slowed their retreat. The wounded were tied upright in the saddles so that even when unconscious, the group could maintain a blistering pace. Such travel was so painful and jarring that many died in transit, but the Nez Perce would not leave their wounded behind.

Flying Horse rode up the steep slopes of the ravine, leading her father's horse through the chaos. Nez Perce sharpshooters held off the soldiers long enough for the massive herd and human caravan to scale the mountainside to the plains.

Evening was coming, and the gulches and cutbacks filled with shadow. Sturgis was forced to make camp. The next morning, troops found the canyon path barricaded with brush, fallen trees, rocks, and dead horses, rendering it impassable. Again the Indians had found uncanny refuge in the land and outsmarted him.

Sturgis's only consolation was that the Indians in their haste had abandoned 400 of their most exhausted or lame horses. Sturgis had promised the Crow their pick of any animals they could wrest from the Nez Perce. Like the Nimiipuu, the Crow coveted fine horses, especially Nez Perce Appaloosas. Throughout five months of fighting and forced marches over brutal terrain, the Nez Perce horses had consistently outdistanced the Army's freshest, finest mounts.

The animals left behind were gaunt, broken shadows of their former magnificence. But the Crow were jubilant. When they drove the herd to the Crow reservation and others saw their new wealth, more Crow were persuaded to join the whites.

Sturgis pursued the Nez Perce for two more days, but the Indians outdistanced them. With his troops exhausted and their horses spent—100 mounts, a quarter of their total number, had been killed or wounded—the colonel reluctantly gave up the chase.

The Nez Perce trekked doggedly across the Montana north, now less than 200 miles from the Canadian border and freedom. They saw large herds of buffalo and antelope and elk. At night they watched the northern lights striate in sugared waves across the sky. They beat their drums solemnly, keening in chant a final goodbye to their ancestral lands. And they remembered how it had been before the white man had dragged their world beyond the edge of the sky and taken it from them.

FIFTY NINE

AMONG SOARING EAGLES

AFTER ESCAPING Sturgis's columns at Canyon Creek, the Nez Perce traveled fast across the plains, covering seventy-five miles in thirty-six hours. They numbered about 700, including 250 warriors and some 30 badly wounded on travois or horseback. Their horse herd had dwindled to 1,600 horses—many killed or wounded or too lame to sustain the punishing pace. They wildered on, forced hard against a cold north wind under a bleak, indifferent sky. They climbed to high, sharded country carved out by the upper Missouri and flanked by wind-sculpted gulches and jagged cliffs of red stone. The Nez Perce called it Attish Pah, "Cave of Red Paint."

The Nimiipuu came upon a military supply depot at Cow Island, where a small detachment of US soldiers guarded fifty tons of freight. It was late September. The depot was well stocked with food, home goods, machinery, ammunition, and niceties like fabric, clothing, and tobacco. Two Nez Perce warriors rode up to the depot to buy food, but the sergeant offered only a side of bacon and a half bag of hardtack.

Insulted by the niggardly gesture, the Indians began looting the supplies. The sergeant and his guards made a hasty retreat, lest they become part of the carnage.

Despite the chiefs' entreaties, young braves gathered foodstuffs and ammunition and tied bolts of fabric to their horses' tails and ran about the prairie, unraveling the cloth in colorful streamers. The women replenished their larders, which had been desperately depleted at the Big Hole battle. They gathered flour, bacon, beans, and coffee, and loaded cooking utensils, pots, and fabric for bandages onto their pack animals.

What the braves did not want they burned, including 500 sacks of bacon, which ignited in terrific sizzling until the fire leapt so high it could be seen for miles and the smell of frying pork fat filled the prairie. Despite the raucous behavior of the braves Chief White Bird admonished as "bad boys," no soldiers were hurt. They huddled in their rifle pits throughout the night, the reflections of the inferno dancing upon their terrified faces.

The Nimiipuu caravan swam their horses across the Missouri, now ice cold and freezing at its edges from the cold Klondike Chinook winds. They pitched camp two miles upstream near Cow Creek. The brutal pace had caused great suffering among the wounded, and five had died during travel. Flying Horse and Fire Bear, with other warriors, volunteered to stay behind with several dozen wounded, including her father. They would follow the trail of the main body and hope that the US forces would not overtake them.

Flying Horse watched the large caravan depart until it was only a thin line on the northern horizon. She wondered if she would ever see her people again.

Flying Horse and Fire Bear set up a tipi and bedded down for the night with the other warriors and wounded. She re-dressed her father's wounds, tried to pour some water down his throat, and covered him in a buffalo robe, even though he was burning up with fever and his face beaded in sweat. Flying Horse was grateful her father's pain was masked by deep sleep, but she knew he was dying.

She woke to her father calling out in the night. He mourned in his unconscious sleep, outstretching his hand toward a restless phantom—his dead wife or his lost home, Flying Horse did not know. His arm dropped. His chest rose mightily, then rattled and was still. Her father was finally free of pain.

But a frenzied panic shook her. Her father was gone. Lost forever. She put her hand on his cheek and sat in stony silence, tears running down her cheeks until Fire Bear woke at dawn.

Together, they dug a grave. The ground was already frozen, and it was hard work digging with bone tools. Flying Horse's heart was riven with bitterness: she could not lay her father's bones next to her mother, who lay alone, her limbs stiff in the frozen earth in a strange land, far beyond the hoary, naked horizon.

They wrapped Tall Tree in a blanket—buffalo robes were saved for the wounded—but she could not cover his face, knowing she would never look upon it again. Fire Bear put his hand on hers, then covered Tall Tree himself.

With her father dead, there was nothing to hold them to the ragged group of wounded, so Flying Horse and Fire Bear volunteered to scout the southern reaches for soldiers, Bannock, and Shoshone enemy. From Yellowstone north, Nez Perce scouts reported seeing more and more tribes join the whites to pursue them. First the Sioux and Cheyenne, then even their old friends the Crow. Now, in north country, Bannock and Shoshone, longtime nemeses of the Nez Perce. It seemed all were against the Nimiipuu, and their hearts were heavy. Still, they pushed on, Canada their only refuge.

The Bannock were especially vicious fighters, scalping and mutilating the dead and wearing the scalps, fingers, and other macabre mementos of their coup. General Howard employed many Bannock but was appalled by their mutilations of Nez Perce dead on the Big Hole battlefield, even disinterring women's and children's bodies for booty and scalps.

Fire Bear and Flying Horse made their way west on the Missouri River, searching for signs of soldiers from Fort Benton and enemy scouts. From the towering cliffs above the Missouri, they spied a ribbon of riders on a far horizon. As they advanced, Fire Bear saw that they were Bannock dressed in battle garb, as many as twenty warriors.

Fire Bear and Flying Horse mulled what to do. The bluffs afforded them excellent cover for an ambush. The pursuers would have to cross at a landing where the river was broad but relatively shallow and less treacherous. They could surprise the band as they crossed with no cover. They thought they could pick off most of them.

Fire Bear now carried a Winchester repeating rifle and a Colt .44 revolver—both Army issue, taken from a dead soldier—as well as several cartridge belts slung over his shoulders and a parfleche of cartridge boxes tied to his Indian saddle. Flying Horse carried her Winchester Yellow Boy and a rawhide bag heavy with her own cartridges. Between the two they had more than enough ammunition to dispose of the Bannock riding from the west.

Flying Horse and Fire Bear turned their horses and rode back along the cliff, keeping below the Bannocks' line of sight. They rode to a point overlooking the place where they would ford the river. They decided to split up on two different cliffs to confuse the enemy and make their numbers appear greater than they were.

Flying Horse dismounted and pulled several cartridge boxes from the rawhide bag. She handed them to Fire Bear. "Use them well, husband."

He reached down and touched her cheek. "I married a fine warrior. An eagle in a woman's body," he said. "I have often wondered how pleasant our lives would have been living in peace at Wallowa. But it is not to be."

"We will live in peace again, but in Canada," she said. She mounted Alla, and both wheeled their horses in opposite directions. Flying Horse rode a hundred yards, then dismounted and lay behind some rocks to wait. She took some cartridges from the box, opened the breech of her gun, and began filling it one by one. She was ready.

She raised her head slightly and peered through the rocks, watching the Indians approach the pass, now perhaps a quarter mile from the river. She and Fire Bear would wait until the party was out in the middle of the river before starting to fire. Fire Bear would take the leaders, Flying Horse the last riders. They had thirty shots between them before they would need to reload. They had to make them count. They could not let any riders get away without at least shooting their horses out from under them.

Flying Horse propped the Yellow Boy between two rocks and peered through the sights. She had learned its feel—the burnished walnut stock gracefully curved so that it nestled in the crook of her arm, the brass-clad butt that rested against her shoulder, the comforting, clean click of each cartridge as she loaded it into the gleaming brass receiver. It felt like security itself. She aimed at the middle of the river, imagining her targets.

It was afternoon, and the sun shimmered on the water's surface, but the sun was behind her and would not obscure her aim. Rain had left the pungent scent of wet sage, like her mother's herbal pouches. She felt a trickle of saliva in her mouth and a thin line of sweat on her upper lip.

The breeze high up on the cliff felt cool. Her body readied itself for battle. She yearned for the riders within her gunsights.

The faint talking and laughing of the Indians below drifted closer. They came into view, and she breathed deeply and waited. Bannocks. Her heart flared with hate. *Ten, eleven, twelve,* she counted, and they kept coming. The first two had reached the water's edge, and the horses plunged into the current. *Fourteen, fifteen, sixteen.* Sixteen of them, strung out three or four abreast. The leaders were approaching the middle of the river. Fire Bear had told Flying Horse to wait for his first shot. She drew a bead on the last rider as his horse lurched down the bank into the water.

Fire Bear's rifle shot cracked the air, echoing off the high cliffs. Flying Horse pulled the grooved trigger of her rifle and sent her first shot true to its target. The last rider toppled into the water and floated lifeless below his horse. She felt the satisfaction of the kill.

She cocked her rifle and ejected the spent shell and aimed again. Her second shot, too, hit her target. The rider fell backward into the water as his horse reared in panic. Now the riders began to mill around, uncertain if they should make a run for the far bank or turn around. In only seconds, Fire Bear and Flying Horse had downed five enemy, and they continued firing methodically: aiming, shooting, cocking, aiming again, their breathing timed to the rhythm of their shooting.

The leaders scrambled for the far bank. Flying Horse could see that Fire Bear's aim was indeed deadly. A trail of bodies floated across the river, horses lunging riderless up the far bank. One rider had managed to crouch low behind his horse while the horse was swimming, and Fire Bear, not wanting to waste any bullets, shot the horse near its spine in an effort to down the animal and perhaps hit the rider too. The horse screamed and reared up, kicking the water, and fell to its side on top of the rider. The rider resurfaced several feet from the carcass of the horse, limp on the water.

Flying Horse had killed or badly maimed at least five now. She shot two horses to keep riders from reaching cover. Her eyes scanned the river, waiting for the warriors to bob up. They would have to climb the bank and run across open ground for cover if she didn't get them in the water. The crown of a head emerged near the bank. She aimed and fired. Seconds later, the body bobbed to the surface.

Several riders had dismounted to swim behind their horses for cover. Flying Horse shot the horses and waited for the riders to surface. She had six cartridges left before she had to reload. She now saw riders slogging up the river's edge and galloping to cover behind rocks. Others who'd lost their mounts were running for cover too. She shot into their midst, managing to kill one and wound another, but others had made it to safety.

She was reloading her rifle when shots rang out. They had not come from the river but from the rocks below. And Fire Bear had not answered them. Alarmed, she hurriedly finished loading her gun, then jumped on Alla. Galloping toward Fire Bear's position, she spotted several enemy warriors riding up the rocks.

She pulled Alla to a rearing stop at Fire Bear's position, but he was not there. Then she saw blood splattered on the rocks. She jumped off to find him crumpled below on a ledge, a bullet in his chest. His eyes were still open, and he looked up at her and tried to speak. She scrambled down the rocks to him, pulling him to her.

"Go!" he whispered hoarsely. "They are coming! I will die soon."

She knew what he said was true, but she would not leave him. His eyes were full of love, then suddenly pride. His mouth curled gently into a smile, like peace to a parting soul. His eyes flickered. "An eagle in a woman's body. Fly, my eagle!"

She held him in her arms, chanting in choked notes his death song. Her tears fell on his handsome face. The cliff was his stony catafalque. She could not give him an honorable burial, but in her fierce covenant she would not let the Bannocks defile his sacred body. She kissed him, touched his cheek. Then she rolled him over the edge, releasing him like a mountain stream tumbling toward a greater current, a slipstream to eternity. Her love was liquid fire pouring from her heart, falling with his body into the river below.

She heard hooves rough upon stone. Her spirit was numb, but she scratched her way up the rocks, grabbed her rifle, and ran to Alla. The Bannock whooped and screamed 300 feet behind her, stripped for battle and painted in colors so bright they seemed phantasms of a nightmare. She pressed Alla, and he exploded into a full gallop up the rocky path.

Higher they went, the Bannocks behind her, yelling war chants. She looked frantically for cover, for a place to make a stand. She was looking over her shoulder when Alla suddenly came to a stop, falling back on his haunches. She looked forward and saw that the path had run out: they faced the maw of a thousand-foot drop.

Her instincts told her what she must do, even as fear denied her fate. She wheeled around and readied her rifle. The Bannocks came charging up the path, and she fired into them. One rider fell. She cocked her rifle again and pulled the trigger. But many rifles were aimed at her, smoking with savage fire. A bullet hit her in the shoulder and nearly knocked her off Alla. Another hit her stomach. Still she fired, her body going through the motions of a warrior. But her spirit wandered, searched. Time seemed long. Lingering.

She thought of her mother, Sings Like Lark, and her father, Tall Tree; she thought of Sorrel, whom she had left behind; of Fire Bear—fine, gallant Fire Bear. Her fierce love burned for his bones, his heart, his smile.

Flying Horse looked to the sky and began a low mournful chant in Nimiipuu: "*Neiz uetes*, Mother Earth; take me in your arms."

She turned Alla and looked down into the abyss. She felt strangely alive, exhilarated—filled with the truth of the place. All seemed close and vivid beyond life. She squeezed her thighs gently around her horse's ribs. He gathered himself, shifting his hooves at the edge, unsure, then plunged into the air. Even in this, her last request of her warhorse, he did not falter in courage. And her chest wrung at his brave heart.

They touched the sky. One moment of the earth, the next passing through a veil beyond knowing, the sky embracing their souls. They soared, her arms clinging to Alla's neck, their fearless souls bound. A bald eagle rose above them, lifting them. Her wyakin was with them. Their warrior hearts were strong and good. And there was honor in it. She hugged her body tight around Alla and whispered into his ears through the high-cliffed wind: "Hokahey, nayaz, hokahey." My brother, today is a good day to die.

SIXTY

WINTER OF DESPAIR

THE NEZ PERCE refugees had traveled ceaselessly north and were now only days from the Canadian border. By night they camped in the treeless swells before the Bear Paw Mountains, girdled by shallow bluffs that gave meager cover from the winds and driving snow. The grassy landscape offered only sage and willows as poor firewood. Buffalo chips were good fuel and plentiful but frozen and took much effort to chip from the hard ground. The people were exhausted.

But hands borrowed from the years, their ancestors reaching through the cold, gave strength. They were so near the border that they could taste freedom, and their white pursuers lay far behind. At last, they would be free.

Chief Lean Elk, who knew the territory well, drove the people hard. The horses were so footsore they could barely walk. Five months of grueling travel with meager forage had reduced them to racks of bones. Spine sprung and ewe necked, their once beautiful lines were no longer the taut geometry of fine horseflesh. Rib cages gaunt as rake tines hung from spines like sagging axles. Many suffered festering battle wounds. Each day, more horses were left behind, unable to keep up.

Looking Glass, who had fallen out of favor after his disastrous judgment at Big Hole, again urged the chiefs to rest a bit, that Howard's army was days behind. Pushing the people so hard brought undue suffering, death, and great loss of horses, he argued. They desperately needed meat for coming winter, and the Bear Paw abounded in buffalo and antelope.

After council of chiefs and warriors, they decided to slow their pace through the Bear Paw so they could hunt and butcher meat and doctor the wounded. But Lean Elk, who felt they should not rest and were in danger as long as they were south of the Medicine Line, left the council in disgust: "We must save ourselves! We will not be safe until we reach Canada! Hear my words: if we rest now, our people will die!"

On September 28, the Nimiipuu camped at the northern flank of the Bear Paw, only thirty miles from the Canadian border. The cold arctic wind whipped across the bleak land. The people set up their lodges in deep coulees along the Snake River.

The Nez Perce scouts were correct in their pronouncements: the nearest armies were days behind them. But they did not know General Howard had realized he could not catch the Nez Perce before they reached Canada. So he telegraphed an order to Colonel Nelson A. Miles several hundred miles northeast, who had nearly 800 men. There was a chance that Miles could head off the fugitives and hold them until Howard caught up.

Colonel Miles was an ambitious officer married to General Sherman's niece. He hoped to be promoted to brigadier general. Decorated at Antietam, Appomattox, Chancellorsville, and Fredericksburg and a seasoned officer of Indian campaigns, he was in charge of crushing the Sioux and Northern Cheyenne after Custer's disastrous end. Now came his biggest challenge ever, and he was hell-bent for success. His men thought him a glory seeker like Custer, but they also knew he was competent and ruthless.

In addition to Miles's veteran soldiers, he had forty wagons, a mule train with a month's worth of supplies and ammunition, and two large cannons loaded on ferries to cross the Yellowstone River. He began a forced four-day march 200 miles west, then north, hot on the Nez Perce trail. Cannons and wagons were left behind to follow so as not to impede their speed. The terrain, mostly rolling hills and prairie, was easily traversed. They made excellent time.

On September 30, Miles's scouts spied a group of Nez Perce hunters running buffalo. They waited for the hunters to ride back to their camp and trailed them. Miles's massive column rode overnight to be ready for a morning attack on the Indian camp.

Frederick was reading the Idaho City *World* about his old friend Chief Joseph and his struggle when the telegraph boy walked into his studio. The boy handed him a telegraph: "It requires your urgent answer, sir."

The message was from Colonel Miles, requesting Frederick's immediate services. The colonel anticipated he might be on the receiving end of the surrender of one of the nation's most infamous renegade Indian chiefs. Miles wanted the historic event photographed for posterity. *And for his own career*, Frederick mused sourly. The colonel suggested Frederick take the steamboat up the Missouri to Fort Benton. From there, soldiers would escort him to the Bear Paw. Time was crucial. Miles demanded immediate confirmation.

Frederick's blood rushed in a turmoil of emotions—excitement, guilt, fear, anxiety. How could he photograph the ultimate humiliation of such an honorable and dignified man? How could he betray his friend Joseph? How could he break trust with Ollokot, whom he had photographed in Spotted Horse with his brother? He had photographed Flying Horse and Fire Bear at their wedding on a mountain cliff just a year before. How could he forsake them?

And yet his government—his *country*—asked this of him. He had not served in the Civil War when every family in the nation had sacrificed. Was he going to shirk his service now? Was it not his patriotic duty?

He thought of Two Head Otter, the proud father of Storm Horse. Surely, both father and son were now fighting for their survival with Chief Joseph. And the little Nimiipuu children he had photographed with their pets—how many of them were dead?

But how could he refuse to photograph one of the most significant historic events of his lifetime? He was a photographer, was he not? This was his living, and his legacy. If he refused, he would never get another government assignment again.

He grappled between guilt and opportunity, duty and shame, searching for middle ground. Finally, he pounced on expediency. Wouldn't it be prudent, honorable even, if *he* was the photographer rather than someone unsympathetic, a stranger who reveled in Joseph's humiliation? Frederick would portray Joseph in a dignified manner. Surely Joseph would understand that this was history. That this was Frederick's job.

The telegraph boy cleared his throat. "Will there be an answer, sir?"

The bronzed faces of Joseph, Flying Horse, Fire Bear came to him, haunted him. *Quick, you must decide.* In his mind's eye, Frederick saw his photograph engravings in newspapers across the country: *The San Francisco Chronicle*, *The New York Times*. He had been born for this day. Fate had chosen him. He shut out the faces in his head. Pushed away his guilt to a disembodied place far back in his mind. He turned to the boy.

"Send this answer: 'Yes. Will come to the Bear Paw posthaste. On my way.'"

While Frederick was in transit to the Bear Paw, Colonel Miles's columns reached the Snake River and, under the cover of darkness, made camp only two miles east of the Nimiipuu refugees.

The next morning at dawn, Miles saw from a distance the Indian herd milling. He feared the Nez Perce had seen the troops. About a mile from the encampment, he ordered his trumpeter to blow "double quick" and yelled, "Charge! Damn them!"

With that, the men shouted excitedly, and 800 troops broke into full attack.

Indeed, the Nez Perce scouts had frantically warned the people troops were coming. They barely had opportunity to grab rifles and cartridge belts and run into the hills. Warriors took their posts just in time to see a cloud of ominous dust behind a flood of horses and soldiers thundering toward them across the plains. The sound was like the rumble of a mighty buffalo herd.

At 200 yards, the Nez Perce braves opened fire, and the massive column shattered in the deadly volley, horses crashing in spectacular falls and troops crumpling to the ground. The back columns drew rein and milled in confusion. Smoke lingered on the battlefield from hundreds of guns, yellow flashes pocking the haze. Soon the soldiers retreated in the withering fire. Within minutes, the Nez Perce had repulsed the charge.

Off to the west, however, an attack by the Second Cavalry broadsided the camp and crashed into the Nez Perce horse herd, stampeding the animals. Chief Joseph had already ordered warriors to drive the horses away from the soldiers, but there was no time. The cavalry whipped the sickly beasts brutally into pathetic gallops, effectively cutting the Indians off from their horses.

Before the attack, about 100 horses had already been packed to begin the day's trek north, with many more secured as mounts. Joseph ordered those who could not fight to make a run for Canada and Sitting Bull's protection. Sound of Running Feet, Joseph's eldest and most favored daughter, was helping her father prepare for the day's march when they spotted the wave of soldiers a mile off. Joseph grabbed a big paint for his daughter.

"Ride fast, daughter! Ride to freedom!" He hugged her hard, then lifted her onto the horse. He looked up at her and wondered if this would be his last look at his beloved daughter.

Running Feet pleaded: "I want to stay here with you, Toe-ta. I want to fight."

Joseph was touched by his daughter's bravery. "Daughter, help those riding to Sitting Bull's camp. If you are safe in the north, my heart will be full. Be free of the white man."

His heart was glad that his daughter would escape. But now he saw that the soldiers had split the village nearly in half, and he was cut off from his wife with the baby and little children. Armed only with resolve, he grabbed a horse and charged through a smoking gauntlet. Bullets sang in his ears and tore through his buckskin shirt. His charger was grazed in the shoulder and stumbled. Still, he was not hurt. He reached the lodge to find his wife shooting at the soldiers, unafraid: "Here is your gun. Fight, husband!"

The fighting was furious and close range. Joseph saw several Nez Perce killed before his eyes. He rallied the men to drive back the invading soldiers, and white and red men tangled in a swirling, bloody melee. The soldiers wilted in the ferocious onslaught and ran. Joseph and his people quickly gathered guns and ammunition from the dead.

On higher ground in the hills, Ollokot, Lean Elk, Lone Bird, Toohoolhoolzote, Pile of Clouds, and others were ensconced in gullies. They let loose a deadly fusillade that stopped Miles's charge and sent veteran troops scattering in chaos.

But the toll for such bravery was deadly: one by one, all five warriors were hit and lay dead in the cutbanks. Ollokot, Lean Elk, Lone Bird, and two medicine men—Pile of Clouds and Toohoolhoolzote—who had foreseen their own deaths in dreams.

Ollokot's wife, Wetatonmi, ran to Joseph. He saw in her face the terrible truth. "Our Ollokot is gone," she sobbed. Petite and beautiful, she was also brave of heart and admired in the tribe. She had been well matched with her handsome husband.

"I am sorry, sister." He touched her shoulder. "A mighty warrior." He choked out the words but could speak no more. She saw in his eyes a ragged, broken grief, and her heart ached for him and for their people.

Joseph had not the luxury of honoring his brother's memory, but he helped carry Ollokot's body from the rifle pit to his lodge. Wetatonmi wept with her husband's head in her lap. She stroked his hair even as bullets ripped through her tipi. Joseph saw that she did not care; she did not fear death. He left to fight but saw her gather water at the creek, although it was dangerous to do so. He knew she was bathing Ollokot for burial.

Miles had sustained serious casualties, and many soldiers lay dead or dying, littering the plain. He retreated to wait for Howard's reinforcement, but his troops continued to fire on the Nez Perce from the far bluffs.

While Nimiipuu braves gathered their dead and guns and ammunition from the battlefield, the women dug graves in the far bank away from the battle. The wailing women, covered with dirt and blood, dragged the blanketed bodies of twenty warriors, women, and children to the graves. Ollokot was placed in the grave first, his head toward the east. Wetatonmi chanted a death song as she covered him with dirt and small boulders. Together, they covered the bones of women and children, the bones of warriors.

Wetatonmi's heart burned, but her husband spoke to her from the grave: "Do not linger, wife! Fight for your people!" She swallowed hard and ran to the battlefield. Drawing fire all the while, she collected ammunition and guns from fallen soldiers, running as if she did not exist inside her skin. Longing only to be with Ollokot in the earth with his body, in the sky with his spirit.

Night pulled frigid darkness over the battlefield. Joseph asked Wetatonmi to help the women and children escape on the packed horses. Nearly 300 refugees, many wounded, were secreted away in the darkness by Chief White Bird.

Before Wetatonmi rode into the dark, she bid Joseph adieu and told him that she would watch over his daughter, already on her way to Canada. They embraced in deep sorrow that their family should be ripped asunder like an oak's roots in a whirlwind.

The remaining Nez Perce once again found refuge in the land. A broad coulee flanked on both sides by deep slopes provided the people a protected avenue to the hills. While warriors fought, the remaining women and children carried utensils, guns, tools, even bayonets taken from enemy troops, into the ridges. Through the dogged night, they dug entrenchments and rifle pits so warriors could move from ravine to ravine. There could be no campfires that would draw gunfire. Their work became even harder as the cold north wind whipped up and snow began to fall.

Women used camas hooks, butcher knives, and bayonets to dig while children and the old emptied the dirt on top of saddles and dead horses to build barricades above the trenches. In this manner they dug forty breastworks and fifteen long rifle pits.

Babies and toddlers huddled asleep under furs in tipis as their mothers and siblings toiled through the bitter night. When dawn broke, the hands of the diggers were raw, but their hearts were strong to see the deep pits that would give their warriors protection.

Miles's army had improved its positions as well. Their scouts had noted the activity in the folds of the hills far away but were unable to get close enough to the coulees without becoming targets for Nez Perce sharpshooters. They resolved to reposition the Hotchkiss breech-loading gun, a prototype and the first of its kind, which could shoot a devastating two-pound explosive percussion shell 1,500 feet. They pointed the big gun straight at the ravines and pits where the Nimiipuu huddled.

The next morning, five inches of snow carpeted the ground and shrouded the broken, frozen bodies of dead soldiers and horses left twisted where they had fallen. Sharp cracks of gun reports echoed into frigid nothingness, and a haze of gunpowder blanketed the wasted prairie like a funeral pall.

SIXTY ONE

DUSK OF A DREAM

THE NEXT DAY, Miles's mule train of ammunition and cannons arrived. Among them was a monster, a bronze Napoleon cannon drawn by a team of six mules. It weighed 1,200 pounds, and the murderous maw of its barrel threatened destruction of the blackest kind. This cannon, Miles ordered, should be positioned directly on the noncombatant Nez Perce trenches.

The soldiers began firing the cannons. The shells from the Hotchkiss and Napoleon ripped ragged black craters in the bald shell of the earth, and the ground quaked with new terror as the Nez Perce crouched in their trenches. But their deep earthen breastworks proved steadfast against heavy artillery.

The lone Nez Perce sentries scattered along their rifle pits were impregnable islands of resistance too. The sharpshooters' deadly accuracy once again impressed white soldiers. The Nez Perce strategy of targeting buglers and officers was especially lethal.

"Any insignia of rank was a death warrant," Portland's *Daily Standard* reported. Sergeants suffered the highest casualties; eight died at the Bear Paw. "Those Indians were the best shots I ever saw," Miles's lead scout, Louis Shambo, was quoted.

As a result of the Nez Perce's punishing aim, the field surgeons were overwhelmed doctoring the wounded. Newspapers quoted Dr. Henry Tilton: "The Nez Perce marksmanship was excellent, and from the opening fight, we had our hands full." The standard treatment was dressing, bandaging, and a stiff drink of brandy and opium.

But Joseph's warriors fared far worse. The people's store of bandages, herbal medicines, poultices, and painkillers had long been depleted. Even basic comforts like blankets and furs were dwindling and used for the children. Campfires could not be lit. On both sides, many wounded could not be rescued and suffered frostbite or froze to death.

Snow fell on the open eyes of the dead, melting first from the fading warmth of life, finally freezing in crystalline hulls, like frosted marbles. From a trench, Young Willow gazed out at her dead husband, who lay not far from her on the open field. She cried to see the snow take the sight from his dark, once smiling eyes. She waited until his eyes were eerie cataracts of ice, then turned away into the pit, alone with her tears.

White soldiers stranded near Nez Perce positions were terrified the enemy would come in the night to finish them off and mutilate them. But their fears were unfounded. Some wounded soldiers were visited by Nez Perce, but none were harmed. One disabled sergeant testified later that he had his revolver ready when approached, but the brave spoke to him in

English, assuring him he would not be harmed but that he must hand over his arms. A warrior gave another wounded soldier a bladder of water after relieving him of his gun and cartridge belt. Several soldiers lived to tell of their kindly treatment by their enemies, their accounts published in newspapers.

The long lulls in shooting prompted bizarre colloquies across the killing expanse. Late in the afternoon, an Army scout fluent in Nez Perce yelled out a challenge: "Come out and fight, you bastards!" A Nez Perce warrior answered in plain English: "You come! Try to take our hair!"

Warriors overheard Miles yell to his men, "Charge them to hell!" A Nez Perce adept in English cursing taunted: "Charge, hell! You sons o' bitches! You aren't fighting goddamned Sioux!" Nimiipuu laughter and whoops erupted from rifle pits across the hillside.

After two days fighting in plummeting temperatures and driving snow, they were at an impasse. Both feared the other had reinforcements coming. The Nez Perce worried that Howard would arrive soon, and the whites imagined the dreaded Sitting Bull would come from his camp just north of the Canadian border to aid his red brethren.

At one point, a murmur arose among the Nez Perce warriors: "Look there! Horses! Sitting Bull!"

The soldiers panicked. "We were very anxious until we determined they were buffalo marching in single file with all the precision of soldiers," Army surgeon Dr. Tilton was quoted. The humps and faces of the buffalo had been covered in snow, creating the illusion of spotted horses.

Chief Looking Glass, believing they were Sitting Bull's warriors, stood up in his rifle pit for an instant, and a white sharpshooter shot him dead with a single bullet to the forehead.

With Looking Glass dead, White Bird gone to Canada, and all the other chiefs killed, Joseph was the last remaining chief, and his heart was heavy.

Meanwhile, Miles was racked with worry that Sitting Bull *would* come to Joseph's aid. He was nearly as troubled that General Howard would arrive and take the glory of defeating Chief Joseph for himself. Both scenarios prompted Miles to take action.

He sent a soldier with a white flag and a message that he wished to talk to Chief Joseph. A warrior named Yellow Bull rode out and took the message back to Joseph. They held quick council. Most were fearful, pointing out that other tribes—the Spokane, Palouse, Yakima—had been imprisoned, then hanged, under a white flag. But Joseph wanted to buy time in hopes Sitting Bull would come.

Joseph, with several warriors following, rode out to meet Miles in a hollow. The warriors trained their guns on Miles as insurance he would not hurt their chief. Miles asked Joseph to surrender. The chief answered that he would not surrender but that he wished to return to the Wallowa to live in peace. Miles told him that he could return to his homeland, but only under unconditional surrender. No agreement was made, and Joseph returned to camp.

The white flag stayed up. Gunfire ceased. The no-man's-land between the opposing camps was strewn with carnage, the craters of exploded shells, and dead and wounded, both white and red. Both sides buried their dead and retrieved their freezing and wounded in the field. Many dead horses remained splayed on the battlefield, the slow crumble of their bones into the ground their only eulogy.

Miles and Joseph attempted another council. But Joseph suspected Miles had called a truce only to gain information about the Nez Perce condition. Second Lieutenant Lovell Jerome accompanied Miles and reconnoitered Nez Perce entrenchments: warriors were well armed with Winchester and Henry rifles, "three guns each, including a repeating rifle for close-range."

Frederick arrived on the fourth day of fighting, accompanied by a cadre of six soldiers from Fort Benton. He had seen battlefields before, but never during the throes of slaughter. He was horrified by the many corpses discarded like the dross of death, covered only by indifferent snow.

The unsteady truce did not last. Miles finally surrounded Joseph's camp with a thin skirmish line. The Nez Perce were essentially under siege. Artillery fire continued in raw, blustery weather. On the fifth day, the big Napoleon gun landed a shell in a Nimiipuu pit shelter, exploding and burying four women, a small boy, and a twelve-year-old girl. The people dug furiously to uncover them, but the girl and her grandmother were found dead.

At dusk, riders appeared on the southern horizon. The Nez Perce knew it could not be Sitting Bull. Indeed, it was General Howard, and Joseph lost hope that Sitting Bull would come. His people were freezing and starving. The wounded suffered terribly. Their refugee spirits were raw nubs. Sleep brought no escape from the living nightmare.

Joseph found himself held by what was but pulled by what could never be. He struggled in his heart. How did the shining legacy of his people come to this? Robbed of the land that was part of them, it seemed they had ceased to be themselves. How was it that all the great chiefs were dead and so many fine people, old and young, lay in shallow graves or dying, mangled in the cold? His heart was sick, for he knew the only thing left to do was the thing he could not do.

On Friday, October 5, the sixth day of battle, General Howard ran up a white flag again and told Joseph that he and his people could return to their homeland in spring if they ceased fighting and gave up their weapons.

Joseph rode out to the foot of the bluff on his stallion, followed by several braves on foot. Miles and Howard were waiting for him. He dismounted and with quiet, erect pride walked directly to General Howard. Towering over the officer, he held out his Winchester carbine in surrender. He had many graze wounds and bullet holes in his shirt and leggings. He tore from his tongue the bitter words he could not say.

Through an interpreter he spoke slowly, solemnly:

> Tell General Howard I know his heart. I am tired of fighting. Our chiefs are killed. Looking Glass is dead. Toohoolhoolzote is dead. The old men all dead. Ollokot, who led the young men, is dead. The little children are freezing to death. Some of my people have run away to the hills and have no blankets, no food. I want to have time to look for the children. Maybe I shall find them among the dead. Hear me, my chiefs! I am tired. My heart is sick and sad. From where the sun now stands, I will fight no more, forever.

Frederick had been standing behind the officers with his camera. The colonel turned and motioned for him to step forward. Joseph looked at Frederick, his face inscrutable, then nodded slightly. Frederick nodded back but felt sickened, shrinking in shame before the big, quiet chief. Frederick's thoughts seemed to taunt him: *I cower before this great man who stands at the brink of his lost Eden, clothed in blood and tattered rags and his own righteousness. And you, profiting from his ruin?* He set up his camera, fumbling, unworthy.

General Howard stepped away and allowed his subordinate, Colonel Miles, to stand alone with Chief Joseph. Frederick slunk under his shroud. In his camera he saw Joseph standing tall and solemn, his big hands crossed before him, the ends of his fingers blackened with frostbite. He had bullet grazes across his forehead and chest, and his buckskin shirt was shredded from gunfire.

Frederick wanted to run away. To shut his eyes. He tried to focus his viewfinder, but his eyes welled with tears, and the image blurred. He swiped them with his sleeve, closed his eyes and swallowed hard, and clicked the shutter. He was in the presence of greatness. In the presence of history. And unalterable tragedy.

The prisoners totaled 418, but only 27 were warriors, the rest women, children, elderly, and wounded. Although General Howard, Colonel Miles, and the American public did not know it, among the destitute prisoners was an old man whose father had been one of the most esteemed figures in American history, a white man who had altered the destiny of a nation and the fate of Native tribes of North America. Among the prisoners was Daytime Smoke, the aged son of the explorer William Clark. Seventy-two years before, the Nimiipuu had saved William Clark and Meriweather Lewis. They had not known that by doing so, they were embracing the ancient oracles' predictions: that their way of life would come to an end.

The victory had come at great cost to the Army, not only in lives but in the public's regard. The American press and public had come to admire the Nez Perce as a desperate, innocent people fighting valiantly against all odds for their existence.

Strategically, the Nez Perce had outmaneuvered, outfought, and outsmarted the Army and its most seasoned generals through 1,500 miles and eighteen engagements. Nez Perce strategies would come to be taught at West Point. The Nimiipuu and the "Red Napoleon" had been outnumbered and did not have the benefits of modern technology: telegraphs, trains, ferries, and, especially, modern weaponry.

In sheer numbers, both sides had suffered almost the same numbers of dead and wounded, but most Nez Perce dead were civilian women, children, and elderly. In terms of *fighting* men, the Army lost three times the casualties of the Nez Perce.

The battlefield was studded with the bodies of warhorses and Nez Perce dead in hoary, frozen repose. A people who had dared to be free. Thirty miles from the Canadian border and freedom, a 10,000-year-old culture gasped a death rattle on the windswept prairie. At the Bear Paw, Joseph saw the dusk of a dream swept into oblivion with snow fine as the dust of bones.

SIXTY TWO

BLOOD TO RUBIES

IT HAD BEEN FIVE YEARS since Sorrel had bid Flying Horse goodbye. She thought of her often and hoped with all her heart that she and Fire Bear were living free in Canada. In that time, Sorrel had happily watched her daughter grow to toddlerhood.

Sorrel stayed home doing chores while Ransom and Ella went to town in the buckboard to get supplies. They planned to stay overnight at the hotel. Sorrel was sharpening a plow blade when there was a knock on the barn door. She turned to see the most unexpected guest she could have imagined: Spotted Horse's black madam, Magnolia. She was not wearing her fancy flounces and elaborate hat but instead had donned a drab calico dress. Her face was more grim than her dress, and Sorrel thought something very dire indeed must have brought the woman to her farm.

Sorrel peered out to see Willie McGee sitting in his buckboard. Magnolia nodded back at him: "Mista Willie brought me out here. He not sech a bad sort." She gathered herself. "Miz Lanning, ah knows you don' know me, but ah need yo hep. Ah don' know where else to turn, septun' maybe miz Houston, but she live too far fo' me to go, and ah need hep now."

Magnolia explained that she knew Sorrel had helped the Blades woman escape her husband, but he was "up to no good again." A Chinese girl had come to the black madam's door—how on earth she got there, Magnolia did not know, for the child was nearly naked, covered with bruises. The girl asked if she could work for Magnolia, and the madam thought, *What I need with a little chile?* But when the girl told her she "be veddy, veddy good to man," Magnolia realized she was a boat girl, a prostitute.

Magnolia asked the girl where she'd come from. The girl dropped her eyes and wrung her hands, mute with fear. The madam could see the girl had been mistreated and was terrified she'd be sent back to the place she had escaped. Finally, after feeding and clothing her warmly, Magnolia got her to admit that Cornelius Blades had bought her in San Francisco. The little waif began to cry. Her twin sister was still with Blades. She was afraid he would kill her.

Sorrel already knew that she would help Magnolia and calculated in her head how long it would take to get to Blades's place. The homestead was about five miles away, and they would have to ride horseback, for the country was too rough for a surrey or buckboard.

"Can you go astride?" Sorrel asked.

"Ah brought ma old mule, Lester," Magnolia said. "He ain't much to look at, but ah keeps 'im around for ole time sake. He serve me well back when ah was po'."

"I'll go saddle my horse," Sorrel said. Sorrel and Magnolia lit out through the valley, around the base of a mountain, then across a stream. Lester proved to be a good trail mount, even carrying the amply fleshed Magnolia. Sorrel saw that Magnolia had packed a revolver, a Webley Bull Dog five-shot, which hung from her saddle horn in a holster. Sorrel brought her Winchester, knowing Blades would only respond to high-caliber coaxing.

The two women traveled together for nearly an hour in silence. Then Magnolia nudged Lester up abreast of Dagda and cleared her throat.

"What you do fo' Miz Blades, dat be mighty brave," she said. "Dat Blades, he a killer. He kilt so many folks, niggers an' yellow an' ah 'spect white too. He near kilt ma mama years ago. She was white an' nigger an' Cherokee, all mixed."

"He knew your mama?" Sorrel asked, turning to Magnolia, stunned.

"Well," Magnolia sighed, and she then took a deep breath as if the telling would take some effort. "Befo' de war, Blades be a slave trader, an' he bought ma mama at de auction. He beat her an' beat her and dishonor her sumtin' awful. An' den she get in de fambly way an' he near beat her dead an' want to cut dat baby right outa her belly. He sell her. Den I was born," Magnolia said. She suddenly seemed limp and small and slouched like a heap of rags on Lester. She looked straight ahead down the trail, avoiding Sorrel's stare.

"You mean Blades is your father?" Sorrel asked incredulously.

"Dat be de truth of it. He don' know. Ah wish it weren't so, Lord knows. 'Cuz ah woulda kilt 'im dead way back, but ah be afraid de Lord have a special punishment fo' de chile dat kill her own pa, no matter how bad he be. But he deserve to be dead. Ah don't know why de Lord see fit to let 'im live affer all de bad he done. Ah maybe kill 'im yet. But dey hang me fo' sho. A nigger whore killin' a white man. They'd come fo' miles to see big ole Magnolia hangin' from a rope. Now, dat be a sight!"

The big black madam began to chuckle. But the smile faded, and hardness dragged down her dark features.

Sorrel asked if Magnolia wanted to stay behind, but Magnolia insisted this was her fight too. "It 'bout time ah stood up to dat son of a bitch for what he done to my mama," she said. And her jaw tightened and her lower lip protruded in resolve.

They rode down to the front of the log cabin together and noticed the front door flapping open with the wind. Magnolia and Sorrel stepped into the doorway and reeled as a powerful stench accosted them. Sorrel recognized it as rotting flesh, the same smell that had overcome her when she rode over a swell on the prairie to see hundreds of skinned buffalo carcasses rotting in the sun, left by a white hunting party.

Magnolia was nonplussed. "Well, dat sure as hell be de smell o' trouble. Gawd knows what po' creature dat man has kilt in dis here house." She shook her head, waddling through the debris, peeking warily in corners, into the bedroom. Nothing.

She finally pointed to a filthy rag rug. "Ah 'spect dey's a cella' hatch under dat rug."

They pulled it back to reveal a wooden door. Sorrel pulled the door open, and a putrid current of air rushed out as if anxious to escape the terror in which it had been trapped. Sorrel staggered back and vomited on the cold potbelly stove.

Magnolia lit a kerosene lamp from a table. "This ain't gonna be pretty. You sho you wanna do dis?"

Sorrel, ashamed to appear like a weak white woman to the tough madam, gritted her teeth and nodded resolutely.

Magnolia waved the lamp over the opening. At first there was nothing but a dirt floor below, but then in a corner they saw a hand. Sorrel knelt on her knees and lowered the lantern down the hole. She was not prepared for what she saw. Lying in the dirt was a wisp of an Oriental girl huddled in a fetal position. Her long black braid lay splayed out in the dirt like a shriveled umbilical cord. Her slender legs and arms bore whip marks. Her small face was bowed down, her diminutive hands clasped under her chin as if in prayer.

"Lord Gawd," Magnolia said as she peered down. "Dat po' chile. Ah surely hope what de preachers say be true. Ah hopes dat lamb be in heaven now and Blades be bound fo' the devil's kingdom. But look to me lak hell be too good fo' 'im."

Sorrel leaned on one knee, and Magnolia stood beside her. The two were silent for a moment as their minds absorbed the horror of the place.

"One thing fo' certain," Magnolia began. "Dey be no justice on this sorry earth fo' dat little chile. Dey never gonna punish a white man for killin' a little yellow slave whore. Dat da way dey gonna look at it. An' dey ain' no way we can prove he kilt dat chile either." Magnolia shook her head. Sorrel knew what she said was true. It was the way of it.

Sorrel looked out the open door and into the hills, pondering. She saw a whip coiled up on a nail by the door, its smooth-plaited leather the texture of scaled snakeskin. It looked as ominous as a coiled timber rattler. She took the whip off the wall. She wanted Blades to suffer in some way for this crime, make him feel fear and pain in the same way the little girl had.

But Sorrel knew Magnolia could not be involved. If she were implicated in any way, her punishment would be severe. A white woman might be forgiven, perhaps even admired, for giving such a vicious man a good whipping.

She knew that Blades was probably up at his mine. She didn't know its location but knew what pass he'd have to take to get there. She would wait there and surprise him.

"I'm going up into the hills to find him. I'll try to bring him in. But he won't go easy. It's better I do this job alone," she said to Magnolia.

Sorrel could see Magnolia gauging the worth of revenge against losing all she had built—her business, her freedom, perhaps even her life. She had been a free woman for seventeen years. Did she want to be the white man's chattel again, as a prisoner?

"Ah sure would lak to see dat man grovel," she said, relishing the image in her mind's eye. "I surely would."

"Can you find your way back to town?" Sorrel asked. "If you can get Willie and the coroner, we can at least give this poor little girl a proper burial."

Magnolia thought on this proposal, then said: "Ah believe yo' right, Miz Lanning. Dat little chile needs to be put to rest. Yes'm. Ah'll go back to town. I knows Mista Willie will hep." She nodded as if affirming to herself that she was doing the right thing. Then she added: "Townfolk won't bury a Chink chile in their boneyard. But there be some plots ah know for niggers and half-breeds by the creek outside of town. We can bury 'er there."

Magnolia went to mount Lester, but she turned around. "Ah'm much obliged to you fo' comin' out here wit' me, Miz Lanning. Ah wished we found dat little chile alive. Ah hope she be wit' de angels in heaven now. Dat be my hope."

She mounted Lester with much effort and grunting and gathered the reins. "Now, you take care. Dat Blades a viper. He kill you dead if'n you don' watch yo'self. You take care."

Sorrel rode Dagda up into the hills, her Winchester in its long holster and the coiled whip tied to her saddle. Up in high country, they hid among the rocks overlooking the path Blades would take home. Finally, in late afternoon, she spied him coming up the path. When he was only twenty-five feet from her, she stood with her gun pointed at him and yelled at him to stop. She strode down the path, stopped in front of him, and ordered him to dismount.

"What in the hell you doin'?" he demanded through a huge chaw of chewing tobacco wadded up in his left cheek. He dismounted and spat tobacco juice in front of her boots, his disdain clear. He was unarmed.

"You murdered a little Chinese girl," she said. His face clouded with rage, for he suddenly realized that Sorrel must have been on his property, meddling in his private affairs.

"You goddamned bitch! That little Chink whore wasn't worth the dirt she slept on! She was sick. Died from the fever. You can't prove shit!"

He saw in Sorrel's face that she knew what he said was true, that a jury of white men would never make him pay for what he'd done. He had friends in high places—the banker Slickum, for one. He laughed and jutted his chin in arrogance, unafraid, exposing his knotted Adam's apple on a neck scrawny and ugly as a plucked chicken's. She hated him.

She lowered her gun at his crotch and shot between his legs, close enough to graze his miner's pants. He jumped and shuffled backward. Now, finally, she saw fear in his face, a hesitance in his swagger. She loved the power rendered by the business end of her gun, the obeisance it brought to her wishes, even from an obstinate sort like Blades.

The carven image of the dead girl in the cellar flashed in her mind like a lightning strike, a ragged effigy refusing to be unseen. She thought of the little girl under Blades's cruelty, what she must have suffered.

She felt the grooved familiarity of the trigger, a tiny ellipse of deadly power at the tip of her finger. A tiny squeeze, barely detectable except in its result, would put down this scourge. She could mete out some small justice for each blow, each devilment he had rendered upon the helpless for so long. How many had he hurt? To what depths had his depravity plunged, unfettered in dark, secret places?

For a terrible moment, her memory was porous to the unremembered violence in her childhood, the guttural grunts of release, the silent ripping of her child mind. His eyes raked her body, the arrogant grin. What fetid thoughts sprang from his memory? He made her feel small. The stench and shabby darkness of the New York tenement rushed back to her. Her memory recoiled, stuffed in a dark corner, a big dirty hand smothering her screams. And she was a speck, nothing at all.

But from the dark came a roaring rage, searing her chest, her fingertips trembling, alive in unwilling restraint. She pointed the gun muzzle square at his face. Her fingertip felt the curve of the trigger beckoning. It squeezed.

A ribbon of smoke spiraled leisurely up from the mouth of the barrel. Sorrel stood like a statue, the rifle suspended in the air with both arms braced. She rested her chin on the smooth wooden stock as if it were a ledge and she were weary. She felt nothing but release as she looked down at Blades's corpse convulsing like a beheaded fish, not knowing its futility. The mortal wound had rearranged his face, ruined in bloody ragged bone and flesh encircled by a rind of hair, his grin, studded with stumps of rotten teeth, now a rictus of death.

Sorrel heard scuffling, and small rocks tumbled down the ridge above her. She jerked her gaze up to see two men scrambling behind some boulders. She did not recognize them, nor did she know if they had recognized her. But she knew what she had to do. Kneeling hurriedly, she untucked Blades's blood-splattered shirt from his trousers and pulled the flannel over his mangled face. His stomach was grayish yellow like a fish's belly and flabby as pork fat. She wrapped the cloth around his head, dragged the body to the precipice of a cliff, and pushed it over.

She listened through an eternity of thuds and scrapes as the rocks battered the body in the fall, the head striking stone like a melon hitting pavement. Then there was silence, finally punctuated by a resonant splash far below. She could tell by the sound that the river water was deep under the cliff, and she felt relief. The current was fast with the spring thaw. The terrible flotsam would be carried quickly downriver and mauled by the rocks and fish into an unrecognizable bolus.

She grabbed handfuls of weeds to sweep up telltale smears of blood in the dirt. She swung atop Dagda and galloped down the mountain trail, hoping that the voyeurs did not get a good look at her or her horse.

Blades could no longer cause pain. He'd needed killing. If his demise meant she would have to pay, so be it. It was a good trade. She did not fear. She did not regret.

She rode through the mountains, suddenly tired of the business of being human. Of its flabby vicissitudes and sordid vanities. She longed to be part of the glorious rocks and trees around her. Stalwart. The sky. The earth. Flesh to stone. She longed for sinew marbled with justice, like blood turned to rubies, embedded with raw truth.

SIXTY THREE

LAND OF MY FATHER'S BONES

THE BATTLEFIELD at the Bear Paw was quiet now but for the whining north wind. The Nimiipuu prisoners totaled around 420—half the original refugees who had started the grueling 1,500-mile journey five months before. A fifth of the original band had been killed in battle or died of their wounds during the trek.

Some 300 Nez Perce had escaped to Canada in ragged remnants, in darkness during the siege or after the surrender. Fifty Nez Perce led by Yellow Wolf were the last to leave the battlefield for Canada. At dusk, Frederick was riding on the horizon above the Bear Paw battlefield when he spotted the group riding north. Yellow Wolf led them on a bay

Appaloosa, followed by Earth Left by the Setting Sun, Joseph's fourteen-year-old nephew. He was swathed in bloody bandages covering burns from Big Hole and a gunshot wound at the Bear Paw.

To Frederick's amazement, hanging from the boy's saddle pommel was the King Arthur flour sack that held the magic hooves of Custer's horse, Vic! Frederick recalled Captain Wheeler sawing the hooves for souvenirs at the aftermath of the Little Bighorn. He found strange comfort that Earth Left by the Setting Sun had them now. Frederick pulled up his horse and watched the weary warriors pass before him, nodding to Earth Left by the Setting Sun and others he recognized. They disappeared over the bluff and into the dark toward Canada.

Frederick left the battle of the Bear Paw with another contingent of soldiers to return to Fort Benton. From there, with his horse and mule, he boarded a steamboat heading south on the Missouri River to Helena. He would then ride through rough country, retracing the arduous journey Chief Joseph and the Nimiipuu had taken to the Big Hole, on his way back to Spotted Horse.

He stood at the rail of the steamboat, looking back over the wide Missouri. It was dusk, and the river reflected a pink band of light stretching to the northern horizon, calm but for the boat's wake rippling away from his backward gaze.

The land seemed melancholy to him, washed in yearning with the rushing sunset. He could not shake Joseph's image on the Bear Paw battlefield. He was haunted by the children crying. Ollokot's makeshift burial, marked by his shield. The women digging graves, the mothers he had recognized from his visits over the years to their villages. And Earth Left by the Setting Sun, his inscrutable face old beyond his years, a warrior boy in a broken, bloody body. They had looked at him askance. Betrayal in their eyes.

He felt like a vulture picking at the wounds of a broken people. His heart railed against his own ambition.

His Bear Paw photographs would be on the front page of every newspaper in the country. They were history. The nation had been following Joseph's struggle for survival with rapt fascination. Frederick's photographs of the defeated "Red Napoleon" would be the culmination. Joseph in his bullet-riddled buckskin, extending his rifle, solemn as stone, the end of his people's civilization. But those images plastered across the nation would trap Frederick in regret, drowning him in a waste of shame.

He found himself walking to the upper deck of the steamboat, where his packed camera equipment was stored in his small berth. He pulled two negative plates from his leather bag. They were dated with a grease pencil: the images he had taken of Chief Joseph's surrender. The metal cases seemed to burn his hands with recrimination, the images on the negatives like raw nerve endings. He wished he'd never come to the Bear Paw. He wished his eyes had never seen it, his camera had never captured it. To do so was to give witness to the unholy, to carve into stone the unspeakable.

He returned to the lower level of the boat, approached the railing. *Hurry, while I still have the courage,* he thought. *Hurry, before it's too late.* He leaned over the rail and held the metal cases out into the darkness, then dropped them from his fingertips. He heard them splash in the Missouri. Looking down at the river, he saw only black water swallowing his stain.

The nearly 300 Nimiipuu fugitives who had escaped to Canada left behind them the sound of guns and cannons and the death wails of mourning Nez Perce and dying soldiers. They trudged north in the bitter cold, their tears freezing on their faces, starving, some without horses, most without buffalo robes, which were too heavy to carry. Many perished. They swaddled the children to keep them from crying and alerting the soldiers.

When White Bird's caravan and then Yellow Wolf's finally reached Sitting Bull's camp in Canada, their hearts were full of trepidation, for the Lakota Sioux were traditional enemies of the Nez Perce. But Sitting Bull welcomed the beleaguered fugitives with sadness in his heart.

When the Nez Perce told of their long trek and desperate battles, the Sioux broke into sympathetic chanting and weeping, for they had suffered as the Nez Perce had and understood.

After Chief Joseph surrendered at the Bear Paw, the Army fed the prisoners hot food, the first they'd had in six days, and roaring campfires were started to ward off the cold. White soldiers shot buffalo, skinned them, and wrapped the fresh hides around the children and wounded to keep them from freezing to death.

While the people were rounded up from the hillsides and rifle pits and their arms collected, Nez Perce horses were also gathered. They were now officially the property of the US Army. The Indian scouts for the Army had been promised five horses each. Officers, and then soldiers, also took their pick. The Nimiipuu watched as their prized horses were taken from them. It was as if their hearts were being ripped out. They turned away.

Shortly after the surrender, *Harper's Weekly* reported:

> Colonel Miles requested Chief Joseph's buckskin shirt as a souvenir, for it bore twenty bullet holes. It was visible evidence of the fierce fighting and that Joseph had been where lead was flying.

The article continued:

> Chief Joseph's face is gentle. . . but intensely strong and full of character. A photograph does not do him justice.

The defeated Nez Perce began the 270-mile trek to Fort Keogh, Colonel Miles's headquarters on the Tongue River. When the caravan reached the Missouri River, now sluggish and turbid with cakes of ice floating in its current, the Nimiipuu men stripped and jumped in, to the amazement of the Fifth Infantry soldiers escorting them. The Nez Perce, always meticulous in their grooming, had not been given many chances to bathe.

The imprisonment of such a proud people was nearly unbearable, and many wounded died. The press reported that white soldiers wept at the tragic end of the Nez Perce.

Nimiipuu fighters would have preferred a warrior's death on the battlefield. Lauded Nez Perce warrior Shot-in-the-Head told newspaper reporters, voicing the anguish of his people:

> I was not made to suffer bondage! I would be as the coyote and the wolf . . . seeking to die in the wild forest alone . . . to be eaten by the wolf's fang—instead of the slow dying of bondage!

Miles planned to keep the Nez Perce at the Tongue River cantonment until spring when they could return to Idaho and their ancestral lands. But he received orders from General Sheridan that they were to be transported to Leavenworth. Miles's father-in-law, General Sherman, concurred. Miles and General John Pope, commander of the Department of the Missouri, beseeched Sheridan not to move the Nez Perce, informing him of the dire condition of the captives. But Sherman and Sheridan vetoed the requests.

Joseph objected vehemently. After several conflicting directives regarding the fate of his people, he shook his head in disgust: "When will the white man learn to tell the truth?"

The weary entourage arrived at Leavenworth to be imprisoned in filthy, disease-infected tents where many more died. By spring, three-fourths of the people had contracted malaria. One writer reported:

> The camp, situated between a swamp and the Missouri River, brought to mind the horrors of Andersonville [the notorious Civil War concentration camp].

The struggle of Joseph's people was not over. The next spring, instead of being allowed to return to their verdant homeland of rushing rivers and forested mountains as Miles had promised, they were ordered to move to the Quawpaw reservation in Oklahoma, a dry, desolate place they called Eeikish Pah, the "Hot Place." There, more Nimiipuu died, and the infant cemetery filled with a hundred tiny graves. Joseph was devastated. The suffering of his people sickened his heart. Still, he traveled all over the country to plead for his people's return to their ancestral land.

Frederick followed accounts of the Nez Perce's suffering after the surrender. Every word weighed on him like heavy stones of reproach.

A year after the Bear Paw surrender, the *North American Review* interviewed Chief Joseph. Frederick read the article recounting the chief's terrible dilemma and subsequent betrayal:

> I knew we were near Sitting Bull's camp and I thought maybe the Nez Perce who had escaped would return with assistance. . . . My people were divided about surrendering. We could have escaped from Bear Paw Mountain if we had left our wounded. But I could not bear to see my wounded men and women suffer any longer; we had lost enough already. General Miles promised we might return to our own country with what stock we had left. I thought we could start again. I believed General Miles, or I never would have surrendered.

The article continued with Joseph's words:

> All men are made by the same Great Spirit Chief. They are all brothers. The earth is the mother of all people and all people should have equal rights upon it. You might as well expect the rivers to run backward as that any man who was born a free man should be contented penned up and denied liberty to go where he please. . . . [I] have asked some of the great white chiefs where they get their authority to say to the Indian that he shall stay in one place, while he sees white men going where they please. They cannot tell me. I only ask to be treated as all other men are treated. . . . Then the Great Spirit Chief who rules above will smile upon this land and send rain to wash out the bloody spots made by our brothers' hand upon the face of the earth.

Later on, Chief Joseph went to Washington to speak to President Rutherford Hayes. Along with much of the country, Frederick read his speech in the *New York Herald*:

> I have shaken hands with a great many friends, but there are some things I want to know which no one seems able to explain. I cannot understand how the Government sends a man out to fight us, as it did General Miles, and then breaks its word. Such a government has something wrong with it. If the white man wants to live in peace with the Indian he can live in peace. There need be no trouble. Treat all men alike. Give them all the same law. Give them an even chance to live and grow.

After his speech, Congress and the nation praised Joseph. Sympathy swelled for the "Red Napoleon" and his lost nation. Colonel Miles concluded in his report to the secretary of war: "The Nez Perce are the boldest and best marksman of any Indians I ever encountered, and Chief Joseph is a man of more sagacity and intelligence than any I ever met."

Even the general most responsible for the plight of the Nez Perce, the old warhorse Sherman, not known for sentimentality, admired the Nez Perce, saying theirs was "the most extraordinary Indian War in history," that they "elicited universal praise" and "fought with scientific skill." Nevertheless, he remained intractable. Joseph would not be allowed to live in his ancestral land—not until 1903, a year before his death, when Joseph met with President Theodore Roosevelt. His old conqueror-turned-advocate, now *General* Miles, hosted the visit.

Joseph would be allowed to return, briefly, to the land of his father's bones, the Wallowa Valley. When he visited his father's grave, he found it had been ransacked and that a local dentist was exhibiting his father's skull in his office. At the desecrated grave, amid a plowed field, his daughter Running Steps tried to comfort her father as he melted in grief. His chant was full of yearning, and he felt the wind of leaving begin to blow.

SIXTY FOUR

LOST HORIZON

FREDERICK was returning from the Montana prairie on the Lolo Trail through northern Idaho. It had been five years since the Nez Perce had traveled the ancient trail in their epic struggle. He rocked in his saddle and thought for some time of Ollokot and Chief Joseph and the photographs he had taken of them. His mule Elmer was in tow, packed with all of Frederick's photographic supplies, which jangled gently with the mule's walk.

Frederick had been hired to take a portrait of a Missoula frontiersman in a wilderness setting for a book of memoirs. The author, Jebediah Emmett P. Weston, had begun his long and adventure-filled career first as a Hudson Bay trapper forty years before, then a scout for survey and mining companies, then a US Cavalry scout, and, finally, a famed Indian fighter and buffalo hunter. His tales had been featured in many eastern magazines, and a publisher had approached him about compiling his memoirs for a book.

Frederick knew the terrain south of Missoula and suggested they ride to a prairie area that abutted rocky foothills, with a backdrop of the mountains, snowcapped and spectacular. Frederick directed his subject to sit on a boulder jutting from the grass and pose pensively, as if reminiscing about his many adventures and brushes with death. Quiet integrity, wisdom about all things wild, stoic toughness hard and sharp as a woodsman's axe—these were the qualities he wanted to capture.

Frederick had known plenty of scouts and trappers and survey men. These were men who spent most of their lives alone in nature. They were often close lipped and independent, hard to fathom, and suffered fools in silent resentment. Their commodity was knowledge of the land, and they had been used to exploit the land they had come to love. Frederick wondered how old-timers felt about what was happening to the land and the wildlife and the Natives who had once roamed free across the continent. He wondered if they were nostalgic for the way it used to be and thought, probably, they were.

So he added one more entry to the list of qualities he wanted to capture in his photograph: reverie—reverie for a lost horizon, reverie for a wild land the frontier scout had helped, unwittingly, to tame.

Elmer the mule had been with Frederick a long time, since leaving St. Joseph, Missouri, and the old mule was getting slower by the mile. He was overdue for retirement. But Frederick couldn't quite bring himself to retire his old friend and wasn't sure what to do with him. He was thinking about asking Sorrel if she would take him so the old boy could live out his days in the lush prairie meadows with other horses.

Elmer plodded along the trail behind Red, Frederick's bay mount, so slowly that it looked as if both horse and mule were slowly lapsing into sleep along the trail, which was dreamily shaded, soft, and strewn with pine needles and moss.

They had six more miles to go until they got back to Spotted Horse. He was about ready to fall asleep in the saddle himself when he spotted Sorrel, Ransom, and Ella in the distance, picnicking in a meadow. He was instantly hungry, for he smelled fried chicken and hadn't had anything worth tasting for several days on the trail. He reined Red and Elmer toward the picnickers and sauntered through the high grass.

"You're a long way from home, Frederick. Ya lost?" Ransom called out. Frederick grinned.

Ever since discovering each other as fellow voyeurs years before—spying on Sorrel, no less—Frederick had felt a special affinity for Ransom.

"I'll come a long way for fried chicken," Frederick joked. He tied Red and Elmer to nearby trees with lead ropes so they could graze. Massaging his lower back with his left hand, he complained that he was getting too old for fieldwork, even though he was only in his late thirties.

A blue, speckled enamel coffeepot sat in the coals of their campfire. Ransom handed him a cup. Sorrel offered him fried chicken and warm, powder-milk biscuits.

The three adults lolled on a blue gingham tablecloth laid out on the meadow grass, drinking coffee and eating. They talked about the new farmsteads in the area, the upcoming turkey shoot, how soon the snows would come, and what photography Frederick had done on this most recent trip. Frederick brought up the topic of Elmer and his idea for retirement at Sorrel's farm. He would, of course, pay for the service and the feed.

Sorrel loved the idea and said Elmer was surely welcome and that Old Gentleman, also in the twilight of his years, would be happy for a wise old compatriot.

Ransom turned to Sorrel, feigning a secretive tone: "I s'pose this means we'll have to put up with more of his company!" Sorrel and Frederick laughed.

Frederick looked back at the scenery behind Ransom and Sorrel and commented that he had never seen this spot before. There was a beautiful backdrop of mountains with a slender waterfall. He said he might set up his camera and take some photographs and excused himself.

Ella came running through the grass, yelling that she had found something. She ran up to Ransom and Sorrel, her skirt full of findings. She had a four-leaf clover, a milkweed pod, a squirrel skull, an arrowhead, and a hawk feather. But she was most excited about the prize she held out in her left hand. It was a small beaded amulet on the end of a long, beaded necklace. Sorrel recognized it immediately as an umbilical necklace. When she turned over the amulet, a terrible emptiness took her breath away. On the front of the amulet was a beaded green frog on a yellow field: it had belonged to Flying Horse.

She caressed the amulet. Emotion filled her chest, and her throat tightened. "Oh, Ella!"

But she could say no more. Ella looked inside the amulet and, with tiny fingers, pulled out a twisted, withered little cord, deep red, almost black, cut clean at one end, the other end ragged and knobby.

"What is it, Mama?" Ella asked. Sorrel held it in her hand. Sorrel felt the hair on the back of her neck prickle and a breeze brush her skin like the presence of impossible truth.

"It is the umbilical cord from an Indian baby," Sorrel said. "There is powerful medicine in it, Ella. It carried life to the baby inside the mother. The Nimiipuu believe it holds great power. Here, wear it around your neck. It will keep you safe and strong."

Sorrel gently nestled the wizened umbilical inside the amulet and placed it around Ella's neck. She felt a sharp pang, fierce with longing. Sorrel hugged Ella hard and looked up at her proudly. She would be a fine, strong woman someday. Ella kissed her mother, then squirmed away.

"I'm going to look in the woods for more things. This is a magic place!" Ella declared and took off, gamboling through the grass, happy at her thrilling discovery.

Ransom lay on his side on the blanket, propped on one elbow, lazily chewing on a stem of foxtail grass. He pointed out a cloud of dust across the valley near their farm. "Look there, Sorrel. Looks like a group of men riding to our place. Wonder what that's about?"

Sorrel had not told Ransom about her bloody encounter with Cornelius Blades only days before, nor about the drifters who might have seen her. She assumed the cloud of dust in the distance was a posse coming to arrest her for murder. It raised in her a moil of emotions, like a storm coming to sweep her world away. She did not fear dying. She did not fear being hanged. But she did fear the loss of all she loved. Her daughter. Her husband. Her farm. Her horses. Watching Ella grow up. The lost years she'd never know.

She didn't mind being punished for the deed, though she thought, in a better world, she'd be given a medal instead. But she did mind hanging for murder because of Ella. Her little girl didn't deserve such a reputation by association. She was innocent.

Sorrel looked up into the sky and thought about the world. She thought about how much injustice went unanswered, unpunished. She thought about Flying Horse and her people and why such good people had been visited by such an end. And she thought about Ella and Ransom and what their lives would be like without her, how lucky she was to have had them.

Ransom looked down at Sorrel as she stared up into the sky. Her eyes looked like crushed violets, the pigment broken and watery and melancholy. He had noticed a strange distance in her the last couple of days, as if preoccupied with some internal struggle. But he knew her well enough not to try to draw out her secrets.

"What are you thinking about?" he asked as nonchalantly as he could, stretching out beside her, resting his head on his hand.

She stiffened a little in her broken reverie. Sorrel smiled at Ransom, but her smile was vacant, not there, still beyond in the blue of lost thought. Her love seemed far away, deep and echoing in the hollow of her hardness, like pebbles dropping into the dark water of a well.

He stroked her cheek, pulled a wisp of golden hair behind her ear. Ransom thought he saw a pooling in the corners of her eyes, like little gullies collecting rain.

"What is it, love? Tell me," Ransom pleaded so softly his words were barely audible.

But Sorrel only closed her eyes and did not speak. She could not tell Ransom that she had killed Cornelius Blades. She could not tell him his life and Ella's life would be changed forever. She could not tell him that she felt Flying Horse among them, ethereal but quickening. That she felt her in the breeze, beckoning in the amulet Ella found. She could not tell him that she had felt the pounding of Flying Horse's heart as she fell from the sky, felt her pulse like hooves upon the ground of some distant horizon. How could she share such visions that were strange beyond understanding, meant only for the inner reaches of her own heart? Her chest was heavy with the weight of parting worlds, and she could only close her eyes to keep the sorrow in.

She whispered to him: "How lucky I've been that you found me, Ransom. Do you know how much I love you and Ella?"

He looked at her, searching, alarmed at her sudden uncharacteristic tenderness. But he realized that some dark, impenetrable force was working here, something that he could not pierce or plumb. He wished desperately that he could help her, that he could reach into her heart and hold it in his hands and protect it for all time. But all he could do was reach out to her and whisper: "Yes, love, yes. I've always known."

They sat on the blanket in the warmth of the sun. Suddenly, from the edge of the meadow came a scream from Ella, spine-ripping like a mountain lion's caterwaul.

Sorrel sprang up, grabbed the Winchester, and charged across the meadow in a streak. She had seen the danger before anyone else, perhaps a mother's instinct.

Peering through the viewfinder, Frederick beheld the commotion with horror. As little Ella wandered giggling through the tall grass, a monster grizzly had caught her scent. The animal was a huge she-bear, rearing to a magnificent height like a totem. She roared a warning that she had cubs nearby and shook her immense skull back and forth menacingly, the jaw wide open with serrated terror.

Sorrel ran like a tigress, wild with fear for her baby. Frederick saw her blurred image skim the surface of the feathered prairie grass. But in his mind's eye, her motion slowed, deliberate, like a deadly ballet. He himself stood frozen, small, his will frail in the face of monolithic fear.

Old Gentleman awoke from the scent of the grizzly, and perhaps human fear, rank in the air. He was up on his old legs and bounding past mother and daughter with the swiftness of his youth. He reached the bear first, snarling terribly. He leapt at the bear's neck, and its jaw roared opened, a great maw of savage, glinting teeth. The bear sank its jagged incisors into Old Gentleman's neck, then, with one swing of its massive head, snapped it. The old dog yelped softly and was dead.

Sorrel whisked past her daughter and charged the grizzly head-on. Frederick thought for an instant she would attack the beast with her bare hands. But ten yards off, she halted and raised her rifle to her shoulder.

This, then, was the supreme test of her courage. She knew that panic was her enemy and that only a clear head would save her daughter. Her courage compressed into an instant of explosive focus, tamped down by ramrod will.

Sorrel drew breath, held steady, and marked a bead on the huge head. The bear charged. But Sorrel was pure logic laced with adrenaline. She waited and didn't shoot. The moments were interminable, murderous.

Finally, she fired a shot from no more than twenty paces and hit the bear square in the skull. But still the bear came. Undaunted, she found the crosshairs yet again, the bear only three rifle lengths away, and shot before it collided with her full force. It reared up to its full height before crashing down on her, its enormous claws like the ribs of a whale, its sawtooth mouth bared for the kill, seeking the neck, as carnivores do.

Sorrel stood intrepid, subverting the fear that comes with instinct—her destiny for her daughter's life. Courage was her final comfort.

The bear's mouth engulfed her neck, breaking it instantly. The creature fell with a groan, the bullet having finally found its target. Its monstrous paws wrapped around her as her body crumpled under the bear's dead weight.

Sorrel lay still under a mountain of fur, the bear's jaw locked around her neck even in death.

SIXTY FIVE

SCATTERINGS

FREDERICK HELPED Ransom bring the bodies of Sorrel and Old Gentleman back to the farm. They laid Sorrel on the rope bed and Old Gentleman beside her. Ransom asked Frederick to ride to Gert's farm to get her. She'd know what to do.

Ella stood silently crying and wringing her hands, as if all her anguish had pooled into her fingers and she did not know what to do with it. Ransom was struck by how much Ella was like her mother, strong, stoic, how she corralled everything inside her. He thought it best that he give Ella some tasks to divert her grief. He asked her to find a rock for Old Gentleman's gravestone and a blanket to wrap him in. And could she draw some pictures for her mother and Old Gentleman to bury with them? They would like that.

She dutifully gathered a quilt for Old Gentleman, wrapped it around the old dog, then laid down beside him and her mother and cried herself to exhausted sleep. She awoke to Charlie rubbing against her and purring. Then he looked down at Old Gentleman, and his purring stopped. He put his pink nose tentatively to the dog's head and gave out a high, mournful yowl that made Ella sob. Charlie put his paw gingerly on Old Gentleman, gently, barely touching him, as if afraid to wake him, then slowly curled inside the dog's belly like a nesting doll, where he remained.

The next morning when Ella woke, she could not stir Charlie. He must have left to be with his old friend, Ransom told her. She seemed to accept that, even find comfort in it. They would be together with her mother.

Ella suggested that Old Gentleman and Charlie be buried between her mother and Grampa Seamus. Ransom thought Sorrel would have loved the idea, even though the local Christian ladies would cluck about burying people and animals in the same plot.

Gert and Bull and Frederick were present for Sorrel's burial and, by circumstance, those of the old dog and the cat, too. Gert had dressed Sorrel in the blue silk dress Ransom bought her years before. Ransom lifted her body and laid her in the raw pine coffin he had spent the day making. He helped Ella place her crayon-rendered picture within Sorrel's folded hands. It was a family portrait, including Old Gentleman and Charlie, Dagda, and Grampa Seamus, all standing together in the yard.

Just as Ransom and Bull were putting the pine top on the coffin, Ella yelled, "Stop!" She stood above the coffin and her mother and took off the beaded amulet of the frog, intertwining it in her mother's hands. "It will keep Mama safe," Ella said, as her final goodbye to her mother.

Ransom asked Gert to say some words for the burial. She was about to say she wouldn't know what to say, but then pursed her lips and agreed. As they stood over the graves, Gert cleared her throat and began haltingly.

"Sorrel, you know I ain't much for words. Neither were you. You didn't talk. You *did.* I liked that about you. You faced life and you faced death and you didn't flinch." Gert paused and looked down and fiddled with the watch chain hanging from her waist, pondering what to say next. "You loved life. You loved your farm. You loved your little Ella. You loved Ransom. You loved horses. You loved the wild. You were a wild thing yourself. You knew we're all part of the firmament. We all become one in the end. You're beyond us now, with the trees and the mountains and the cougars and the wild horses. You'll always be a part of us." Gert looked to Ransom and nodded that she was done.

Ransom and Bull took up the shovels and began shoveling dirt into the three graves. The yawning holes were darkling and lonely, like abandoned wells. It occurred to Ransom that he did not want Ella to know that those she loved were put in such a desolate place. But it was too late. The dirt landed in hard, hollow clumps on the pine coffin, the sound harsh in its shocking permanence, jarring after Gert's soft words. Old Gentleman and Charlie were wrapped together in an old quilt, cocooned in death as they had so often been in life. Ella helped her father push two big rocks, like lumps of grief, atop the graves of the dog and cat.

Ransom had given Frederick written directions for the stone he wanted ordered from the undertaker in Spotted Horse. When Sorrel's stone was ready, Frederick would take care of transporting it out to the farm and putting it atop her grave. Hers would match Seamus's stone. They would remain together on the farm they had built together with their own hands.

"Da, what will we do with Dagda?" Ella asked, her eyebrows knitted. She touched Dagda's soft muzzle, and the horse nibbled at her fingers, hoping for carrots.

Ransom stroked the horse's neck. "I don't know, Ella. Mama was the only one who could ride him."

"We should let him go," she said thoughtfully, "so he can be with the wild horses."

Ransom gazed down at his daughter with soft revelation. "Yes, Mama would like that, Ella. He can be wild and live free. And he can be a father to babies just like him. That's what we'll do," he said softly, gazing out toward the mountains as if in a trance. "And they'll be together out there." His voice trailed into the ether, and Ella knew he was far away.

The liberation of Dagda would be Ransom and Ella's final act on the farm. Ransom packed all their bags for San Francisco and loaded them into the buckboard. He had asked Frederick if he would live in the cabin, free of charge. For several years, Frederick had been talking about moving out of his apartment above his studio. It was small and filled to brimming with his photographic equipment and piles of old photographs, stacks of metal negative plates, and newspapers and books. If he moved to the farm, he'd be with his old mule, Elmer, too. Ransom had sold most of the livestock, saving a cow for milk, chickens, and a couple of hogs for Frederick.

A powerful irony stabbed at Frederick as he helped Ransom load the buckboard. The two friends had discovered Sorrel years before, swimming naked in the mountain lake. It was fitting that they should bid her farewell together now. Ransom had been with her in life. He did not begrudge him that. But Frederick would have her in death.

He was used to living with ghosts. His photographs were ghosts, paper-thin specters that stayed with him long after the flesh and bones had departed the earth. Sorrel. Flying Horse. Fire Bear. Ollokot. The Nez Perce children he had photographed.

Despite his hard reckoning that Sorrel was gone from the earth, or, rather, in the earth, he felt an odd displacement of emotion. An unfathomable sorrow, a panic that she was gone. Lost. But also, strangely, a feeling of possession. He felt an urgency to be alone on the farm. To touch the things she had touched, to sit in her rocking chair inside her cabin and open his Chinese box of clandestine photographs, Sorrel sequestered among them—now forever young, never to wear the tattered rags of old age. Time had saved her.

At dawn, Frederick walked with Ransom and Ella out to the dew-sparkled meadow. Ransom called to Dagda. He whinnied and trotted to them. *Odd*, Ransom thought. The horse never came for anyone but Sorrel.

"Yes. I can see you're ready, big fella," Ransom said. He slipped the halter over the horse's head and opened the gate, taking the lead rope.

"I'll help you, Da," Ella said, and she dutifully took up the dangling end of the lead in her little hands and assumed a position on the other side of the horse.

They walked out into the valley, the man and the little girl, the spotted horse as docile as Old Gentleman sauntering between them. His big head hung down to Ella's level, bobbing as he clopped. Frederick followed behind, feeling an interloper in such a sacred moment.

Dagda was calm, almost acquiescent, as if the horse understood this was the last time they would be together. Ransom wondered if the animal knew his mistress was gone. Perhaps he had smelled the scent of her death, even from the grave. Sorrel always said animals had extraordinary powers humans didn't understand.

They walked up to the lake where the wild horses often watered and stopped in the grassy meadow near its edge. Ransom asked Ella if she wanted to help him take off the halter, and she quietly reached up, standing on her toes. Together they unlatched the leather strap and pulled it gently down the horse's head and over his speckled muzzle.

"You're free now, boy. Go to your ladies fair," Ransom said. The horse only stood looking out toward the mountains. He pricked his ears at a distant whinny, then neighed a clear clarion call, his body shuddering with the deep reverberation. Ransom patted the horse, partly in affection, partly to urge him to the wild.

"Go! You're free!" Ella ordered the horse, and as if in obeisance, he nickered softly and nudged the little girl. Then he lunged forth, his head held high and his tail flaring out beyond his strong back, mane and tail rippling in silken glissando.

Ransom, Ella, and Frederick watched him gallop up the valley slope. Frederick felt a surge of the rightness of it. Dagda suddenly stopped, statuesque, at the top of the ridge. He pawed the ground and swung his head up and down, as he had so often done in his paddock when he smelled the mustangs near and the lure of the wild filled his lungs, agitated his soul.

Ella pointed. "Look, Da! Dagda is saying goodbye!"

Frederick noticed a reflection in the lake below, the mirror image of Dagda atop the ridge. A gentle ripple undulated across the glassen image, from a mountain breeze or a falling seed or the touch of a dragonfly wing. It started as a mere droplet, a kiss dimpling the water, emanating liquid rings like echoes of stone, expanding, embracing. For only an instant, Frederick thought he saw the image of Sorrel's face in the satin water, the ripples her purling hair.

Dagda whinnied and reared, pawed the sky, his distant silhouette imperious against the rose dawn, like an ancient hieroglyph. Then he breathed in the world he'd been given and carried it beyond the horizon into a raw, wild land. And was gone.

A WORD ABOUT THE PHOTOGRAPHS IN

BLOOD TO RUBIES

The use of photographs in conjunction with fiction is a concept rarely used in literature. During my many years of research for this book, I referred to thousands of history books with amazing historical photographs that profoundly intermingled with my imagination. They became visual guideposts for the story and gave me valuable information: the dangers and terrible injustices of the world of our immigrant and Native ancestors; the ancestral land of the Nez Perce, some of the most rugged and spectacular on the planet; the heart-wrenching decimation of species and land in the wake of Manifest Destiny.

The images became so much a part of this story that I wanted readers to experience what I had experienced. Since my main character, Frederick Cortland, is a frontier photographer, these archival images, many by famous frontier photographers, seemed natural companions in helping to tell this story through Frederick's eyes.

I have used poetic license in the use of some images. Movie makers call this the "suspension of disbelief." *Gone with the Wind* was filmed in California, *Doctor Zhivago* in Spain, and *Gladiator* in England; they are technically and geographically inaccurate, but we willingly suspend our disbelief, and the stories utterly engulf us, aided by the haunting power of images to create a world new to us.

Not all the images in *Blood to Rubies* are archival. Some are contemporary images by some of the best photographers in the world, many leading American West photographers, but also some from Poland, Spain, Wales, and England. Their images capture magnificently the power of landscape, horses, and the Native and Nez Perce cultures.

In a few cases, images are composites, many beautifully created by Bob Pecher of B&L Photo Lab in Shorewood, Wisconsin, and the design department at Koehler Books. Some images came from pictures of my friends' dogs and cats, old family photos of my ancestors, public domain images, or stock photographs from Dreamstime.

I hope the images in *Blood to Rubies* resonate as profoundly with you as they do with me and bring you closer to the experience of Chief Joseph and his people, as well as the millions of immigrants and pioneers who braved a new world to journey west.

SPECIAL THANKS

My sincere thanks to the many world-class contemporary photographers who generously donated their spectacular images for this book. I hope readers visit their sites listed in these credits and view more of their work.

A huge shout-out from the mountaintops to the many librarians and researchers in North America and in Europe for their invaluable help in the research for the photographs for this book, especially at the National Archives, Library of Congress, the Smithsonian, the Beinecke Rare Book Library at Yale University, the National Park Service, the Nez Perce Historical Park Service, the Polish Digital Equestrian Library, special private collections, many state historical societies, and especially my local libraries: Mequon Frank L. Weyenberg Library, the Milwaukee Public Library, Whitefish Bay Library, Northshore Library, Shorewood Library, Cudahy Library, West Allis Library, Wauwatosa Library, and so many others.

Librarians—mild mannered but fierce when they have to be—are the protectors of knowledge and literature and the backbone of our learned society. Mark Twain called public libraries "the most enduring of memorials." Librarians are their unassailable sentries.

PHOTOGRAPHY CREDITS

FRONTISPIECE: Chief Joseph portrait, Edward E. Curtis, 1905, Library of Congress, #USZ 62-49148. Perhaps the most famous portrait of Chief Joseph and the most famous photograph of frontier photographer, Edward Curtis, as well as one of the most famous portraits of the American West. Curtis photographed many thousands of Native Americans, as well as many portraits of Chief Joseph.

PAGES xii-xiii- DOUBLE PAGE PHOTOGRAPH: "The Tetons and the Snake River", Ansel Adams, 1942, National Archives and Records Administration, Records of the National Park Service. (79-AAG-1). Possibly Adams' most famous photograph, the Snake River in Nez Perce territory, now the Grand Teton National Park, Wyoming (only thirty miles from Yellowstone National Park). The United States Government employed Adams as part of the series, *Ansel Adams' Photographs of National Parks and Monuments, 1941-1942.*

CHAPTER NUMBER AND TITLE, PAGE NUMBER, SOURCE, YEAR, AND DESCRIPTION

1. *prelude:* 1, main photograph, Eadweard Muybridge, 1872, "Yosemite Falls from Glacier Rock"; University of California, Los Angeles, Department of Special Collections, Research Library. Composite.

2. *prism of the sun:* 5, William Henry Jackson, 1874, "Castellated Rocks near Monument Park"

3. *silk & simpatico:* 9, McBride Museum, Whitehorse, Yukon Territory, today northern Canada, Yukon prostitute

4. *buried treasure:* 16, E. Garrett, Peter Palmquist Collection, two babies who died from poison milk on the trail

5. *westering muse:* 21, scene from movie *The Covered Wagon*, 1924 Paramount Pictures

6. *confluence of fates:* 26, George Catlin, Ba-da-ah-chon-du (Crow Chief He Who Outjumps All) on Horseback, circa 1856–1870, from the Paul Mellon Collection

7. *vermin & verité:* 31, composite, B&L Photo Lab

8. *far side of paradise:* 35, William Henry Jackson, 1880s, Denver Public Library, Glacier Point, Yosemite Valley

9. *whiskey & wrath:* 39, Kansas State Historical Society, Photographer unknown, 1870, #FK2.E3.H77*22, two dead cavalrymen reputed to have been gunned down by Wild Bill Hickok, Hays City, Kansas

10. *motherless child:* 44, New York City street children playing next to a dead horse, 1903, Library of Congress, #det1994000613

11. *molten dreams:* 49, *The New York Tribune,* July 16, 1863

12. *thy kingdom come:* 54, Brigham Young University, Harold B. Lee, Photographic Archives, Provo, Utah, 1860s, three children and their dog on the Mormon Trail

13. *intimate illusion:* 59, composite, B&L Photo Lab, base image Dreamstime image, #198519236, PHOTO CREDIT: Siarhei Dzmitryienka

14. *iron sharpens iron:* 64, composite from the archival collection of my family's 1800s Iowa ancestors

15. *the bowels of hell:* 69, Arthur B. Foote Collection, Berkeley, California

16. *tread the earth lightly:* 72, Smithsonian Institution, (#NAA 76-13355) Assiniboine youth on his horse with his proud father

17. *thunder rolling from the mountain:* 77, Edward E. Curtis, famous Nez Perce Chief Joseph portrait, 1905, Library of Congress, #USZ 62-49148

18. *stowaway heart:* 83, Paul Wakefield, rugged shoreline of Traethllyfn, Dyfed, in Wales, from his book Wales: The First Place, Brockhampton Press Ltd., 1998. Paul Wakefield is a world-renowned photographer who has had exhibits all over the world and won many awards, including the prestigious D&AD (Design & Art Direction) Award, Association of Photographs Gold Medal, and the Grand Prix de L'APPM. View more of his work at paulwakefield.co.uk.

19. *best portion of a life:* 88, Whyte Museum, Banff, Alberta, Canada, V#469/2771, 1907, an Assiniboine family, Sampson, Frances Louis and Leah Beaver

20. *soiled doves:* 93, Lulu White, about 1910, famous New Orleans madam, photographer Ernest J. Bellocq, The Historic New Orleans Collection & Museum. View Bellocq's images at the International Center of Photography in New York City at their website: www.icp.org.

21. *a fern unfurled:* 98, painter F. M. Bredt, 1896, *Chopin*

22. *modesty redressed:* 104, San Francisco Maritime Museum

23. *from the earth rising:* 110, Yellowstone National Park Archives, National Park Service

24. *ashes of roses:* 116, Emma Wixom, the Nevada songstress known as "the Comstock Nightingale" at her 1885 San Francisco debut, The Graham Hardy Collection

25. *siren song:* 123, Dreamstime image #118357899, PHOTO CREDIT: Siarhei Dzmitryienka

26. *sweet-smelling straw:* 129, composite B & L Photo

27. *clap of condor wings:* 135, William Henry Illingsworth, New York Public Library, #NYPG 90-F80. Also, Devereaux Library Archives, South Dakota School of Mines & Technology, 1874, Custer's advancing column, Castle Creek Valley in the Black Hills.

28. *sumac dreams:* 140, Erika Larsen, photograph of Nez Perce woman Katie Harris and her Appaloosa horse, Ollokot (named after Chief Joseph's warrior brother), both in full Nez Perce regalia. This photograph was featured in *National Geographic*'s 2014 issue, in the article "People of the Horse." Erika Larsen's work has appeared in the world's leading publications, including *The New York Times Magazine* and *National Geographic.* She has also been commissioned to do portraits of famous persons, including Dr. Jane Goodall, Oprah Winfrey, and Nancy Pelosi. View more of Erika's photographs and buy prints of her work at www.erikalarsenphoto.com.

29. *wild at heart:* 146, Adobe image #231648637

30. *from souls of great beasts:* 151, George Catlin painting, *Buffalo Hunt,* circa 1856-1870, from the Paul Mellon Collection

31. *manifest destiny:* 157 (LEFT) Stampeding buffalo: Western History Collections, University of Oklahoma Library, Campbell #1667. Page 159, Mountain of buffalo skulls: Detroit Public Library, Michigan Carbon Works, Detroit, 1880s.

32. *dark luster:* 162, William H. Illingsworth, 1874, South Dakota State Historical Society

33. *savage seduction:* 165, Peter Palmquist Collection

34. *creature comforts:* 171, composite, B&L Photo Lab

35. *two spirits:* 176, composite, B&L Photo Lab

36. *cloven tongues of fire:* 180, A clearcut mountainside in Washington State, Darius Kinsey, photographer, about 1900. Library of Congress #USZ62-113600, Whatcom Museum.

37. *gilded granite:* 186, Colorado Historical Society, 1894, Becker sisters branding on their Rio Grande Ranch

38. *commerce of need:* 191, Denver Public Library, Western History Collection, #X-11682

39. *long squash, round melons:* 196, Solomon D. Butcher, 1886, Solomon D. Butcher Collection, Library of Congress and Historical Society of Nebraska, Girl with produce, Custer County Fair, Broken Bow, Nebraska.

40. *echoes of stone:* 201, David Jensen, Lostine River, near Wallowa Lake, Chief Joseph's ancestral home. David Jensen is an award-winning fine art and landscape photographer who has lived for thirty years at the foot of Wallowa Lake. His work has appeared in *National Geographic, Time-Life* books, *Sierra Club, Audubon,* numerous other magazines, books, and calendar publishers. His photography was also featured on Oregon Public Broadcasting's *Art Beat* program. Fine art galleries across Oregon feature his work. You can view his photographs at www.djensenphototgraph.com or purchase his prints at www.agpix.com/djensen.

41. *broken hoofbeats:* 207, George Catlin painting, *Indians Racing Horses on the Plains,* circa 1856–1870, from the Paul Mellon Collection

42. *of human bondage:* 211, Peter Palmquist Collection

43. *beseech the earth:* 217, Marian Gadzalski, Farmer with plow horses. Polish photographer Gadzalski (1934–1985) was internationally famous for his magnificent equine photography. Special thanks to his daughters, Hannah Gadzalski-Syfert and Ola Gadzalski, for generously granting permission to use their father's photographs in this book, and to Artur Bober, director of the Polish Digital Equestrian Library. See Gadalski's work at www.polishequestrianlegends.com and Polish magazine Blok website, www.blokmagazine.com/marian-gadzalski-konie-1978/.

44. *wilderness of desire:* 222, Dreamstime image #239663978, PHOTO CREDIT: Noah Ragone

45. *of wind & fire:* 229, Adobe image #346147022

46. *ride the devil's spine:* 236, Main image: Studio Tavera, Pinerola, 1905, Spanish Military School in Zarzuela, composite, B&L Photo Lab

47. *pavane of passion:* 244, composite, Dreamstime image #241700587, PHOTO CREDIT: *Noah Ragone,* the Columbia River Gorge

48. *old truths trodden:* 254, Smithsonian Institution, National Anthropological Archives, 1900; Nez Perce boy Joseph Ratunda with typical Nez attire of otter-skin breastplate, hair roach, and floral beadwork

49. *pound of flesh:* 259, Base images: Skeletal remains, IStock image. Cheyenne shield, mid-1800s, Gift of George Armstrong Custer to the Detroit Scientific Association. Image of Eton College coat-of-arms,

50. *worlds apart:* 264, main image: Wallowa Falls, Randolph Fritz. Wallowa Falls is near Chief Joseph's ancestral home of Lake Wallowa. Randolph Fritz is an award-winning Idaho photographer known especially for his magnificent western landscapes of farms, ranches and nature. His prints are for sale at Saatchi Art: saatchiart.com/account/profile/1132600 and Fine Art America: fineartamerica.com/profiles/randolph-fritz

51. *footfalls under a full moon:* 272, Marian Gadzalski, "Night horses"; see note for chapter 43 for more information

52. *milk of human kindness:* 279, Sharlot Hall Museum Library Archives, Prescott, Arizona

53. *a good day to die:* 286, Northwest Museum of Arts and Culture, 1877, Chief Joseph's Band at Lapwai, Idaho, during the Nez Perce War of 1877

54. *handful of stars:* 294, William B. Post, "Apple Trees in Blossom," 1897, Renwick Gallery, Smithsonian American Art Museum

55. *sun of big trouble:* 302, Chuck Haney, the Big Hole Valley in southwest Montana, where the Nez Perce suffered devasting losses in 1877 during a US Army ambush. Chuck lives in Whitefish, Montana, several hours east of Bear Paw Battlefield. He hosts photography workshops at some of the most beautiful places in the West and beyond. His work has been featured in numerous publications and more than a dozen books. View his work, learn more about his photography tours, and purchase his prints and coffee table books at www.chuckhaney.com.

56. *bleeding edge of a shaman dream:* 307, E. Jane Gray, about 1890, National Park Service, Nez Perce Historical Park

57. *eye of the needle:* 314, Kansas State Historical Society, Topeka, Kansas, 1890s, quilters at the Pendroy, North Dakota, post office

58. *two worlds colliding:* 321, Northwest Museum of Arts and Culture. Chief Joseph, Looking Glass and White Bird near Lapwai, Idaho, the spring of 1877 during their exodus from the U.S. Cavalry.

59. *among soaring eagles:* 329, composite, B&L Photo, main image: Taft Point in Yosemite National Park, from Wikimedia, photo by Nirvana. Image of woman on horse: Library of Congress, Prints & Photographs Division, famous equestrienne Eunice Winkless

60. *winter of despair:* 338, John Hale Fouch, 1877, portrait of Chief Joseph, the first photograph of Joseph after his surrender, taken near Bismarck, North Dakota, during his imprisonment. Fouch was the official photographer for Fort Keogh, Montana. Smithsonian Institution, National Anthropological Archives, Photo Lot R92-39. James Brust Collection.

61. *dusk of a dream:* 347, Beinecke Rare Book and Manuscript Library, Yale University, Blackfoot village around 1900

62. *blood to rubies:* 354, composite, PHOTO CREDIT: Anthony Giacomino and B&L Photo Lab; main image, Hughes Photography, 1980 Tevis Cup endurance race at infamous Cougar Rock, the summit of a brutal mountain climb of 2,550 foot in four and a half miles. Hughes was the official photographer for decades for the world's longest running equine endurance race (100 miles in one day), which was started in California in 1955, following the historical Western States Trail through iconic towns of Tahoe, Deadwood, Last Chance, Devil's Thumb, and Chicken Hawk, ending in Auburn. View Hughes Photography work and images of the Tevis Cup at Hughes-Photography.com or TevisCup.org.

63. *land of my father's bones:* 363, Edward S. Curtis, Library of Congress, #USZ62-113091 Spokane village, WA

64. *lost horizon:* 371, William Henry Jackson, 1874, "North from Berthound Pass"

65. *scatterings:* 379, E. Jane Gay, 1897, Idaho State Historical Society, #46.30764, 3116.40774. The Clearwater River where Lewis and Clark continued to the Northwest Passage.

HEARTFELT ACKNOWLEDGMENTS

My endeavor to write *Blood to Rubies* has been a lifelong passion. I almost didn't make it. Several years before this book was published, my congenital kidney disease from infancy finally degenerated to a heart attack, then end-stage kidney failure. But, I am blessed with wonderful family members who volunteered to save my life: my two sisters, Sue Schoen and Scheila Hufford, who were both disqualified when they discovered they had the same congenital kidney disease I had, but not life threatening; my 90-year-old mother, Dorothy Hufford, who was rejected because of her advanced age; my dear nephew Marshall Dorman, who was disqualified after he lost his leg being a Good Samaritan; and, finally, my husband, Evan Jones, who at first was disqualified but went on a yearlong campaign to lower his blood pressure, so he was finally approved.

Eternal thanks to the amazing staff at Aurora St. Luke's in Milwaukee and their kidney transplant program, one of the best in the nation, founded by Dr. Ajjampur Vidyaranya; the ICU; Center 8th; and Interventional Radiology; Dr. Matthew Hanna, my nephrologist for thirty years, and Julia Kashou, his nurse. Their diligence, excellent training, and genuine caring saved my life.

The very same day my husband was approved as my kidney donor, my book got a publisher. Two miracles in one day! Many thanks to Koehler Books and all their staff, especially editors Hannah Woodlan and Greg Fields, book designer extraordinaire Christine Kettner, and Publisher John Koehler. They are all simply magnificent. It's been a joy to work with them.

I would like to thank the many friends and family who helped me throughout this long endeavor, especially my wonderful parents, Dorothy and Tom Hufford, and my dear mother-in-law, Erla Enochson Jones. There are so many others I must thank. Please see my author site at DeborahHufford.com for further important acknowledgments.

I am most sincerely grateful to the best-selling authors who, early on, were supportive of my work on *Blood to Rubies*. Their generosity in reviewing my galley copies and providing testimonials is a gift I can never repay, except to pay it forward. Those authors are Kathleen Grissom, William Kent Krueger, Lisa Wingate, Peter Buffett, Gretel Ehrlich, Karen Fisher, and fellow Wisconsin writer Leslie Kagen, all of them best-selling and much-loved authors.

Many thanks to Dr. Steven Evans, thirty-three-year professor emeritus of Lewis and Clark College, who helped vet my book.

Most importantly, I want to thank Nez Perce elder and scholar Allen V. Pinkham, Sr., who co-authored with Dr. Evans a seminal work, *Lewis and Clark Among the Nez Perce*, that provides rare and little-known Nez Perce perspectives of the Lewis and Clark Expedition.

Allen Pinkham is a descendant of Chief Joseph and Chief Red Grizzly Bear, who helped save Lewis and Clark from starvation in 1805, as well as the Nez Perce warrior Wahlitits, who fought next to Joseph and died with his pregnant warrior wife in the War of 1877, a scene depicted in this book. Allen is also a leading elder of the Nez Perce tribe. (Please view Allen's impressive bio on my author site.) He spent many hours vetting *Blood to Rubies* and very generously wrote its Foreword.

Among Allen Pinkham's extraordinary accomplishments, he is the founder of the Chief Joseph Foundation in Idaho, which empowers and educates Nez Perce children through their work with Appaloosas and helps youth become first-generation students at college or trade school. Because I grew up with horses myself, I know firsthand how profound a difference horses make in a child's life. I am donating a percentage of my *Blood to Rubies* royalties to the Chief Joseph Foundation (ChiefJosephFoundation.com). When you purchase *Blood to Rubies*, you support the legacy of Chief Joseph and help Nez Perce children, many who are descendants of Joseph or those who fought beside him. I hope you find in *Blood to Rubies* inspiration and new appreciation for Native cultures, especially the Nez Perce, and for their most esteemed leader, Chief Joseph. All the world should know his story.

ABOUT THE AUTHOR

I grew up an Iowa farm girl with all kinds of critters, especially horses. And I was a rodeo queen! My childhood horse, Sundance, was my greatest joy. I attended the University of Iowa. While a graduate student there, I taught students at the Iowa Writers' Workshop and was exposed to the best literature in the world. I got my first job writing at *Better Homes & Gardens* publications. Later I would be the lead editor for many wonderful magazines and the publisher for *The Writer's Handbook*. My work has appeared in many national publications, including the *New York Times, NYT Magazine, Connoisseur,* and many other titles.

I've taught writing, magazine editing, and publishing at the University of Iowa, Northwestern University, Marquette University, and Mount Mary University. I am most proud of my volunteer work for causes I believe in: for veterans, women and children, the environment, animal rescues, refugees, and especially the Chief Joseph Foundation (CJF). A percentage of my book sales goes to CJF.

Several years ago, I launched a historical blog, *Notes from the Frontier,* as a precursor to my debut novel. The blog now has more than 100,000 readers. (See link below.)

My life dream was to write a novel. Now, late in life and after a kidney transplant (I now have my husband's left kidney) I've accomplished that with your help and that of so many others! Thank you with all my heart ♥.

You can read more at my author and historical blog sites at the links below:
www.DeborahHufford.com
www.NotesfromtheFrontier.com
www.Instagram.com/DeborahHufford.Author
www.facebook.com/deborah.hufford.3

BOOK CLUB DISCUSSION & READING GROUP GUIDE

Available on my author site at:
www.DeborahHufford.com/BookClubGuide

Made in the USA
Middletown, DE
22 November 2024

65232642R00248